FELICITY'S GATE

FELICITY'S GATE

A THRILLER

JULIAN COLE

Minotaur Books
A Thomas Dunne Book
New York

30529 0973

L

A THOMAS DUNNE BOOK FOR MINOTAUR BOOKS.
An imprint of St. Martin's Publishing Group.

FELICITY'S GATE. Copyright © 2009 by Julian Cole. All rights reserved. Printed in the United States of America. For information, address St. Martin's Press, 175 Fifth Avenue, New York, N.Y. 10010.

www.thomasdunnebooks.com
www.minotaurbooks.com

Library of Congress Cataloging-in-Publication Data

Cole, Julian.
    Felicity's gate : a thriller / Julian Cole.—1st U.S. ed.
        p. cm.
    "Thomas Dunne book."
    ISBN 978-0-312-58592-1
    1. Private investigators—England—Fiction. 2. Police—England—Fiction.
3. Murder—Investigation—Fiction. I. Title.
    PR6103.O4415F45 2011
    823'.92
                                                                    2011001276

First published in Great Britain by Quick Brown Fox, a Quick Brown Fox Publications Book

First U.S. Edition: May 2011

10 9 8 7 6 5 4 3 2 1

For Margaret

ACKNOWLEDGEMENTS

The author would like to thank literary agent Shelley Power for all her efforts, Adam Kirkman of Quick Brown Fox Publications for keeping faith, and Gina for being there.

FELICITY'S GATE

PROLOGUE

WHAT does a murderer look like? Much the same as anyone else. But I would say that, wouldn't I? All I have to do is look in the mirror. Murderers look like you and me. Well, certainly like me, that goes without saying. And how do I look? Unexceptional, ordinary, much the same. I have the appearance of an everyday person.

You might think murder exciting and perhaps it is, but there is nothing exciting about me. Dullness personified, that's me, at least on the surface. You have to look deeper to find the hatred and the resentment, the broiling jealousy. Most people don't realise, and if only they were a little more observant, if only they took care to notice me properly, these things wouldn't happen. People should have a responsibility for the way they treat other people.

Is there a flaw in my psychological make-up to explain what I have done; or in my background? Was my childhood deprived and unhappy, full of abuse and neglect? I could tick a box or two, but are those honest ticks, or am I seeking to excuse the inexcusable? Who knows? You decide. Clearly I have considered these matters because I have taken the trouble to commit my thoughts to paper. Strictly speaking, I committed my thoughts to the computer, then on to paper, and later shredded the paper so that no one would find what I had written. Then I zapped the file.

So I go about my life, doing what I do, and avoid drawing attention to myself. But my hands, these hands that do the mundane tasks hands do, day in and day out, have blood on them. Oh, yes, there is no doubt about that.

CHAPTER ONE

MOSES Mundy could not have picked a finer day for his life to fall apart. All the good years came to an end under a clear blue November sky. As he stood in the cemetery he could hear the leaves falling from the copper beech tree. These dead things crackled as they turned in the air. In his hand he carried a large square parcel; on his back a rucksack he had packed earlier. In the distance he could hear a siren and he knew they were coming for her.

Moses stood before the gravestone and his fingers traced the familiar inscription as if he were reading Braille. He smiled at the name and heard her speaking it in everyday moments, asking him if he wanted tea, or to go for a drink; and he heard her cry out his name when passion was carrying her away. "God, Moses, you've worked out what to do at last."

He turned and walked beneath the high wall until he reached the padlocked gate. You could see the house from here. Craning his neck, he saw the attic skylight window. He liked to sit under that window and look over the serried gravestones, her half-completed paintings behind him. He loved the woman yet found her creativity unsettling. How could someone paint? Such mysteries were contained in the act of capturing something on paper. He never understood how she managed it. "That's because you're a big old ignoramus," she said, laughing, teasing, and putting a blob of paint on his nose.

The sirens were getting closer, so he turned away from the house and carried on. The sun picked out his profile, emphasising the large nose, the broad forehead and the shaved greying stubble of his head. There was stubble on his chin too, where once an impenetrable beard had grown, and a tear threaded through these rough facial hairs. He paused by her special spot and managed a smile. "Moses – someone will see. We can't have sex here." But they did, after he spread a blanket on the chilly night ground ("Like in that country song," she said, laughing, before pulling him down). As he walked, more quickly now, he saw her smile, saw her hand pushing back her strawberry-blonde hair with painted fingers. He saw her younger self and he saw her middle-aged self, a few grey hairs now, and he loved them both.

A ginger cat, not much more than a kitten, curled on the path in the sun. He didn't much like cats. His foot swung on a pendulum of rage, but the cat was quick, all sudden liquid motion, and flowed between the gravestones and up on to a garden fence.

Old instincts, long dormant but stirring, told him not to head the obvious way to the station. They would be looking for him. So he walked along the main road in the wrong direction until he found the unprepossessing street with a second-hand Volvo garage at the end. A path led to the Millennium Bridge, built to mark the occasion of its name, and vandalised soon afterwards. In the middle of the span he looked down at the River Ouse, its broad flow impervious to his or anybody else's problems. Then he headed back towards town on the opposite bank. People walked their dogs, jogged, cycled or wandered; didn't they know what had happened? He scowled at the sun-gilded river and the handsome houses on the opposite bank that stood tall and proud, even if their feet were nearly wet.

At the station he remembered the day when he got off the Edinburgh train on impulse, liking the look of York. He never got back on that train. Now the wary sensibilities were stirring, the watchfulness and the waiting. He had been out of the game for a long time. His new life had been so complete it had blocked out the past. He had moved on and remade himself. Now he would have to do it all over again.

CHAPTER TWO

THE body lay at the bottom of the stairs. The head was twisted cruelly and the back of the skull had been lethally indented by unkind application of a heavy object. The likely instrument of injury had not survived the assault and lay in pieces around the corpse, glittering in the pooled blood. From the fragments that remained, the murder weapon appeared to have been a heavy glass juicer designed to press into halved citrus fruit in order to squeeze out juice. This had fallen with the body and smashed on contact with the hall floor. Shafts of sunlight filtered through the stained glass panel above the door and decorated the body with coloured leaves of light. How many different types of glass, and how many different uses. The glass above the door had been artistically tinted and shaped into a design incorporating the house number and garden flowers. The glass used to make the juicer had been substantial enough to do its accredited job, and weighty enough for its illicit use. The handle remained intact, while the spindle curves designed to ease and force the flow of juice had smashed into pieces.

Detective chief inspector Sam Rounder recognised the juicer because his wife, if that's what she still was, had one at home. He guessed what it was from the bulbous handle. She bought it in a kitchen shop off Stonegate. It cost an exorbitant amount. She teased him about being a mean Yorkshire bastard. He said he took that as a compliment.

Sam recalled the conversation now as he navigated his bulk around the body. They rarely spoke and most of their conversations were repeats. He had gone for a pint after that discussion. She hadn't accompanied him although he had asked. You are getting fat, she said. All that beer. So what, he replied, like you care. He followed the first pint with another, then one more. When he went home to continue the argument she had gone out.

Sam stood and the white disposable one-piece overall made an irritating scratchy noise as it stretched over his stomach. He hated wearing these things. The other officers around him were similarly dressed, as were the forensic boys and girls. The over-crowded hall seemed like a final insult to the dead woman.

Sam had seen many bodies but never got used to it. He felt sad and revolted at what had been done. Now he would again have to go through the frankly knackering process of meeting a dead person. He would sift the minutiae of the dead woman's life and "ruffle about in her bloody knickers".

Sam set about exploring the house. It was a thrill of sorts to enter the sanctuary of another person, whatever the circumstances. Misfortune allowed him to exercise his curiosity. He felt his life was measured in misfortune, his own and that of other people. Was it a misfortune to have a wife intent on leaving him for a younger man? He supposed it was, although not of the same magnitude as having your head bashed in.

The stairs creaked under his weight. The house was nicely cared for, decorated in quiet good taste, with paintings hanging on the walls. He paused in front of a floral scene, executed in madly bright colours, with splashes of thick gold paint marking out the stems and rimming the petals. He absorbed the details, squinted in puzzlement, moved on. At the top of the stairs, a landing ran to the left and the right. He turned right and went through the only door in that direction. This gave access to a large back bedroom with a view over other houses and gardens. It appeared to be the main bedroom. Sam liked to have the first look. It let him take ownership of a crime scene. He liked to soak up the details, let the floating atoms of what had happened enter his skin. Sam tried to explain this to Rick once, in the days before his brother stopped being a proper copper and turned into a bloody private investigator. A look of astonishment surprised his brother's face, even though he tried to hide it.

"I'm not just some fat-arsed Yorkshire plod, you know," Sam said.

"I know." Rick's reply came a little too quickly.

There were two other bedrooms on this floor and neither seemed to be in regular use. Suitcases were stored in the smaller room, which faced the stairs, while the larger room at the front appeared to be for guests. It was neat and lacking in clutter. Sam parted the lace curtain and looked into the street. A black mortuary bag was being loaded into a van, and two squad cars were squashed on to the pavement. Neighbours gathered on the other side of the street in a congregation of nosiness. Some of them would soon be telling reporters this was a quiet street where "nothing like that" ever happened. Most places, in Sam's experience, were quiet until they weren't.

Another flight of stairs wound up to the top floor, and Sam puffed his way up, passing more paintings. These also depicted riotous garden scenes, with the stems burnished in gold. Sam peered at one and saw the initials JFW etched in gold in the bottom right-hand corner.

The room at the top assaulted his senses in a number

of ways. It was such a jumble of industrious mess. Two skylight windows, one at the front of the house, the other at the back, admitted a rush of cleansing light. Blinking against the November sun, Sam let the room settle about him. The smell took him back years to primary school. This was a functional place, with a wooden floor and bare walls, one with a disused fireplace. A table was filled with pots, brushes, pencils, charcoal and filthy cloths. To the right of this there were two easels, standing back-to-back and each positioned to catch the light.

One easel held a painting in progress. Sam eased himself round to look. A frenzy of colour filled most of the canvas. Her work was almost done, the canvas more or less filled, and now it would remain undone. Sam squinted, trying to make it out. He was too close, he decided, and so he stepped back and leant against the doorframe. Distance helped and he saw that the painting depicted a border packed with competing colours. Tall grasses swayed, pink poppies smudged open, while abundant roses dipped heavy heads as their petals began to fall away. One departing petal was captured in the first slow curl of its descent. Sam was transported for a moment and almost swore he could hear bees, silly sod that he was.

Then he let out a great, tearing fart. "Better out than in." There was something disturbing about the painting in what it showed or in the way it captivated him. Paintings didn't usually mean much to him. He wasn't an arty sort, so why had assorted colours arranged on a canvas pulled him in so?

In the street outside, a diesel engine shook into life. The body was being driven away.

Sam squeezed by the table and caught a whiff of his own breath. He had only been in the attic for a few minutes and already he had contributed at least two unwelcome odours to its atmosphere. Still, that's what we are, human machines that eat, chew, digest and shit out the consequences. Sometimes he felt lost inside the person he had become, but everyone had to become someone, and this blunt fat man was what he projected to the world. This was the form he had taken. He sometimes thought about a diet, but never for long: counting calories was better suited to over-anxious women.

There was a small pot of gold ink on the table. Sam remembered the signature on the painting hanging by the stairs. This was what the artist had used to sign off her paintings. She had dipped a nib into this pot of liquid gold and put her three initials to her artwork in a final flourish, the tiny full stop after the 'W' indicating her work was done.

A collection of books stood at the end of the table, their spines cracked with use. He pulled out a book about Claude Monet, which fell open at a painting entitled Still-Life With Anemones. The corner of the page was turned over. Sam tried to return the book but it would not fit amid the others. He inserted his large hand into the small space it had occupied and pulled out a small leather-bound volume. He returned the Monet and examined his discovery.

The book was about the size of a thin paperback novel. He flicked through its pages and saw a blur of gold. He stopped and turned the pages again, slowly this time. It was a diary, written by hand, the letters neat and perfectly formed. He had never seen such immaculate writing, yet it was easier to look at than to read; all that gold did strange things to his eyes.

The first page was inscribed "February, 1987". What followed were words Sam would come to know intimately. He would live the dead woman's life again or at least part of it; he would resurrect her; and in his weakest moments he would almost fall in love with her. Sam closed the book. The diary was evidence, but he wanted to read what it had to say before anyone else saw it. He owed the dead woman that much. So he took the diary home and told no one. It was her secret and now it was his.

As he prepared to leave, Sam noticed a chair by the skylight window at the front of the house. The window was low enough so that a person sitting in the chair would be afforded a decent view of the cemetery, so long as they angled themselves some degrees to the right. An empty glass stood on the floor. Sam picked the glass up and sniffed it. The inside was coated with a film of stickiness. It smelt of whisky.

Chief inspector Sam Rounder later conveyed the official version of events at a press conference. He revealed that Jane F Wragge, an artist, of York, had been bludgeoned to death in an attack at her home close to York Cemetery. The police were extremely anxious to talk to Jane's partner, who had not been seen since the discovery of her body. Anyone who knew the whereabouts of Moses Mundy should contact them immediately. There was no mention of a diary.

Sam gathered his team about him, including his indispensable sidekicks Inspector Iain Anders and Sergeant Sallie Lane, and the cold bureaucracy of murder began.

Phone calls were made, doors were knocked on, papers were read and sifted, samples taken, blood splatters stored. Everything about the dead woman became of interest, her friends, the twists and turns of her life, her likes and dislikes, and her art – it was all evidence.

CHAPTER THREE

SAM should have been proud of where he lived. Plenty of people would have been, and many visitors succumbed to property envy, sometimes thinking the elegant house and the overweight policeman seemed an odd fit. "You didn't know I had such good taste, did you?" Sam would say, or something similar, aware of the small hypocrisy: he had fancied a semi somewhere off Stockton Lane. The classy old town house had been Michelle's idea. Nagged him rotten about it, she had.

The sight from the gate could still catch Sam by surprise, as he looked along the path that wound up the long garden to the imposing front door, with windows on either side, an arrangement of elegant simplicity. The house was in a Georgian terrace that stood back from Huntington Road, a short distance from the centre of York. It was a very fine house, but now it seemed to stand in mockery of what he had become: overweight, middle-aged and cuckolded. This was the house of a successful man, not a fuck-up with furred arteries and a swelling belly.

Another path led down the long back garden to a garage with a room on top. It had slanting ceilings and a skylight window, a single bed, an armchair, an old television and a tiny kitchen. There was also a lavatory and a shower, tucked under the eaves. Self-sufficiency was his. This was where Sam retreated as he immersed himself in the story of Jane Wragge, as told in her diary beginning in February 1987. He began the first entry while sipping from a bottle of beer, squinting at the golden calligraphy. The diary looked beautiful, a regular work of art, but it wasn't easy to read and Sam was a slow reader at the best of times. Getting to know Jane was going to be a struggle.

HERE is the first entry in the diary of Jane F Wragge, immaculate in gold…

February 23,1987

THIS week I met a man at the cemetery. He calls himself Moses Mundy, if you can believe such a thing. He seems a strong man, quiet and solid. For some reason I fancy my future could lie with this man. And if he wants to lie with me, he certainly can. It has been a while. What was his name, the last one? I shall affect not to remember, even though I painted him. I have painted all of them. The sex with the last one was good, then it wasn't, and the conversation was never up to much. So good riddance to that member of the male species, and to his male member too (thank heavens no one else will ever encounter these ramblings).

I first see Moses as he stands with a collection of tools, a spade, some shears and other implements. Painting is my thing, gardening too. I love to garden and love to paint gardens. So I volunteer at the cemetery. Moses is new in York and wants something to do. He likes to work with his hands, he says. Strong hands, by the look of them. He is tall and solid and very hairy, a regular fur-ball.

York Cemetery has been in a terrible state, but now it has been bought for a pound from the Crown by a trust that intends to put things right. I want to help. My life, although filled with art, flowers and some friends, sometimes feels empty. Do we all sense this emptiness, this vacuum of spirit? I suspect so.

The cemetery, overgrown and ramshackle, remains a place of wonder. It is so large, 24 acres I think, all that space contained amid the crowded streets of York. It is a garden of death, which sounds creepy, but there is comfort in that description. It comes from the inscription on the tombstone of Charlotte Hall, buried when the cemetery opened in 1837. Her tombstone says she was "the first transplanted into this garden of death".

Well, it's not a bad place to be transplanted to.

We are allocated the same patch to untangle. The undergrowth rises to meet a sad-looking tree, making a green whole. Brambles twist through the greenery, like nature's barbed wire. Soon I am tugging and pulling, working into a sweat and a fury, pulling out bindweed and ivy. I roll my sleeves, exposing a length of arm between the tops of my old gardening gloves and my scrunched-up jumper. It is a tug of war, me against the incredible green monster. Moses laughs at my feeble efforts, letting out a delightful rumble.

Do you want me to do that?

Why do men always do that?

Do what?

Patronise…

The words are lost in my fall. The ivy tendrils unearth with unexpected suddenness, throwing mud and leaves into my face. A cruel lash encircles my right arm, a curlicue of bramble. I cry and swear. Moses places his left hand on my arm, just above the injury. With the large, strong fingers of his right hand, he gently uncurls the bramble and uses a hanky to clean my wound. I want to swoon and collapse into his solidity. What calm blue eyes he has, yet his eyes are haunted by something, some shadow of the past. His eyes have seen things to fear or regret…

SAM put down the diary and flipped the crinkled top on another beer. He sat still, resting the bottle on the swell of his stomach. He was pooled in light from the lamp, alone in a room at the bottom of the garden. His family would be gathering in the house, the daughters and the semi-estranged wife. Would anyone notice? No one had been in when he walked through the house. They would think he was working or drinking. He ought to go inside and get something to eat, to show them he was still alive, but he wanted to read more about Jane Wragge and Moses Mundy, one murdered, the other disappeared. What had Jane seen when she had looked into Mundy's eyes after her small accident in the cemetery? Sam picked up the diary again. The next entry had been made the following day in February 1987…

WHAT a fool I am. How can I have seen something haunted in his eyes? Moses smiled today, a proper smile, broad and surprising, that split his serious face in two. There was nothing haunted in his eyes. We were clearing again, attacking the undergrowth at the spot where the bramble had lashed out. As I stepped up to the thicket, Moses laid a hand on my shoulder. Watch out for the monster, he said.

I had not seen him smile like that before.

The thicket has receded a little. The garden will be tamed, the dead will tell their tales again as their inscriptions emerge through the greenery. Never have I felt so close to the past as when working in the cemetery. There is almost a tangible sense of lost lives. So many lives and so many stories, all ending in this peaceful yet neglected place.

Moses stands with a black bin bag in one hand, overflowing with what we have removed. His blue eyes flicker and I sense a blush beneath his beard. I am not sure about this facial adornment. What a thicket, as overgrown as the greenery we are trying to tame. When I said yes to a drink his thanks come in a deep mumble. What a strange, entrancing mix of strength and gentility is this man. What enigmas are curled inside him, or so I decide, and I do like a puzzle. Perhaps happiness lies this way. Oh, it's foolish to gush so. This is 1987 and I am a grown and intelligent woman living independently in York, and not some Jane Austen heroine banking everything on her man, on The One, and hoping for a fortuitous meeting while promenading with ancient aunts in Bath.

SAM emptied the bottle and placed the diary on the small single bed by the chair in the cell-like room. He stood unsteadily, thanks in part to the beer, but also to the struggle with gravity involved in getting himself perpendicular. Standing up wasn't always easy.

Over the days that followed, Sam ran his investigation on two levels. Officially, he drove everything forward, sifting the evidence and leading his team. The forensic evidence confirmed that Jane had been hit from behind. She had been standing at the top of the stairs when assaulted. The blow had fractured her skull, and she had received additional injuries as she had fallen down the stairs, further fracturing her skull on impact with the tiled floor. When he wasn't leading the official inquiry, Sam read the dead woman's diary. He told no one. There was no good reason for behaving in such a fashion, but the more he read, the more he wanted to discover.

In a short briefing with Inspector Iain Anders and Sergeant Sallie Lane, Sam asked what progress had been made in tracing Moses Mundy. He was playing his accustomed role, speaking as he found, not caring who he upset. His way was the only way. It had always been like this. The years had given him weight and confidence, and while being overweight had its disadvantages, his persona was tied up in his shape. He had become this fat man, this blunt-speaking middle-aged policeman, and that was that. He was not sure how he would operate without this greater circumference.

"So where are we on tracing Moses Mundy?"

"Disappeared without trace, boss."

Sallie Lane was small, slight and tough. She cut a comical figure next to Sam, Laurel to his Hardy. She was a working mother with two children under ten. Her husband taught maths at a state secondary school in York.

"When was he last seen?"

"No one seems sure. He seems to be a quiet man, from what we can surmise, with few friends, aside from Jane."

"And what about her?"

"She had friends, quite a lot really. Well, you know what women are like. They do need their friends. Someone to natter to, someone to share a gossip,"

"So I am given to understand. I am married to one, at least I was the last time I looked."

"What did he do for a living, Iain?"

Inspector Iain Anders was older than Sam, but a good deal fitter. He was lean from running with Knavesmire

Harriers. He was the same height as Sam, but weighed a lot less.

"We are having trouble finding out. As far as we can tell, Jane Wragge owned the house, which she inherited from her mother. So there was no mortgage. She earned money from selling her paintings, and from teaching and lecturing."

"Whereabouts?"

"Some part-time lecturing at St John's, teaching at York College. And her paintings sold for good money. She had shows in the local galleries, and a gallery in Covent Garden in London had taken her on, too. She was in discussion with the gallery about producing a book, too. So everything was going well."

"So what about Moses?"

"Like I said, the money mostly came from her, so far as we can tell. Mundy did odd jobs for people, property maintenance – that sort of thing. A bit of building, a bit of gardening. A useful man to have around, by all accounts."

"Can't have earned much?"

"Their needs weren't high. No mortgage, no kids…"

"God, sounds like heaven…" The interjection came from Sallie. She was drawn and tired, but the men in the room did not notice, or pretended not to.

"So he's a bit of an enigma, our Moses Mundy."

Mundy was less of an enigma to Sam. Not the disappeared, suspected murderer – he was a puzzle; but the other man, the romantic hero of the diary, who was slowly coming into focus. Sam wanted to get back to that book now, to settle into his isolation at the bottom of the garden, to open a beer and lose himself in the dead woman's past. But the bloody present was making too many demands.

"So we think that Mundy could have killed her, then disappeared."

"That seems to be likely, boss." Sallie yawned and apologised. One of the kids had been ill in the night. She hadn't had much sleep.

"Any indications as to motive?"

"None at all. A domestic, an argument of some kind. But the fact that he disappeared – that doesn't look good, does it?"

Jane found him strong and gentle, so why would he do that to her? Sam couldn't say out loud what he was thinking. He needed to read more of the diary.

"What about Mundy's family? Anyone local?"

"No one at all, not a thing. He seems to have arrived in York from Mars, from all the evidence we can find."

Sam knew Moses Mundy had arrived in 1987. He had no idea where he had come from, but Mars seemed unlikely.

"Who told us about the murder?"

Iain laughed. "Our old friend anonymous. He rang from a phone box in Heslington Road."

"Mundy?"

"Yes, we think so."

"What did he say?"

"That was the odd thing. He said…" Iain flicked through a notebook. "He said: 'I would like to report a dreadful occurrence. The artist Jane Wragge has been injured, fatally so. You will find her in the hall of her house. The front door is open'."

"A 'dreadful occurrence' seems an odd way of putting it. A bit ponderous for someone who has just killed his long-term partner and friend."

"That's what he said, boss. And we don't have any other suspects at present."

Sam went in search of a coffee. The Moses Mundy in the diary did not seem like a murderer, but people did kill those they loved.

Later that day, much later, Sam would return to his hiding place and to reading a dead woman's lost romance…

February 25, 1987

WE CLIMBED the cemetery walls last night and crept to my secret gate. We kissed against the stone wall, then fell to the grass. His large hands cradled my face for a moment, almost as if he were fondly embracing a child. It was a kind touch, a touch without sexual intent, or so it seemed fleetingly. I stopped to look at his large and lovely face, and told him that it was all right, I was ready for him. His hands left my face and when he touched my still clothed breast, I jumped with shock. He wandered lower still and I jumped again. It has been a while since a man touched me there, well a few months at least. I felt a warm liquid swelling of excitement, I felt ready in a way I hadn't felt for ages. Then he began to undress me, buttons, hooks and zips succumbed to his large fingers. His serious lips kissed my nipples and I began to swoon. His beard brushed over my stomach, his fingers freed the last elastic and I was quite naked. He removed his T-shirt, exposing a barrel chest covered in hair. A hairy man, a proper man. I like that. My fingers fiddled with his belt, then the button fly on his jeans. I lay back as…

SAM had to stop to reposition himself. He eased his bulk in the chair to better accommodate the unexpected physical excitement. She certainly knew how to set the scene, didn't she? But something about what he had just read bothered him, aside from the reminder about his own lack of activity in that direction. How long had it been? He didn't care to remember. He had a memory of Michelle above him engaged in unenthusiastic bouncing, and then detaching herself too quickly.

He returned to the diary...

ONLY kidding. It's February. I would have frozen my tits off. Just a little exercise in self-arousal. I can remember how it goes, it hasn't been that long. But I can't remember anything like I have just imagined. Cool it, girl! Anyway, at least we are going for a drink.

The mysterious Moses picks me up. His shadow fills the stained glass window in the hall. He really is a sizeable man. He steps inside and waits for me as I get my coat.

Nice house, he says. And he sees the paintings.

You buy a lot of art?

Sometimes, but these are mine.

You paint?

Yes, I do. That's what I do when I am not falling over and being attacked by brambles.

I didn't realise.

Oh, I thought I told you.

No.

Well, I'll tell you now as we walk to the pub. You haven't really told me what you do.

This and that.

I'll tell you about my painting, and you can tell me about yourself.

Oh, man of mystery, that's me.

So I am beginning to realise.

It's early evening and Moses fancies a walk. He doesn't know York and leaves the pub to me. So we go up the hill towards Heslington. He walks quickly but without apparent effort, taking long, almost lazy strides. To look at him you wouldn't think he was moving so fast. I have to walk quickly to keep up, three quick steps to one long stride. We go down the lane by the Retreat, and skirt through the edge of the university.

Did you go to university, Moses?

Do I look like I did?

I only asked.

I know, sorry. I didn't mean to be so, what's the word, abrupt. But no, I didn't. I survived school, and that was enough.

And then?

Oh, you know, the this-and-that business.

Most of the university is new, in that it was built in the 1960s and onwards. We pass Heslington Hall, one of the few fine old buildings, and cross by the roundabout. Heslington is an old village that woke up one day to find a university squatting all around. You can still see how it must have been, the nice old Yorkshire houses and cottages arranged either side of the long street. You could almost be in the middle of nowhere, except you are in the middle of a university.

The pub is full of excitable students, but we find a quiet corner. I have a half, Moses a pint. The glass looks minuscule in his hands, and the liquid it contains is drained fast. We talk and fill in more details. Most of the sketching in comes come from me; Moses keeps hold of his secrets.

He tells me a little about his childhood in Bermondsey, by the fattening flow of the Thames. Mostly I do the talking, about school in York – The Mount, a posh girl, you see – and my time at the Slade. I tell him about all my youthful high hopes, and what I have become, a successful artist, a good artist, but not yet a great one. The house was left to me, I say, so there is no mortgage, and this lets me live off the art, and I have just started teaching too, to help with the bills. All this I tell him. Should I reveal so much about myself? Who knows, but Moses is a good and patient listener.

He goes for more drinks and I watch him at the bar. His shoulders are square and strong, but he is shaped well, with a narrow waist, before a proper meaty man's bum. He smiles as he returns, revealing a flash of white amid the black facial thicket.

I try to learn more. He used to live in south London, working for people.

That could describe anything, working for people, I say. Any job is working for people.

You're not wrong about that. If I could, I wouldn't work for people, but generally it's unavoidable.

I have to smile at that. He has a sort of gloomy flippancy about him. What he says can sound miserable, yet there is an underlying teasing humour. His hands cradle the beer and I recall my vision. I feel a blush coming on and excuse myself. In the ladies, student girls apply too much make-up in front of the mottled mirror. They look so young, gorgeous, full of life and themselves; yet seem little more than children.

We walk back in the dark. Students throng at the bus stop, waiting for a night out. I used to be that slim, like that girl flashing her midriff. I'm far from fat, but you wouldn't catch me exposing myself on a chilly night in February.

Moses walks me to my door.

You haven't told me where you live.

Oh, in lodgings. Other side of town, near the football club.

I suppress the urge to invite him in, to offer him a room even. Why does this large and far from vulnerable man make me feel like this? I wonder about coffee, think yes then no, but already Moses is turning away.

That was very nice, Jane. We should do it again.

Yes, we should.

We'll choose a pub where all the clientele are not all about 16.

Sounds like a good plan.

It's too late to paint, and the alcohol won't help, but I lock the front door and climb to the top of the house anyway. I put on my painting overall, a baggy shirt left by one of the other men, and sketch Moses on to a blank piece of paper, working quickly before the details fade. There is something contradictory about the result. It suggests, oh I don't know, a sort of furious gentility, if such a thing can exist. I shall try again after our next meeting. Perhaps he will agree to sit for me. That would be exciting.

SAM spent the night in his retreat. This avoided more cul-de-sac conversations with Michelle. The way things were going, he would have to get used to sleeping alone. He slept surprisingly well, and awoke refreshed and ready for the new day. Twenty minutes later his back hurt from the soft bed and he was slipping towards a bad temper.

CHAPTER FOUR

RICK Rounder ate the world and the world spat him back. How had he ended up back where he had started after all that travelling: what sort of a journey was that? He was happy enough, but the world was a big place and York wasn't. It was a small and crowded city, the big village, as they used to say.

There was beauty in the city, no one could deny that. Certain views of York Minster could tilt the soul sideways. He also liked to watch the River Ouse from Lendal Bridge in the pink dusk. The broad flow of the river made him feel insignificant, put him in his place. He loved the walk down from the station after a trip away. That felt like home.

It wasn't only the city he was getting to know again. There was his brother, too. If travel broadened the mind, staying put had broadened Sam. Just look at the size of him now.

Rick, ex-cop, ex-traveller, relatively new-spun private eye, sighed as he entered the pub in Goodramgate. He was doing all right, sustained by the infidelity of others, and occasional industrial work. Spying and telling tales – that was what he did: he had become a hired pair of eyes, a professional watcher, a paid sneak, an arbitrator in the moral minefield of life.

"She not feeding you then, that girl of yours?" Sam stood at the bar, a pint in his hand and another on the bar. Were they both for him? The belt containing his circumference seemed more taut than ever.

"What?"

"That girlfriend. She must have put you on a diet. You look even slimmer. Here, I took the liberty."

He handed Rick the surplus pint.

"Michelle's not done the same for you, then?"

"She couldn't much care if I exploded in an Hiroshima of calories or faded away to nought."

"Things not going well, then?"

"You could say that."

They retreated to the furthest corner in the bar. As Sam eased into the chair, air was expelled from various flesh-folded crevices.

"You got a stiff back or something?"

"I've been sleeping in the room above the garage. And don't ask why."

"The usual marital reasons?"

"Something like that. Anyway, I can't stay long. A murder inquiry doesn't run itself."

"I read about that. The artist woman who lived near the cemetery."

"Had her head bashed in, poor woman."

"Any suspects?"

"Just the live-in boyfriend."

Sam swallowed half of his pint in one go, placed the glass on the table.

"No trace of him yet?"

"No, disappeared off the face of York."

"What was their relationship like?"

"How the hell do I know, Rick? She's dead, he's scarpered. I guess you could hazard a guess that the relationship wasn't at the hearts and flowers stage."

Rick saw a flicker of something in Sam's eyes. Wondered about that, then moved on.

"You'll catch him in the end, I'm sure."

"So how's the private eye lark, then? Still sitting in cars spying on people while pissing in bottles?"

"Never had to do that yet, Sam. But, yeah, it's going all right. I have an appointment soon."

"Another poor sod worried about their partner's shagging habits?"

"Something like that."

"There's a lot of infidelity about. And I should know."

"Infidelity keeps me solvent and in a relationship, ironically enough. But you two, you've still not made up, then?"

"There's about as much chance of that as me moving to Lancashire and having a sex change."

"Parts of Lancashire are very nice, you know."

"God, travel's turned you into a traitor."

"It's a big world out there, Sam."

"So you keep telling me."

Sam drained his pint, eased himself up.

"I'd better get back."

"We should do this again, Sam, but properly, instead of just grabbing a pint in the afternoon."

"You mean that girlfriend of yours lets you out at night?"

"You know she does, Sam. And she's got a name, as you know too: Naomi."

They left the warm sanctuary of the pub for the cold street. Rick's mobile rang and he patted his brother on the shoulder by way of a farewell. Sam went towards whatever illegal spot he had found for his car. For a weighty man, he walked with a quick rolling gait. He headed towards Monk Bar, then disappeared down an alleyway.

★★★

MIRANDA Inchcliffe was not a happy woman and perhaps she had never been. Her present unhappiness could be laid at Bill's door, or more accurately at what he kept in his trousers. He was not a faithful man; in fact his lack of faith was the one constant thing about him. His affairs always involved younger women. By a process of mathematical progression, his illicit partners would end up so young he would get himself arrested. That, at least, would solve her problem. If he ended up in prison, having to watch his arse in the showers while he bent to pick up the soap, she wouldn't have to worry about him. Did that really happen in prison showers? She had no idea, but felt happy to accommodate the cliché.

Why had she stayed with him? She asked herself this many times, and squirmed when friends asked it too. Especially when Helen had been doing her concerned friend act. Helen was insufferably smug, and sometimes she wondered why they were such friends. Were they even friends, real friends? Increasingly she found it hard to tell.

"Of course, my John would never do such a thing." That was Helen last week, speaking with a frightful simper. "He's just too faithful to his sexy kitten."

"I am sure he is." Miranda mentally calculated that her friend, if that was indeed what she was, looked more like an over-fed cat than a sexy kitten. As for poor, faithful John, he made monogamy seem like a sentence rather than an achievement. Was it possible for a man to be any more boring and still remain upright? Anyway, he had roving eyes, terrible undressing eyes. She had caught his piggy eyes looking her way when he thought she was unaware of his sexual prying. Perhaps she should go and shag the unpleasant little sod just to burst her friend's marital complacency. That would show her.

"My John's a one-woman man," Helen said, while this unpleasant thought wormed through Miranda's mind.

"What, even inside the confines of his own smutty head? I bet he is."

Miranda regretted saying this immediately, because it brought on one of Helen's tearful turns.

"Oh, I don't know how you can be so beastly about my John."

Beastly was such a Helen word: anything bad was beastly, while anything good was marvellous. Her language knew no further poles. Mascara tears leaked down fleshy cheeks, and Miranda rooted for a tissue in an approximation of feminine solidarity.

"Sorry, I was being mean. It's just all this latest trouble with Bill."

"I don't know why you stay with him, Miranda, I really don't."

"Me neither, but I am heading towards a resolution on that matter."

"Really, Miranda, you do say the strangest things. That's why we are such friends, plain me and glamorous you; simple-minded me and clever old you."

Miranda told her friend not to utter such nonsense. She was far from plain or simple-minded, she said, almost meaning it.

As for Bill, she had hired a man, although not for sexual reasons. She was quite good looking enough to fund her own infidelities, should the desire take her. There had been a man, two when she stopped to think. She hadn't enjoyed either entertainment. One act of betrayal had taken the form of a short trip to Edinburgh, or an "away-day fuck" as she thought later, when the thrill had worn off. In reality, the thrill had worn off immediately, if it had ever even "worn on" in the first place. She didn't see that man again. The second diversion had taken her to a bed and breakfast in the Yorkshire Dales, with the man who liked hills. Miranda felt that the problem with hills was they went up. She was not keen on exertion, at least not of that kind. They walked up too many hills in the rain, then ate heavy food in an over-heated pub. Miranda fell asleep the moment she got into bed with her hill man. In the morning she rose early and asked to be driven home immediately after breakfast. So hardly any betrayal was involved at all.

No, she had hired a different sort of man to help her out this time. Miranda was always hiring in men, usually to carry out some improvement or other to their house in Copmanthorpe. Barely was one room painted than another needed decoration, a new carpet or a fresh piece of furniture. Something always required updating, improvement or moving. Life was too short to spend in tatty surroundings. She could only survive with the best, as if in compensation.

Her predicament found her sitting upstairs in a coffee shop in the centre of York, waiting to meet a stranger. In the street below, which she could just glimpse from her window-side seat, the inexorable Christmas throng had already started. The sight of all those shoppers left Miranda fancying a touch of retail therapy herself. Where did that expression come from, she wondered? Whatever, it contained a lie of sorts. She loved shopping, loved buying things, almost anything, yet few of her many purchases ever made for lasting happiness. There was a drug-like rush, a flurry of excitement, followed by the slow fuzzy comedown. That was just what life was like.

RICK bought a cappuccino and took it upstairs. His client had described herself on her mobile and he spotted her beneath one of the large windows. She was "stranded in the middle of her thirties, but didn't look it, or so people said. She had dark, shoulder-length hair – helped out a little by dye – and was slim, and slightly tanned in appearance, as if she had just had a holiday (which she most definitely had not, thanks to that mean bastard)."

Rick sat and extended his hand. She smiled but kept her scarlet-tipped fingers to herself.

"That was a very full description you gave of yourself on the phone just now."

"Well, I have had plenty of opportunity to look at myself lately. You might suppose that a woman in my position would not wish to look at herself too closely, but I find that it helps. I like to confront myself, to see myself as others do."

The story unfurled like a tablecloth that had been put away dirty, and the details were familiar. When you dealt in other people's betrayals and miseries, the plot was often the same. Miranda Inchcliffe sipped a chilled mineral water as she relayed the details. She was certain about what was going on, but wanted confirmation. A younger woman was involved, she was sure of that. It was always a younger woman. She just wanted to know, before deciding what to do next.

Rick blew on the foamy surface of his cappuccino.

"Either they slipped something in that coffee for you, or you had a beer before meeting me, Mr Rounder."

"Not a crime, is it?"

The foamed milk tickled his lips, the sprinkled chocolate sweetened the bitter coffee. He put the cup down.

"Well, you are right, as it happens. And I'll tell you something for nothing: cappuccino tastes weird after a pint."

"I'll have to take your word for that." Miranda took another chilled sip.

She handed him a computer memory stick. "You'll find everything you need on here. I'm into my computers, and thought it might help."

Rick took the stick and twirled it in his fingers. "What...?"

"You place it in the socket on the front of the computer, go to 'my computer', and open the relevant file. The one you want is called 'lying twat'."

"Right, thanks for that. I'll have a look and give you a call."

She stood up, brushed invisible dust from her jacket, and left. Rick watched her go, admiring her shape, idly wondering why her man was such a cheat, then he turned his attention to his coffee. It might taste strange after beer, but he had paid for it and he was going to drink it.

CHAPTER FIVE

RICK sat in his office, a tiny space stolen from the far end of the garage. As the computer hummed into life, the Minster bells tolled, their resonant musicality dimmed by the walls of his townhouse in Ogleforth. He looked at the memory stick and wondered what went where. He hadn't liked to ask. There did not appear be anything resembling a connector or whatever. Fiddling fingers discovered a top that came off to reveal a small metal plug. Squinting at his computer, he found a slot into which the stick would fit. A few misdirected clicks got him nowhere, then he discovered what he was looking for. Clicking on the folder marked "lying twat" revealed a number of files, each with separate titles.

The first he opened was called "the man".

"Bill Inchcliffe is 38 years old, six foot tall, with brown eyes, curly brown hair threaded with corkscrew threads of grey. These he leaves uncoloured. Every inch of his body is familiar to me, or so it once was. His chest is surprisingly smooth, almost hairless, and leads to the swell of a slim man's overweight stomach; in truth, he is beginning to fill out too much, as if he is being slowly over-inflated. His arms are still long and lean, if not strong. His legs are long too, but a little thick about the thighs and calves. What he keeps in his pants once struck me as rather magnificent, but now I see it as a foul instrument of male betrayal. He has a good smile and knows how to use it. He is charming, but in a slightly wolfish way, and his grin can be unsettling, a sudden warm flash of total insincerity. His smile says he wants to be liked, at least until he gets what he wants.

The charm can disappear in a moment if he does not get his own way. This summary can be dismissed as the sour ranting of a disappointed woman, but as I am the medium through which you will have to get to know Bill Inchcliffe, there is not much we can do about that."

Another file was entitled "adultery vitae". This contained details of suspected assignations, favourite pubs and restaurants, Inchcliffe's place of work – a large insurance office in the city – and his car registration number. There were also a number of photographs featuring Inchcliffe. In one he displayed the wolfish smile, while another showed him minus the grin, in which he appeared handsome, or so Rick assumed.

Another file was called: "What he's missing." This puzzled Rick and he clicked with no expectation of what he was about to see. A box opened, filling the screen with pictures. The woman who had just employed him was shown in a series of naked poses, artfully done, nothing too graphic. He heard the front door, minimised the file and the naked pictures disappeared as Naomi squeezed into the office.

"Hi, love. Working?"

"Yes."

"Not surfing for porn or anything?"

"Why would I want to do that when I've got you?"

"Hmm, isn't that something men sometimes do?"

"Oh, not this one."

She leant over and kissed him. "Glad to hear it, mister investigator."

"It's been a little while since I investigated you."

"So it has. Well, your luck's out there. Time of month and all that."

"Oh."

"Have you cooked anything?"

"No, sorry, I met Sam, then a client, and I got back just now."

"Well, I'll put some pasta on. We've got a jar of sauce somewhere."

Naomi was half-Australian and half-American, tall and black, and beautiful. This was an unusual and striking combination anywhere, but particularly so in York. She had followed him to this ancient city out of love. The journey had not been without its complications. As to her heritage, Rick liked to tease her about which half was which, the American or the Australian. Where did the one stop and the other begin?

They had met on his travels, after Rick had left the police, quit his home city of York, the only place had ever lived, and embraced the world as a way of forgetting the girl who died during a siege. He blamed himself and always would.

Rick and Naomi had lived together in Queensland, a wonderful life, and then he brought her home – home to him, but not to her. She missed the sun and the wide skies, the beaches and the surf. She had an uninteresting job in a large office connected to credit insurance. Whenever Rick asked her about it, he could never concentrate long enough to take in what she was saying.

As she went to cook, Rick opened the box again and looked at his client. Why had she had those pictures done? They obviously weren't for his benefit alone. Perhaps she had been trying to spice up a failing marriage. If so, her tactic did not appear to have worked.

He was still looking when his mobile rang. It was Miranda Inchcliffe.

"Oh, hello."

"So you've been through everything?"

"Yes."

"And what do you think?"

"About what?"

"About whether or not you can help me."

"Yes, that can be arranged."

Rick discussed his fee, she agreed without hesitation. He said he would start as soon as he could. She thanked him and rang off before he could ask her about the pictures. He went upstairs to eat and to not listen properly to what Naomi was telling him about her day. He really should pay more attention. He loved this woman who had come halfway round the world with him, but he worried that a dull life was not doing her any favours. They washed up, watched television, drank wine (Australian, red) and went to bed. Naomi curled into sleep in an instant, while Rick lay with the light on, reading. He read for what seemed like ages, trying to like the Jane Austen novel Naomi had insisted he try, and was about to surrender to sleep when his mobile rang. He silenced the phone before it could disturb Naomi, and walked to the window, where he stood naked in the shadows, looking up at the dark outline of York Minster.

"Yes?"

"My name is Harrison Hill, and I would like to employ you in a delicate and difficult matter."

"Fair enough. Adultery?"

"Nothing of the sort."

"Sorry, it's just that it often is. Matters of the flesh and all that."

"No, this investigation would be of a different nature altogether."

"Fire away, then."

"No, I would prefer to meet in person."

"Whereabouts?"

"The Yorkshire Dales."

"That'll add to the mileage."

"No problem. Just charge me what you need to."

"When and where?"

"Early tomorrow at Arncliffe, in Littondale."

"All right."

"And do you cycle?"

"Yes, why?"

"Bring a bike and we'll go for a ride to get to know each other a little. The cycling is very good round here."

The man gave directions. "If you get as far as Kettlewell, you've over-shot the mark."

Rick, cold and shivery, returned to bed and fell asleep quickly enough.

CHAPTER SIX

SAM was still awake, propped up in the too-soft bed in the room above the garage. He liked his hideaway, and he enjoyed the way the bedside lamp cast shadows round the room, picking out the sloping ceiling, with its skylight window, and the tiny kitchen, where he had earlier heated up a meal from Marks & Spencer. One of their healthy meals, it had left him dissatisfied and grumpy, so he had compensated for the minuscule sustenance with three bottles of beer. Now he was faced with the unavoidable consequence, and so he rolled himself from the sponge-like bed and took the few steps to the toilet. There he stood in all his flesh-garnered glory, a big, powerful man gone to seed more than somewhat, his weighty, collapsing buttocks supported on heavy legs, podgy fingers holding his penis, which was located somewhere beneath the rolling mound of his belly. Finally relieved, he shook himself dry and returned to bed and the diary, which had moved on a few days..

March 7, 1987

THE days have settled into a pattern. Art, cemetery and Moses. There is an intimacy between us, we have become confidants, friends and mates, or whatever word you wish to use. Whichever one it is, this friendship can't come between a girl and her art. My painting is a comfort and a curse, in that I love to paint but I cannot escape it. Painting flows round my veins and seeps into my brain. I am good tempered only if I paint. You don't want to meet me in one of my dry, barren, blank-canvas periods – what a restless, headache-numbed pain in the arse I am then.

When we are not together, I ascend to my lovely attic, the safest place in the world. Just me and my paints and my whirring brain, so long as it is whirring. Sometimes it won't whirr at all, and those are the days when you do not want to meet me. What a strange thing is creativity, the motor that fills all that blank whiteness.

Where do the ideas come from, what generates them? Don't know, but without them I am nothing. This creativity defines who I am. Without those paintings I am nothing at all.

So I paint, and Moses does whatever it is he does. When we are at the cemetery I talk about everything and nothing, and he soaks it all up, listening intently. What a good listener he is, but he offers only a cautious reciprocity of information. He is kind and generous, but not about himself. On that subject he remains more or less a closed book. Perhaps this should worry me and maybe it does, but it intrigues me too.

The outside world still turns as we untangle the cemetery and build links between us. A terrible thing has happened to a ferry. It tipped into the sea, capsized because its doors were not closed properly. I have been on these ferries and there is a name for them, to do with the way you can drive on at one end and off at the other.

RORO, says Moses, when I ask.

Ro-what?

Roll-on, roll off.

Oh.

That's what the Herald of Free Enterprise was. A RORO ferry, one with a stupid capitalist name. Its sister ships have similar names. Pride of Free Enterprise and Spirit of Free Enterprise. All that aspiration didn't help the poor drowned sods. They say that 193 people, passengers and crew, perished in the water.

I know, how sad. So you're not any sort of a capitalist, then?

I don't think I am any sort of an 'ist'. Not a socialist either.

Just an individualist.

Ha, yes. Probably one of those, yes.

His eyes glint blue and his beard parts to reveal a smile, wide and white. Then the smile goes and the beard takes over again. I step closer, stretch my toes, and kiss almost-hidden lips.

There I've done it now. Or gone and done it, if you're not pleased and I've done something I shouldn't have, and…

Oh, stop all that fussing with words, woman. There are weeds here to untangle, roots to pull up, thickets to, oh I don't know, unthicket or whatever the word is.

No such word.

Thought as much, but never mind.

When we're done, you could come back for a coffee.

Aye, I could.

Moses turns and works, putting his powerful shoulders into the task. I feel small besides this man. The last one was slight and almost skinny, attractive enough and nicely proportioned too, but without that mass of male presence, that unquestionable solidity.

The pulling of weeds reveals so many stories. Lives summoned in stone, the brief details chiselled into a hard surface, the final hardness. Some are long, but many are not. Brevity was often the way and when we find a child, I feel sad. Four or five years, no life at all. Some are measured in months.

Later I make coffee in the kitchen, trying to get warm. He teases me about the procedure. The beans kept in the freezer, measured in tablespoons, then ground, and placed in the glass jar, before adding water just off the boil. Boiling scalds the coffee, burns it, spoils it, I say. Stir the dark liquid, put the plunger in place and set the kitchen timer to four minutes.

Then plunge and, hey presto you have a coffee.

I could have made and drunk an instant coffee by now.

Maybe, but it wouldn't taste this good.

After the coffee, which Moses admits is nice if you don't mind the fuss, I take him on the grand tour. Every door is opened for him, each step trodden on. I feel a blush rising as he stands in my bedroom, filling out the door, so I turn and he follows, into the spare room at the front, and then up to my studio.

A painting is nearing completion, arriving at that point when further brush strokes would spoil it, yet still it feels unfinished somehow. It is always hard to know when to stop. Too much work can spoil a thing, too little leave it feeling not fully defined. Yet, paradoxically, a sketch can say so much, the freshness of the strokes conveying or suggesting meaning.

The painting is one of my impressionistic garden scenes, poppies in red, pink and orange, the petals overlapping with lazy grace, the stems edged in gold, not because poppy stems are gold, but because I like them that way. A blue-and-white sky can be glimpsed between the flowers, with their black-eye centres.

Moses stands and looks, then speaks.

There's a lot of heat in that painting. You can feel it shimmering. How do you paint heat?

You don't, as such. You suggest it. But the heat is something you bring to the painting, not necessarily something I put there, if you see what I mean?

Maybe, I do, maybe I don't.

I'm trying to decide if the painting is finished.

It looks complete to me, like a thing in its own right.

Thank you. Perhaps I won't add to it now.

Moses moves to look around, ducking his head to miss the sloping ceiling. The erotic trepidation that has exercised me intensifies, and for a moment I feel like a silly teenage girl rather than an artist in her thirties. He looks out of the skylight window, the larger one at the front, by the top of the stairs.

Good view of the cemetery, he says.

I squeeze into the space next to him and we both look over the cemetery. From this angle, the place is still untamed, abandoned to the undergrowth.

A good project, that, says Moses. He turns and we are so close it seems we cannot escape. We kiss, tentatively at first, then with passion. We fall to the floor beneath the window and undress each other. I lie naked on old dustsheets discarded under the window and he looms above me, all male and hairy, a proper man in every respect, as I now see. His fingers slide down my stomach.

Don't worry about that, I say. I just want to feel you inside me.

He enters with gentle force, causing a rush of something like pain that soon melts into warm pleasure.

Our love making is over quickly and lacks the sexually charged intensity of my imaginings, but it is very welcome. No outcome for me this time but that will take practice. I'll show him soon enough, like I showed the others.

Moses rolls away and props himself under the window. The black curled hairs on his chest are wet with sweat, his stomach protrudes but with solid flesh rather than flab. His penis rests thickly on his hairy thigh.

You look lovely, he says.

Thank you. You don't look so bad yourself.

Soon we are cold and start to feel self-conscious, so we dress and go downstairs.

Do you fancy another coffee? I say.

Not sure I've got that much time to spare.

Moses chuckles, kisses me once more, and leaves. I shall have to paint him, like the others.

CHAPTER SEVEN

RICK reversed his Golf out of the garage and into Ogleforth. Then he wheeled out his bicycle and lifted it on to the racks on the roof. He hadn't got round to removing these after a trip into the country, the Wolds that time, with Naomi.

It was early and he escaped York without difficulty, even managing to avoid being trapped in traffic on Gillygate, and was soon driving at a speed that could get him into trouble with his brother's lot. The car was sporty, fast and responsive. His spirits lifted until Harrogate, where the traffic gummed up. It was a slow haul up to the Stray, bumper to bumper with four-by-fours ferrying children to school. At the big and mildly terrifying roundabout, much of the traffic drifted left towards the town centre, while he carried straight ahead.

After Skipton, he found the road he had been told to take, and followed its twists and turns, savouring the morning freshness of the Dales. The countryside looked so appealing, clear skies and gentle undulations. He knew this was illusory, that the weather could blow up a hellish storm in the blink of a passing black cloud. But he enjoyed the show nature was putting on for him this morning. The road wove through attractive villages, under canopies of thinning trees, and then the landscape surrendered its softness to a harder Dales beauty.

He nearly missed the Arncliffe turning, but spotted the junction on a bend at the last minute, then sped down a twisting road that ran along Littondale. All about him, valley bottom fields and steep green hillsides of open pasture and hanging woods created a sense of calm, while craggy outcrops and exposed moorland suggested something hard beneath the picturesque scene. The Dales could do hard and soft like a geographical good-cop, bad-cop partnership. One minute's calm green and clear blue skies could be blown away and replaced by howling winds and relentless rain. The place didn't get to be so green without rain, and the sunny-day visitor could forget this unavoidable meteorological fact, only to be cruelly reminded later, perhaps up high and unprotected on a rocky outpost.

He thought he had arrived before he had, which was often the way on journeys in the Dales, and after a few false arrivals, he finally entered Arncliffe. The road twisted sharply to the right, following the valley bottom, but he kept straight on to the centre of the village. Small cottages and larger houses faced each other across the broad green, and in the far corner sat an impressive old Dales pub, the Falcon. Rick stepped out of his car and took in the view. He had to admit that for all the wonders he had seen on his travels, this place could hold its own. It was beautiful in a solid, no-nonsense manner, with the rocky hills standing guard on either side. This old farming village had much to offer, although big money business types were more likely to be found there than farmers these days. They were the only ones who could afford the property.

Rick rang the number on his mobile and a couple of minutes later, a door to one of the small cottages opened. The man calling himself Harrison Hill stepped out, or so Rick assumed. He approached and introduced himself.

"That's strange," the man said. "A Yorkshire accent with a touch of Australia, unless I am mistaken."

"No mistake there, and well spotted. York-born, travelled the world, lived in Australia for a few years, then did a prodigal returning act. There you have it, my potted history."

"So what did you do before you got wanderlust?"

"I was a copper in York."

"So you've returned to your roots, but from the other side of the fence, as it were."

"You could say that."

Hill extended his hand and treated Rick to a powerful grasp.

"That your Golf over the way with the bike on top?"

Rick said that it was.

"Had any breakfast yet?"

"No."

"I better fix something then. You are going to need it."

They went inside the cottage, which was an image of compact cosiness. Hill busied himself at a range cooker, sizzling bacon and then toasting bread. He made coffee too, and when he had finished, he handed Rick a toasted bacon sandwich and a steaming mug of coffee.

"Let's go out the back."

The garden behind the cottage was long and narrow, with a view to the hills behind. They stood and ate the sandwiches, then drank coffee from mugs fingerprinted with fat from the bacon.

"Good breakfast, that. Now do you want to tell me what this is all about?"

"Not yet. We'll ride first, then we can talk. I have a route in mind, 20 miles or so, nothing too strenuous."

Rick liked to cycle and thought that sounded fine. This was his first mistake. York is flat, famously flat. The Dales are famously inclined in the opposite direction. Rick often managed 20 miles – or 20 York miles. The distinction was important, as he was about to discover.

Rick went outside to free his bike from the roof and gather his cycling gear, and soon they were standing by their bikes opposite the pub. It was a cold clear morning and goose-bumps had broken out on Rick's bare legs and he shook with shivers.

"Time to get going, I think."

Harrison Hill mounted his bike.

"It's the tough stuff soon on this ride. So I hope you're up for this."

"I love long cycle rides."

"But only in York?"

"Mostly, yes, but what's that got to do with anything?"

"You'll soon find out."

They set off, passing over a small bridge, and the road rose in front of them, gently at first. Rick couldn't understand the fuss. He sped along, tagging behind Harrison Hill. To their left a steep valley climbed sharply, its vertiginous slopes sectioned with apparently haphazard arrangements of dry-stone walls. Soon the road started to resist their efforts and Rick felt his breathing race in protest, but he kept on, changing down through the gears. He lasted for a couple of minutes, then stopped, heart pounding. Up in front, Hill was still upright and mobile, and he stayed that way, his solid calves marbled with veins, all the way to the top, propelling the seemingly tiny bike with effort and strength.

Rick, pushed and panted, hopped on, managed a few yards, surrendered again, and via this unsatisfactory means of propulsion he eventually caught up with Hill, who was waiting by a dry-stone wall at what Rick took to be the top.

"Plenty more hills to come, but that one's the worst."

They drank water, Rick got most of his breath back, and set off again, climbing more, then descending, brake pads screeching in protest, down a zigzag arrangement of sharp bends, shot through a farm, climbed again. The ride continued in this vein, with long ups and swift descents, and breaks while Hill waited for Rick to catch up, until they could see the grey glint of Malham Tarn. Hill pointed out the stretch of water as he handed a red-faced Rick a drink and a plastic bag containing a mix of chocolate, nuts and dried fruit.

"There's a fast section coming up, then more hills. There are always more hills."

He smiled in a way that could be interpreted as pleasant or slightly mocking; Rick couldn't decide. He was right about what was to come. A couple of miles on, the road turned into a Tarmac rollercoaster and their bikes swooped and sped with unstoppable momentum, requiring no effort, other than a steady nerve and a careful eye.

There was a long descent towards a cattle-grid, then a steep climb past a farm, and after that they began turning to the right, heading back. They stopped by the cars parked below Pen-y-Ghent, one of the Three Peaks, towering over Ribblesdale and the head of Littondale. Some have likened the peak to a crouching lion, something Rick was too busy panting to notice, although he did take in the towering cliffs and escarpments.

"We could always park up and climb to the top, just by way of a break," said Hill.

Rick found the breath to say: "Is that your idea of a joke?"

"Well, yes, I suppose it is. Nice scramble up to the top, though, and fantastic views. On a very clear day you can see Blackpool Tower, or so I've been told. Never managed it myself."

Hill took a swig of juice, offered the bottle to Rick.

"Not so far now. And there's a thriller of a hill coming up."

And so there was. After two or three easy miles, the road fell away to the hamlet of Halton Gill, and the steep hill sucked them in and claimed them for its own, as the two bikes flew in an unstoppable gamble with gravity. Rick had never been so fast on a bike, never felt so excited, so joyfully terrified, on two wheels. There was no point trying to use the brakes, nothing could stop him now. Staying upright was the thing, the thrilling, giddying thing. A stray thought entered his head – he wasn't wearing a helmet, was this wise? – but this was blown away as his bike accelerated madly. There was a bridge up ahead and the road looked bumpy. Rick managed to use his brakes and jolted over the bridge, coming to a stop at a junction.

"That was fantastic. Biggest thrill I've had in ages."

"Yes, it's a good one, isn't it?"

They set off again, passing a bunk barn, and rode along the valley bottom, following the river. At the village of Litton, the pub had just opened, so they pulled up and Hill went in to get them two pints.

"Brewed out the back of the pub, this is," he said, on returning. "Lovely stuff."

Rick drank deeply, looked around at the attractive

village, recalled the thrills of the ride, and felt suddenly and completely at peace. This was the life, he thought, taking another gulp. Exercise and beer was such a perfect partnership. Then he remembered that he was working.

"That ride was wonderful – as is this beer. But what is it that you want me to do?"

Hill was silent for a moment, and Rick wondered if silence was his way, an astute enough observation, as this was a man who liked to shun unnecessary noise. A troubled look clouded his blue eyes – Rick hadn't noticed the colour, but they were definitely blue, a clear deep blue – and his large features were still as granite for a moment. Then he sighed, a long exhalation that seemed to come from the very centre of his being.

"Well, it's a long story. But you will know some of it already. I've told you that my name is Harrison Hill, and so it is, in a sense. I even have the passport to prove it. But I have lots of other passports too, all with equally plausible identities attached, none of them exactly true, none of them entirely a lie. Identity is a funny thing to pin down, don't you find?"

He spoke deliberately, as if considering the weight of each word before rolling it out.

"I have lots of different identities and aliases, but you may know me as Moses Mundy."

CHAPTER EIGHT

DOORS were knocked, phone calls made, criminal records scoured. Friends supplied what details they could, fellow artists mourned one of their own, sometimes at greater length than the investigating officers strictly had time for, but no one had a plausible theory about why Jane Wragge had been murdered. What had spurred someone to kill a respected York artist, a woman whose work had brought pleasure to, if not exactly many, then to a good, cultured few? Wragge's paintings had been selling well before her abrupt death, and now their cachet had increased. Death rarely harms art, even if it doesn't do much for the poor artist.

Jane Wragge's house had been searched already, but Sam Rounder sent his team back. They had been working there for a couple of hours when he turned up. It was another cold and crisp morning, the same one on which his brother, unknown to him, was breaking the speed limit en route to the Yorkshire Dales.

Sam entered the house near York Cemetery and saw in his mind the body twisted at the foot of the stairs, the clever, frail and fallible bundle of humanity that had been a woman until shortly before he had first encountered her. It was an oddity of his job that sometimes you only got to know someone after fatal mischance had intervened. He first met Jane Wragge as a corpse, a fresh corpse, the life hardly fled from her, and their relationship picked up from that point. It was unusual to get to know a victim so well, and so intimately, but he felt he had an inside track on Jane Wragge, even if he had no idea where that track might lead.

Sam climbed to the attic studio, panting heavily. He should do something about all this weight, everyone was always telling him; the trouble was, the more everyone told him something, the less he felt like obliging.

Somewhere inside his middle-aged swollen self there was a young, fit and slim man, who played rugby, a bit of football, went for the occasional run, even a game of squash. Sam wondered if he would ever find that inner self again, but he wasn't banking on it any day soon. Life had assaulted him in layers and now he had a very physical representation of that accumulation. His weight stood as an accusation of self-indulgence and lack of care, but it also represented the years in an all-too physical manner. Unlike his roving brother, Sam had stayed put, and now he felt mocked by the youthful promise represented by the golden young man trapped somewhere inside. Sam had hit the plateau, the mid-life flatness in which nothing got better, no further achievements were made, ambition ground to a halt, and the bright-eyed hope of the twenties had dimmed. He sighed and told himself not to be such a self-pitying bastard.

Perhaps it was time he bought a sports car. Then again, those cars could be a tight fit.

"Morning."

He eased himself into the crowded studio. He liked this space and could see why Jane, as he now thought of her, thanks to the intimacy of the diary, had enjoyed her time up here.

Sergeant Sallie Lane and a couple of PCs were sifting through the half-completed paintings and sketches, upending the books.

"Morning, boss," Sallie said. "Nothing to report yet. What exactly are we looking for?"

"Not sure, but there is something here we have overlooked." He couldn't tell her the line from the diary – "I think I shall have to paint him, as I did with the others" – because officially the diary did not exist. So he had to dress it up as a hunch.

"Just a feeling, you know."

"Didn't know you could do feelings, boss."

"The unfeeling fat man does have a soul, you know."

"Just teasing."

Sallie smiled and yawned.

"Those children of yours being keeping you up at night again?"

"The youngest one's still ill."

"Never mind, they'll grow up eventually – and then present you with even more problems. Or ignore you altogether, apart from when they want money or a lift."

"Quite the ray of sunshine this morning, aren't you?"

"More of a bloody great cloud come to glower over you lot."

Sam stood by the skylight. He was rewarded with a good view of the cemetery and an unexpected erotic image. He was standing where Jane and Mundy first made love. Cosy spot, he thought, turning back towards the studio. Then he thought of moving the table. Why hadn't he thought of this before or why had no one else either?

"Anyone moved that table yet?"

"Don't think so, boss."

"Why the bloody hell not? Do I have to think of everything round here?"

They removed the books, paintings, half-filled paint pots, and glasses of stale water. Then the easels were taken down and moved aside. The floorboards were splattered with paint, but the area under the table was relatively clean, aside from curling caterpillars of dust.

"Looks like Jane kept the table in the same place," said Sam.

Sallie wondered why Sam was talking about the victim as if he had known her? The dusty floor brought to mind her neglected house. She worked full time, they both did, but most of the domestic duties still came her way. She'd left the kitchen looking like a bombsite and it would still be a bombsite when she got home.

"Any of those boards loose?"

"Not sure, boss."

Sam got down on to his knees with much wheezing and displacing of inconvenient flesh. He ran his fingers over the dusty floor. One of the boards seemed a little loose. He pushed and fiddled, and then the board lifted. Some minutes and much wheezing later two boards were removed. Sam put his hands into the space under the floor, hoping there wouldn't be spiders, because he hated the little buggers. He flinched as something touched his hand, but he persisted. Then he encountered something that felt like paper. A moment later he extracted a thick role of drawing paper. He blew the dust off his discovery.

"Let's take this downstairs. There's not much room in here. If you wanted to swing a cat you'd have to find one with a short tail."

The roll was laid on the kitchen table. It was tied with green garden string and Sam's fingers struggled with the knot. Sallie stepped in and did the job. Sam noticed how big his fingers were next to hers.

The outer paper was unrolled to reveal five paintings of men, all naked. The poses were not provocative or overtly sexual. The subjects all appeared to be calm, as if captured after making love, or so Sam supposed. There was no erotic anticipation in their nakedness, no expectancy, but a loose, unthreatening nakedness.

Annoyingly, Sam thought, their features were not clearly portrayed. Each face was thrown in shadow or caught by direct light, like an over-exposed photograph.

"Bloody artists. Why can't they paint things that look like they are meant to be?"

"It's a start though, boss," said Sallie, brightly. "And anyway, you can certainly make out something about their faces."

"True enough, my optimistic friend. We need to get these scanned and distributed."

So there had been five men in Jane's life, five partners she wished to paint in such an intimate manner. One of the men was Moses Mundy, Sam was sure of that. They had found no photographs of the mysterious Mundy. Perhaps he didn't like having his picture taken. Sam guessed the solid, shaven-headed man was Moses and the back of the sketch confirmed this hunch, as the words "My Moses" were written in gold ink.

But who were the other four men?

The painting of Moses was the most recent, but it was still dated 1987, the year he and Jane Wragge met. The other four paintings were dated between 1982 and 1986.

"One man a year," said Sam. "She got round a bit, didn't she?"

"Maybe she was just trying to find herself," said Sallie Lane. "Or maybe she just liked men, liked relationships, enjoyed having sex. Some women do, you know."

"So I am given to understand. Five men, pictured naked, across five years. Intimate paintings, but not smutty or anything. Respectful paintings, tender paintings. At least I think so. Truth is, I know bugger all about art. But that's the feeling I get."

He sent the constables back to the studio and sat at the table, staring at the paintings.

"No woman ever painted you naked then, boss?"

Sam scowled at Sergeant Sal.

"They'd need a big canvas nowadays."

"You could always do something about that, you know. Go on a diet, take some exercise."

"And you could always mind your own business. Why is it that everyone feels free to comment on a person's weight? Have I got a sign around my neck saying 'Pity the fat man'? 'Open season on the fat git' – or something like that?"

"Just trying to be helpful."

"You can help by getting these down to the station, then coming back here with a big bacon sandwich for my lunch."

"With or without coronary sauce?"

"Brown sauce… and no more sodding sauce from you."

"Fair enough, boss."

But it wasn't fair enough. Resentment bubbled through her at the unfairness of things and all those males: one husband, two sons and a grumpy boss. Sometimes she felt she didn't fit into her life at all.

Sam stayed behind to root and to count the moments to

that bacon sandwich. No further discoveries were made, or nothing large enough to excite interest. Jane had liked to cook, judging by the recipe books in the kitchen. She liked her music too, with CDs stored throughout the downstairs, with a couple of racks in the kitchen, and more in the front room. Her tastes ran to Van Morrison, John Martyn, bits of jazz – including some Jamaican ska – and some classics, including two requiems: Mozart and Verdi. Plenty of Bach, too. Sam ran his eye over the spines, recognising some titles, skimming others. He liked music, knew a bit about it, but not a lot; Rick had always been the more cultural one, the big ponce.

JANE was 35 years old and had 14 years of life remaining. Somewhere between her late twenties and her mid-thirties, she had five boyfriends whom she immortalised in the flesh. Was this unusual, weird or kinky? Sam had no idea, but supposed not. People, in his weary experience, did all sorts of odd things. Some filmed themselves having sex and posted the pictures on the internet; who on earth wanted to watch anyone doing that? God, but modern life was a puzzle sometimes.

Sam ate the bacon sandwich. Eating helped him to think, and eating a bacon sandwich concentrated the mind so magnificently he ought to be able to get the things on prescription. Sadly, Sam suspected all he would get from his GP would be an earful about salads, exercise and cutting down on the beer.

Aside from Moses Mundy, the errant boyfriend, only a Christian name or a nickname identified the remaining lovers. These were Mick, Rich, 'Himbo' and Pablo. The penultimate one was a puzzle. Who would be called something like that? And was the last one Spanish or something?

The disappointingly impressionistic paintings were copied into North Yorkshire Police's computers and turned into posters that might or might not jog a memory somewhere. The posters went out to local newspapers and the television news. Look North ran a short item, which was followed by the male presenter asking his female co-host if she had ever painted any of her boyfriends in the nude. She graced his remark with a smile that could have frozen a penguin on the spot. Sam, watching when the report went out, decided he was not the only male in Yorkshire to be in trouble.

CHAPTER NINE

THE man calling himself Moses Mundy emerged from the bar with two more pints.

"You still warm enough out here?"

"Fine, but I've got to drive back to York, so I don't know if I should drink that."

"You can cycle it off on the way back to Arncliffe, then sleep at the cottage. You'll be fine."

It was easier to drink than to argue and Rick accepted the pint. Their bikes were propped against the table, a tractor passed the pub, exhaling clouds of diesel, and a minibus full of glum teenagers drove off towards whatever hill they were going to be forced to climb.

Rick looked at Moses, locking on to those clear blue eyes.

"Let me get this right. You are Moses Mundy and you are the chief suspect in the murder of the artist woman."

"Yes. Jane Wragge, friend, partner, love of my life."

"So you didn't kill her?"

"No, absolutely not."

"But why do the police think you did?"

"You'd have to ask them that. I suppose they often think the boyfriend did it. They don't have much imagination."

Rick sighed and wondered whether to come clean, but Moses was speaking again.

"Someone wanted to punish me, and they did so through Jane. By killing her. I think my past caught up with me, or rather with poor Jane."

"So why didn't you stay put and wait for the police?"

"I ran because running is what I always did when I was in trouble, in the past."

"So you found Jane?"

"I came back after a walk and she was lying at the bottom of the stairs. I knew she was dead immediately, knew before I checked her pulse. I howled and cried, then ran about the house packing a couple of things, and then left. I rang the police anonymously from a phone box."

The blue eyes watered and Rick wondered what was expected of him.

"Why would someone go to all that trouble, and do something so terrible, just to punish you?"

"I upset a lot of people in a former life."

"From what I understand, the police can't find out anything about you. You're a man of mystery, Moses Mundy."

"Well, that's probably because Moses Mundy doesn't exist."

"Where did you get the name from?"

"You're a private detective. Find out for yourself."

"Fair enough. So what do you want me to do?"

"Prove my innocence."

"How?"

"By uncovering the people who set me up."

"How will I do that?"

"I'll prepare something for you, get some information together. But you will have to go down to London, south of the river."

"Why?"

"It's a long story and not a very nice one. So are you prepared to take on this assignment?"

Rick took a long pull at his pint.

"You need to know something about me first."

"What's that?"

"My brother is leading the investigation into Jane Wragge's murder."

"Does that present any problems for you?"

"Well, there's certainly one."

"What?"

"I'm sitting here talking to a wanted man who the police, in the shape of my brother, can't find. Quite funny, in a way."

Moses finished his pint and sat back.

"You have to decide what to do, Mr Rounder. But don't bother telling your brother, I will move on, to somewhere else in the Dales, or further afield. But I do love the Dales, such a fundamental place, don't you find?"

"Yes, it is. Fundamentally knackering, too."

"It's flat all the way back now. A nice easy ride."

Rick sighed and wondered if he would regret what he was about to say.

"All right, I'll do it."

They cycled off, leaving Litton to enjoy the fast bends and the gentle valley-bottom views. Dry-stone walls blended to smoothness, silver spokes spun, the rush of cold clear air invigorated the riders.

Rick surrendered to the purity of the moment. Sometimes it just felt good to be alive, in touch with his working body, in consort with nature.

Then he remembered that he was on a cycle ride in the Dales with a suspected murderer who was on the run from North Yorkshire Police.

Back at Arncliffe, he changed out of his cycling gear, put the bike back on the roof of his Golf, drank a strong black coffee – "Where would we be with caffeine, eh?" said Moses, or whatever he was called – and drove back to York. The hills had tenderised his legs, Moses was troubling his conscience; but he had a case to follow up, and that always felt good. Two cases, he remembered.

CHAPTER TEN

WHERE Clarence Smith lived was, as he would joke with his guests over breakfast, a dead-end road in the most literal sense, in that it ended with a cemetery. The witticism had done valiant service over the years. It helped warm things up over the eggs and sausages, the fried bread and sizzled bacon. He let out three rooms, usually to couples visiting York for a day or two. He liked the company, enjoyed the ebb and flow of companionship. He ran the place by himself. A girl came in to clean; well, he said girl but she was pushing forty. On days when all three rooms were booked, she arrived early and helped with the breakfasts.

Some might think of him as lonely. He lived in an attic apartment, one floor above where his guests slept, made love, watched television, or did whatever it was guests did. Skylight windows in the sloping ceilings let light into a simple but comfortable arrangement of rooms. There was a small lounge, an en-suite loo and shower, and the large main bedroom, with its king-sized bed, one of those brass jobs, with shiny globes on top of the vertical struts. A big bed for a man on his own, but life went on. He had found love once and hoped it would return.

Mostly, Clarence entertained himself with the help of late-night television on obscure satellite channels; sometimes he managed the real thing. The last one had been an Australian on the European tour. She was not as young as the usual rucksack crowd because she had to fail at being married before she could travel, and by then she had fine lines round her sad brown eyes. She booked in for two nights but stayed a week. She wanted to get accustomed to sex again, after her ex, and thought the skinny Brit at the guesthouse would be a start.

What was her name? Clarence thought for a moment. Julie, that was it. Perhaps they could have made a go of it, stayed together longer. He enjoyed the sex but found her New Age-y conversation dull. Could good sex and boring talk be the foundation for a relationship? Often since he had thought it could have been, but by then it was too late. Besides, they had argued and that was that. What about? He wasn't sure he could recall.

Their parting played over in his head – recalled the way he liked to remember it. She shot him a regretful glance, a lover turning back into a stranger. That was how he recalled the moment. He had turned it over in his mind quite often, imagining her at the station as she waited for a train to Edinburgh. She promised a postcard but the card never came; well, it wouldn't now, would it? The passing intimacy faded to a smudge. He returned to sleeping alone, swapping her warm but imperfect body for the cold perfection of soft-porn TV. He forgot Julie's face and put aside her tedious conversation, but the shadows of their lovemaking would rise late at night, when nubile nothings were cavorting for his benefit on the television.

He sighed away the memory and concentrated on work. A couple had booked in for the night and he knew they were up to no good. One thing about this job was that you noticed things: they brought no luggage, only food and wine. Then there was a flush of anticipation on the girl's face, too. They were having sex when they shouldn't be. They had arrived on foot, unusual because the guesthouse was a fair stretch from the station. Besides, he suspected they were from York and wouldn't have needed the station.

Clarence was almost right. The couple had walked from the station, but only because the man had left his car there to back up his story (an expensive act of subterfuge, given the parking fees). His wife thought he was in London for the night on business, and she wasn't above checking. So he parked at the station, as he did when he went away on business.

Bill Inchcliffe was playing a dangerous game but couldn't help himself. Really, he couldn't. He supposed he must be one of those sex addicts he had read about in one of his wife's magazines. One woman, the same woman night in and night out, just wasn't enough for him. This wasn't Miranda's fault, and besides she was quite a woman herself, certainly in the early days. How exciting everything had seemed then. His dalliances since were merely an attempt to recapture that sexual excitement. He was chasing up the old tingle. Anyway, if he was one of those addicts, it wasn't his fault; addicts couldn't help themselves.

Bill was disappointed in his latest conquest. Not Catherine herself, Catherine was lovely. Slim and shapely, quite short, sporty, played squash or something. A sweet-faced blonde, 15 years younger; he liked them younger, which was part of the problem, or would be if he stopped long enough to think about it. No, the disappointment was because Catherine was his secretary, and shagging your secretary was a bit of a cliché. It was also risky because Miranda knew he wasn't above committing a sexual cliché, so she would know where to look. Still, she wouldn't look down this dead-end road near York Cemetery. The guesthouse had been Catherine's idea and he went along with it keenly enough. Now they were naked in the late afternoon on rented sheets, her on top of him, her strong little body moving up and down, wavy blonde hair flopping around, sweat running between her small, delightful breasts. Then they were done, or he was, and they lay on the bed for a while in post-sexual glow, him more aglow than her, before dressing and switching on the television.

"Let's have the picnic."

Catherine spoke brightly but felt let down that the sex hadn't lasted longer or ended somewhere for her. She had gone on top to slow him down, but never mind. There was still time, so long as Bill didn't drink too much. She was beginning to notice he liked his wine.

She unpacked the food while Bill uncorked the wine and poured two glasses, making sure he took the fuller one. No need to get Kate drunk, they had done the sex bit already; besides, he needed a drink. It was that time of day, and this adultery business was wearing on a man. They said a man couldn't do two things at once, didn't they (they being women), well carrying on with two women was doing two things at once, wasn't it?

"Here you are."

Catherine lay out the supermarket feast. Sandwiches, salads, posh crisps – gruyere and shallots, which translates more familiarly as cheese and onion – and two slices of blueberry cheesecake, each in a see-through plastic wedge.

They ate and drank, and Catherine asked the question again.

"Do you think they know, at the office?"

"Know what?"

"About us."

"Dunno. Don't see why they should. None of their business anyway."

"True."

"So where does you wife think you are?"

"In London, for an overnight meeting. That's why I did that business with the car, leaving it at the station. In case she checks."

"Oh, and will she?"

"Who knows. She's a devious cow when she wants to be. Anyway, what did you tell your man?"

Catherine blushed and a stamp-sized patch of red appeared on each cheek.

"Nothing. Well, there was no need to tell him anything. We split up. I finished with him, because of us."

Bill glowered at her over his wine, taking a big gulp before he spoke.

"But there isn't an 'us', is there? Not in any lasting sense. This is a bit of fun, a frolic and a fuck, then on with our lives. Isn't it?"

She looked crestfallen, and suddenly so young, and this made Bill feel guilty. He hadn't behaved well for years, he knew that much, but there was a kernel of honesty somewhere inside. It was just that a passing pretty woman easily extinguished the little glow of decency.

"Sorry, Catherine, love, I didn't mean to be unkind, the words came out wrong and…"

"Don't use that word."

"What word?"

"Love… you called me love. You don't love me, it's just a bit of fun, a whatever it was you said. A frolic and a fuck, and…"

"I've never heard you swear before."

"Lots you don't know about me, I'm sure."

Bill privately doubted it: nice girl, well behaved at school, bright but nothing too taxing, sporty, a little dull, and hoping for a life of domestic harmony, children, occasional holidays, the usual mundane stuff stretching out to meet the horizon. Given all that, why was she here with him? Because he had flattered and seduced her, like he always did. And because he had wanted to see that tight little arse unclothed, and because he couldn't stop idly wondering what her breasts looked like, and because he was so generally hopeless.

"I'm sure you are a proper woman of mystery."

"You're teasing me now."

"Like you teased me that day when you came to work in that tight pencil skirt and the high heels."

Catherine smiled and a flicker of naughtiness illuminated her innocent-seeming face.

"Well, it worked, didn't it?"

She had started this exchange wanting to leave, to storm out, but she had to admit there was something about Bill. She felt guilty about the wife, and knew that she wasn't being very sisterly. Nice girls didn't do things like this, but she was a nice girl and she had (God, if her mother knew, she'd blow her tight Catholic lid right off).

"Put that wine down, Bill Inchcliffe. I want to show you something."

She stood in front of him and undressed. She ran her hands over herself, circling over the slight mound of her stomach, then went further down.

"This is what you have to do, see?"

As she attended to herself, her head thrown back, Bill was suddenly excited again, and that didn't often happen twice in a row.

She was all husky urgency. "You take over now, Bill. Just like this."

Later, both satisfied and glowing, they ate the cheesecake and finished off the wine.

ALL the while they remained unaware of the figure in the street outside. Rick Rounder was used to lurking and shadows. Sometimes he thought that was all he did, skulk in the dim corners of other people's lives. He looked up at the Cemetery View Guesthouse, glanced at his watch, and mumbled something into a small digital recorder (a new purchase, Naomi's idea). He would type up the log of infidelity when he got home. He was about to leave when on impulse he went inside. He tapped the breast-shaped bell in reception and waited for an answer. The lobby was just the smart side of scruffy.

Rick rubbed his tired eyes and stretched his muscle-sore legs. That cycle ride hadn't done him any favours. When he opened his eyes a man seemed to have materialised from nowhere.

"How may I help you?"

Funny the way some people could make a polite inquiry sound like the purest impudence.

"It's a matter of some delicacy, but basically I have been hired to observe two of your guests, and I wonder what you could tell me about them."

"Any reason why I should?"

"Not really, but it might help me out."

"And who might you be?"

Rick handed over one of his cards. Clarence Smith glanced at it.

"Who hired you?"

"Can't tell you that, client confidentiality."

"The wife then, I guess."

"You are free to guess what you like. I just wondered when they arrived, how long they are planning to stay, what names they gave."

"Not asking much, are you?"

Smith made a show of looking at the visitors' book, even though he knew the details. "Arrived this afternoon, just for the night and booked in as Harry Belafonte and Sally Bowles."

"When Harry met Sally, eh?"

"What?"

"Never mind, but I think those may not be their real names. In fact, I know for sure the man is not called that."

"How come?"

"Oh, that old client confidentiality thing again."

"Not much more I can tell you then, is there?"

"Nope, but if they come again, would you phone me – or text even."

"Can't get the hang of that."

"Me neither, really. My girlfriend helps me out. So will you phone me?"

"Might do."

Rick looked across the desk and down a little. Smith was fairly short, but he probably didn't calculate it that way. He looked like a man who knew his height, and never mind what the measurements said. His head was shaven to make light of encroaching baldness and he fidgeted about on the balls of his feet, made impatient and itchy by the small bit of power he had just been given.

"Might do, might not."

"Fair enough."

With that, Rick left.

Upstairs, Bill finished off his 'half' of the bottle and fell asleep. Catherine sat in front of the television, wearing a cheap dressing gown bearing the guesthouse logo (an askance sign with tombstone-style lettering). Bill was snoring and she began to wonder what she had been thinking. Wasn't an affair meant to be exciting? Still, he'd do for now, she thought. Until something else cropped up. There was that guy at the squash club, the one she had lost to the other night. Now he was delicious.

Chapter Eleven

Moses, Mick, Rich, Pablo, and Himbo – it sounded like the names of a band, something manufactured and silly, like The Monkees or whatever they were called. Sam had a fuzzy grasp of popular culture. He turned the names over in his mind as he walked up the long path to his front door. Five lovers – how many had he managed? Fewer than that, for sure. Three, but maybe there was a 'half' in there too, a nearly lover. He almost smiled as he thought about the almost one.

He reached for his keys and stood before the handsome entrance. There was no skulking and hiding this time. It was his front door and he was going to walk through it, boldly and like a man. This he did without difficulty or witness. The house was empty. In the large kitchen he found two notes, one from each daughter. He remembered when they used to wait for him, red with excitement. They would rush up to him, arms flung out, and he would grab them up for a cuddle, whirling them round in a dizzy embrace. He switched on the kettle and knew that this was a lie – not a big lie, but a partial truth. That had happened, certainly once or twice. More often he had loomed over their sleeping forms to breathe a silent, beery goodnight. Had he been a bad father? He had no idea. It was a bit late to start worrying now.

There was no note from Michelle.

Sam put pasta to boil and went outside to retrieve the diary from his garden retreat. He was going to sleep in his own bed tonight. Back in the kitchen, he fried garlic, black olives, chilli and anchovies, threw in a chopped tomato, then poured the sauce over the hot drained pasta. He drank half a bottle of red wine with the meal while watching the TV news and then disconsolately channel-hopping. Then he went upstairs without washing up, had a shower and took the diary to bed.

March 8, 1987

MOSES has found me out. At least he thinks so, although he can hardly have expected me to arrive complete and inviolate at my age. Perhaps other women haven't painted their lovers, but they aren't artists.

Another day at the cemetery, a good day. Much hard work is done and my muscles ache. Moses is strong and purposeful. He braces himself against tangled old roots like an old salt tugging a boat in (or something, nautical images not being my thing). He digs out beds, wheels barrow-loads of greenery. A man at peace with himself, a man best kept busy.

Arousal surprises me as I watch while continuing my own more feeble efforts. That first time on the studio floor swims back to me and I smile. Moses stops and the stern concentration lifts. He is smiling too.

What are you thinking about, Jane?

Oh, nothing much.

It must be a nice sort of nothing much to get you smiling like that.

Well, yes.

Well yes what?

Oh, I was remembering that first time. When we worked here then went back to my studio.

That day when your luck was in?

Something like that.

We carry on working and Moses is quiet for a while. He is quiet a lot of the time, but I don't mind. There is peacefulness in his silence.

I straighten my aching back and Moses surprises me. His hand, warm from the work, even on a chilly day like this, rests on the small of my back. His black beard parts into a smile as he speaks.

Time for a coffee, I think.

We store away the tools and get ready for the long walk round to the house. It isn't far, but seems long when you can see your destination over the wall. Suddenly, Moses grabs my hand and lifts me up, so strong and sure, and balances me on the old wrought iron fence. His hands stretch between the bars and he steadies me as I climb down. Then he hauls himself up and jumps down in one swift movement, landing lightly for one so large.

Coffee now or later?

My question is barely out when he kisses me, pushing me up against the hall wall beneath my paintings. Then we climb the stairs, passing hot colours and the gold, the passion and the decline.

Later we lie in bed, me panting...

That was the first time for me.

First time for what?

You know, resolution.

Oh, I see. Never heard it called that before. Well done me and you then.

Moses dresses and goes to make coffee. I lie there for a moment, tired, a little sore, but complete. Then I dress and follow him downstairs.

Moses is finishing his coffee ritual. He has taken over this task since more or less moving in. He still has his rented rooms, but I don't know why. It seems a waste. He presses the plunger, pours the strong coffee, adds the frothed hot milk.

I want to paint.

Sounds like a good idea.

What are you going to do? I don't mind, you can do what you like. No need to go back to that pokey little room of yours.

(I don't know why I said this, because I have never been to his room off Bootham, so have no idea about its size).

I am giving up the room.

Oh, so where are you staying now?

Here, if that's all right.

Of course it is. Why don't you go and get your stuff while I paint?

I got it already.

He points to a single suitcase by the back door.

So that's all right then.

I paint for an hour or two, maybe more. Time condenses. I don't know whether or not to be happy with my latest garden. Closeness stifles judgement. Only later will I have any idea, and perhaps not even then. Sometimes the complete is unobtainable. The stairs creak and Moses comes in. He pokes round the studio while I tidy up.

You could restore that, you know. Might keep you warm up here in your garret.

Moses is looking at the fireplace. Suddenly I feel uneasy but I don't know why. He shouldn't be doing that, but I cannot recall why. Moses is squatting in front of the fireplace, appraising it like a professional hired in for the job. This'll cost you, missus, he says inside my head, tutting – not an easy job, that.

Moses removes the board I'd put there to keep out the draught. He ferrets around in the black hole and peers up the chimney. When he withdraws a long roll of paper, dusted with soot, I remember.

Oh you don't want to look at that. Just some old paintings I nearly threw away.

Moses places the dirty package on the table and unwraps it. And there are my four men, posing naked. Mick, Rich, Pablo and 'Himbo', although the order isn't right, of course. Pablo should be the last.

Moses is dark and furrowed. He looks at my naked lovers and he looks at me, alternating his rage. Then he speaks with a quiet sort of fury.

I am going out for a while.

Don't be angry. There were bound to have been others. I like to paint my men. I'd love to paint you. You're much nicer than them.

Why did you keep the paintings?

Good question. Because I painted them, because I turned these imperfect men into my perfect images of them. Because I'm an artist and that's the sort of thing artists do.

I thought you only painted flowers.

Mostly, yes, that's what I do.

He turns and leaves. The stairs creak and in the distance the front door shuts. I look at my quartet. Not one of them was a good idea, although two seemed so at the time. It hurts when you are wrong about people.

When I go downstairs, the suitcase is still in the kitchen, which is something. A good sign.

SAM put down the diary and turned off the light. He was asleep in a happy instant. The big marital bed took him and embraced him. The untroubled purity of sleep embraced him. His snores rang out and there was no one to complain. After a while the snores subsided and Sam was perfectly at peace, still with replenishment. Until he was woken by a scream.

He sat up, rubbed his eyes and tried to work out where the hell he was. He wasn't in his penitential cell above the garage, he was here in his bed, their bed. And a woman was screaming. Gradually he realised that the screaming woman was his wife.

Michelle sat on the bed.

"You gave me a start. I wasn't expecting you to be in here."

"Can't a man sleep in his own bed?"

"You've been hiding away in the garage."

"I know when I'm not wanted."

"Oh, Sam, can the self-pity. Anyway, it's late. I haven't got the energy for this. I'll go into the spare room."

"No, don't do that. Stay here with me. It's all right, I won't try anything on. You'll get no unseemly advances from me."

"All right."

She went into the en suite to undress and clean her teeth, and came out wearing a nightie. Not the sexy, your-luck-might-be-in-tonight nightie, but the prim no-nonsense nightie. She smelt of toothpaste and wine. Her lips were stained red.

"Good night?"

"Er, yes."

She didn't want to talk, it didn't seem worth the energy involved. But Sam sat up, displacing rolls of flesh.

"I'm awake now. You woke me up with your screaming."

"Sorry about that."

Michelle yawned.

"I'm tired, I need to sleep, I've got work tomorrow."

"Me too, but I'm awake now. I think I'll read for a while."

They needed to talk, Michelle knew they needed to talk, but she was too exhausted for conversation, especially that conversation. Sam sat in the light from his bedside lamp. Michelle breathed deeply. He watched in a curious, passionless gaze. This woman who had meant so much to him, whose mere presence once caused such excitement to his rushing flesh, now slept a few inches from him and he felt nothing, aside from a dead sort of regret. He supposed it was over, but he didn't want to think about it, so he returned to Jane. She was better company and she was dead.

March 9, 1987

I DON'T know when he returns, sometime late. I think I hear something but do not wake properly. My sleep is populated with naked men. Normally this would be a good night's sleep, but not tonight. Tonight their presence troubles me deeply. Eventually it is morning and I awake still indented by sleep, and stagger about, finding dressing gown and slippers.

In the kitchen Moses is enjoying the coffee routine. I

need tea, not coffee, this early in the day. I want to say this, but I accept the cup.

So you came back, then?

Clearly so.

Where did you sleep?

In the front room, under my coat.

Weren't you cold.

A bit, but it suited my mood.

Oh. How are you this morning then?

Mulling.

What?

Mulling things over. Other than that, I'm all right.

Glad to hear it.

Anyway, I'm not mulling – I've mulled. I've decided how to resolve this.

He hands me his coffee and picks up a plate of toast (how had I not noticed this toast?), then heads upstairs, with me in tow. We climb right to the top, to my studio. Moses places the plate on the table and picks up a piece of toast, which he eats before gulping down coffee.

That should fortify me.

Standing under the skylight he quickly undresses.

So how do you want me? I thought the chair might be good.

His skin prickles with the cold, but he does not attempt to warm himself, although he does make a comment.

You may have to exaggerate my manhood a little. The cold is having a diminishing effect. Wouldn't want anyone questioning how much of a man I am.

So I paint Moses, too early in the morning, with gummy eyes and a headache for company. He sits patiently with a blue sky framing his large head. Sunlight frizzes the hairs on his chest. His stomach is a solid swell, more muscle than fat. The hairs on his folded arms stand up in the cold. His penis lies thickly pink across a hairy thigh. His legs are crossed at the surprisingly shapely ankles. He looks magnificent and I strive to do him justice.

When my sketching is over, he rises and turns to the stairs without a backward glance, leaving his clothes in a heap on the floor. His muscular arse fills the narrow door and then he is gone. A short while later, when the sketch is finished, and watercolour pencils have begun to smudge life into the lines, Moses returns with a towel pulled round his middle, water dripping from his hair. He views the result but makes no comment on the likeness. He says nothing, makes no criticism, but he does smile. A Moses smile is good enough for me.

Now you can put me away with the other men, shove me up the chimney or wherever.

Yes, I'll do that.

But I don't. I work on the painting for the rest of the day, and when Moses is out on one of his walks, I move the table. There is a loose floorboard under there, I am sure of that. I roll my boys up, lift up the board and hide them under the floor. Then I put the table back and everything is as it should be.

SAM woke feeling tired. Michelle was up, showered and dressed presumably. She had stayed the night, but left the bed early, like a guilty lover – or a pissed-off wife. There was a mug of tea by the bed. Tea was just what a man needed after half a bottle of red the night before. He reached gratefully for the mug and his fingers touched cold china. The tea was old, there was dust on the surface. God only knew how long it had been there. Sam swung his legs out of bed. There was no point staying in bed until Michelle brought him a cup of tea. He'd be waiting a long time for that.

CHAPTER TWELVE

RICK'S tea was warm and so was Naomi. It had been a while since they had done that in the morning, thought Rick, as he lay back, mug in hand. He could hear her singing in the shower. He didn't recognise the song, yet he felt as if he had known it forever. She was always singing that song, whatever it was. He smelt of sex and could feel her imprint on him. He smiled to himself and then set himself thinking. It wasn't his own sex life he had to worry about: it was Bill Inchcliffe's. He would have to go back to the Cemetery View Guesthouse and see if he could come to an arrangement with the owner. What had he been called? Clarence someone or other.

Naomi whisked into the bedroom, kissed him, and left, casting a smile over her slim shoulder as she went. "See you later, private dick," she said, laughing. "Or see your private dick later."

Her laugh danced out of the house with her.

Rick showered off the sex, dried and dressed, then ate a healthy breakfast of yoghurt and muesli, washed down with orange juice. By unseen synchronicity, his brother was eating too, half a mile away in the large kitchen of his Georgian home. Light flooded through the glass roof of the garden room, picking out the crumpled material of Sam's un-ironed shirt (she'd been too tired and Sam didn't know how), and illuminating the greasy smears on the empty plate in his hand. He had just eaten a sausage sandwich and it had been bloody marvellous. He'd bought the sausages from the farmers' market, proper Yorkshire sausages, made by a proper Yorkshireman after his own clogged-up heart.

As Sam burped in satisfaction, Rick swallowed a couple of the pills Naomi always lined up for him, a multivitamin and a fish-oil supplement. Then he began tidying the kitchen. Sam, meanwhile, took one bite out of an apple, and lobbed the barely mutilated fruit through the open door and into the garden. He hadn't lost his touch: it landed just where he wanted, in a big pot containing one of Michelle's favourite plants. He had no idea of the plant's identity and no curiosity either. It was a plant, it was called something or other, and that was all he needed to know. Sam locked the French windows and, on his way out of the kitchen, just as Rick was washing up half a mile away, he deposited the greasy plate on the work surface and grabbed a couple of chocolate biscuits from the tin. The dirty frying pan stayed on the cooker and half a loaf sat nearby skirted by crumbs.

The brothers were embarking on more or less the same journey, Rick on his bike, and Sam in his Audi. Rick was easing his bike round the Golf in the garage, while Sam was squeezing into his car, having opened the doors into the wide back lane. Soon Sam was bouncing down the lane, which brought him on to Huntington Road, opposite the tiny riverside motor mechanics. Then he headed off on a short journey across York to the road where Jane Wragge had lived and died. Sergeant Sal was due to meet him there, with a sheaf of posters, for a spot of door-knocking. As he turned into the dead-end street, Sam had to brake to avoid a bike.

"Bloody cyclists! String the lot of them up, the inconsiderate bastards. Sweaty too, no doubt, the soap-dodging free-wheelers."

He wound down the electric window so that his thoughts could be communicated to the cyclist.

"I was about to give you a mouthful."

"What for?"

"For being a cyclist who got in my way."

"Oh, carry on, if it makes you feel better."

The window whirred back up and Sam harrumphed out of the car.

"So what are you doing down here then?"

"I've come to see the owner of that guesthouse."

"Why?"

"To follow up a line of inquiry."

"What, some errant husband been putting it where he shouldn't?"

"Something like that."

Sam turned to his sergeant, who had been watching her boss and his brother.

"You got those posters, Sergeant Sal?"

"Yes, boss."

"Let's get going. Oh, how rude, I didn't introduce you. This is Rick, my brother. He used to be one of us, but he's gone over to the dark side."

"How's that?"

"He's a private investigator."

"I remember," said Sallie. "You were in the force when I joined. There was a case in the Groves, a girl killed by her own father or something."

"I left York to sort my head out."

Sam mimicked his brother: "To find myself. Daft bugger went backpacking or something. Away for ten years he was – until he returned to get in our way."

Rick smiled at Sallie, not his brother.

"Well, I'd better be going. All those naughty shaggers won't incriminate themselves."

CLARENCE Smith emerged from the kitchen where he had been cooking breakfasts for his guests, two middle-aged couples from middle America. He asked them where, and smiled politely when they told him, but forgot their answer immediately. A haze of breakfast fat enveloped him. He liked to shower after breakfast, and he was tidying up the kitchen in readiness for a welcome spell under hot spouting water when the reception bell rang.

"Yes, how can I help you?"

Clarence offered a brittle smile.

"Oh, it's you again. What do you want?"

Rick held up his hands as if miming offence.

"You never called."

"Perhaps because I didn't wish to speak to you."

"I'd like to set something up in one of your rooms."

"What do you mean?"

"Hide covert recording equipment in there. A tiny camera with a feed to a laptop, so that I can record my client's husband when he comes back with his girlfriend."

"How do you know he's coming back?"

"Well, I don't. But he may well do. It's worth a try, isn't it?"

"How is it worth my while, though – what do I get out of it?"

"Oh, I'm sure we can come to some arrangement."

Rick rubbed his forefinger and thumb together. Clarence was tempted, but not for the reason Rick thought.

"Go on, then. I expect we could strike a deal."

"I was hoping you'd say that. If you could show me the room they used last time."

"Sure."

Clarence led the way upstairs from the lobby and into a corridor with three doors leading off.

"These are my guest rooms, and the happy couple were in this one."

The room was large and pleasant and had a view over the street. Rick saw his brother and Sallie Sidekick knocking on a door. Sam moved like a man weighted by life.

"Is that where the artist was murdered – the house over there?"

"Yes, I believe so. Nice woman, apparently. They reckon the boyfriend did it, don't they?"

Rick turned back to face the room.

"What's upstairs?"

"My rooms."

"May I have a look?"

Another staircase led to a door with a private sign. The rooms had slanting ceilings and large skylight windows. Rick looked around the lounge, which led off to another room, a bedroom by the look of it, then took an interest in the floor.

"The room we were in – is that below this one?"

"Yes, right under."

A large rug covered the floor, leaving varnished floorboards on show at the edges.

"What I'd like to do is set up something in the room below that could be monitored from up here. A couple of tiny cameras with transmitters should do the trick. Then if they book in, I'll set myself up here with my laptop."

"And how do I occupy myself while you're busy with that?"

"Oh, glance over my shoulder, I shouldn't wonder."

"There's no need to be rude," said Clarence.

TWO things happened as Rick left the guesthouse: his mobile chirruped its annoying tone and his brother loomed into view.

"Must take this," he said, flipping the top on his phone.

"Moses Mundy here," said the distant voice.

"Oh, where are you now?"

"Not telling. I've got some background material ready for you."

"What about?"

"My life in south London. I'm sure you'll find a lead there. Those people, the people I knew, they are not big in the forgiving and forgetting department. They threatened to track me down, and I guess they took their time. They didn't find me so they took revenge on Jane instead."

"Isn't that a bit extreme?"

The line went quiet for a moment. Rick stood in the street, looking at Sam and listening to the silence. When Moses spoke again his voice sagged with sadness.

"You don't know these people. They have their own codes, their own ways of operating. If it suits them to bide their time, they will. And if it suits them to kill a man's girlfriend as a way of getting to him, then that is what they will do."

"So what's this material then?"

"Details, addresses, photographs – the lot. I've just put them in the post to the address on your card. I'll call again in a day or so."

"Fair enough, and…"

Moses rang off and Rick tired to get his head round what he had just been told. An alarm bell began to ring somewhere deep inside his being, but he silenced it: he could do with the sleuthing, he told himself; what harm was there in a trip to London?

"Another wife wanting her husband caught?"

"Something like that."

Sam wondered what his brother was smiling about.

"You're looking pleased with yourself."

"Am I? Oh, don't know why. Nice day, isn't it?"

Rick unlocked his bike.

"You ought to be careful on that thing, you know. It's best to be careful at our age."

"Age has not nothing to do with it, Sam. I'd worry about circumference more than age, if I were you."

As his brother left, Sam tried to remember if Rick had always been that smug,

CLARENCE Smith was finishing up in the kitchen and looking forward to a de-greasing under the shower, when he heard that bell again.

A large man was standing in reception.

"Morning," said Clarence.

"It is, that's true."

"What are you after?"

"Not a room, fortunately, or I'd walk right back out of this guesthouse and find one with a more welcoming host."

"Sorry, busy morning. Cooking breakfast and then I just had some private detective in here asking me questions."

"I know. Saw him on the way out. Always was a nosy

bugger, ever since he was ten and I caught him spying on me and my first girlfriend."

"How's that?"

"Here's my card."

"Oh, I see, another Rounder."

"Yeah, I'm the official one: chief inspector Sam Rounder. I've got some posters here I'd like you to look at. These four men are connected in some way to Jane Wragge, the artist who was murdered over the road."

"Terrible business, but like I just told your brother, I didn't really know the lady. Only to nod to, that sort of thing."

"I'd like you to look at this and to put it up in your lobby here, see if it jogs any memories."

"Mostly tourists coming in here. What are they going to know about anything?"

"Well, you never know? This poster has pictures of four men, as painted by Jane Wragge. We are assuming that the men were her lovers, thanks to the intimacy of the poses. Sadly, she didn't just paint them as they looked, she did them all impressionistic, or whatever the word is. Anyone look familiar to you?"

"Nope, don't think so."

"If you could put the poster up, sir, it might just nudge someone's memory."

"All right."

"Oh, what did my brother want?"

"We were discussing an arrangement we might be able to come to."

"What about – some illicit shagging no doubt?"

"Something in that general vicinity. Why don't you ask your brother?"

"I might just do that."

As Sam left, his head swam with thoughts about lunch, mingled with images of underhand sexual goings-on. It had been a while, but at least he had spent the night, or part of it, with a woman, even if it was his pissed-off wife who had upped and left long before he awoke. He wondered if he would ever wake up again with someone pleased to see him at the start of another day. Somehow he doubted it. Then he told himself to can the self-pity, and trudged off to find Sallie Sidekick.

CHAPTER THIRTEEN

BILL Inchcliffe began to plot his next assignation. He should not be doing this, but he could not help himself (that sex addict curse again). Besides, he should cash in on Catherine before his attention wandered. He had got himself into a corner over this one. Catherine was his secretary and that would make it difficult when he moved on, as he would. He knew fidelity was the proper thing, and Catherine was a lovely girl, so why didn't he stay with her? Or even with his wife. Miranda was the forgiving sort, perhaps they would be all right, if he kept it zipped up.

The truth was he enjoyed the hunt, the chase and the challenge, but quickly tired of the prize. He wasn't sure what this said but suspected it was not flattering.

"I am who I am" – that was his personal philosophy and it had served him well.

When Catherine came into his office that morning, the sun was shining in a blue November sky. The world looked good, and so did Catherine. She was wearing the pencil skirt again, the one that made her walk in tight, restricted steps on her black high heels. Usually she dressed for practicality, choosing grey suits and pastel blouses, no nonsense clothes with only a hint of sexuality. Mostly she favoured flat-heeled shoes on which she carried herself briskly.

"You look fantastic."

"Office talk, please, Bill. We need to keep all that private."

"Why come dressed like that unless you want me to notice you all over again?"

"Perhaps I was hoping some of the other men might notice me."

"Why would you want to do that?"

"Oh, a girl likes to have her admirers. Besides, you're a married man."

"Oh, but she doesn't…"

"Understand you?"

Bill sat back in his leather swivel chair.

"No, she understands me all too well. But let's not spoil the day by talking about my wife. She'll divorce me soon enough, and then I'll be free… we'll be free to do what we like. Anyway, why don't you book us into that funny little guesthouse again? Then we can have another naughty night."

"What will you tell her this time?"

"Oh, don't worry about that. You make the booking and I'll concentrate on the fabrications."

"All right. But now we need to work. You've got a meeting at 11, then another at 12, and one more this afternoon. And there are three reports waiting to be signed off."

"My, you are being strict with me this morning."

He stood and moved closer, and ran his hand over her tight arse. She flicked him away and walked over to her own smaller office. Through his blinds the firm carried on its business, betting on assorted risks and dangers, balancing cover against profit, calculating the many ways of misfortune.

Bill wondered exactly how he had ended up in such a job. His marital recklessness hardly chimed with such a careful profession. How had he chosen such work? He could hardly remember. Perhaps one day he would discover what he really wanted to do, but at least he wasn't bad at this work and it gave him plenty of opportunity to pursue his hobby. That's the way he liked to regard his dalliances, as a pastime. Other men threw themselves around the mud while trying to pull each other's shorts down, or whatever the muscle-bound fools did in rugby; slithered around after a football; found boring hills to ascend; played computer games; even collected stamps (did anyone do that still?); whacked small white balls around a big field. He liked to collect women. And he felt good about Catherine, so perhaps he should stay with her.

Bill spent the rest of the day constructing a suitable lie. He also thought of what lay ahead again. Perhaps Catherine would do that thing to herself again. That had been a real turn-on. What a surprising girl she was turning out to be.

CHAPTER FOURTEEN

THE posters started to do their work. This was how Sam found himself in the playground of his old secondary school, which was now a primary. It was lunchtime and shrieks tore the air. Sam was transported back as he crossed the playground. Memories lined up to taunt him.

"Noisy lot of buggers, aren't they?"

"Oh, no noisier than any other year. You don't notice after a while. It's like those people who live near roads who manage to block out the traffic noise. I can manage to exclude the noise of children."

Mick now preferred to be called Michael Stilton and was a head teacher. He had seen the poster on Look North, the local TV news. Sam was suspicious of people who volunteered themselves and, to be fair, suspicious of people who didn't. He once read about a political pundit who always thought, when interviewing politicians, "why is this bastard lying to me?". He felt much the same with suspects, even voluntary ones. They all had their secrets.

Stilton led Sam into his office. He sat at his desk and formed his fingers into a pyramid. His wife said this made him look precious, but the habit stuck – especially when he was nervous, which added deeper tones to his already red complexion. Sam slid a copy of the poster across the desk. Stilton glanced down, then away.

"Dear me, I was younger then, wasn't I? You can see that even in her impressionistic swirls. And I was in better shape then, too, which I think she has caught. Jane was a good artist and a lovely woman too, but we didn't last long. We spent a couple of months together one summer... 1985, I think it was.

"After we'd slept together a few times, she asked if she could paint me in the nude, and I was flattered, I suppose. Excited even. No one had ever asked if they could paint me before. Plenty have since, but they've all been children – and I've definitely kept my clothes on."

He let out a strange titter of a laugh that didn't seem to fit with his height and sober bearing.

"Yes, well. Like I said, it was a long time ago."

Stilton fiddled with his hair, which was arranged in a vain attempt to disguise his baldness.

"Did you keep in touch?"

"Not really, although I did go to one of her exhibitions once. There really isn't much more I can tell you. After we parted, I then met the woman who would become my wife and that was pretty much that. I heard Jane had moved on a couple of times, maybe more. I don't think there is anything else I can add."

"One thing about being fat is that you can't disguise the problem," said Sam, pushing himself upwards.

"Not sure I get your drift, Mr Rounder." Stilton worried a loose strand of hair back into place.

"I'll be in touch again," said Sam. Why did he think this man was lying to him? Maybe it was something as simple as the hair. The smallest thing could make you suspicious of a person, even a bit of foolish vanity; precious, too, the way he steepled his fingers. Sam passed through the cacophonous throng in the playground, as waist-high children swooped and dodged, weaving round this large intrusion into their space. The noise was still ringing in his ears as he drove off in his silver Audi.

It was Rich's turn now.

Richard Whitty was a York artist who worked from a

studio in his house in Heworth. He, too, had come forward after seeing the item on Look North.

Sam drove up one of York's less attractive streets, passing industrial units and the huge rusty gas tank, which rose and fell throughout the day like a gigantic metal toad, then entered one of the city's nicer addresses. The difference between the two roads always struck him. Pass over the small roundabout by the toyshop and you entered somewhere altogether different. He parked outside the house and sat still for a moment. He had still not eaten and his stomach was complaining. He eased himself out of the car and walked towards the house. This was a nice street with a few local shops, a bowling green, a down-at-heel tennis club, as well as two specialist businesses, one stocking posh Norwegian electrical goods, the other selling upmarket cookers, stoves and fireplaces. Sam had never bought anything from either establishment.

Whitty came to the door wearing a paint-splattered shirt and old jeans decorated with spills and dribbles. There was a paintbrush in his hand, another inserted behind his ear. Sam showed his identity card.

"Ah, yes, sorry. I forgot, got myself wrapped up in what I was doing. Come in, come in."

The hallway was tiled and a door to the left offered a glimpse of sofas and a large television.

Ahead a handsome staircase rose to do its job with confidence. The hallway diverted to the left of the stairs and ended at a closed door decorated with two panels of stained glass depicting sunflowers. Another door to the left led to a room Whitty used as his studio. A sash window offered a view of a yard and garden beyond.

The room they entered suggested a comfortable sort of

chaos. A radio kept up a sonorous commentary. There was an easel in the middle of the floor, a couple of small tables to the side, and a canvas covering on the floor that spoke of years of creative spills. Half-completed paintings were spread on one of the tables, while sketches were pinned to the walls. Finished paintings decorated the walls. Sam squinted at one of the paintings, trying to make out what it was supposed to be. He never could be sure, although he liked Jane Wragge's garden paintings. He could tell what they were.

"Can you see it yet?"

"What's that?"

"The painting. Is it translating for you?"

Sam looked again. Two forces appeared to have gone into its creation. A formal, technical display of skill had captured York Minster in all its majestic scope; then afterwards chaos had been imposed on the picture, smudging and half-obscuring what had been carefully painted before.

"Not much of a one for art myself – and the last time I painted anything was at primary school."

"Did you keep any of your childhood art?"

"What do you think? No, although my mother kept some framed on the kitchen wall, for some reason. But she's been dead for years, so my artistic contributions are lost to the world. Mind you, I don't think Turner ever felt threatened."

"Sorry, I haven't offered you anything. Tea, coffee?"

…or a nice big sandwich, overflowing with sliced beef, maybe some red onions, and lashings of pickle…

"Coffee would be good."

"Feel free to have a nose round."

Sam felt hugely weary as he looked for somewhere to sit.

He placed himself on a chair by one of the small tables. The table had been tidied and was neater than anywhere else in the room. On top of a pile of sketches was a framed watercolour nude showing a woman with strawberry-blonde hair raised in a precarious pile. She leaned forward on a hard wooden chair. She was in good shape, Sam couldn't help but notice, although something about the painting troubled him. He was inching towards the answer when Whitty returned.

"Ah, I left that out for you. Thought you might be interested."

"Why is that?"

"That's our lady, poor Jane."

He handed Sam a steaming mug of black coffee, and Sam drank deeply of its hot dark bitterness.

"Sorry, I didn't ask the milk and sugar question."

"This is fine."

"When Jane said she wanted to paint me naked, I said that I will if you will, lover. She seemed happy with this, so she did me first, and then I did her. In between, we did each other, if you get my drift. I hope I have captured something post-coital in my brushwork."

"I'm sure you have. So how long did you know Jane Wragge?"

Whitty rubbed paint-stained fingers over the grey stubble decorating his head.

"I've aged a bit since Jane painted me. No grey hairs back then. It was 1986, I think. We spent a few months together, lovely months, and I was sad when we parted."

"Why did you part?"

"Oh, artistic differences, I guess. Two artists do not necessarily make for a happy union. But it was fun while it lasted, and I missed her afterwards. I've been married and lost my wife since then. Cancer it was, horrible, a terrible time. But I made it through and here I am, still with my paintings. And a new younger girlfriend, as it happens."

"So you didn't keep in touch with Jane?"

"Not really. I went to one of her shows and we gave each other a shy cuddle. That was about that. I did see her around occasionally. York's a small place, you bump into people."

"But nothing else? You never went back to her house or anything like that?"

"The funny thing is, even after I lost Mary, my poor wife, my mind often went back to Jane. Isn't that awful? I was married to Mary for, what, 11 years or something, and yet Jane inhabited that small alcove at the back of my mind, that special place.

"What do you have in your alcove, inspector?"

…right now a big steak sandwich, or maybe one of those Italian toasted sandwich things, dripping melted mozzarella…

"Plain empty."

Whitty drained his mug. It was time for this policeman to go. He wanted to paint again, he wanted to lose himself in what he was doing, to submerge himself in his work. It was better that way, better to lose himself. When he emerged he didn't always like what he found. He handed over a large brown envelope.

"What's this?"

"I took the liberty of having my painting of Jane copied. I thought it might be useful to your investigation."

Sam felt almost absurdly pleased as he took away his souvenir. Would an old nude help in any way? He had no idea, but he was happy to have the painting. It made him feel closer to Jane again.

"Thanks for speaking to me, Mr Whitty, but I'll be back."

As the door closed and the inconvenient policeman left, Richard Whitty leant back against the wall, his face drained of expression, and he felt exhausted from the effort he had put into his performance. What a curse Jane Wragge was, still with her tentacles round him all these years later, even after her death. It made no sense, he had Sarah, the new girl, and yet still she haunted him. She's gone, really gone now at last. He wondered how one relationship could have stained his life so, making more of an impression even than his marriage.

He pushed himself away from the wall and went back to his painting, only to find that the inspiration had left him. Instead he picked up his painting of Jane. It was a good painting, he had to admit as much, and her remembered nakedness could still arouse him all these years later, even though she was gone. He thought of their times together, all the fun and sex they had; but not the last time, best to put that out of his head.

Chapter Fifteen

SALLIE Lane was having no luck in her search for Pablo and 'Himbo'.

"That woman managed to fit more men into her life than I ever have."

She scowled as she spoke. Sam had worked with Sallie for years and he saw the scowl as endearing. It reminded him he wasn't the only pissed-off person around.

"It must be something about those artistic types."

He was trying to find pleasure in a station cheese sandwich: God, but wasn't food meant to be enjoyable in some way? Not this pappy bread and flaccid cheese, slithered with limp lettuce.

"Always wanting to express themselves. Maybe it gets them all excited or something."

He washed down the disappointing sandwich with a mouthful of tepid coffee, and then upended the half-full cup into his bin.

Sallie listed her men for Sam, who didn't want to hear, but she told him anyway: one 'proper' boyfriend, followed by one husband. "The sum total of my sexual experience." She sighed as she ate a mouthful of salad from a plastic box.

Iain Anders had no progress to report either. It was that sort of afternoon. Not easy, he said, having to door-knock and make calls asking about someone called "Himbo". He had heard more than enough jocular remarks and putdowns on the subject.

"I thought I'd got somewhere for a while, but it turned out to be someone taking the piss. Again."

He stretched his long runner's legs and crossed his trim ankles. He was eating, too, a sandwich he'd made at home that morning.

"That looks better than the rubbish I just ate," said Sam.

"Ham and roasted pepper on wholemeal bread I made myself yesterday afternoon."

"Bloody hell. There's Sallie with her salads and you with your posh sandwiches on home-made bread. How did I ever get landed with two such disgustingly healthy underlings?"

"Here, try this."

Iain offered a sandwich. Sam, who tended to steer clear of anything wholemeal or brown, took a suspicious bite, nodded in appreciation, and then polished off the rest.

"Not bad. Maybe I should have a go at this healthy eating lark. Then perhaps I could join you and your jogging chums for a canter."

"Knavesmire has been there for a long time, boss, but I don't think it's ready for that yet."

"Very amusing. And for that insolence, and for consuming all that healthy food in my presence, you two can carry on looking for our Mr Himbo."

THE irregular hours weren't popular with Naomi, but she wasn't around to complain. She was out with her girlfriends, probably being chatted up by some romantic chancer or boozed-up Romeo. Naomi always attracted the men.

"Don't worry. Most of them are idiots," she said. "Anyway, it's just a bit of fun, harmless flirting and all that. It does the soul good. You should try it."

Rick sent a text as he left home and she replied straight

away. They were in a bar by the river. Rick drove off with images of Naomi and strange men in his head. Maybe it was all the betrayal he saw.

He parked in the dark street. His other life held its attractions on a night like this. He could still be on the other side of the world with Naomi, but instead he was sitting in his car in a dead-end street by York Cemetery, waiting to capture evidence of an insurance boss shagging whoever it was he wasn't meant to be shagging. His secretary, from what Rick had weaselled out after a few calls. While he was sorting out somebody else's mess, Naomi was on the razz and available to please other men's eyes. For the first time in years, Rick felt the hot uncoiling of jealousy. This wasn't getting him anywhere. He went into the guesthouse, where Clarence Smith was positively ecstatic about the subterfuge.

"Spy cameras linked to a laptop – it's like something off the television."

He spoke all too eagerly, as he led Rick up the stairs and showed him into the room.

"Right, I need to be busy. So can you leave me in peace?"

"Sure. How shall I let you know when you need to be out?"

"Ring my mobile."

Rick gave Smith a card with his name and number on it. Alone in the room, he looked for the best locations. After unpacking his bag of technological tricks, he decided to use two cameras: one hidden underneath the television and facing the bed, and the other secreted in the lampshade above the bed. He had just managed to attach the second camera when his mobile rang.

"I couldn't get a signal. They're on their way up."

As Rick slipped out of the room he heard footsteps on the stairs. He hid and watched through the strengthened glass of the fire door, seeing distorted shapes rather than people. His heart beat faster than the last time he had risked a game of squash.

He gave them a couple of minutes and then went upstairs. Sitting in front of his laptop, he wondered what exactly he was doing. One floor below, a man and woman were undressing each other and he was perched above preparing to watch and record their lovemaking. Until he became a private eye, Rick had never witnessed another couple having sex, but now it seemed to be an occupational hazard. At least the wireless technology worked. They were at it right now on the screen in front of him. Miranda Inchcliffe would have all the evidence she needed.

"THAT was the best one yet."

Catherine slipped off and lay next to Bill. He smiled without replying, and reached for his wineglass.

The difference in their ages was illustrated by their nakedness. Where Catherine was still slim with only a slight mound for a stomach, Bill was starting to fill out. Where once he had been tall and slim, now he was tall and not so slim. If his arms were still lithe and his legs betrayed little sign of added weight, the same could not be said of his stomach, which had started to swell a few years ago, slowly, almost imperceptibly at first, but now there was no denying it. He was the shamed owner of a thin man's stomach, which protruded from beneath his skinny chest as if he had swallowed a football whole.

"All that wine's to blame."

"For what?"

"Your stomach."

Bill frowned and swallowed, which is harder than it sounds to do simultaneously.

"I could stay at home and get nagged."

"I wasn't nagging. I was just teasing, having a bit of fun. Don't be touchy."

It had been a long day and Bill wasn't sure he had got the better of it. He didn't think Miranda had believed his story about a last-minute meeting in London, but she had accepted his excuse with equanimity, which was unsettling. She had smiled pleasantly and told him he was working too hard, and should perhaps consider taking up a recreational activity. He hadn't like to point out that he already had one.

Now he felt overcome by lassitude. The sex had been nice, sex always was, but Bill understood at some level that he only enjoyed sex he shouldn't be having. Other men looked at Miranda with longing, and if he wasn't married to her, he might feel the same. He wondered why he couldn't stop chasing other women. Somewhere deep down he just wanted to be 19 again and possessed by excitable virility, ever ready to have sex, an erection on legs. Nowadays it was all more of an effort, but still he couldn't stop himself chasing up more partners in the hope of capturing something that had gone.

Bill smiled at Catherine and refilled his glass.

"Funny sort of a place this, isn't it? Perhaps next time we should find somewhere more romantic."

"Oh, I don't know. I like it. It's our secret, isn't it? We're tucked away in bed and nobody knows we are here."

A few feet above the naked couple, Rick was wondering

how much longer he would have to keep on filming. He wanted to be at home, he wanted Naomi. Instead he was spying on two naked strangers. It was a funny sort of way to earn a living.

Chapter Sixteen

SAM was engaged in a desultory conversation. Michelle was cooking, if making a salad can be called cooking. As she chopped and grated assorted healthy ingredients, they talked in tight gloomy circles. Hostility swarmed the air between them, waiting to sting.

"What's for tea?"

"Salad for me and the girls. You can have that too, or you can make yourself something unhealthy and fat sodden that will end up killing you instead."

"This isn't going to be one of those conversations about my diet, is it?"

"I've given up having those."

"What, because you don't care any more?"

"Because you don't listen any more."

Sam accepted a plate loaded with a distressingly large pile of greenery, took a bottle of white wine from the fridge, and retreated to the garden room while the others ate in the kitchen. He had the diary with him and needed a comforting break with Jane. He began to wonder about poor Jane, with her beautiful brains bashed out. Surely she would have understood. Then he laughed sourly: women never understood him.

March 13, 1987

MOSES is such a dear man, yet a man of silence too. His wordless spaces allow me to paint. After capturing all that muscularity, and rolling him up to lie with the other naked boys, I have returned to my imagined gardens. No garden, however beautiful, can match what I conjure. The plants are recognisable, accurate, yet there is something deeper, something impenetrable in my gardens. I don't think too deeply because it would spoil what I create, but these gardens are my Eden, I suppose, with latent sin slowly uncoiling in the undergrowth.

Life has returned to normal again after the naked portrait, or so I tell myself. Or it had until last night.

Moses exudes power most of the time and especially in the company of men. He has no male friends or none he tells me about. He says I am all the friends he needs, which is sweet, but a bit of a responsibility. We bumped into Rich the other day and I almost told Moses about him, about what he did to me, but decided not to. He seemed nervous and it occurred to me how big Moses is, the sheer size of him.

Then there was last night, and how my hand shakes still. Here is how it happens. We have a lovely meal in town, fish for me, steak for him, chips times two, a bottle of red, and ice cream for me, coffee for him. We walk home via the bridge in Fossgate, that cobbled hump over the River Foss, which coagulates beneath us, unseen and unloved. We are full and happy. The encounter with Rich has flickered almost out of sight.

That was a lovely night, Moses.

Glad you appreciate it.

Along Walmgate he puts his arm around me, and he is holding me still as we pass under the dark arches of Walmgate Bar. We cross the busy road, walk round the corner, dodge up the narrow terraced street that rises slightly, cut through another and come out on to our hill. It's not much of a hill, but it is ours, and it stretches up to the university. We cross the road, dodging the taxis carrying students who are starting their night while ours is ready to end, and submit ourselves to the shadows. There is a full moon and scudding clouds, so the light is luminescent, then darkness pulls over, in a pattern that repeats every minute or so.

It is always restful here. I like the way this street runs to the cemetery: all that quiet and eternal peacefulness lies just over the wall. So much space, so many lives lived, just beyond where we are living ours.

Funny, Moses, how a place for the dead made our introductions.

The dead have their uses.

You do say the strangest things.

I say the strangest things! That's rich coming from you.

Don't know what you mean.

We are nearly home and the street is in shadow, then it is flooded with pearly light, before the moon clouds again. The returning moonlight delivers a shape. The man, when he speaks, has a rough London accent. He addresses Moses as 'Harrison', which confuses me. I assume he must have got the wrong person, and I am about to tell him this, when Moses blocks out the stranger.

Go inside, Jane.

Why?

Just do it, please.

I open the door and step into the hall, the beginning of my sanctuary, the place where everything always seems right and no harm can befall me, yet I don't go all the way in. I watch from the door. Moses is bigger than the wiry tough stranger. As he manhandles the man down the street, towards the cemetery, I see a flash of something, then hear the clatter of metal. Has Moses been hurt? Moses and the dangerous whippet stranger move towards the wrought-iron fence, grappling in a vicious cha-cha. Their struggle forms an almost comical dumb show yet watching makes me feel sick. The shadow men slip round each other, made insubstantial by a passing cloud, then as the moonlight returns, I see that Moses is lifting the other man clean off the ground. The man wriggles but Moses has him tight and he is risen high until he is level with the top of the fence, then he goes over, falling to the ground on the other side. Moses steadies himself, then leaps over, landing next to the slumped stranger. He drags the man up, who is limping now, and they are absorbed into the darkness, gone missing among the dead.

I drink black coffee in the kitchen. The meal churns to acid in my stomach and the coffee adds to the unease. The clock on the wall above my head deals the minutes like a miser handing out coins. Two long hours let me worry about might have happened. When Moses returns, his face is dirty, mud decorates his shoes, his trousers are ripped, and there is a gash in the arm of his jacket. He removes the jacket gingerly, and I see that the gash goes all the way through.

Please don't ask me too much.

What do you mean? I've been sitting here waiting for two hours, wondering what the hell has happened. I wanted to call the police, but didn't know if I should.

Moses permits himself a wry grin.

No, that wouldn't have helped.

Who was that man?

He came from the past and was not welcome.

What does that mean?

It means what I say, and he won't be troubling us again.

What have you done to him?

I have conveyed a message to those who sent him.

Moses, why are talking in this strange way? You don't sound like yourself at all.

Well, I don't entirely know who myself is, but I like the self you turn me into. The self I am with you is a good self. You didn't know my other self, my other selves, so you need not trouble yourself about them.

You are scaring me, Moses, talking like this.

There is nothing to worry about, lover girl, not now. I had to do something, now it is done. Here, help me with this.

Moses rips at his shirt and pulls off the sleeve to reveal the wound. I get hot water and cotton wool and clean the gash. The wound is about three inches long and the flesh parts in a way that makes me feel dizzy.

That must hurt.

Naturally, but I've had worse.

I have seen the scars when you undress.

Each one tells a story, none of them very nice.

Oh.

I dress the wound with lint, then bind it with a roll of plaster.

You should get that seen to properly.

It will find a way to heal, flesh usually does.

It is 2.30am when we go to bed. My sleep is fitful, made uneasy by the friendly sounds of my old house. Every familiar creek or rattle seems menacing. Voices overheard from the street can only speak of harm to Moses, my Moses.

★★★

SAM put down the diary and drained the last of the wine – warm now, lacking the cleansing thrill. His plate was empty so he must have eaten. A pool of spent dressing gathered round a sodden slice of cucumber. He rose on aching knees and went upstairs to his own bed. Michelle was already asleep and she had risen by the time he awoke. The first thought to crawl into his skull as he lay alone in the big marital bed was that he needed to check the dates for March 1987. Perhaps there was a body, an unexplained death, something to pinpoint the stranger who accosted Moses Mundy, and was last seen being lifted into the darkness of York Cemetery.

CHAPTER SEVENTEEN

LATE autumn fog obscured the morning. It nudged against the guesthouse windows as Bill Inchcliffe and Catherine Whiting curled round each other, her youthful curves slotted into the contours of his incipient middle age. Then she unlocked herself and, shivering, leapt out of bed, lithe and quick, while Bill admired her well-turned nakedness through sleep-smudged eyes. His uprising was slower and he felt for a moment the treacherous pull of gravity as he tested unsteady legs.

"How's your head?"

"It's fine," he said, lying. Catherine smiled and said he should watch the wine.

"Like I said, I could stay at home and get nagged like that."

She came close, wrapped in a towel now, and threw her slim arms around his neck. Her eyes were clear and blue, and free of make-up her face held a faint scattering of freckles. He thought about removing that towel, but his back ached, his head hurt, and his penis was shrivelled and sore. Sex and alcohol wasn't doing him any favours.

"Shower and breakfast."

She pirouetted towards the bathroom. He followed and soon they were enveloped in steam and soap. Once dry, they dressed. A fresh outfit for her, the same clothes he had arrived in last night for him.

"You should have brought a change."

"I forgot."

"Well, at least I'll be wearing different clothes when we get back into the office. We don't want to arouse suspicion."

"True enough."

Bill spoke for the sake of saying something. He had form when it came to arousing suspicion and gossip followed him wherever he went. He wasn't as accomplished at deception as he thought, and perhaps Miranda was wasting her money – or, strictly speaking, his – on a private investigator. Proof might as easily have been got from casual conversations at the office, yet she had wanted something definite: the sort of proof that could not be argued against. That evidence of marital betrayal would be delivered soon, but for now Bill continued to believe he was inviolable, quick and clever enough to keep one step ahead of his compliant wife. That he saw her as compliant showed just how much a man can misunderstand his wife, even after ten years of marriage.

Breakfast should help the hangover, Bill thought, as he descended to the dining room. The funny little man who ran the guesthouse offered him a full English, and he accepted the lot, a plate piled with bacon, sausages, scalding hot tinned tomatoes, baked beans, and fried bread, and a mug of coffee too. Catherine had yoghurt, fruit, half a piece of toast. Then she whisked herself upstairs to pack and be gone, as had become the pattern. She was already navigating the fog by the time Bill was finishing his breakfast, fully satisfied and cured in the happy interim before the weight of greasy food met the swill of half-absorbed alcohol. Soon enough she would be at her desk, armed with something vague to say about last night's television, just in case anybody asked (she had swotted up on the Radio Times); a quiet night in by herself watching ER.

In the kitchen Clarence Smith stared out of the window and could see only fog. How depressing. Then he saw the washing up. How depressing times two. He couldn't do anything about the fog, but left the washing up for now, thinking the "girl" would do it later. He returned to the dining room, which was too small for the number of tables it contained and pushed unwanted intimacy on the guests. This morning there was only the man who was up to no good, his girlfriend, and two visiting Americans. The girlfriend had already gone back upstairs. The middle-aged Americans were pulling away from their table. They smiled and went up to pack. They had done York yesterday, now Edinburgh beckoned.

"Busy day ahead?"

Bill was already beginning to regret breakfast, which had just met the wine residue and it was not proving to be a happy union. A bubble of indigestion popped somewhere deep inside.

"Oh, just the usual. Work."

"Do you work here in York?"

"I think that's probably my business."

"Just making conversation. Has your, er, friend gone already?"

"That's my business too, but, yes, she wanted to make an early start."

"Oh, I see."

Bill was thinking that this annoying man didn't see anything at all: he didn't see that he was still a virile girl-getter who could enjoy dalliances with women almost half his age. Whereas Clarence was thinking that this cocksure twerp didn't know that his illicit cavorting had been filmed to provide evidence of his extracurricular shagging.

The two men exchanged tepid smiles. Bill went upstairs to clean his teeth. Clarence remembered the "girl" wasn't due in today, and surrendered to the suds. He wore yellow gloves for the task, which wasn't very manly, but washing up was a casualty of the job and he didn't want to ruin his hands. He had nice hands, or so he had been told once, long ago. He savoured the memory, then pushed it away. That wouldn't get the day started. Instead, he wondered if the private eye could be persuaded to give him a look at his laptop. That girlfriend was a pretty slip of a thing.

Across the city, fog nuzzled the windows of the kitchen where Bill should have been having his breakfast. From where she stood, the long garden was virtually hidden, with only shadowy trees still visible. Miranda spent hours outside, digging and planting, pruning and planning. A garden was something you could plan, unlike a husband. She wanted to keep hold of the garden after Bill had been dealt with. Would she find herself another man? Almost certainly, but she would have her fun first, have sex for the sake of having sex, play the field like a man.

She wasn't quite young, but she was not middle aged. Men still found her attractive, still looked, and sometimes she felt empowered by that realisation. It was good to be looked at and she didn't even mind when men gazed unashamedly at her tits. At other times, self-doubt would ambush her, unpicking her confidence stitch by stitch, so that her attractive, open face seemed plain and closed, and the body she maintained so carefully betrayed her with sags, bulges and other imperfections. Some mornings she stood naked in front of the full-length mirror in the bedroom and cried at the punishing self-exposure, seeing the girlish ghost of herself through her tears. But not this morning, this morning she felt good. She regarded a night in by herself as a treat, having made a necessary pleasure out of Bill's absences. She never knew when he was truly away on business, so had decided to treat moments of solitude as a treat. She took long scented baths, and watched what she wanted on television – ER last night – while drinking Bill's most expensive white wine (just the one big glass) and then eating dark bitter chocolate (just the two tablets, nibbled round the hard edges until they dissolved to sweet nothing). She turned her bed into a luxury rather than seeing it as a symptom of abandonment. Or she tried to and often succeeded, being strong willed that way.

As for sex, she could look after herself until she decided what to do next.

She had work today, at the university. She worked part-time, three days a week, in one of the offices. She enjoyed the job as much as she had enjoyed any other, which is to say not an awful lot, and when she tired of the office politics, or grew weary of the thin superiority of some academics, she was perfectly employable elsewhere. In truth, she had yet to find herself, to use that woolly imprecision, yet she knew she was capable of much, if she could only put her mind to it.

Miranda tidied the kitchen, which was hardly messy at all with Bill being away, and then prepared to leave. God but that man could make a mess. Sometimes she wondered how one man could cause such domestic chaos, a scattered trail of discarded socks curling in their own foul scent, crumpled clothes, scrunched beer cans, abandoned mugs of coffee, and washing up that never got washed unless she gave in and did it herself. As for the vacuum cleaner, she doubted if Bill even knew where it was kept.

It was a short drive to the university, and normally she enjoyed speeding round the ring road, overtaking numbskulls who stuck to the speed limit, but the fog would deny her that pleasure. She would have a slow and anxious journey. She hated fog. She set the burglar alarm, locked the front door and climbed into her sporty German car. She was about to leave when her mobile rang.

Some miles away, in the foggy heart of the city, Rick Rounder stood by the bedroom window above Ogleforth. The gothic heights of York Minster were shrouded. Naomi had left for work feeling grumpy, denied a run by the fog. She ran to work most days, going the long way round. Her route took her through town, up Micklegate – offering that rare thing, a hill, in flat old York – under the bar, in front of the Odeon, and then over the iron bridge at Holgate, before curving towards her destination. She showered at work then changed into the smart clothes she kept in the office. Today she had taken the bus and how dull and depressed everyone appeared in the fog-shrouded vehicle.

Rick sensed Naomi wasn't fully satisfied, knew his job was pushing them apart. He would devote more time to her when he had finished the jobs he had on at present. One case concerned the call he was making now, and the other would see him taking the train to London in an hour or so.

"Hello, Miranda, Rick Rounder here."

"Oh, hello."

"Have I got you at a bad time?"

"No, I was just about to drive to work, that's all. Key in the ignition and all that."

"Be careful in all this fog."

"I will. Do you have something for me?"

"I have the information you require."

Rick wondered why he started to use such stale official language.

"Evidence of what my husband has been up to?"

"Precisely so, yes."

He was growing used to other people's secrets, to trading in their lies and deceptions. But he wondered how good it was for the soul to be the means by which a woman discovered the full grisly truth of her husband's infidelity.

"I'm about to go to London for a day or so."

"Ha, that's just the sort of line that Bill spins."

"Well, it happens to be true in my case. Another investigation I'm working on. I can post the information to you before I leave."

"Yes, do that. I need to see what you have. I don't want to see it, but I need to have the irrefutable proof put in front of me."

"I'll post it to you before I go to London. We can meet up when I return, if you want to."

"Yes, and you need to send me a bill."

Miranda spoke briskly, as if she were settling another mundane account, a bill for decorating or building work.

"I'll send it with the material you require. You should get it in the post tomorrow. And feel free to contact me again if you need anything else."

"Thank you, I will. Although I suspect it will cost me."

"We all need to earn a living."

"And that's how you have decided to earn your crust?"

"It is."

"A strange kind of occupation, isn't it, Mr Rounder?"

Before Rick could answer, Miranda rang off. As she edged towards the university through the fog, her errant husband came downstairs into the reception at the Cemetery View

Guesthouse. He settled up, exchanged a wary farewell with the owner, and prepared to leave.

"Until the next time then," said Clarence Smith, smiling. It was not, Bill concluded, a very nice smile. How curious that a smile, that indicator of happiness or pleasure, could have a sting like that. He parried with one of his own, a smile considered wolfish on occasions.

"Maybe."

"Goodbye then."

Clarence Smith thought he was unlikely to return if his wife saw the evidence first. He was thinking that he wouldn't like to be in his shoes when that happened, although he would quite like to have been in – or rather out – of his shoes last night. Late-night television could only sustain a man so far.

Bill stepped into the fog. Instead of walking out of the street, he approached the railings and looked at the cemetery, standing at just the spot where Moses Mundy had heaved a stranger over the fence, many years previously. Swirls of fog wrapped round the gravestones, grey plants were weighted with damp. Despite the cold, it looked peaceful in the cemetery, a place apart. He had never been inside and should visit one day. Maybe go for a walk with Miranda. She liked that sort of thing, or he thought that she did. Sometimes he lost track.

He turned up his collar and set off for work, passing, although he did not know this, being incurious about the wider world, the house where Jane Wragge had been murdered.

Bill had seen Jane Wragge's paintings, although he did not recall doing so. Miranda had taken him to an exhibition at a bookshop in York for an opening. There had been wine and real fires. Bill had helped himself to three glasses of cheap red wine, which was two more than everyone else. Miranda wanted to buy a painting, but Bill wasn't encouraging. She nearly went ahead anyway, but lost confidence. They had muttered hot words amid the polite conversations of strangers. The day had been spoilt, Miranda said.

It was still foggy when Bill approached work along the banks of the River Ouse. Great blankets of chilled air and condensed droplets unfurled beneath Lendal Bridge. Inside the office it was warm and air-conditioned, so even the air they breathed was controlled.

People chatted about last night, what had been on television ("Did you see...?"), or discussed sporting clashes and compared holiday plans. Catherine had a workspace just outside his office. He smiled at her as he walked by. She smiled back and asked, a little too shrilly, if he had been up to anything last night. He wondered what on earth she was on about, then flashed a lupine grin and said that, yes, indeed he had. Catherine reddened. She had supposed he would take the hint and say something about going to the pub or watching television, a mundane snippet to be overheard by others; but he did not.

At around the same time, Rick Rounder walked across Lendal Bridge, going past the office where Bill Inchcliffe worked. Fog wrapped his hurrying feet. He was booked on the next train to London.

As Rick entered the station, his brother began searching the records for evidence of death or disappearance to tie in with the stranger who had paid an unwelcome visit to Jane

Wragge and Moses Mundy, all those years ago. Iain Anders and Sidekick Sallie continued to search for the remaining two members of Jane Wragge's quartet of painted lovers. Mick and Rich were accounted for, if not free of suspicion, but Pablo and 'Himbo' were still to be found.

CHAPTER EIGHTEEN

IT WAS damp where they had brought him. Mossy bricks curved into the gloom above his head. Dank droplets blessed his bruised cheek and reconstituted the dried blood smeared across his face. Trains rumbled above his head. His hands were tied behind his back and a rough wooden chair supported his weight. They had pushed him underneath railway arches somewhere. Some god-awful corner of the capital he wished he had never visited. He steadied himself as a bright light burned out the darkness. A face loomed and spoke in the harsh tones of south London.

"So pal, what are you doing sniffing round here asking about Harrison Hill?"

"I'm a private eye, Hill employed me. Rang me up wanting help. Said I should follow up leads down here, to help prove his innocence. He isn't Harrison Hill now, he calls himself something else."

"That fucker has called himself all sorts of things down the years. None of them true. And I know what I'd call him."

The light scorched and tiny white worms wriggled across Rick's eyes as he tried to work out how he had got himself in this mess.

The day started so well. This well-travelled man, this "trendy bloody globe-trotting hippie", as his brother put it, was looking forward to a short trip to London. He enjoyed the journey, surrendering himself to the pleasant forced inactivity of travel, the forward rattle of the tracks and seeing his reflection flung across the scenery. On arrival, he was swallowed up at King's Cross and discovered again the rank intimacy of travelling on the underground, the mandatory, wordless companionship. He didn't mind. He was on the move again, a traveller once more, if only for a day or so.

He gave himself a couple of hours in Greenwich Park before visiting the people and places Moses Mundy had suggested. How he loved that park, high on a hill above the widening Thames, with front-row seats for the view across the river to the City. He didn't even mind the towers, slicing into the sky with boastful ease, although he preferred the Royal Naval College, a picture of symmetry neat at the bottom of the hill.

The day turned out sunny and clear. A pristine blue sky stretched above as he stood on the highest point in Greenwich Park, savouring air that was fresh for a polluted city. Earlier, he had walked through the fumed centre of Greenwich, so he appreciated the difference.

He walked across the park all the way to the Blackheath side, where he discovered deer fenced off among the trees. Then he had stepped beneath the Royal Observatory, and followed a precipitous path towards the gates at the bottom of the park. He passed a theatre, asked the way to a decent pub, and was directed to a small pub in a terraced street. Even the beer was good, not that Sam would have admitted as much. No, Sam believed that praise for anything southern uttered without the application of torture represented a grand betrayal. This especially applied to beer, which was uniformly awful in the south, flat, tasteless and over-priced. But never mind Sam, the beer was good, bright and bitter, and Rick felt happy as he drank it. Sometimes perfection came in small things.

He could have stayed longer, but had work to do. After

re-reading the instructions from Moses Mundy, which he slipped back inside his jacket pocket, he took a noisy, smelly bus to Deptford. The journey did not flatter the destination. Where Greenwich had been classy and historical, Deptford was sooty and run-down. He asked for directions and was pointed towards a pub with grimy windows. Inside, the pub was musty and uninviting. The beer tasted as if it had died in the barrel some time ago, but he took small sour sips anyway, not wanting to get off on the wrong foot. The place was almost empty, and he might have felt happier if it really had been empty. The locals lurking in the shadows glowered at him. He offered to buy the landlord a drink. The landlord accepted with a nod but little grace. He was a big man, taller than Rick and with greasy tendrils of hair hanging over a square forehead. He looked like an ageing rocker. Life had left its marks on his face, a tracery of scars and scratches.

"You passing through?" he said, leaning towards Rick, thick wrists crossed on the bar.

"Sort of."

"Only we don't get many tourists in here."

"Oh, I'm not one of those. I'm working."

"At what?"

"Finding things out."

"Are you some sort of a journalist?"

"No, not at all."

"Copper then?"

"No to that one too, although I used to be."

"So what is it, then?"

"I'm a private investigator."

"Don't get many of those in here."

"I'm working for a client who is in some trouble and he

suggested that I come to south east London to chase up his past."

"And he said you should come in here?"

"He did."

The big landlord fell silent, and the pub did too. The place hadn't exactly been noisy when Rick walked in, now it was almost silent. There was a dog behind the bar, Rick noticed, something large and menacing. He wasn't hot on dogs and didn't like the look of this one. It exposed its teeth at the side of its mouth, eyes flashing black.

"Down, Bruno, down."

Relieved of the necessity to threaten, the dog disappeared out of view. Rick was relieved - he bloody hated dogs. The landlord stayed put.

"So what's he called, this client of yours?"

"Well, he seems to be called lots of things, but when he lived round here, I think he was called Harrison Hill. It was a long time ago, maybe you won't remember him at all. A long shot I know, and…"

Rick sensed the name had meant something. A flicker of recognition animated the tapestry of scars and nicks that made up the landlord's face. Strange that such a face should have eyes so blue and clear, he thought. He was wondering at the disparity when the landlord took away his pint, which he had barely touched, and poured it down the sink.

"You don't want to be drinking that muck. It's off today. Seeing as you're almost a regular, what with your connections, have this instead."

He flipped a lid and passed a bottle. Rick sipped and nodded his thanks. This beer was much better, and Rick said so.

"Glad to hear it."

"So is there anything you can tell me?"

"About what?"

"Harrison Hill."

"Like you said, it's been a while… thirteen, fourteen years. He kept himself to himself, liked to sit over there at the table under the window, watching and occasionally talking to people. He was a pleasant man, considering."

"Considering what?"

"Considering how he earned his living."

"And what did he do?"

"Somebody will be along in a minute to tell you, another friend of mine, and Hill's. One of the old gang."

A certain level of noise had resumed, but Rick still felt exposed. If he had acted on his instincts a moment or two earlier, he might have got away to ask more questions elsewhere. But he ignored what his finer senses were telling him, sipped his beer, and glanced about the pub at the truculent locals.

"I bet you do a lively karaoke in here," he said.

"Oh, yes. Johnny over there by the dartboard does a mean Frank Sinatra, while I do a passable Edith Piaf."

Rick laughed at that, genuinely, freely, forgetting the danger.

"As for Ethan here, who's just come through the door, you should see his Bruce Springsteen."

Before Rick could think of a song-theme response, saying that he was born to run, and doing just that, the new man in the bar had put his arms round his shoulders.

"Nice to meet you. Now I think I know someone who can help with your inquiries."

Rick found himself propelled from the bar by the man

called Ethan and an unnamed sidekick. Both shared certain characteristics of size and head meets razor encounters. Their shaved craniums escorted him, one each side, burly arms directing him. Rick had managed to grab his bag before they commanded him, but other than that his freedoms were limited. Outside the pub it was almost dark and he wondered where the day had gone. The fine blue sky had surrendered to drizzle and dusk An old white van was parked outside, blocking the traffic. Cars squeezed by, horns tooting. The traffic stretched in a long impatient queue. Some cars had their headlights on already and the reflections spilled across the wet road.

"Dear me, we seem to be causing a nuisance," said the man called Ethan. The other man opened the back doors and went to shove Rick inside. Rick swung a punch at the man. Rick wasn't a small man and he was fit and strong, but his attempt at an assault bounced ineffectually off the man's muscle-bound chest. The man hit him back, one punch to the side of the face, then manhandled Rick inside the van. The door clanged shut and his burly chaperons walked round the van to climb in the front, with Ethan driving. Rick's face felt red and stinging, and blood dripped from a cut beneath his eye. The inside of his mouth tasted metallic as he spat blood.

The van slowed and Rick tried the doors, vainly hoping to escape, but they had been locked. He sat back against the side of the van and allowed himself to be rattled inside this tin can on wheels to wherever it was they were taking him. The journey lasted ten minutes or so, which gave Rick time to wonder what he should have done differently. Another job was leading him towards trouble. Had he been foolish to agree to Moses Mundy's suggestion that he should go to south London and look around? Possibly, but he wasn't sure what else he could have done. He didn't know this part of the world and the secrets of Mundy's past weren't going to reveal themselves. He didn't even know for sure that Mundy was innocent. The world at large, even his brother at large, assumed he was guilty of murder. Rick believed Mundy or Hill or whatever he was called, but he was gambling on a hunch. And this was where his intuition had got him.

The van jolted to a halt. The back doors were unlocked and Rick stepped out. Before he could get a bearing on his location, he was pushed through a small door cut into a much larger door that reached up high above his head.

It was damp where they had brought him. Mossy bricks curved into the gloom above his head. He couldn't make out much. There was a counter or desk of some sort, a large shape, possibly a car, under a cover. He was pushed into a rough wooden chair and had his hands tied behind his back. As he waited in the dark, his breathing seemed harsh and uneven, and somewhere inside his chest his heart raced and hammered. He took deep breaths and tried to bring himself under control.

Then the harsh light was turned on and the man started to talk to him. It was going to be a long night.

CHAPTER NINETEEN

THE face behind the light was hard and unforgiving, the voice rough and fag-worn. The shadow raised his hands in an expansive gesture, palms upward, as if intending to convey reasonableness. He didn't sound like either of the men who had brought him here. Maybe they were the goons.

"Perhaps you could just tell me, Mr Rounder, where I might catch up with Harrison Hill or – what did you say he was calling himself these days?"

"Moses Mundy."

"That's quite a name. I'm sure it suits him. Yes, if you could tell me where to find our Mr Hill, or Mundy, then we could part friends, no harm done."

"The thing is, I don't know."

"Why should I believe that?"

"Believe what you like, it's true."

"From where I'm sitting, a little more politeness might be in order, pal. You are not in a position to strike a bargain."

"Last thing I heard, he was hiding out in the Yorkshire Dales. But he won't have stayed there. He's a man on the move, the police want him."

"What for?"

"They suspect he killed his girlfriend."

"Hill got himself a woman, did he? How sweet. Then he went and killed her. Now isn't that just typical."

"He says he didn't do it."

"Well, that's all right. An honest man gave his word. So we can all go home."

The man chuckled, or Rick assumed that was what he was doing behind the burning globe. It wasn't a pleasant sound. As the mirthless laugh stopped, a match flared. Smoke curled from the end of a cigarette, the man exhaled. The smoke parted round the light and Rick closed eyes already raw and itchy. He coughed and spat. His spittle hit the bulb, hissed and evaporated.

"Any chance you could point your sun-lamp in another direction? I think my tan is done now."

"Very amusing, Mr Rounder. But I'm not sure a man strapped to a chair with his hands tied behind his back is in a position to make demands."

"Here's something I don't understand: why didn't you go after Hill before?"

"He disappeared off the face of the earth. Well, off the face of south London. We heard a whisper and one of our crew went off on a solo mission to find him. The thing is, he didn't tell us where he was going, we only found out afterwards. He told his girlfriend he was going after Hill. But he didn't say where he thought Hill was and we never heard from him again. Not a squeak, never been seen to this day. So we can only assume he found Hill."

"And Hill had quite slipped your mind, until I started sniffing around, asking questions?"

"Not exactly, but you brought him back to mind. He sent a message, you see."

"He contacted you? But he sent me here to find information to clear his name."

"That's a good 'un."

The man emitted an unpleasant gurgle.

"Glad to have caused you such amusement."

"Oh, you aren't amusing me at all. You, my friend, are pissing me off something rotten."

"What did he say in his message?"

The man sighed and fidgeted.

"He said his circumstances had changed suddenly, that he had certain needs, that he wanted money he felt we owed him from years ago. The cheeky bastard."

"And did you pay up?"

"Oh, let me see… no, course we didn't."

"So what will he do next?"

"Show up for a nice nostalgic chat, I shouldn't wonder. Talk about the old times."

"What did he used to do for you?"

"This and that, bit of the other – some of it not very nice. Good at what he did, though."

"Hill swears he is innocent, so could someone from down here have caught up with him and killed his girlfriend, just to settle an old score?"

"Yeah, it's possible." The chair fidgeted again, scraping on the hard floor. "Anything is possible, isn't it? But I ain't going to sit around here chatting all night. It's getting late and I need my bed."

The man stood and sent his chair clattering to the floor. This set a dog barking and snarling.

"Shut it, mutt."

The dog whimpered into silence. Rick hadn't realised there was a dog. Shit, he hated bloody dogs.

The man moved to the side of the harsh bulb. Rick still couldn't see clearly, but he could distinguish the outline of the man's face. It was large, framed by lank grey hair.

"Well, I'm off to get my beauty sleep. I hope you find the arrangements to your liking."

"What, you're leaving me here?"

"You won't be alone. You've got the mutt for company."

The man came out of the light and moved behind the

chair where Rick was tied. Rick could feel breath on the back of his neck.

"Now I'm a reasonable man. You've told me what you say you know, and maybe you are being straight. What should I do with you now – let you go now and send you back to sheep-shagging land, or wherever it is you come from?"

"York, I come from York. Not many sheep there."

"Never been there myself."

"You should, you'd like it."

"Now would I? How, what's the word, presumptuous of you. We've only just met and already you are telling how I might like to spend my valuable free time."

"You could come and visit me. I could repay the hospitality. I must have an old chair and a rope somewhere or other."

"Very droll, Mr Rounder. Anyway, that's enough chat. It's been very nice and sociable, and all that, but I'm off home to sleep in my nice big bed next to my nice big girlfriend. You, my friend, are sleeping in this shit-hole next to a big hairy dog. One of us has got the better of this arrangement."

As he spoke, another man emerged from the shadows. The first man put his arm round Rick's neck. Muscles flexed beneath the man's shirtsleeve and Rick swallowed. The unseen man undid the ropes round Rick's wrists.

"Stand up."

Rick did as he was told. His legs cramped beneath him and his wrists were chafed. His head hurt from the bulb.

"We've made up the spare room for you."

Rick was manhandled away from the bulb and into a far corner of the arched space. His hands, released and free, were grasped and tied again, this time in front.

"It even has en suite facilities," said the main man, laughing unpleasantly. "I'm sure I left it round here somewhere. Ah, yes. Our en suite bucket. And we've kindly tied your hands at the front, in case you need to piss."

"How very considerate."

"I know, my friends always say I am too kind. So, that's it: one ratty old mattress, one en suite bucket, and one hairy mutt guarding the only way out. He's on a chain and he shouldn't bother you if you stay put. Try to get by him, though, and he'll have your bollocks."

"So my bollocks will become the dog's."

"Yes, very amusing. I'll be round with your breakfast in the morning, and then I'll decide what to do with you."

The man turned off the bright bulb and left, taking his sidekick with him. Rick sat on the mattress until his eyes grew accustomed to the dark. He couldn't make out much at first, only shapes. Gradually, he could distinguish the curve of the ceiling, and in the far corner a crack of light. That must be the door, he thought. He stood and took a tentative step towards the door. Nothing. So he inched nearer, keeping his eyes on the crack of light. The light grew brighter, then disappeared. A car could be heard driving off. Up above, the last train of the night rattled towards its destination. The train shook drips and dust from the ceiling. A dirty droplet landed on Rick's forehead as he made one more tentative step. He took shallow gulps of air and his heart pounded. He was steadying himself for the next step when the dog shot out of the darkness, barking furiously. The terrible sound shocked the silent space. The dog was caught in mid-leap, barking and foaming, inches from Rick's face. But the chain contained it, and the beast – for it was certainly that to Rick – fell to the ground. It continued barking and Rick could smell its rancid breath. Christ, what were they feeding that thing on?

Eventually, the dog relaxed and slunk back to its place by the door. Rick let his heartbeat settle, then found that bucket. The beer he had been drinking earlier, a lifetime ago it seemed now, had turned his bladder into a furious ball of nerve-twanging agitation. His tied hands made the job difficult, but he managed to free himself and fired off a stream of hot urine into the old bucket. Splashes and spray came back at him, but he didn't care. The relief was a sort of ecstasy in his present bleak circumstances. He put the bucket down as far from the mattress as he could, then lay down and started planning what to do next.

CHAPTER TWENTY

HE SLEPT well, betrayed by exhaustion, and was woken by the first train when dirt trickled on to his face. There had been a plan in his head when he fell asleep. Now it was gone. He sat up, his aching hands tied together in a rough simulacrum of prayer. Fitting, really. He could do with someone answering his prayers.

It wasn't fully light, but he could distinguish more of his surroundings. He was in a workshop or garage beneath railway arches. Standing, he used the facilities again. The splashing woke the dog. The big hairy creature of indeterminate breed yawned, then lay with its jaw on the floor, one eye watching.

"Morning," Rick said. The dog made no reply.

There was only the one door, behind the dog. Rick considered the foul bucket. Perhaps if he threw its contents at the dog, he could get out somehow. He picked up the bucket, no other plan in mind, and made one step towards the door. The dog decided it didn't want to be placid any more and leapt in one swift hairy movement. The chain yanked it back inches from where Rick stood, bucket in hand. The dog snarled and snapped. Rick replaced the malodorous bucket, its liquid sloshing unpleasantly, and took a step back. The need for aggressive animation having been removed, the dog returned to the door. Rick sat on the smelly mattress. Other than emptying a bucket of his own urine over the guard dog, he didn't have a plan.

Then he noticed that his bag had been left with him. That was something at least. As he picked up the bag, he wondered what Naomi would be doing. Waking up, preparing for a run, or out already, striding and skipping across the pavements of York. Not round the bar walls because they wouldn't be open yet. She was fitter and fitter, always running. She was making her own life, with him and apart from him.

Naomi wouldn't be worried. He had said he was going away for a day or maybe two. His phone was still in his bag. He wanted to hear Naomi's voice, but he didn't want to alarm her. What could she do anyway? He would phone Sam instead. His brother could contact the Metropolitan boys. Even as he flipped his mobile he could see the weakness in his simple plan. There were countless railway arches, so how would the police know where to look? What category of idiot was he? He pushed on anyway and hit the stored number. Would Sam be up yet?

As it happened, Sam was attempting to do sit-ups on the bedroom floor. Years ago, when he still played rugby, he had been able to push himself up and down with mechanical rapidity until he was rewarded by a warm spread of muscle pain across his stomach. Now his muscles were hidden beneath a mountainous aggregation of unwilling flesh. He counted out ten, twenty, then collapsed, panting. Still, it was a start.

Rick looked at the screen: "no network". He flipped the lid shut.

Rick was overcome with a sense of his own foolishness. He had come to London at the bidding of a man wanted for murder in York. His only reasons for trusting this man lay in a vague sense of his innocence. He still didn't believe Moses Mundy had murdered Jane Wragge, but the man had an unsavoury past. What had he been thinking? Nothing much beyond asking a few questions at locations suggested by Mundy. That had got him locked up underneath the arches somewhere in south London, with only a bucket of piss and a hairy dog for company.

Rick had a signal and tried the number again. Sam was now attempting push-ups. His arms were strong, always had been, but they were barely equal to the task. He pushed against the floor and raised his body, lowered himself, pushed up again. Then collapsed on to the carpet. His mobile rang on the bedside table.

"Yes?"

"Morning, Sam."

"Bit early for a chat, isn't it?"

"Less a chat, more a brotherly cry for help."

"So what bother have you got yourself into now?"

"Locked up under a railway arch in south London, with only a big hairy dog for company."

"How did you manage that?"

"It's complicated…"

"What do you want me to do?"

"Call someone in the Met, ask them to look out for me and…"

"Where are you?"

"Dunno exactly. Under a railway arch somewhere near Deptford."

"Where's that?"

"Down from Greenwich."

"Even I have heard of Greenwich. There's a big boat there. A tea clipper or something."

"Yeah, the Cutty Sark…"

Rick saw the door move and heard a rattle of a chain.

"I need to go, Sam. Someone is at the door."

"Any other pointers to where you are?"

"No, underneath a railway arch somewhere in south London, like I said."

"Hopeless…"

Rick cut the call and stood. Sam rose from the carpet, stretched and tried to touch his toes. Perhaps it would be easier if he could see them in the first place. He gave up and made a few calls. He wondered where Michelle was.

The door swung open and the light flooded into this place of stale confinement, along with the smell of bacon. God but he was hungry, he hadn't eaten for hours. The hairy guard dog jumped up and barked with enthusiasm rather than menace.

"Down, mutt."

Rick recognised the voice, but not the face. He hadn't been able to distinguish much the night before, but he was certain that the man holding him captive was not George W Bush. Neither, he felt sure, was his taciturn sidekick Tony Blair.

"Morning, Mr Rounder."

George Bush was speaking to him, but it wasn't easy to hear what he had to say. His mouth didn't appear to be a good fit.

"We had a disagreement outside. My friend here said he didn't want to be that public school ponce Blair, but I told him he had no choice. I'm the boss so it was only right that I should be the leader of the free world, the pretend Texan cowboy."

"But you always make me be Blair," said 'Tony'. The sulk didn't fit the grin on his face. Unkind commentators liked to point out that the Prime Minister's hair had thinned since the heady early days in Downing Street, when the sun used to shine on Tony Blair. From where Rick was standing, the prime ministerial coiffure gave way to a gleam of skull. The mask did not fit and bulges of stubbled flesh protruded from the side of Blair's face. Bush was a better fit, although lank greasy hair hung either side of the president's face.

"We brought you a sandwich. Bacon, hope that's all right. You not one of those vegetarians, are you, mate?"

"No."

Rick accepted the sandwich with dirt-grimed hands.

"Here, have a chair."

Bush swore at Blair, who found the chair Rick had been tied to the night before and placed it behind him. Blair didn't like having to answer orders this early in the morning.

"That's why I like to be Bush, you see. Means Blairy boy here can be my poodle."

Rick took the sandwich from its greasy wrapper and ate it with dirty tied hands. He was ravenous and the sandwich was good, a regular symphony of bread and thick-cut bacon.

"They say that it's a bacon sandwich that often betrays the vegetarians, don't they?" said Bush.

Blair, who didn't get to speak as much as the real thing, disagreed. "Sausages are better. Nice fat sausages."

"I think Mr Rounder is happy with his bacon sandwich."

Rick nodded as he finished off his breakfast and wiped his mouth with a wrapper made translucent by grease. Then he scrunched up the paper.

"Very nice, thank you."

"Now," said George Bush, stretching and trying to yawn

behind the wrong mouth, "what are we going to do with you, pal?"

Blair chipped in again. "We could take him on a tour of the sights and lose him somewhere in Thamesmead. We done that a few times before."

"Don't get carried away, poodle. I know you like it when we take inconvenient people on that particular tourist trail. But maybe Mr Rounder here could have other uses."

"Like what?"

Rick was wondering as much himself. He also calculated that when Blair had said "lose him", he was employing some grim euphemism: that sort of losing wouldn't see you found again in a hurry. A train rattled overhead, loosening more dirt. People were going to work. Normal life was going, just like it always did when someone else was having a shit day. Rick supposed it was good that life always continued. It would carry on when he was dead, and he was glad of that. That acceptance was a comfort, an indication of human immutability, but it wasn't going to get him out of this situation. He needed a plan and all he had was a headache. Bush and Blair stood either side of him. Then Bush extended a hand and rested it on Rick's shoulder.

"Right, Mr Rounder, time for us to get going."

CHAPTER TWENTY ONE

THE day broke bright and free of fog. In the allotment behind York Cemetery, a project was taking shape. A man began to attack the rampant greenery, thistles and brambles that choked his plot. The man, who was neither young nor old but stranded somewhere in the middle, did not own the land, but was determined to make the most of his rented soil. He had always wanted an allotment and today marked the first day of his fruitful new venture. He imagined this fruitfulness in a vague but satisfying manner. The fruit and vegetables had already sprouted and shot forth in his mind, spring or summer meals having been cooked, and jars filled with preserves and bottled fruit for winter. Self-sufficiency was the thing, especially with the way prices were going in the shops. In truth, the prices weren't that bad, but the man, who was called Freddie Smithson, needed some form of motivation. He knew growing food would be hard work, although his notion was a little hazy and based on his grandfather. As a small boy, it had puzzled Freddie why his grandfather needed an allotment. The garden at the back of his grandparents' house had a garden with room for vegetables. In truth, the allotment, although productive, had been a place of solace from the sometimes sharp-tongued attentions of his wife. His grandfather had hidden away, working the ground, planting and harvesting, talking to his fellow refugees, and occasionally retreating to his shed. This ramshackle construction of random wood held together surprisingly well. Inside, there was musty carpet, a collapsing armchair with disembowelled springs curling below, and a small paraffin stove, on which tea would be brewed, to accompany the smoking of hand-rolled cigarettes. Occasionally, the old man treated himself to a bottle of beer, and it was in the shed that Freddie had first tasted beer, grimacing at its thin bitterness. His grandfather had laughed so hard the phlegm had rattled in his chest.

Eventually Freddie acquired the taste, as evidenced by the thickening of his waist all these years later. He hoped the digging might take away some of what the beer had endowed. In memory of his grandfather, and in pursuit of a place of male solace of his own, he also fancied a shed.

This plot had a shed, which had been one of its attractions, although it would take a morning's deforestation to reach it. Some hours after he began, Freddie – he knew the name sounded childish, but it had stuck since childhood – reached the door. Sore of back by then, hands raw and ripped, face stung from a vicious encounter with a bramble, he stood panting. When his breath settled, he tugged at the door. It stuck, blocked at the bottom by banked up soil and matted grass. He retreated across the cleared space and retrieved his spade. He used this to cut and lever away what looked like a grassy carpet tile. Resting again, he wiped sweat off his face with a dirtied hand, which left a streak of mud, perspiration and bramble-pricked blood. Then he tugged at the door. It opened this time, swinging back with ease. The shed was dark and dusty inside, with a shaft of sunlight passing through a broken pane of glass. Old tools lay in an unproductive heap against the wooden wall, a rusty fork, a spade encrusted with ancient mud, a tangled-toothed hoe. The plot hadn't been tenanted in years and no one on the allotment could recall who had last worked the land or used the shed.

Freddie stepped inside from the bright day and breathed

the ancient dust. The shed was about the same size as his grandfather's, from what he could remember. There was no chair, but room for one. He imagined sitting here, away from the classroom, away from home, safe from the attentions of his friends. Sometimes he felt there were too many people in his life. He did a quick calculation as he bent down inside the abandoned shed: one wife, four children, two or three good friends, one surviving parent, countless colleagues at the secondary school in York where he taught. There was much love and affection wrapped up in those relationships, to varying degrees, but sometimes he craved solitude. To be a man alone, the man with no name, the Clint Eastwood of the local allotment. He laughed at the absurdity, stood, and turned to discover the remains of what had once been a living, breathing, regrettable man much like himself, or so he would later assume, as he wondered about the identity of the body in the shed. Freddie had no way of telling the sex of the dead person lying in the corner of his shed, but he assigned maleness to him instinctively. At first he wasn't even sure what he was seeing. His mind skittered about as he tried to make sense of what his eyes were showing him. "All skin and bones" was a common expression, and suddenly he saw the inadequacy of words used to describe a skinny person. What he was seeing was all skin and bones, more bones than skin, but just about identifiably human. The remains were curled at the far end of the shed, suggesting the last refuge of a creature seeking a place to die. But did they really convey that? Freddie wasn't sure, although the image would stay with him.

He extracted his mobile from the pocket of his jeans,

not an easy task given the taut way the material strained against his stomach, and rang the police.

Soon a police patrol car, which had been in the area, arrived. Shortly after that, other vehicles drew up to the allotment, more patrol cars, and a big black van, anonymous and vaguely menacing. Then another car, a silver Audi, joined them. The door swung open and the car tipped a little as the occupant eased himself out. Chief Inspector Sam Rounder had arrived. He walked over a little stiffly, his back sore from his morning exercises. Freddie Smithson felt positively slim as the policeman began asking him questions.

"So how long have you had this patch of earth and weeds, then?"

"Just this week."

"Who had it before?"

"No one seems to know. I did ask round, but it seems to be a mystery. Maybe the council will know."

"Since when did they know anything."

Sam smiled at his own remark, moved towards the shed. There wasn't room inside, so he peeped inside.

"What do you reckon then?"

The pathologist looked up from the skeleton. Justine Haxby was still in her thirties, young for the job. Sam liked the Haxby woman, as he called her when trying to affect a brusque lack of interest, and always enjoyed meeting her. The trouble was, a dead body usually came between them.

He had a stab at charm, remembering roughly what shape it took.

"Another dead one on your hands! Perhaps you should give up being a doctor."

151

The Haxby woman smiled, and spoke. "You said that about the last one. And I'm a forensic pathologist, as you well know."

"Did I say that? Oh, well. That's middle-aged men for you: always repeating themselves. So what do you think did for this one then?"

"Not a lot to go on at first glance, but we'll run some tests later during the autopsy."

"Should you be able to put an age to the victim, and give us some idea of when he died?"

"Might do. But then that wouldn't give you a lot to do, would it?"

"What about DNA?"

"Seems unlikely, but you never know. How did you lot do your job before DNA came along?"

"With the same level of skill and professionalism we have always employed." Sam smiled as he spoke.

The human remnants were removed from the shed, tenderly sheathed in black, and placed inside the anonymous van. Sam stood by the cemetery wall and stretched his sore back. He was wondering if the soil was good in this allotment, thanks to its proximity to all those bodies, leeching out their minerals or whatever it was that bodies contained. His knowledge was fuzzy. He wondered if the bag of bones might be connected to the stranger who had surprised Moses Mundy. The trouble was, his only witness had herself been murdered, and his knowledge of what might have happened rested on her diary, whose existence he was keeping to himself. Why was he doing this, following a solo offshoot into the past? He could not say for sure, but he had never felt so close to a murder victim as he did to Jane Wragge. Perhaps it was a mirage, a self-deluding fantasy borne out of his disintegrating marriage and the mess of his life. Maybe he was being a fool, and an unprofessional one at that, but he still wasn't going to tell anyone about the diary. The dead woman's words were calming and cleansing. He almost felt ready to sort his life out; the push-ups were only a start.

He made the calls to London, as Rick asked, but he wasn't sure what good it would do. Irritation prickled over his skin. He loved his brother, or supposed he did; wasn't that what you did with brothers? Sibling resentment broiled away, but Rick was all that remained of the original Rounder clan; their parents were long dead, most aunts and uncles gone. He returned to his car and offered a silent prayer to whatever gods were out there.

CHAPTER TWENTY TWO

MIRANDA Inchcliffe phoned in sick and imagined the resentment her call would cause. She was good at her job, as good as she needed to be, but her commitment was fragile. The other women would be dissecting her now, freed by her absence. There was always a ringleader and she saw her now, charming and bright on the surface, so long as everything was going her way, yet with a mouth on her when events were less obliging, and still affecting to speak like a slangy teenager; her sentences buttressed by "d'you-know-what-I-means?".

Miranda had the measure of her opponent. When she was being charming, especially to the bosses, she would look at her and think: underneath this shiny veneer, beneath the too-loud laughter and the tedious accounts of your boyfriend, hair-style, clothes, vacuous favourite television programmes – underneath all that shiny wrapping, you are just a nasty cow. The revelation emboldened her, then made her feel small and stupid. She remembered moments of friendship among her colleagues, touches of kindness from the women; and recalled her own catty lapses.

Miranda opened the padded envelope. Similar packages arrived in the post most days containing CDs, DVDs or computer games ordered by Bill. That man could certainly spend money.

"I earn it, I spend it," he would say, flashing the wolfish smile. Once she had been wooed by that smile. She had thought him handsome and charming, but charm could come in shades. Now she saw that smile for what it was.

She made tea and took the steaming mug through to the lounge and steadied herself, aware of a happier routine.

The house to herself, a slushy DVD, chocolates and the most expensive bottle of white wine in Bill's collection – such was her self-reliant routine when Bill was not around. "Not here" was the phrase she used when on the phone to her mother or to deflect a call from Bill's office, if that was where such calls came from. He was absent now, at work, or so she assumed.

The lounge was large and tastefully done out, full of stuff, yet oddly empty, as if in cautious emulation of what its owner had seen in a glossy magazine. Miranda slipped the silver disc into the DVD player – the biggest and best when bought, although superseded since – and turned on the wide-screen television. Bill's acquisitiveness had been endearing at first. She had teased him about his need to have everything new, and smiled at his impulsive purchases, his latest must-have desires; eventually she began to realise she, too, had had once been a must-have desire, an object of immediate, easily spent fascination.

The image occupied a screen as wide as easy credit could buy. It was grainy, but there was no mistaking it. She watched as her husband and a young woman entered a room, a hotel room or guesthouse room, she supposed. Miranda had seen the woman before, at some do or other. It was Bill's secretary. Her heart leapt at the recognition and she felt sick. She could have guessed, perhaps had even guessed, yet still the confirmation hurt. The couple stood by the bed, kissing. Then the orientation changed and she was looking at Bill and the girl from above. Ha, she thought, trying to grasp on to some sort of normalcy, you can see his bald patch from this perspective. He's so vain he would hate knowing that. The angle reverted and now the little bitch was undressing herself. She was slim and pert, hardly any fat on her at all. She slipped out of her underwear and was quite naked now. Bill was still struggling with his trousers, which were becoming a tight fit round his stomach. He had been so slim when they had met, not an ounce on him, a proper washboard. Now he was swelling in the middle. Unencumbered, Bill fell on to the bed while the little bitch climbed on top. Soon she was bouncing with glee, her hair flying about and lashing Bill on the face. Their lovemaking continued for a while longer but Miranda no longer took in the details. She sipped her cooling tea and remembered when she had been that girl. There had been a holiday in Greece spent island-hopping, sunbathing and making love. There were other happy times too, but hidden behind the hateful present. At this moment she knew what she had to do, knew as certainly as she had before having her suspicions confirmed in such a graphic manner. She would have to get a man in. After extracting the traitorous silver disc and turning off the DVD player and TV, she went into the downstairs bathroom and vomited up the tea and the breakfast she had eaten earlier.

CHAPTER TWENTY THREE

THE big man looked around and knew why he had left. He sniffed the petrol-infused air as he crossed a busy road, weaving between the slow-moving cars with a balletic ease surprising in such a large man. The old sensibilities came back, the watchfulness and the waiting. He had been out of the game for a long time, and had not wanted to present himself again. His new life had blocked out the past. He had moved on, made himself invisible to those he had walked among before. He had become a different and happier man, but there was no avoiding what had to be done. Events had been set in motion and the pieces were spinning as he had arranged; now he was back for one last time.

FLESH painted in the glowing moment had outlasted the love or lust that occasioned its uncovering. Three of her naked boys had already revealed their secrets, two more remained hidden. Jane Wragge, murdered in York while her paintings looked on, the only witnesses apart from the perpetrator, or 'perp', as American TV dramas have it, had left personal runes in the shape of five paintings and a diary. The memoir remained the illicit property of Chief Inspector Sam Rounder, while the still undiscovered naked men were mostly now the concern of his staff, in particular Sergeant Sallie Laine and Inspector Iain Anders. Today, they were working together, following up an anonymous phone call. The caller had said she knew the identity of one of the naked men she had seen in the evening newspaper and on the local TV news. Anders had taken the call and their witness had been garrulous in providing the details…

"I know the one calling himself Himbo. And that's a joke, too. I've seen him without most of his clothes on and I can tell you he doesn't deserve that name. I've met coat hangers with more flesh on them. Not that I was doing anything I shouldn't have been doing, at least not with him, Mr so-called Himbo. It was a barbeque and he had taken most of his clothes off and was strutting his bony body around. And it wasn't a turn-on at all. Mind you, I'm quite a big woman and he wouldn't last long under me. He'd snap like a twig once I got to work on him. I have to be careful with my John, and he's a bigger sort of man. And I'll tell you this for nothing, I like the look of the boyfriend, the one they think might have done her in. Now he looks like my sort of man, a proper full serving of a man, both scoops full, if you get my drift. This artist woman seems to have had a few, doesn't she? Perhaps I should have paid more attention in art at school. Looks like these artists have a right sex life. Anyway, the man you want, he lives in New Earswick, at the far end, getting on towards the school."

A name and address given.

Anders and Laine drove along a short and twisting stretch of road that might almost have been in the country. In the spring this route was painted pink and white with blossom; even in the autumn, with the leaves turned and fallen, it still felt almost rural. They passed the cottage on the corner that looked as if it belonged by the side of a canal, and drove through the canopy of branches, a few still green with leaves. Now houses could be seen between the trees.

New Earswick owed its origins to Joseph Rowntree, from the chocolate family. The garden village had been built in an attempt to provide better housing for the working classes in York. The idea had been to create a balanced village community where all the houses had gardens with fruit trees and enough ground to grow vegetables. Laine had been told about it more than once when she attended the local comprehensive school, which was named in honour of the village's founder. She had grown up nearby and still had a couple of aunts living in the village. Joseph Rowntree would have been pleased with the way the place had turned out, although he might have been surprised by the graffiti in the bus stop. He had failed also to predict the need for the mini mountain range of speed bumps that had sprung up, forcing vehicles to lurch and wobble.

Laine and Anders were negotiating the tarmac impediments when they saw the turning they wanted. The houses in the road were well kept and the place felt mature and settled. There were trees and gardens, and a sense of space. The house they sought was the scruffiest looking one. They knocked on the scratchy door and a dog sent itself into a paroxysm of snarling, barking and scratching.

"Shouldn't we tell Rounder about this?" said Laine, while the dog continued to worry away at the door.

"Later."

"He's been taking an unusual interest in this dead artist."

"Yeah, I noticed. There's something funny about him at the moment."

"Dodgy marriage can't help."

"Yeah, I know. But it seems to be a bit more than that."

"Perhaps he's having a mid-life crisis."

"Could be. His door was shut the other day and I could have sworn he was trying to do push-ups."

Laine giggled at the revelation. "God, I'd have paid good money to see that. Did he manage to get off the floor?"

The door opened to reveal a man restraining a dog by its collar. The man was tallish but rake thin. His Adam's apple protruded from a long neck and two or three day's worth of stubble decorated his sunken cheeks. He was wearing a vest and shorts, from which his thin legs protruded in a manner that wouldn't have embarrassed a stork. It was a bright but cold morning in November and he looked under-dressed and under-fed.

"Yeah?"

"Police. We're looking for a man used to call himself Himbo and we believe that you fit the description we have been given."

Laine looked up as she spoke. The man and his house smelt of lack of care and too many fried breakfasts.

"That's a stupid name, isn't it? Who'd call himself something like that?"

It was Anders's turn this time. "According to the anonymous call I just took at the station, it sounds like you do."

The man paused and the dog, a Staffordshire bull terrier, snuffled around the edge of the door, a wary upturned eye directed at the visitors.

"So what's all this about then?"

"We're following up leads in a murder inquiry."

"Murder? Shit, I've never done owt like that."

"We never suggested you had, sir. But we would like to come in and have a word."

The house was scruffy inside, too. Washing had been left

to dry hanging from two bikes in the hallway. They went through to the kitchen, where the smell of old breakfast was at its strongest. The bony man sat at the table.

"Park yourself down."

The officers did as advised, although only after removing more washing, arranged in two untidy piles.

"Don't mix them up. One pile's clean."

Laine tried to decide which was which; she couldn't tell, so placed both neatly on the floor.

"Not there, the dog will mess with them."

The dog was already sniffing at the clothes. The skinny man leant over and moved the washing up high, next to the grease-gummed cooker. The squat muscular dog went through an open door into the back garden.

"Live here by yourself, do you sir?"

"Just me and the dog, and the girlfriend, when she can be arsed to come round."

"Is it your house?"

"Yeah, used to be a Rowntree one, but me mam bought it from them. When she popped it, she left the house to me."

"Did she leave you any instructions on what to do with it?" said Laine.

"Yeah, but I lost them. I'm not the most house-proud man, but I try me best." He made to stand, saying: "I didn't offer you a drink. Would you…?"

Anders declined: "Just had one at the station, thank you."

"Me too."

The man settled back into the chair, eyes in a furtive flicker.

"What was it you said about a murder?"

Laine spoke this time. "We are following up leads in the murder of an artist, Jane Wragge, who was killed in her house near York Cemetery."

"Yeah, terrible thing. I read about it, in the newspaper. What's it got to do with me?"

"Possibly nothing, but the artist, Jane Wragge, left behind a series of paintings."

"Yeah, well, she would, wouldn't she, what with being an artist and all that. That's what artists do, isn't it?"

"How perceptive of you, sir. So why don't you stop playing games and tell us about your relationship to the artist."

"I'm not playing games."

"So are you the man called Himbo?" Laine only just got the words out. She felt like a newsreader struggling with a comically difficult name. A giggle was rushing up to incapacitate her.

"So are you him... Himbo?"

The word just made it out this time. Laine bit on the side of her index finger, where the skin was rough from habitual chewing. Anders took over.

"We have reason to believe that you are Himbo, and..."

It was no good, the giggles had hold of Anders, too. Now both of them were laughing. Laine had gone pink in the face, and Anders was trying to speak, but his words were lost in an outbreak of spluttering.

"Glad to see I'm keeping you two amused."

Laine regained some sort of composure. "Sorry, sir. Very unprofessional, it's just that name, you see."

"Her idea of a joke."

"Whose idea of a joke?"

"The artist woman, Jane."

"So you did know her."

"Yeah."

"And are you one of the naked men?"

"Yeah, and I was right embarrassed. I hoped no one would recognise, but they did. Got the piss taken out of me something rotten by me mates."

"But why didn't you think to tell us you were one of the old lovers? We've been trying to track you down, to find who did this terrible thing."

"I don't usually go out of my way to help you lot. Reckoned you would figure it out eventually, and you did. So well done, Sherlock."

"Which one of us is Sherlock?" said Anders.

"You mate, She's She lock."

Himbo seemed pleased with himself and his slightly bulbous, melancholy eyes lit up.

"So why don't you tell us about your relationship with Jane Wragge."

"Yeah, all right, but I'll just put the kettle on for a brew."

He stood while the kettle boiled and then dropped a teabag into a mug rimmed with the evidence of many other drinks, a tarry archaeology of stains. He agitated the teabag with the wrong end of a fork, pushing as much flavour out as he could, then topped up the mug with milk. He sat down again, with his thin legs apart and the mug cradled in his bony hands.

"I'd rather you didn't sit like that, sir," said Laine. "I think you might up end revealing more of yourself than I would like to see so early in our relationship."

"Yeah, sorry. Haven't got dressed yet."

"So we can see. So tell us your story, then. And what's your name, we can't keep calling you by that nickname?"

"Jim Whitehorn. James me mother used to call me. Nobody much else does. She, the artist woman not me mother, took the Jim and turned it into Himbo. It seemed to amuse her. She said it was because I was so skinny. Ironic, she said it was. I looked the word up later in me mum's old dictionary. Still wasn't sure what it meant."

"So how did you meet her?"

"It was down to me mother. She was still alive then, see, and she thought I should, you know, improve myself, the daft cow. She signed me up for an art course Jane was teaching. I really took to it for a while, took to the teacher too. Younger then, better looking. Me, not the teacher. She's dead, isn't she? Anyway, she was encouraging and she seemed to like me. I asked her out for a drink in town one night, and she said yes. Well chuffed, I was. We had a few and got to talking, and she told me she was in between men or something. We went out again, one thing led to another."

Jim was lost to a private reverie. Jane was middle class, educated, older. He could see her in her studio, working like mad while wearing that man's shirt covered in paint. He had never met anyone with that sort of skill. The people he knew didn't have aptitudes, at least not ones you would want to boast about in public. She drew him into a different world, showed him the possibilities.

"You've got some talent here, some rough, unfinished ability – take it and work at it, push yourself, make something of what you've got. Be yourself."

The words followed him down the years. She inspired him, made him want to fill all the blank canvases in his mind. Taught him a few tricks in bed too, giving him an anatomical pointer or two, showing him how to make her happy. Before that he had been an in-and-out man, fulfilled in a selfish instant. The girlfriend, the fat one he had now, she had been surprised when she discovered what he knew.

"You must have struck people as an odd couple."

Jim blinked away the memories. The tidy looking policewoman was speaking to him.

"Yeah, I guess we did. Nice middle-class artist and her bit of rough. Looking back, I think she was playing with me, having, you know, an adventure or something. Having her fun, but she was a nice woman. I really liked her."

"So what happened between you?"

"We fell out over something and she finished with me."

"What did you fall out over?"

"I don't recall."

"And the art?"

"What, my art? It all came to nowt. Sketch and scribble when watching television, that's about it."

"What do you do for a living?"

"Helping out friends, that sort of thing."

"Successful?"

"What do you think? Never been successful at anything, but I get by. No rent or mortgage to pay on this place, just need a bit of money to get by."

"It's legit, this work you do?"

"What's all this got to do with the dead artist?"

"Probably nothing at all sir. We just like to follow up all possible leads. And you're a lead because you were one of the men painted by Jane Wragge. Here, I've got a copy."

Laine pulled out a photocopy of the painting and handed it to Jim Whitehorn, Himbo as was.

★★★

HE LOOKED at the creased image of himself from 1985. He'd been young then, 17 years ago, only 23. The man in the painting was slim and his flesh had yet to give way to scrawniness. She asked him to look at her, but not directly at her, to gaze off over her shoulder, as if dreaming of something. He didn't know what she was talking about, but he did what she asked. It took ages and she stopped occasionally to allow him to warm up. He put on a dressing gown and drank tea. When he had warmed through, she took off his dressing gown and arranged him into the same pose again, and he sat, fighting against pins and needles and boredom. One tea break they made love under the skylight window, the afternoon sun streaming in. She had showed him by then and she cried out in delight. Then she slid from him, pulled her paint-splattered shirt over her head, formed her hair into a precarious pile to keep it from her eyes, and told him to arrange himself as he had been before the interruption.

"There's a look in your eyes after we've fucked that I want to capture."

He hadn't heard her swear before and the word on her lips upset him. It was a familiar word, one he had heard spoken often; used it himself enough times, too, unthinkingly, inserted into his speech like rhythmic punctuation. If you came from his background fuck was just what you said; but Jane was something else, she was better than that.

"You shouldn't swear like that," he said, standing.

"Himbo, sit. You've broken the pose. Oh, what did you have to do that for? I had you just right and there was that look in your eyes I wanted. Now your eyes are blazing and angry, and it's gone. These moments are so hard to get right. We had it just then. Everything was just right for my painting, just as I wanted it. Now you have gone and ruined it. My concentration is all shot to pieces. You might as well get dressed and leave."

He stepped closer. "You shouldn't have used that word. It's not right."

"That's very sexist of you, if you don't mind me saying."

"No it's not, you're better than them."

"Better than who?"

"The girls I hang out with. Tarty girls with tattoos who dye their hair, wear too much make-up and swear all the time. Not classy like you; not natural like you, with no make-up and no coloured hair, just natural."

"Well, thanks for the compliment, I suppose, but I do in fact take good care of myself, and I even have a little make-up on right now. But I don't know why I'm telling you that. I'm not having this conversation any more. You've broken the spell, ruined the moment. So you can go. Come on, get out of my studio and leave me alone."

He stepped closer and the compliant, gentle nakedness of moments earlier took on a new form. His stance was aggressive, his muscles flexed and angry, his eyes cold and dead. He reached out and grasped her shoulders, scrunching up the paint-patterned shirt.

"You can't talk to me like that. Who do you think you are?"

Panic streaked through her, but she regained her composure, and removed his hands.

"That's it. Will you kindly get dressed and remove yourself from my studio. People like you don't understand how difficult it is to be an artist, how hard it is to capture the moment. The more I think about it, the more I am drawn to only painting flowers. They don't answer back or go off on a big sulk."

He let go, contrite now. A departing ray of sun gilded his slim shoulders and long neck as he occupied himself with his clothes. He felt angry and stupid, pupil to her teacher again. Jane removed the painting from her easel and replaced it with a rose that was beginning to fill the canvas, the petals almost like flames as they ate up the virgin white. By the time he had dressed, she was already inside the painting, distracted by drunken pollen-dusted bees, watching out for the malicious wasps; cursing the relentless sun and mourning the falling petals. She knew people bought her paintings because they "looked nice" and this infuriated her and drove her to a fury. Didn't they understand the loss, the sense of menace, the useless beauty of it all? There was such sadness in a garden, the fleetingness of it all, the heady poisoned loveliness.

Jane was transfixed by the beautiful disintegration of her rose. She painted until the light was gone, stood back and squinted at what she had done. Released from the work, she was dog-tired and hungry. She hadn't eaten in hours. She went downstairs, still wearing only the shirt left by another man, which she now used as an overall. She fixed herself a salad, poured a hefty glass of red wine, and went into the lounge to watch the television news. The parade of tragic events barely impinged on her; the political manoeuvring failed to make an impression; even the weatherman, the one she liked, did not communicate with her. She was still inside that rose, was still herself that rose, that doomed and dying thing. She blinked and thought she should go and shower. She hadn't washed that day. Not once did she think of the man who had left earlier. She wouldn't see him again, she thought.

LAINE and Anders left the scruffy house in New Earswick, and headed back to Fulford Road to tell Sam Rounder about what they had discovered.

"You can see why she called him Himbo," said Anders, as he negotiated another speed bump.

"Yeah, it fits. What did you make of him?"

"Bit of a sad character, I guess. Not much spirit about him."

"Still a suspect, though."

"I guess they all are."

"Who?"

"The naked men."

"The boss has seen two of them, we've spoken to one, the other's gone missing – so there's just one more out there somewhere."

AFTER they left, the skinny man thought of showering, but had a desultory wash at the bathroom sink instead. He dressed in his bedroom, glancing at the painting, seeing his reflection in its glass. He wondered if he should hide it somewhere, but felt that the room wouldn't look right without it. He went downstairs and put the lead on the dog. It was called Buster, or was when he wasn't calling it Bastard instead, which was his idea of a joke, shouting out the word as the tough dog scuttled off to find sticks or to menace passers-by and other dogs. He walked alongside the River Foss, skirting the riverbank house he had tried to break into once, and failed, having set off a very noisy alarm. He joined Haxby Road for a short distance, then cut across the meadow, where he let Buster/Bastard off his lead. The dog romped off in search of trouble, and its owner thought of a time when he might have been a painter, of all the unlikely things; a time when he had a classy and tasty girlfriend, who taught him things, things he had never understood or glimpsed before. She knew a lot for a posh girl, did Jane. He felt like company now, but the fat lass was working at the factory. Well, one of them had to have a proper job and he didn't see why it should be him. Besides, his girlfriend was no Jane. She was overweight, dull from too many soap operas, nearly always too tired for sex. Not like Jane.

Chapter Twenty Four

RICK squinted at the sun and glimpsed the wide river. He wondered if they had worn the masks while driving him here. He supposed not, because George Bush and Tony Blair in the front of an old van might have raised suspicion. They were wearing the masks again now. He could see the masts of the Cutty Sark in the distance. Not far away, tourists were starting their happy day's toil. Ordinary life was doing that thing it does, continuing its tidal flow, whatever shit was happening to someone else. Rick felt weighted by his own insignificance. Perhaps it didn't do to think about things; then again, maybe it was lack of thought that got him into trouble. His heart raced and bumped as the masked men pushed him. He could have run for it, he was fit enough, but they had shackled his ankles, so the only action available to him was shuffling compliance. No one was around to see George Bush and Tony Blair as they escorted the private eye from York down an anonymous looking alleyway near a pub that faced the river. They stopped in front of a large door in a high blank wall. A hefty padlock secured the door, and Tony Blair fiddled with the key while George Bush stood next to Rick.

Despite the grin on his face, Blair was unhappy. He swore at the key and kicked the door.

"Here, try this one," said Bush, passing another key.

"You could have given me this one first."

"Oh, what's a poodle for if not to do a bit of extra work, to go that extra mile?"

This time the padlock slipped open. Blair unhooked it and the door swung heavily.

"That's better," said George Bush, his voice echoing round the space before them.

They pushed him inside. The place appeared to be a warehouse. Rick screwed up his eyes, trying to make out the space. It was large and high, and sunlight laced through the gaps in the tiles, alleviating some of the darkness. Rick could distinguish shapes, but little else. Were they going to kill him here?

But if so, why bother moving him? They could have finished him off underneath the railway arches or disposed of him any old way before getting here. Maybe they were playing a cruel game, toying with him, before making that final decision. Nausea swelled up and his undigested breakfast threatened to make a comeback.

Blair was reaching round in the gloom.

"Get on with it," said Bush. "It is round there somewhere."

"I know it is. You don't have to tell me that. Why do you always think you have to tell me everything? I'm not stupid, you know."

"I'm sure you have the certificates to prove it."

Rick looked between the masked men. "Do you two always argue like this?"

Bush looked at Blair, and Blair stared back, his eyes furious and sulky in their slits. Bush laughed coldly.

"Oh, you just can't get the staff. This is what I have to work with. That's the trouble with British workers. Perhaps I should get myself a Polish sidekick instead. They'd work twice as hard for half as much money, and cause me far less bother than this numbskull."

"Don't call me that," said Blair. "It's not nice and I don't like it."

"Not nice. I'm meant to be a criminal mastermind. I don't do nice. Find that light switch – you numbskull."

Blair fiddled in the dark, trying to locate the switch. There was a metallic click, followed by an explosion of dazzling light. Rick could make nothing out at first and shut his eyes tight. Even then the light burned through his eyelids.

"Big bugger that light, isn't it?" said Bush.

Then, to his sidekick, he added: "Haul her up."

Rick half-opened his eyes and squinted. A giant industrial light was being lifted on a pulley. It rose before them like a mini sun and came to rest high in the rafters.

"It's so you can change the bulb. Otherwise you'd never reach it."

Bush was speaking in a matter-of-fact way, as if filling in the gaps in a conversation. He placed a hand on Rick's arm and propelled him forward.

"Here, have a seat."

Rick shuffled towards an old leather armchair and sat. There were two other similar chairs, and all three faced each other around a small table. The table was covered in mug rings and cigarette burns, and an old copy of the Daily Mirror. It was a curiously domestic arrangement for such a cavernous space, a little bit of home inside this industrial cathedral.

Rick wondered at the purpose of this place. Cars and trucks were parked up and waiting. Large shapes were shrouded in tarpaulin. More cars, perhaps, or boats. One of the shapes certainly looked like a boat. They were close to the Thames, so boats would make sense. There were two large doors, aside from the small entrance they had used. One, if he had kept his bearings, faced the river, while the other presumably opened up on a road.

Bush sat and told Blair to make tea.

"Nice and strong, just the way I like it. Two sugars."

Blair turned to go, but Bush brought him up short again.

"Where are your manners. Don't forget to ask our guest what he would like."

Rick said that he would like Darjeeling, with just the right amount of milk, and no sugar.

"Dar fucking what?" said Blair. Rick assumed he was scowling, although he couldn't tell under that mask.

"I'm sure our guest will be polite enough to accept whatever variety of tea you bring."

Blair turned and, as he walked away, pulled the mask up and let it rest on the back of his large bald head. The sight would have seemed comical, under less nerve-racking circumstances. Tony Blair crumpled in Latex on the back of a thick skull belonging to a criminal sidekick from south London. The sidekick walked towards a boxed-off area and disappeared inside. Soon Rick could hear water heating in a kettle, a domestic sound amplified so that it became almost a roar. A few minutes later, the tea arrived in old mugs, each bearing an image of the Cutty Sark. It was the colour of teak.

"I did us all the same, the way you like it, boss," said Blair, his mask back in place.

"So no Darjeeling for our guest, then."

"Well, I won't be coming back to this guesthouse."

Rick took his tea and sipped. It was strong and sweet. Normally he hated strong sweet tea, but he was glad of it this morning.

"How are you two going to drink yours, then?"

"We are going to turn our chairs round and take off our masks."

Bush did as he said, removing a gun from the inside pocket of his leather jacket and inserting it into the waistband of his jeans.

"Just in case you get any funny ideas."

"I'm right out of comedic intentions at the moment."

The chairs scraped round and the masks were pulled up. Rick drank his tea, facing the misshapen features of Bush and Blair. The tea distracted him from the racing beat of his heart. He was trying to think of what to do next, to formulate a plan to get him out of this mess. Could this be how everything would end, killed in a cavernous warehouse by the River Thames, and then no doubt dropped into the cruelly accommodating waters, to be swept away to wherever the river carried him? He wondered how he could have been such an idiot, but knew he had been stupid before. If he survived this ordeal, he would have to get himself some wisdom. His captors had moved him from one anonymous location to another, so there was little chance the police would find him. He was stuck here with only his wits to protect him. Fleetingly, he thought about Miranda Inchcliffe, and wondered how she had reacted to the DVD. She had got the proof she wanted, but what would she do with it?

Bush and Blair fiddled with their masks, and scraped their chairs round to face Rick again.

"Nothing sustains like a good cup of tea," said Bush, letting his weight fall back into the seat. The gun still protruded from the waist of his jeans, held tight by the swell of his stomach. Blair was, Rick realised, larger still.

"So, Mr Rounder, now we have to come to the main item on our agenda. Which is: you and what to do with you. Now if I wasn't such a considerate sort, I could have had you killed straight off."

"So why didn't you?"

"A good question. I guess it's because I wanted to hear more about Hill, or whatever you said he was calling himself."

"Moses Mundy."

"I wonder where he got a name like that from?"

"I've no idea."

"No matter, he's a displeasing old fuck, whatever he is calling himself. So Hill or Mundy or whatever hired you to come to south London and start asking questions in his old manor."

"Yes, he did."

"Didn't you stop to think that might be a dangerous thing to do?"

"Truthfully, no. I fancied a couple of days in London. I used to be a bit of a traveller, you see. Spent years globe-trotting, settled in Australia then came here."

"I've always fancied Australia myself. Where did you live?"

"I ended up in Queensland, near the Great Barrier Reef."

"Sounds like you had a good life, until you messed it up and became a private eye. Are you any good at it?"

"I make a living."

"Well, I'm not sure you'll earn your fee for this job. Perhaps Hill will donate it to charity. Because you'll not need it where you're going."

"Oh, where's that?"

"For a swim, my friend, you are going for a swim. If I'm feeling kind, I'll unshackle your ankles before dropping you in. Well, I won't drop you in, he will. He likes doing that sort of thing. I'm not sure why. Perhaps he had a rough childhood. Did you have a rough childhood, Mr Blair?"

"What do you think, growing up where I did and with a dad like mine."

"So that's it, then. A less than satisfactory childhood has left my prime ministerial sidekick with psychotic tendencies. It's a story to melt the hardest of hearts."

Bush broke off to mime playing the violin.

"Yeah," said Rick. "Mine's melting all over the floor right now."

"That's not nice," said Blair, fidgeting in his chair. "Not nice at all."

Bush turned to his sidekick, saying: "Save it up for later. You know you'll enjoy it more that way. Why don't you go and busy yourself with the boat."

Blair stood and walked towards one of the covered shapes Rick had seen earlier. He pulled at the tarpaulin and, after a few more tugs, managed to get it free, to reveal a large blue speedboat.

"I wanted a red one," said Bush. "I've always fancied a red speedboat. I like red cars, too. I'm sure that says something unflattering about my personality. It probably marks me out as an aggressive and competitive type. You have to be in my line of work."

"And what is your line of work?"

"A bit of this, a bit of that, not much of it legal, some of it positively unpleasant. I do what needs to be done, and I do very nicely out of it. You should see my house, very grand it is. I would invite you round, but you're going for a swim instead, so I won't. Besides, the girlfriend is a fussy sort and she wouldn't like you dripping all over her nice clean kitchen floor."

Bush laughed at what he had said, while Blair pulled on a long loop of chain hanging by one of the two large doors. The door creaked out of view and rolled away high above the opening.

Rick could see a landing ramp and beyond that the grey swell of the Thames. Sunlight skittered across the water, leaving diamonds in the hollows. What an inviting sight it would have been in friendlier circumstances.

"Right," said Bush. "Once my friend here has got this thing started, we are taking you out for a boat ride, with a swim as an optional extra, depending on how the mood takes me."

Blair occupied himself with the boat, fiddling with the outboard motor, and then manoeuvring the vessel towards the river. He panted and swore as he did so, and Rick could hear him breathing harshly through the Prime Minister's mouth.

"Can't I take this thing off? It's bloody murder doing all this with it on."

"You can revert to being your usual charming self soon enough, but we'll keep the masks on for now. We don't want our guest knowing who we are."

"But if he's going for a long swim, it won't matter."

"Look, just do it will you, please. Do what I ask without all that objecting. It really is tiresome hearing you moan. It's beginning to spoil my day."

Blair muttered through false lips. Soon he had the boat at the top of the long ramp. The fresh river air had filled the cavernous space, animating the dust. Rick breathed deeply and watched the two men. He was desperately trying to think of what to do next. He imagined Naomi never knowing what had happened to him until his body washed up months later, if it ever did. Perhaps he would be sucked out to sea, or deposited in a silted grave, where he would lie undiscovered for an eternity. He pulled his legs apart, but the chain held fast.

"No chance, mate," said Bush. "That chain isn't going to break. Can a person swim with their feet tied like that? I don't know, but it seems unlikely. I wouldn't fancy my chances if I were you. But I'm not you, am I? You are you, and you seem to be in the shit, if you don't mind me saying. You should have stayed in Australia. Nice place, by all accounts. Why would someone swap that for being a private detective in York? Beats me."

"It's where I'm from."

Bush shrugged and turned away.

"Oi, Blair, have you got that boat ready yet?"

"A bit of help would be nice."

"Lots of things would be nice, but it don't mean they are going to happen."

"So was it worth it then, however much Hill or Mundy paid you to come snooping round here?"

"He's not paid me yet, the job's not done."

"Not likely to be done now either, is it, mate?"

The boat slid into the water and Blair hopped inside and steadied himself against the motion. He lowered the weighty looking outboard motor and fired it up. Diesel fumes smoked into the air.

"Looks like we're ready for our little voyage and your

first swimming lesson in the Thames. We're trying you in the deep end, I'm afraid, so I hope you've got strong arms."

Panic and nausea spread through Rick. If he didn't think of something soon he was done for. What an odd and inadequate expression that was, he thought. Couldn't he come up with anything better than "done for"? The morning sunshine played on the river and a fresh breeze filled the dusty lungs of the old warehouse. It felt like a good morning to be alive, but a bad one to be facing an unwanted swim with your ankles shackled.

Bush grabbed Rick by the top of his arm and pushed him towards the boat. Although Blair was the hired muscle, Bush was stronger than he looked and his fingers dug into Rick's arm like over-sized claws. Rick was propelled forwards. The boat was swaying gently, invitingly, but Rick didn't want to accept the invitation. He tensed his legs and pushed against a wooden post by the landing. All that cycling should be good for something, he thought; use those muscles. The tactic worked and Bush staggered and fell to the dusty ground. Rick suddenly, fleetingly, felt useful and empowered; he'd done something, he'd caught the bastard out. He tried to hop away, but Bush had picked himself up.

"Now what was the point in all that? You're making me angry and you don't want to go doing that. I started today in a good mood. I fucked the missus, then she made me a nice fry-up. Outside the sun was shining in a nice blue sky. I wandered round my garden and did a little bit of tidying up, did some deadheading, getting ready for winter. Then I picked up Blair boy over there and we came to find you – after first stopping to buy you a bacon sandwich. How thoughtful was that? We didn't have to get you breakfast, you know. And now you're starting to spoil my enjoyable day."

"Thanks for the sandwich, it was very nice. And I needed it. But you forgot to tell me it was a condemned man's breakfast. I'd have had a sausage sandwich too, if I'd known that. With brown sauce."

"Well, pardon me for my manners. I'll make a mental note to be more considerate to the next nuisance who comes sniffing around asking too many questions."

Bush shoved Rick into the boat. The boat rocked and diesel fumes infiltrated his nostrils. He was definitely starting to feel sick.

"I'm not good with boats, you know. So I'd rather miss out on this part of the trip, if you don't mind."

"Very funny, Mr Rounder. Now get your nuisance arse down on that bench."

Rick did as he was told, having run out of options. He was near the stern, not far from the fumy motor. Further down the boat there was a steering wheel. Was that what you called it on a boat? He couldn't remember.

Fleetingly he was back on the River Ouse as a child...

The rocking is making him feel sick. He can see the bank but dry land seems a long way off. Sam and his mates have hired one of those little boats and they have sailed as far as Bishopthorpe, just opposite the archbishop's palace, when Rick vomits over the side. His breakfast floats on the surface, scummy and repulsive. "I guess you're not going to be a sailor when you grow up, then?" Sam says, laughing in a big-brother manner. Rick could hear the laugh now, had always been able to hear it, loud and mocking. Rick is ten, maybe eleven, Sam a proper teenager by then. Two

181

years makes a difference. Rick looks at his rejected breakfast and turns away from his brother and his two friends. His face burns red and he is angry, spurned and stupid. No one but his brother can make him feel that much of an idiot. They are laughing at him now, all three of them, miming throwing up, as the little boat turns round to head back. Just as the boat completes a circling motion, Rick sees a flash of blue and orange in the muddy wall of the riverbank. A kingfisher skims low and rapid over the water, and hovers above the surface. It darts under the water and emerges with a tiny fish in its beak. Then it flies towards the muddy wall and disappears inside a hole. Rick doesn't tell the others about the kingfisher, keeping it as his secret. They can fuck off, they're not having his kingfisher.

Bush and Blair sit towards the front of the speedboat, just like his brother and his friends. The young Rick felt better for having a secret; the middle-aged Rick remembered the secret bird as the boat edged out of the warehouse. The Thames glittered in the sunshine as they left the industrial cavern. Rick wondered what it had been used for in the past.

What happened next took a while to settle. Rick couldn't work it out in the split seconds of sudden frenetic activity. For a moment, Tony Blair was staring at him and miming the breaststroke, his arms stretching forward to form a prow shape, then coming back, elbows bent. He looked like a swimmer, Rick thought, looked like he knew what he was doing. A bulge of stubble-pricked flesh protruded from beneath the ill-fitting latex. In out, in out.

"That'll be you in a few minutes, mate. Swimming for dear life. But sinking like a stone."

"Glad it amuses you," said Rick. The boat was turning

towards the wide expanse of the Thames when Blair, still
doing the mocking mime, leapt in the air and crashed to
the floor. The boat rocked violently as the man fell, then
it steadied. Bush swung round from the wheel, shocked
by the violent interruption of his daydream. He was the
captain, he was always the captain. Steering the boat took
him away, it always did. Made him feel like a different
person. And it was fun, harder than steering a car, and
with all that water to play with.

"What the fuck?"

Bush looked at his wounded comrade. Blair lay still and
blood was leaking from his shoulder.

"How the hell did you do that? You haven't even got
a…"

The sentence ended as another bullet zipped through
the air and embedded itself in Bush's shoulder. The right
shoulder for Blair, the left one for Bush. Someone knew
what they were doing. Bush collapsed too, grasping at the
wound. He had fallen against the wheel and the boat was
locked in a wide arc. It moved out into the wide body of
the Thames, then circled back towards the warehouse.
Rick stared at the wounded men and wondered what the
hell had just happened. He felt as if he were watching a
film. What he had just seen seemed detached from reality.
Events had moved so swiftly, and yet at the same time
a deep stillness had settled on him. As the boat nudged
up against the wooden landing in the warehouse, a man
stepped out of the shadows. He had a rifle by his side.

"It's been a while since I've used one of these things. But
I don't seem to have lost my touch. Nice morning, isn't
it? I'd forgotten how attractive it can be down here. Here,
give me your hand."

CHAPTER TWENTY FIVE

THE room was full and all faces were turned his way, sunflowers to his sun. Sam Rounder had conducted these meetings for years. He projected his usual bombastic confidence, as if he were standing on a stage, which in a sense he was. This was his platform and these men and women his audience, although they didn't have much choice about attending the show.

"Morning, ladies and gentlemen. So let's recap. Jane Wragge, an artist from York, was found murdered in the hallway of her house, near York Cemetery. Our main suspect remains her partner, one Moses Mundy, who has disappeared off the face of the earth. We believe he made the 999-call alerting us to the murder, although we do not know this for sure. If he did kill her, why would he tell us?"

Sam answered his own question before anyone else could.

"Because he had a guilty conscience, because he somehow wanted to put things right. That seems to fit to me. Jane Wragge had her skull bashed in with a heavy glass lemon squeezer. She was standing at the top of the stairs when she was attacked and fell to the bottom of the stairs.

"While Mundy remains our main suspect, we have been following up other leads. Our artist liked to paint naked portraits of her boyfriends, as you can see from our display here. We found the paintings rolled up under the studio floor in her attic."

He gestured towards the naked quintet. Four of the paintings were shown alongside a photograph of the subject, while the fifth had a large question mark in place of a photograph. Sam pointed to the men in turn as he spoke.

"Moses Mundy, our chief suspect. He seems to be a bit of a man of mystery, does our Mr Mundy. But we found a snap on the victim's phone, and we feel certain that is Mundy. We are still checking with Wragge's friends. So, there were five paintings of naked men…"

"Bit of a goer then, this artist…"

Sam glowered at the heckler, PC Tony Wetherby, good enough at his job, but a smart arse. He felt protective and the remark angered him. They didn't know her like he did, they didn't realise what she was like, how lovely she had been; he saw again the naked painting Whitty had given him, saw her slip in and out of bed.

"Five lovers painted over a number of years. The other four, aside from Mundy, are Rich or Richard Whitty, a York artist. Then there is Mick or Michael Stilton, the head teacher of a primary school in the city; and the one called Himbo, who turned out to be one of York's chav characters, one Jim Whitehorn. And the last of the five is known only as Pablo. We are still looking for Pablo.

"I have interviewed Whitty and Stilton, while Laine and Anders have interviewed Whitehorn. Any one of these could also be a suspect, because they all had relationships with Wragge which she subsequently ended. So they could have been spurned lovers who were jealous of the new man on her easel, as it were."

Sam paused to sip his cooling coffee. It was from a machine and tasted oddly of all the different drinks the machine dispensed, as if it had collected a little flavour from each of the available options on the way out. He was sure he could taste soup of some sort.

"God, this stuff is disgusting."

He dropped the half-empty plastic cup into a bin by his feet.

"How do they expect us to think when we are fuelled by such vile alleged coffee? Anyway, that is where we are at present: one murdered artist and five possible suspects, with one gone missing and another still to be identified from his clothes-free portrait."

Sam paused for effect and looked round the room.

"Funny thing is, all the years I've been with the wife and she's never once offered to paint me in the nude."

A titter ran through the ranks at this, as Sam knew it would. He also knew Wetherby would be in with a smart remark. So he got in first, while glowering at the cocky PC.

"And, yes, it would have to be a big canvas. She would have to buy a lot of paint. Anything you lot can think of, I got there before you.

"Before you lot bugger off to do some work, there has been one other development – the body in the allotment shed, close to the cemetery. This body dates back a while and the tests are still being done. There may or may not be a connection with our dead artist.

"Anyway, that's your lot for now. Good hunting."

The meeting ended in a shuffling of chairs, muttered snatches of conversation, and yawning. Sergeant Sal was among the yawners.

"Another bad night?"

"Youngest one's got flu. Up at three for an hour or so. Then it took me ages to get back to sleep."

"At least you still get to see your kids. I can go days

without seeing mine. I reckon if they passed me in the street, it would take them a moment to remember who I was."

"I'm sure you're a very nice dad."

"Oh, not sure about that."

Sam was distracted from further excursions into self-pity by his mobile. He went into his office to answer.

ACROSS the city, under a bright blue sky, Bill Inchcliffe was walking by York Minster, on his way to a meeting at the hotel opposite. He did not usually notice his surroundings, unless they were young and female. But even he could not fail to be struck by the beauty of the Minster this morning. The Gothic cathedral rose before him like a honey-stoned cliff encasing pools of stained glass and ending in rows of tiny towers reaching their stone fingers into the sky. He wasn't sure what these towers were called and made a mental note to look it up. A thought was beginning to take shape about how ancient civilisations left such beauty for other ages to enjoy, and how little of value we were bequeathing future generations. This was quite philosophical for Bill and he was almost impressed with himself. Then a more earthly sight on the hotel steps diverted his higher thoughts. Catherine was looking very nice, in the high heels and tight-skirt number, and she was talking to another young woman, someone he didn't recognise. She looked lovely, too.

"Hello, Catherine."

"Oh, hello, Bill. Are you ready for the meeting?"

"As ready as I ever am for these things. My thrill-meter is fit to explode with the anticipation of it all."

Catherine's friend smiled so Bill tried out his wolfish grin. It was sure to wow her, having done good service so many times in the past.

"I don't think I know your friend, Catherine."

"Oh, no. This is Rachel. She works in the department downstairs from us. Rachel, meet Bill, my boss."

"Oh, so you're Bill. Oh, I've heard all about you."

"Only good things, I hope."

Rachel smiled, but said nothing, and then the two women turned away from him and went up the steps into the hotel, laughing. The wolfish grin disappeared and Bill followed the women into the meeting, eyes flickering between them, but settling on Rachel. After all, he knew what lay beneath Catherine's tight little outfit, and Rachel was a whole new challenge. Something about her reaction to meeting him hadn't been fully encouraging, but he liked a challenge. Not that he wanted to abandon Catherine yet. She had been too much fun lately for that, but it never harmed to look ahead. Perhaps they should go back to that guesthouse by the cemetery. A funny old place, but their own.

The meeting was fronted by one of the big bosses from London whose mere presence could engender general terror such was the power they held over people's lives. These petty vengeful gods could wipe out a person's livelihood in a corporate instant. It was wise to pay attention to what they said. Bill tried to concentrate on whatever it was the man was talking about, but failed. The dreary sentences passed above like distant birds, and in his boredom he forgot that birds could sometimes shit on your head. He drained the good hotel coffee and waited for the meeting to end. It seemed to go on for ages.

★★★

ONCE, a long time ago, he pursued Miranda with all the
sexual cunning at his disposal. She kept him waiting, and
so swept up was he by the chase, so elated by the eventual
prize, that he proposed shortly after they started sleeping
together. She was happy to win the attentions of such a
handsome man, and readily accepted, fool that she was.
How bright and intense their happiness had been, how
unflagging their interest in each other. Days and nights of
lovemaking passed into weeks and then months. Nothing
dimmed their lustful enthusiasm. Looking back, Miranda
wondered when the marital rot had begun to set in. She
could not say, but gradually she knew him for what he
was. Each suspected betrayal, each neglectful lapse, took
away another peel of her love. Now all that remained was
a small hard stone of resentment. Brutally put, she hated
the bastard, yet loved him too; she was repulsed by him,
yet could not give him up either. But now she had proof
of his rottenness, now her suspicions were captured on a
heartless shiny disc. She couldn't still love him after that,
could she?

Miranda was tidying the house on her day off. This
wasn't strictly necessary. The inconvenient clutter of
children never sullied the house. Bill was messy, much like
a sprawling teenager himself, but he wasn't around a lot,
and Miranda liked to tidy. She suspected her cleanliness
might be compulsive, but that was just the way she was.
Anyway, the huge cooker in the kitchen only looked right
if its stainless steel took on a proper sheen. As she rubbed
and polished, bringing the cold surface to life, a fuzzed
image of a woman appeared on the surface. It was her and

yet not her. She moved and the woman moved too. She frowned and the woman frowned too, or seemed to. The reflection wasn't clear enough to distinguish this, but she felt sure it was a frown. She let her fingers slide across the caressed surface of her cold face, then ran them across her forehead. Yes, she was frowning. She finished with the cooker and switched to washing the floor. When this task was completed, the tiles would shine and she loved the unblemished reflection for the short while before dirt and dust reasserted their presence, or Bill wandered in with muddy feet. Really, that man would be the death of her. Miranda had spoken the last thought out loud, as if in conversation with a friend. She spent too much time alone when she wasn't working. Her thoughts wound into a ball so tight she almost felt sick. She told herself to put the image away, and finished off the floor. There, perfect now. She stood and admired her hard work. There was nothing more satisfying than a clean floor.

For a moment Miranda imagined herself as a Fifties-style housewife, with children to cook for, a loving useless husband to care for. She saw herself subsumed into an endless chain of happy drudgery. No one expected her to go out and do a job she didn't really like, and instead she had children who needed her. She worked hard at the cherished domesticity, finding purpose and satisfaction in the smallest things. In the afternoon she drank tea with her friends, while their children played on the floor: small metal cars for the boys, rudimentary dolls for the girls.

The image taunted her, then fled. Perhaps she would have gone mad with boredom. Was anyone truly happy doing all that? She wondered about her mother, who had brought up three girls. She had never worked to this day, at least not gone out to work, and she seemed happy in her dullness.

Miranda wondered what to do next. Then another image came to mock her, the one she had been unable to lose since she first saw it. She looked at her shiny floor and all she could see was Bill fucking that girl.

TWO hundred miles away, the man Miranda had hired to spy on her husband steadied himself against the motion of the boat. It had been a short but terrifying voyage, and he was looking forward to dry land.

Moses Mundy extended a strong hand.

"What the hell are you doing here?"

Mundy ignored the question and busied himself with what needed doing next. The injured men in the boat were groaning. He pulled the boat round so that the bow was pointing out to the wider Thames again. Then, with the outboard motor still burbling, he pushed the boat away. It sailed across the smooth, glittery water in the November sun. Then he called the police on his mobile, and told them to look out for two badly injured criminals, one called Bush, the other called Blair. The civilian operative at the other end assumed he was taking the piss, but he assured her he wasn't. In the end she listened and the river police were dispatched. They found the injured men afloat some distance from the pier at Greenwich where the tourist boats tied up. The incident made the headlines in the newspapers and on the evening news: Bush and Blair shot. It certainly grabbed the attention, making readers and viewers sit up, until the story proved itself to be deliberately unreliable, which is sometimes the way.

Mundy ended the call and threw the mobile into the Thames.

"Come on, it is time to get moving. But we need to do something about your legs. There should be something round here."

Mundy scratched his stubbled head with a strong, trigger-pulling finger. Then he remembered.

"There's some welding gear over there. At least there always used to be."

He rooted around by the kitchen cubicle, then found what he sought. He fiddled with the gas canister, then fired the thing up.

"Right, come over here, Rick, and quickly. I should have done this before calling the police. I must be losing my touch, getting rusty. It's been a while."

"What has?"

"All this."

Mundy swept his large hand, palm raised upwards, through the air.

"South London, those criminal toe-rags who are now taking a voyage in the Thames, and having to do stuff like this."

Rick hopped over to Mundy, warily eyeing the spitting flame.

"Do you know how to use that thing?"

"Oh yes. I know how to do all sorts of things, should the need arise."

Rick stood still, momentarily terrified by the spitting heat. Mundy aimed the flame close to Rick's right ankle. A link went blue and black, then broke. He repeated the action close to the left ankle, and the chain fell away, leaving Rick free to move, but with a metal ring still clamped round each leg.

"We'll worry about those later. Hide the rings under your trousers. Now let's get out of this place."

"What is this place anyway?"

"I guess you could say it was my university, the place where I did most of my learning. Not that anyone gave me a certificate or anything.

"Now come on, let's get going."

CHAPTER TWENTY SIX

THEY left via the door Rick had been brought through earlier that morning. Had it only been a few hours? He felt dislocated from time. He had left York yesterday but it seemed an era away. He staggered, assaulted by exhaustion and a sense that he was still rocking with the boat. The taunting idiot voice of Tony Blair telling him he was about to go for a swim rang in his ears. The thug in the mask raised his arms and mimed the breaststroke, in and out, in and out. Well, the joke was on Blair now. He was lying injured in a boat floating out into the Thames.

Rick was panting already, surprised by the sudden activity after so much tense waiting. The rings felt heavy on his legs.

They ran in front of the pub Rick had seen earlier, and then rushed along a pathway above the river. The masts of the Cutty Sark were in the distance, over the Thames was the Isle of Dogs. It was a nice day to be a tourist, or would be if he wasn't trying to keep up with a murder suspect and crack-shot who had just saved his life. Moses had a rucksack on his back. Presumably it contained the rifle he had used to shoot Bush and Blair.

Soon they were in the centre of Greenwich, shadowed by the great hull of the Cutty Sark. Any other day and Rick would have loved to visit the grounded tall ship, but Mundy was urging him on. The traffic was heavy in the centre of Greenwich. They were at the main thoroughfare now, waiting to cross. Ahead a road stretched up towards the park gates. After weaving through the traffic, they stopped on the other side.

"I expect you could do with a coffee," said Mundy,

disappearing into a cafe. He emerged moments later with two cappuccinos and a paper bag.

"Let's go to the park."

Mundy strode ahead, and after passing through the gates, they walked up the hill towards the Observatory. They sat on a bench facing the City across the water. The towers of Canary Wharf pointed at the sky with what might almost be taken for sexual boasting. The symmetry of the Royal Naval College provided a happier, more ordered distraction. Between the two sights, the Thames widened as it flowed towards the sea. The sky was blue and it was warm for November, just the hint of a chill carried on the breeze. Rick drank coffee and tore chunks out of a Danish pastry.

"This is my second breakfast. Bush and Blair bought me a bacon sandwich earlier."

"They must be getting more considerate with age."

"Not that considerate. They said I was going for a swim – with my ankles chained together."

"Good job I turned up when I did, then."

"Yeah, I was meaning to ask you about that. How come you turned up at just the right moment?"

"Oh, timing is everything."

"I'm sure it is. But why did you turn up just then – and why did you come here at all?"

Moses Mundy took a long pull on his coffee. His eyes shifted, flickering, then he looked directly at Rick with blue intensity.

"I sent you down here to ask around and flush things out. I thought it would unsettle them to hear someone asking about me. And it did the trick."

"It might have done the trick for you, but I was threatened, tied up, kept under a railway arch for the night with only a smelly Alsatian for company, then taken to the riverside for a swimming lesson I didn't need or want."

"Turned out all right in the end, didn't it? I would have freed you last night, but they were using a different railway arch than the last time. They have a number of the dingy places."

Rick sulked and busied himself with the pastry and finishing the coffee. Then the paper cup was empty save for the foamy rings. He ran a dirty finger round the inside of the cup and licked the caffeine-infused froth.

"So you set me up then?"

"Not exactly. I hired you to do a job and you did it. You will be paid. In fact, I'll double the arranged fee to compensate for the inconvenience."

Rick shrugged. "Yeah, well money's money, it won't go to waste. My girl will find something to spend it on."

The flip reference to Naomi had an unsettling effect. He had a sudden longing to be with her. She had no idea what had been going on or how close she came to never seeing him again. Then he thought of Sam.

"I just need to ring my brother, to tell him I'm all right. I got through to him earlier this morning and he passed a message on to the Met."

"You didn't say anything about me?"

"No, Sam knows nothing about you."

"Good. Keep it that way."

He rang the number and his brother answered after three rings, his voice heavy and familiar.

"So you're all right now then?"

"Yeah, in one piece and sitting on a hill in Greenwich Park, looking over the river."

"So you escaped from wherever it was?"

"Yeah, well, sort of. They took me somewhere else, by the river, and threatened to take me for a swimming lesson, but I'm all right now."

"There's quite a lot you're not telling me, isn't there? Did you manage all this by yourself, or have you had help?"

"Yeah, well, I'll tell you about that one day."

"I would ask you to stay away from trouble, but that seems pointless."

Rick rang off and tipped the paper cup back, coaxing out a dribble of coffee.

"How's your brother? I have two brothers myself. Haven't seen them in years. One of them is all right, the other one isn't. I don't even know if they are alive. I cut myself off when I ran off to York. Best way, cutting yourself off. I planted myself anew. After the new me grew, I tried to forget the old me."

Rick scrunched the takeaway coffee cup.

"So who was the old you? You talk about him as if he were someone else altogether."

"That's because he was."

The man calling himself Moses Mundy started to tell his story. Rick Rounder, a private eye 200 miles from home, ankles ringed in steel, head tired and fuzzy, body a collection of aches, listened. A fresh breeze blew off the Thames to where they sat on a hill in Greenwich close to the place where time began.

HE could only remember his mother from one old photograph, which was no sort of memory at all. She died when he was three or four. His father he could remember, but wished he could not. Thomas Hill was an alcoholic left to look after the three boys, so he didn't have it easy, and he didn't make it easy either.

They lived in Bermondsey, long before anyone thought of turning the place upmarket. On the day he left his father was strung out between drinks. They were in the kitchen, which was inescapably greasy and smelt of fry-ups. It was a wonder the boy grew so strong considering what he was fed. Somewhere along the way he ran with the genetic luck.

The father was out of money and told the boy to give him some. The son refused and so the father hit him. The boy who became Moses should have seen the fist but it came out of nowhere. Thomas used to box in the Navy so it was an old reflex. Through the haze of spent alcohol he was in the ring again, dancing on legs that could still dance. The blow caught the boy on the side of his jaw and sent him flying back into the wall. He steadied himself. His jaw throbbed, but he did not touch it, not wishing to acknowledge the hurt.

The boy stared at the parent and breathed deeply. A calm rage passed through him. He stepped over. He had the advantage of height by three or four inches. He could hear the kitchen clock ticking and counted down to its beat, timing what he would do next. The man was breathing raggedly, taking shallow breaths. What came out when he exhaled wasn't pretty. He stank of spent booze, sweat and bad teeth. His eyes were bloodshot, the whites more yellow than white. The boy thought: "This man has nothing to do with me." So he hit him hard and the man collapsed on the kitchen floor. The boy Moses crouched to check if the man was still breathing, which he was. In that moment he awoke to a sense of his own power: he could stop the breathing, finish him off. The temptation fixed him to the spot and he stood and watched. Then he phoned for an ambulance. Before it arrived, he packed a bag and left.

Aged 17 and with nowhere to go and nothing to do, he lived rough in an old warehouse on a wharf by the Thames, venturing out early or late to steal food. At night he would sit in the empty warehouse and gaze across the black Thames, wondering where the water came from and where it went. In the cavernous space above stars twinkled through the ruptured roof.

Then he fell in with a crowd he knew, a bad crowd, but that was the only sort. They thought him handy and he set about making himself useful. Being useful sounds like a good thing, but it wasn't. He was useful at hurting people, adept at damage. He was good at it, too good. Instinct born of muscle and brain guided him in the ways of doing wrong. They showed him how to handle a knife, how to weigh and aim a pistol. Later they taught him how to use a rifle and the skill had stayed with him, as Rick Rounder could testify. He could have shot through the dead middle of their stupid skulls, but he no longer wished to cause such harm. So he took them one shoulder at a time. The bullets went where he told them. Once you have a relationship with guns and bullets, they can be very obliging.

He never saw his father again. The old man recovered from the beating, but died a few months later, collapsed in a pool of his own vomit somewhere. He didn't go to the funeral. One of his brothers, the one he could tolerate, told him about it later.

The years passed and he made good money from doing bad things. He got himself a flat and a good stolen car, then a better one. Girls too, stupid girls who twittered round big men who had ill-gotten money. He enjoyed the girls, especially the prettiest ones, and he told himself that life was good.

Then he had the foolish fight. A scuffle with a stranger in a Bermondsey pub put him away. The irony didn't escape him, sent down for retaliating to someone who hadn't liked the look of him. Six months he got, out after three. On his release, he drifted back. He did a job or two, provided muscle when it was needed, hurt more people if required. It was all he knew, but now he began to desire something else. He took his time dismantling the old life. He sold the flat and the car – a handsome Jag by then – moved some of the money around, and put the guns into storage. Then he packed one leather bag with a few clothes.

He was drawn to the far north of Scotland, a location suggested by the pictures on tins of shortbread or almost forgotten films. He had never been that far north and craved space and fewer people. He liked whisky too, so it was a fit. He bought a train ticket to Edinburgh, planning to stay a few days, then go further north, right on up to the Highlands. But when the train pulled into York, he liked the look of the place, attracted by the curve of the track and the handsome old station, and distant views of York Minster. So he grabbed his bag and got off, reckoning to stay a day or two, then resume his journey. He never got to Scotland, still hadn't been there.

He stayed in a guesthouse near to the football ground, just off the road they called Bootham. He filled his days exploring the city, walking the walls or along the river. He liked to walk out of the city, walking against the flow of the wide river. He passed under a bridge, Clifton Bridge it was called, and then the path became a meadow, and soon he could almost feel himself lost in the middle of nowhere. Once he walked for miles along the riverbank and then on a tiny road which went through a nowhere village. A mile or two later, he mounted a steep bridge by the railway and watched trains heading north. A large sign by the track informed him that Edinburgh was 200 miles away, and he thought, that's where I'm going, one day soon.

Sometimes he walked across Knavesmire, embracing the wide empty spaces, and he discovered a route that took him through the woods at the top. He grew to love Knavesmire when it was empty of all but dogs and their walkers. Some days the races would be on and this empty space would be transformed, turned into one big party, with the women in their dresses and the men in their suits, all elegance and poise, until they drank too much. The horses thundered by with their unnecessary cargoes, the little men clinging on for dear life. Before York he had only ever been to the dogs at Catford, which had its rough charm, but offered little in the way of spectacle.

One of his walks took him by York Cemetery, which was overgrown and ramshackle. It was 1987 and he was about to meet Jane F Wragge, artist and love of his life. The others had been girls and bimbos, bits on the side, inconsequential fluff. Jane, he would discover, was the real thing: lover, woman and friend. He had seen people working in the cemetery, fell to talking, and discovered that they needed volunteers to begin the reclamation. He signed up and fell in love with the place, fell in love there, too. Strange that a garden of death could provide such solace, but it did, and afterwards his life began to make sense. He allowed himself to forget what had gone before. Like many before him, he had intended to stay only a while, but found the city too accommodating. One day he would learn that people sometimes called York the graveyard of ambition, but he did not mind, because his ambition had been only to live a different life.

MOSES Mundy had been a long time telling his story and Rick Rounder was cold. Greenwich still lay below them, the river continued to flow, and across the water in the City, people carried on doing whatever it was they did in those towers.

"Time to get you on a train back north."

They stood and walked down the hill, away from the epicentre of time. They crossed the busy road again and ducked down an alleyway. This took them into a covered market. Only a few stalls were open.

"You should come here on a weekend. The place is buzzing, or at least it always used to be. I guess it still is. Mind you, I don't intend hanging around long enough to find out."

The market was in the middle of what was in effect an island, with the road acting as the river. The cars flowed round the one-way system, an endless stream of tin and rubber. Across the way Rick could see the underground station. He had always wanted to visit Greenwich, but now he couldn't wait to leave the place. He was looking forward to spending two hours on the train, by himself, away from Moses, past and present. He couldn't help liking the man, but the longer he spent with him, the more he found out, the more confused he became. Maybe Moses hadn't killed the artist woman, in fact Rick felt sure he hadn't.

But the police and his brother thought differently, and he was still helping a fugitive, still in the pay of a murder suspect. Yes, that train ride would give him space to think.

The lights changed and they walked across the road. Then the stream of traffic was turned on again and continued its inexorable flow.

As they stood on the opposite pavement, preparing to make their farewells, a car screeched up and a door flew open.

"Get in!" said a rough London voice. "We heard you was back in town. Masters wants to speak to you."

"Does he now."

Mundy affected an air of calm indifference, but Rick could sense something going on beneath the surface, a stirring of instinct and a flexing of muscles. A heavy-set man was stepping out of the car, a low-slung green Mercedes. Mundy stepped closer, as if willing to oblige. The thug was half out of the car now. He looked strong and menacing, but was out of shape, and extracting himself from the car took longer than it should have done. Too much beer and a rotten diet had taken their toll. Fat collected at his middle like a rolled-up sleeping bag. Moses kicked the door. It slammed into his hip.

"Time to run."

Mundy grabbed hold of Rick and spun him round. Behind them the thug was making a low moaning sound. As they disappeared into the station, the other doors in the car opened. Mundy waited behind a pillar and sent Rick to get the tickets. As Rick fumbled with the change, popped coins into the machine, he heard a scuffle. Mundy slammed another thug in the nose. The man put up his hands to his face, as if trying to stem the flow, but blood was pouring out now, flowing between his fingers and splashing down his shirt. Another hired hand was coming at Mundy, but he felled him with a kick to the knee. The man toppled and collapsed. A woman screamed, someone else shouted about calling the police.

"Time to get out of here, I think."

Their tickets disappeared into the slot in the barrier and popped out again the other side. Soon they were on a train that rattled under the Thames and popped up the other side in the City.

"What the hell was all that about?"

Mundy settled back in the seat opposite and smiled.

"Oh, just my past surfacing again."

"And who is Masters?"

"Someone I wasn't keen on reacquainting myself with."

Later they stood in the huge concourse at King's Cross, a place seemingly designed to unsettle and disorientate. Competing sounds echoed round the cavernous space while news of arrivals and departures came and went on the giant electronic board. Crowds of temporarily stranded travellers jostled as they waited.

"This is where we say our goodbyes."

"Are you not coming back north, too?"

"I've got my own route to follow. I'll end up back north, maybe in those Dales. I felt an affinity with that place. It was beautiful, but lonely and hard too. My sort of place."

"Are you going to be all right?"

"You're asking me that? I should be asking you, after the way I rescued you."

"True, although you did get me into trouble by sending me down here."

"No hard feelings, I hope. I'll mail the money to your account."

Moses Mundy extended a hand. His knuckles were grazed and the cuff of his shirt was stained with another man's blood.

"We'll meet again, soon enough. I still need your services. I'll be in touch, but don't tell your brother about me."

His handshake was as firm as Rick had expected, and Mundy squeezed even harder when he said the word 'brother'. Mundy held on long enough to remind Rick of his power. Then he let go and disappeared down the steps to the Tube. Rick turned away and gazed up at the board. The next train to York was due to leave in ten minutes. He didn't think he would ever feel happier to be returning home.

Chapter Twenty Seven

RICK gazed out of the window and his reflection darted across the passing countryside, as it had on the downward journey. One night in London had seemed an eternity; how he hated the place now. Through the glass he saw himself and he saw the world flash by. Something philosophical was suggested by watching his image dance across fields and farms, or flit through towns and weave in and out of the scrappy sites of industry that congregated around stations; something about his place in the world, but he couldn't grasp what it was. He was too tired and his ankles were sore from the shackles. So he fell asleep and was assaulted by strange nightmares featuring Tony Blair and George Bush.

Back in York, Bill Inchcliffe came out of his meeting and began to plot his next assignation with Catherine, while daydreaming about her friend. Meanwhile, at the place he occasionally called home, his wife continued her vigorous cleaning, moving from one already pristine room to another, tidying what didn't need tidying while trying to shake the image from her head. As she threw herself into this maelstrom of furious domesticity, her head found a cold and calm place in which to settle, and this gave her the resolution she needed. Now she knew what she had to do.

Sam Rounder, deciding it was a quiet afternoon, left his boys and girls to continue searching for Pablo, the undiscovered nude sitter. He was owed a bit of Sam time. The job took over and ate away at everything until nothing much was left. He was going to claim back a fragment of an afternoon.

Sam left his Audi in the police station car park, glancing regretfully at its reassuring curves, and headed for the centre of York. He never walked anywhere, but this was the new Sam, the slimmer, fitter Sam; the man with a plan, and a wife who still loved him.

He walked nimbly for a heavy man, but was soon out of breath. Much puffing and panting eventually took up the incline of Fossgate and into Newgate Market. His plan was to buy Michelle the biggest bunch of flowers she had ever seen. That would impress her. He chose a colourful bunch containing blooms of uncertain identity, uncertain to him at least. He could spot the roses, other than that he wasn't sure. The craggy man at the flower stall sheathed them in paper and asked for an amount of money that could surely have bought Sam an arm and a leg. He was tempted to play the grumpy Yorkshireman, to make the obligatory disparaging remark about such extravagance.

Instead he smiled and said: "They're for the wife."

"Very nice," said the flower man.

Sam took the flowers and sat on the low wall round the fountain. As he caught his breath, he wondered how others saw him: a fat and slightly sweaty man with an air of surliness and a big bunch of wife-winning flowers in his large fist, he gloomily supposed. The flowers made him feel ridiculous, but they had a purpose, he shouldn't forget that. The afternoon crowds jostled round the fountain. It wasn't long until Christmas and the seasonal funfair was already on the pavement outside Marks & Spencer. It all seemed claustrophobic and too full of people.

Sam stood and walked heavily away. Despite the cheeriness of his purpose, he felt depressed that Christmas was a month away. What was the point to Christmas if you had a pissed-off wife and two sulky teenage girls? Still, perhaps the flowers would do the trick. You could always depend on flowers.

He wasn't far from home when he paused outside two pubs that stood side by side in the street. He went into the first one for a swift pint, to reinforce his confidence. One pint would do; one pint hardly counted to a man of his constitution. Besides, he had walked all that way from work and was thirsty. What was the point of exercise if you couldn't enjoy a pint of beer? He ordered a nice light ale, sure to be low in alcohol, a choice that proved his virtuosity: no alcohol-heavy ale for him, just a clear, clean pint. The beer tasted so good, and disappeared so swiftly, that Sam felt weighted with regret as he placed the empty glass on the bar. So he ordered another, sticking to the same beer, so low in alcohol it hardly counted. The second pint went the way of the first, although it was consumed a little more slowly. The beer was making Sam hungry, so he bought a packet of crisps and because crisps without beer seemed not quite right, he summoned a third pint. He took this to a table in a room just off the main bar, then remembered the flowers, so he stood, just a little unsteadily, and retrieved the bunch from the bar. Then he sat at the table, enjoying the glow of exercise and beer, and looked around the pub. He hadn't been in here for a while. The last time he went out with Rick they had gone next door. Thinking of his brother, he fumbled inside his jacket for his mobile and then rang him. Rick sounded half-asleep when he answered.

"You woke me up."

"Sorry about that. Where are you?"

"On the train, a few minutes or so out of York. Where are you?"

"On my way home, with a bunch of flowers for Michelle. She'll be bowled over when she sees them. Nice big bunch of beauties. All sorts in there. Not sure what they're called. There are some roses for certain. Roses I can spot, and…"

"Sam, are you in a pub?"

"What makes you say that?"

"Oh, brotherly intuition, I guess. You sound, er, cheerful."

"Well, so I should. Afternoon off, walked all the way from the station, bought flowers, and stopped off for a spot of lubrication. And now I shall wend my way home and impress the wife with these lovely flowery things."

"See you later, Sam."

"Are you going to tell me what's been going on? Why you disappeared to London and got yourself in trouble?"

"Sooner or later, I'll have to, I guess. See you."

Sam put down the empty glass and stood with the purposeful bravery of a man about to do something nice for his wife. The flowers, he mustn't forget the flowers. With bunch in hand, he made to leave the pub. On his way out, he peered at the pump badge of the beer he had been drinking: six per cent alcohol. How on earth could such a light beer be so strong? Still, he could take it.

Outside, it was dark. How had that happened? It hadn't been dark when he went into the pub. Puzzled, he continued his long journey home, reaching the junction with Ogleforth, where Rick lived with that girl: lucky sod, that brother of his, to have such a girl. Perhaps he should give the flowers to Naomi; maybe she would appreciate them more. The swirling thought made delicious sense. Yes, that was what he would do: give the flowers to Rick's girl instead. Then he remembered his original purpose. The flowers were for Michelle, his wife, the woman he was trying to woo back. So he resumed the long walk home. Soon he was passing under the arch at Goodramgate bar, by the model shop filled with toys for middle-aged boys who never grew up. A few more minutes would see him home. He staggered while emerging from the arch and the flowers brushed along the ancient stone wall. Flowers versus wall is not a good argument, and the bunched blooms were not the victors in this encounter. Sam didn't notice and walked on, bedraggled flowers held firmly in his determined fist.

RICK had never felt so glad to see York. As he crossed Lendal Bridge, he had a real sense of home. He gazed along the River Ouse, admiring its broad flow, thinking he could be back with Naomi in ten minutes. But there was a job to do first. He knew just the man to free him and walked to the taxi rank off Colliergate. He felt soul-weary but wanted rid of the rings. Naomi would only ask all sorts of questions. The taxi took him away from the centre of York to an industrial estate on the outskirts of the city. He asked the driver to wait, saying he wouldn't be long.

Rick got out and rang the bell by the shuttered door. He wondered if he should have phoned ahead, but the door rolled upwards to reveal Matt Blackthorn, mechanic, welder and general fix-it man.

"Hi, Matt."

"Rick Rounder, how you doing? I heard you were back."

"Yeah, been months. Returned from my travels."

"What you doing now?"

"Working as a private investigator."

"You not come to investigate me or nowt?"

"No, just to beg a favour."

"What's that?"

Rick rolled up his trousers.

"You joined the Masons or something?"

"The rings," said Rick. "Look at the rings."

"Don't suppose you want to tell me how they got there?"

"It's a long story and much of it is confidential."

"Fair enough, you secretive bastard."

They went inside the industrial unit and Matt signalled a plastic chair for Rick to sit on.

"Are you going to use a blowtorch?"

"No, that might give your legs too much of a suntan. These buggers should do the trick."

Matt wielded a pair of giant cutters. Rick felt a rush of panic as the pinchers were inserted into the tight gap between the metal rings and his calves. He held his breath as Matt brought the pincers together, and exhaled as the metal ring pinged on to the floor. When the other leg was freed, Rick stood and shook Matt by his oily hand.

"Thanks, Matt."

"That's at least a pint you owe me. Always happy to help an old school friend, at least the ones I liked."

"Thanks again. And I'm glad I was one of the ones you liked."

"I didn't say that, exactly."

Rick went outside and got back into the taxi. He told the driver to head for Ogleforth and fell asleep to the chattering of the radio.

THE train disgorged a hundred or so other passengers. Among their number was a young American woman travelling alone and stopping off in York before continuing north, where she was due to meet her mad-assed cousin. After a short stay in Edinburgh, they were heading for the Highlands. At the age of 22, Sherry Smithson was by herself for almost the first time in her life. She lived with her big family in Denver, Colorado, known as the mile-high city because of its elevation. She had grown up with mountains in the distance, and had walked and climbed from an early age. Hills and mountains were her inspiration, so York seemed so flat, with hardly a hill in sight. She did not notice the short, steep climb up Micklegate to the hostel where she was booked in, even though this was just about the steepest hill in York.

Sherry had three sisters and one brother. She was the eldest and the only time she had been alone was when she was a baby, and obviously she couldn't remember that part of her life, so she felt that she had never been alone. Her family meant everything to her, yet she was glad to be away from the bustling interference and love. Sometimes a girl could be loved and bothered just too much.

SAM swayed for his keys. He put down the bedraggled bunch and ferreted in the pocket of his trousers. A pair of lights was attached to the brickwork either side of the door, but the bulb was gone in one. Michelle asked him to buy a replacement, but he hadn't done so, even though she had reminded him. He wondered why she hadn't gone and done it herself, then recalled she had said pretty much the same thing herself. Well, she hadn't because the bulb was still out, so she was as much at fault as he was.

Never mind, she would forgive him when she saw the flowers. Finally locating the key, Sam huffed himself into an upright position. Then he had to bend again for the flowers. Now he held the key and the flowers, so all he had to do was find the lock. A song came into his head. It was a salty old blues number called You've Got The Right Key, But The Wrong Keyhole. He once heard George Melly sing it in concert, all fruity suggestiveness. The memory made him smile, then he wondered if Michelle had done that since this morning. She wouldn't have changed the locks, would she? No, she hadn't. He found the keyhole and was admitted.

After a long day's teaching, Michelle was sitting in the kitchen with her girls, Samantha and Lotte. Until recently, the girls had both dressed in black, usually wearing baggy hooded tops bearing the name of some band or other. Michelle tried to keep up but soon lost sight of whatever it was they were into. Now they seemed to be wearing very brief shorts, fortunately with brightly coloured tights underneath. Without the tights, these shorts would have verged on the disgraceful. Her own mother had been the same with her, complaining about outfits that were too short or too skimpy; tops that were too tight or had too many buttons undone, showing off what shouldn't have been on show, "and you should be keeping your tits to yourself, my girl". Michelle was in a bad mood, so she wasn't receptive to spotting the cruel ironies that afflict daughters who become mothers. A long day at school had left her with a headache and there was still marking to do, once she had finished preparing tea. That's if popping a supermarket pizza in the oven counted as preparation. While the pizzas were cooking, the girls were sorting out the salad, but only because she had shouted at them. She sat at the table watching as they pulled open two salad bags. She sipped the red wine she had just opened and knew its comforts wouldn't do anything for her headache.

"Mix the two salads together, girls. In that big bowl, the one we got from the pottery on Micklegate."

"Whatever," said Samantha, or Sam Too as she was known in the family.

"And quickly fry up some old bread as croutons. Then we'll have a bit of crunch in our salad."

Lotte heated olive oil in a frying pan, opened the bread bin and chopped up the fag-end of a loaf. They were good girls, really, Michelle thought, when they weren't being a pain in the arse.

"Is dad home for tea?" said Sam Too, as she rummaged the salad into the bowl.

"Fuck knows."

"Mum! You swore..."

"Well, it happens. Mothers aren't perfect, you know. Sometimes they swear and sometimes they drink too much, and sometimes they fall out with the men in their lives."

"Does that mean dad? Have you fallen out with dad?"

"Have I fallen out with your father – who knows? I can barely remember how I fell in with him in the first place."

"Was it romantic?"

"Romantic? God, you've met your father, haven't you? In my experience men are useless about romance. Most of them haven't got a clue. But, well, he was quite sweet in those days, when he made an effort."

Michelle almost smiled at the memory, but resumed frowning instead, and sipped her wine, a heavy Zinfandel she shouldn't like so much. The wine tasted lovely, but it was a headache in a bottle.

So it was that Michelle Rounder, working mother and straying wife, and long-time police widow, turned from watching her girls, her precious infuriating girls, to be granted a vision. Sam had walked into the room and was standing unsteadily by the kitchen door, hot and bothered, face pinker than usual. His shirt had come un-tucked and the front flopped over his belly. That belly hadn't been there when they married. For better or worse maybe, but no one ever said anything about better, worse or an enormous stomach, although she supposed the "sickness and health" bit probably covered it. His tie was skew whiff. Why did men wear ties? She was never quite sure. Would humanity soon progress beyond the point when the male of the species was expected to go to work with a scrap of flowered material inexpertly tied about their fat necks?

"Hi dad," said Lotte. She was not yet beyond showing affection, although her sister affected not to. "You've got flowers. Are they for mum?"

Michelle hadn't noticed the flowers. Sam squinted, as if he had forgotten he was carrying them. They made for a fine bunch, although they weren't looking as good as when he bought them.

"The finest York market had to offer."

Sam stood in front of his wife, who was at the end of both her tether and a long day.

"That's very sweet, Sam. But what exactly do you call those?"

"Roses and stuff. All sorts in here. I asked the man on the market, the one with a stall by the sandwich shop, you know, the ugly old sod, to gather together his finest bunch of flowers. Cost me a bloody packet, they did."

Sam held out the flowers, but Michelle didn't accept them.

"So what happened between you buying them and getting them home?"

"I went for a little drink."

Sam had played out this scene in his head, seeing Michelle melt with pleasure at the sight of the flowers, but it wasn't going to plan. She looked tired and cross and the flowers were having no uplifting effect at all. He suddenly felt a swell of weary hopelessness and his upbeat mood of earlier disappeared.

"A little drink! You're stinking of beer and those flowers look like they've just been stolen off the grave of an old lady who died weeks ago."

"They looked fresh when I bought them."

"Well, perhaps you should have come straight home, instead of diverting yourself to the pub."

Sam sighed. He could not deny the logic of her argument, but he wasn't about to admit as much.

"I needed a bit of me time. So I walked from work, all the way to the market, to buy you these flowers, then I walked home. Only I stopped off for a quick drink."

The timer on the oven pinged, indicating that the pizzas were ready.

"Are you two going to stop arguing long enough for us to eat. I'm starving."

Michelle turned away to cut up the pizzas. Sam stood still, or as still as a man can when he has consumed three pints of strong beer on an empty stomach. Then he stumbled forwards and dropped the flowers on the work surface by the oven.

"Not there, they'll wilt even more," said Michelle, without looking at him. He put the flowers next to the sink.

Sam looked away from his pissed-off wife to his two girls. How had they managed to produce such lovely girls? He lurched towards Sam Too.

"Let me give you a cuddle, lovely girl," he said.

She dodged his affectionate advances, saying: "God, dad, you stink of beer. You're not coming near me when you smell like that."

Lotte smiled at her father, but kept her distance. She didn't like the beer smell either.

"Is there enough for me?" Sam said.

Michelle sighed. "Yeah, perhaps it will soak up some of that beer."

The three girls ate their pizzas and salad at the kitchen table, but Sam took his meal into the front room and ate while watching the evening news. After he had finished, he dropped the plate on the floor and went upstairs to their bedroom. He removed Jane Wragge's diary from when he had left it, and went downstairs. In the kitchen, Michelle was tidying up. He helped himself to a banana – see, he could do healthy if he had to – and opened the French doors at the end of the kitchen.

"I'm going to my other bedroom," he said, without turning round. Michelle said nothing.

It was cold outside, pleasantly so after the heat of the kitchen. He stopped for a moment to savour the chill. Then he walked down the long and narrow garden, towards the garage and his penitent's cell above. Before collapsing, he remembered to phone the Met and tell them to stop looking for his brother.

SHERRY was booked in for two nights. She had a shower, talked to one or two people, including a skinny, attractive boy who worked at the hostel, and then, embracing her aloneness, headed back out into York. It was beginning to get dark as she walked down the hill that wasn't a hill at all, and looked for somewhere to eat. Soon enough she found a McDonald's that reminded her of home and, after that, an English pub that did not: the pubs over here were nothing like the bars at home, or at least the few she had entered since becoming legal. Feeling brave, she ordered a pint of beer, because she thought that was what you did in an English pub. When the beer came she was amazed by the amount. How could she ever drink so much liquid? She took the daunting glass and went to sit in the window. The pub was just down from York Minster and she positioned herself so that she could gaze out at the soaring frontage of the cathedral as she took a first sip. It was almost dark and the front of the Minster was illuminated, the spotlights picking out the ancient stonework and throwing interesting shadows. Around her were the comforting sounds of chatter and laughter. When she turned away from the Minster, the pub had a cheery glow. How fab it was to be in England, in Yorkshire, all by herself: two whole days to enjoy. She would visit the Minster first thing in the morning, as soon as it opened, to lose herself in its Gothic interior. She had been on the website, and taken the interactive tour, and couldn't wait for the real thing. Then she would try the National Railway Museum. She wanted to walk round the old walls, too, and to explore the quaint-looking shops she had seen today.

There was so much to do before she headed off to Scotland to meet cousin Emily. Everyone said they made for a proper pair, Sherry and Emily, small giggling girls grown to women more or less. Emily was the same age, shorter and fuller than Sherry, and dark instead of blonde. They were different in many ways, yet such a smart fit too – so good together, everyone always said so.

Most people thought Sherry beautiful, tall and athletic, with a curtain of shoulder-length blonde hair. She couldn't see it herself. Her chest was too flat for a start – how could she lay claim to being a woman with those slight mounds? More than once she had stood naked in front of a mirror and cried at the sight of her disappointing breasts. As for her face, that was on the long side. Still, she liked her legs, which were strong and slim. At least legs were useful too, unlike breasts, unless you counted feeding babies. She reckoned her babies would all have to be bottle-fed, otherwise they would starve, the poor things.

Sherry touched her breasts subconsciously while she had these thoughts, then moved her hand away. Perhaps she would meet a boy on this holiday. She had only had the one serious boyfriend, poor Paul, who had been so distraught when she had said she was going travelling and doing Europe. They had split up, more or less, but she had allowed him one last long kiss. He had been her first love, and she his. Neither of them had had much idea of what to do, but had learned quickly enough; a little too quickly on Paul's behalf, if she was honest, but she knew that was the way with boys when they got over-excited. Everything happened at once and nothing happened for her. Perhaps she would meet another boy on this holiday, an English boy or a Scottish boy. That would be fun. She was prepared for a holiday romance, to have fun and perhaps even sex, with no lasting strings, just tearful farewells. Listen to yourself, she thought, if only your mother knew you had such thoughts. How scandalised she would be, Sherry thought, forgetting that her mother had been young once too.

Sherry did not consider she would be noticed as she sat on her own in the pub near York Minster. Why would anyone look at her? Yet she drew the stares of men in the pub. A group of students stood a few feet away at the bar, and one of them kept looking over, and was then teased by his mates for staring at the blonde in the window. They said he should go and buy her a drink, but he saw that she had one already, a nearly full pint too, so she wouldn't want another. Besides, he was nervous about making that first move. He drank more beer, hoping for courage.

Another man, older than the group of lads, was watching too. He had been eyeing Sherry since she first entered the pub. He watched as she took her pint to the seat by the window. He kept her in his gaze as she looked out at York Minster. So sharp-eyed was he that he even noticed when she appeared to touch her own breasts, and he saw that she reddened a little in the face after doing so. Eyes flitting, he noticed that a group of lads at the bar had seen her too. One of the lads kept staring between gulps of beer. He suffered a prickle of jealousy. He had seen the girl first. She was his, he would make sure of that. He had to make a move before the callow boy summoned the courage.

Sherry took another sip, but regarded the glass with despondence. How would she drink so much beer? Still, she did like the taste, and would have to keep trying. She took a longer pull at the drink and enjoyed the clean bitterness of the liquid as it went down her throat. The beer made her burp and she giggled as she put the glass down on the table. About half of it was gone now, so she was doing well.

At the bar, her young admirer had finished his drink and was hoping it would have done the trick. He'd had a couple in other pubs, so a third pint should make it easier for him to approach the blonde girl. He looked across at the girl and thought of sex, because that was what young men did, some older men, too. Sex was always there on the mind, even if the act itself did not take long. Most of the young man's idle moments were filled with thoughts of sex, or shagging; some of his non-idle moments too. So disappointment swept over him when he saw that the girl was speaking to someone – some old minger of a bloke too, who was middle-aged at the very least. And that was proper old in the lad's eyes.

"Lost your chance now, mate."

His friends teased and joshed him and then, putting down their empty glasses, pulled the disappointed young man out of the pub and set off in search of other adventures, and more drinks in different York pubs.

Sherry was vaguely aware the boys had gone and suffered her own disappointment. They had looked nice and lively, and one of them had definitely been eyeing her up. Annoyingly, a man had started talking to her, just as she had hoped to catch the boy's eye. The boys bundled out into the night as the man introduced himself.

"Hello, I saw you sitting here all by yourself and thought you might like a little company."

The man introduced himself and told her his name. She didn't catch what he said because she was still thinking about the boy who had gone. She didn't ask him to repeat what he had said because she wasn't interested. He was just some man who was talking to her. If only Emily was here. She would have put a flea in the man's ear. Emily had a sharp and a clever tongue. She would have sent him packing. Sherry smiled a watery smile of discouragement, but the man stayed put.

What does a murderer look like? Much the same as anyone else. So how was Sherry to know that she was sitting opposite a man who had killed before and would very soon do so again? He looked like an ordinary man, just another man, and he was taking a polite interest in her. She had been brought up to be polite, so she refrained from rudeness. In the event, rudeness might have saved her.

AFTER the taxi dropped him at the end of Ogleforth, Rick felt weighted with weariness as he walked along the narrow cobbled street. People often assumed all York was like this, narrow and cobbled. In truth, there weren't many cobbled streets, but that didn't stop the reporters on the local TV news from constantly referring to the cobbled streets of York. Once the handy cliché was in place, it was hard to shift.

Rick sighed as he let himself in. Was he in control of anything or was he merely buffeted from one thing to the next? He had nearly got himself killed by a pair of south London hoodlums wearing George Bush and Tony Blair masks. And the man who had hired him for that job, and indeed saved him, was a murder suspect being sought by his own brother. Was he any good at this private eye lark? Well, at least he had managed to find the evidence Miranda Inchcliffe had wanted. That case seemed to have gone without a hitch, and without any harm coming his way or to anyone else. No, the harm was already there and being done by someone else. He decided to look on the bright side, although it didn't seem that bright when he thought of it, because what he had done was illicitly record a man having sex with his secretary. Well, it was a sordid job but somebody had to do it. And that secretary was a tidy little thing, he had to admit, although he shouldn't be thinking such things, not with a girl of his own waiting for him upstairs.

He smiled to himself in happy anticipation as he climbed the last few steps and then kicked off his shoes by the kitchen door. A note stuck to one of the units read: "Gone for a drink with the girls. Well, I've got to find some way of passing the time… N.x"

She hadn't been in a good mood, but had managed the one kiss. Rick had been hoping for more than one paper kiss, and he had calculated that she would be around to cook something for him, too. He could cook a bit, but not when he was this exhausted. So he found stale bread and made cheese on toast. The world always looked better after cheese on toast, he thought, as he watched the cheese melt and bubble beneath the grill. His mouth watered as he marvelled that such a simple meal could be so good. He took a chilled beer from the fridge, sat on the leather sofa and switched on the television, then ate the cheese on toast while channel hopping and trying to find something to watch. What was it Bruce Springsteen sang? Something about 57 channels and nothin' on. Well, Bruce, you are dead right there. There really is bugger all on. Rick wondered if channel hopping wasn't a bit like life. You kept changing in the hope of finding something new, but all you got was more of the same sort of nothing much. With his stomach full, or at least given some food to occupy it, he fell asleep in front of one of the channels with nothin' on.

Naomi found him when she returned an hour later, tired and a little drunk herself. She tried to wake him but he wasn't for rousing. She switched off the television and gently swung his legs round so that he was lying on the sofa. She went upstairs for a blanket. Back downstairs again, she covered Rick and noticed his ankles. There were red marks round one ankle. She looked at the other and that was ringed too. What had happened to him in London? She turned off the lights, went upstairs and climbed into her lonely bed. She had been hoping Rick would be home and in the mood for sex, but only part of that desire had been fulfilled. In a final solitary moment she thought they weren't seeing enough of each other and life had gone dull on her. She wasn't putting up with that. Grasping for a grain of optimism, she told herself it might look better in the morning, then remembered that she would have to get up for work, so it probably wouldn't. Then she fell asleep.

★★★

SHERRY Smithson left the pub in the company of the man she did not know. She said she was walking back to the hostel in Micklegate, and he said that was his way home too. This was not true, but how was she to know that? The man said he knew a shortcut, and Sherry was distracted for a moment by a shop that sold interesting-looking clothes. She would have to return tomorrow when it was open. Then she found herself facing a dark passage between buildings. The walls soared up to form a black canyon with only a slice of night sky on show a long way up above. This was not a place she wanted to be. She turned just as the man said: "They call these snickelways, they run all through York. Dark little arteries through the heart of the city. They're just alleyways, really – snickelway is a daft invention for the tourists, like yourself."

"Snickel-what?"

Only one person was around to hear the last words of Sherry Smithson, a much-loved young woman from a large family, a woman with a life waiting to be lived, and he would not be recording them for prosperity. But "snickel-what?" was indeed the last thing she said on this earth, although not the last sound she made. She cried out, until he muffled her, and then she made some guttural animal groan while he hit her skull and set about doing what he had to do. Soon her young blood was escaping in the dark alleyway in the heart of the old city she had so looked forward to visiting. Her tour and her life were ending right here, at the hands of a randomly cruel stranger.

CHAPTER TWENTY EIGHT

SAM had been too busy to read the diaries for a while, so he was looking forward to spending time with Jane Wragge again. Jane F Wragge, he reminded himself. He wondered what the 'F' stood for and made a mental note to check it out. He undressed until he was naked and then covered his barrelled flesh with the old rugby shirt. The shirt bore the faint stains of muddy conflict from the days when he had still played. Perhaps he should take it up again, once he got himself healthy. He made a start today, with all that walking.

As Sam got into bed he felt a little drunk, more unsteady than he would have expected. It would be easy to fall asleep but he wanted to read, even if the gold hand-written letters always took a while to settle in his eyes. He tried to remember where he was and reread the last words... "Every familiar creek or rattle seems menacing. Voices overheard from the street can only speak of harm to Moses, my Moses."

Ah, yes, they were in the house by the cemetery, the night when Moses Mundy disappeared after being confronted by a stranger, and then returned bruised and alone. Sam suspected the mystery visitor might be connected to the skeleton found in the allotment shed, but there was little to go on. He found his place in the diaries and started to read...

March 14, 1987
IN THE morning, Moses is stiff and tired. This dear man of mine moves slowly as he gets himself out of bed

and he flinches as he tries to lift his arm. In my mind I can still see the parted flesh where the knife tore the sleeve of his jacket and ripped his shirt. The bandage I dressed the injury with is smudged with blood. His big blue eyes are bloodshot, bringing to mind a sun setting in a darkening sky. But no, I should strike that out. That's the trouble with being an artist, I'm too aware of flowery parallels. His eyes do not look poetic in the way just suggested, they look sore and tired. The lines on his dear face are etched deep this morning. His voice sounds rough and sandpapery.

How are you doing, lover boy?

All right.

How's the arm.

Hurts like fuck, but it will repair itself. My body has mended itself in many ways on many occasions. That's why it's a map of scars.

And each one has a story to tell, even if they are not very nice. That's what you said last night, wasn't it?

Something like that.

Do you want to tell me more about what happened last night, or shall I make coffee?

Coffee would be good.

When the coffee is made, we sit in the kitchen, by the French windows. The sun is out and the yard looks pretty. Life is beginning again in the border that runs to the shed, and the big pots by the window are bestirring themselves. In a few months, the yard will again be a riot of colour and form, a real-life painting, as much of a work of art as anything I manage to capture on canvas.

Moses has not said much about himself. His past remains more or less a mystery to me, the sketch before a painting begins to take true form, perhaps. Or maybe I am getting carried away again. Whatever the case, I know so little about him.

You're still a puzzle to me, Moses, a dear puzzle, a conundrum to cherish, but sometimes I don't know what to make of you.

Moses sips his coffee and smiles. His faces lights up for a moment, but then resumes his mask of weariness.

There have been good times and bad times. The bad times were all before I met you, and the good times since.

That's very sweet, Moses.

I know you've had other relationships, other lovers. Like those other men in the paintings.

We've been over this before, Moses. We didn't meet until I was in my thirties, so what did you expect?

I know, that's all right. I accept all that, or I do now. I still feel jealous about those other naked men, but I can cope now.

Well, you've nothing to worry about. None of them was the man you are. Roll them all into one, and they still wouldn't be as much of a man as you.

Why, thank you, fair lady.

We kiss and taste the coffee on each other's lips.

That's better, you sounded almost cheerful then. But you look like you want to tell me something.

Tell you something? Well, maybe it is time I did. But if I do, you must promise not to go off me.

It will take more than a few old confessions to do that, Moses.

I smile as I say this. I have a good smile, I know that, and I understand how to use it. Behind the smile I feel uncertain but I don't want my nervousness to show.

When Moses starts to tell me his story I make an effort not to interrupt, because I know that I do that, jumping in to grasp sentences before they are finished, wanting to hurry the narrative along. So I try just to let Moses speak.

The story he tells concerns a mother who died young and a father who was a violent drunk. He describes to me the abuse he suffered, and the day he struck back, hitting his father hard, and then packing a bag and leaving home. As he speaks I try to see the young Moses. Even though I realise that is not his real name, he will always be Moses to me. He lives rough for a while, in a warehouse by the River Thames. I break my rule about no interruptions and say that sounds interesting and Dickensian in a way, and he says that it was cold, there was nothing to eat apart from what he could steal, and if that was Dickensian, you could keep your Dickens.

Moses looks annoyed at being stopped in his flow. So I promise to keep quiet again. He tells me that he fell in with a bad lot, a criminal gang, and that they used his size. Over a time, he became successful at what he did.

And what I did, Jane, was cause harm with these hands – he raises his beautiful hands before me as he speaks – harm to assorted people of little regard. My victims were of little worth, so was I. It was a life without morals or values, but I did not understand or know any better. I could already use my fists, and I learned how to use a knife, then a gun and a rifle, shotguns too, fire sometimes. And I was good at it all. Prosperous, too, in the end. And attractive to the women, so I have my own sexual history too. All very shallow, but there nonetheless. Assorted dim girls used to hang around me. Pretty girls, but lacking in every other department. I enjoyed the bimbo girls, for a while, I can't deny that. You had your naked men, and I had my stupid girls, Page Three thickos with nice tits and nothing where their brains were meant to be.

That was how I filled the days and then the years. Working as a hired heavy, hanging out with bonehead morons and going to bed with dim decorative girls.

Then a fight with a stranger in a Bermondsey pub put me in prison for three months. All the bad things I had done and what got me caught was little more than a squabble in a pub with someone who thought he was hard enough to have a go. That's the way it goes, I suppose. It's the little things that get you caught.

When I came out I wanted a new start, I wanted everything to be different. But it wasn't. I needed money and my bad companions needed muscle. I didn't want to do it, but I still had the skills, the muscle memory. I didn't have to think about causing harm, it came without thought. But somewhere in my thick skull I knew what I was doing was wrong. Perhaps I had always known that, but now I wanted to do something about it. I wanted a different life, a new start, you know, all the clichés. So I sold up and removed myself from my old life.

I bought a train ticket to Scotland. I'd never seen Scotland, still never have. When the train pulled into York, I liked the look of the station, so I grabbed my bag off the luggage rack and got off the train. And I never got back on that train. I stayed in York and, well, you more or less know the rest.

I don't know what to say when he finishes, so I lean over and kiss him. He has filled in his past for me and the picture seems complete. But is it really? Perhaps I shall never know.

You don't mind that I used to be this bad person?

Oh, you'll never be bad to me, Moses.

Do I mean this? Almost certainly, for he is such a dear man to me. But I am shocked by what he has told me. Perhaps more than I wish to admit but excited too. Bad boys can be so attractive, can't they? And, besides, he has always been a good man to me. He protects me and would do me no harm. No one can hurt me when Moses is around.

You did bad things to bad people, Moses. You were the product of your surroundings and your upbringing. It wasn't your fault.

Oh, don't come all sociological on me, Jane. My background was tough, it's true, but I made my choices. Plenty of people with shit backgrounds manage to sort themselves out. Don't romanticise what I was. I was a tough bastard in a rough place, but I left and found you. Nothing can remove what I was, but I stopped being that person when I met you.

But what about last night?

Sometimes the past catches up with you. That's all that was.

And you sorted everything out.

Yes, I did.

By resorting to your old ways – the old muscle memory thing you said?

I don't want to talk about last night. I did what had to be done. Now I want our life to continue as it was before.

All right, I believe you, Moses. Case closed and all that.

I smile when I say this and stroke my dear man's stubbled chin. I think I believe what I say, I certainly want to believe it. But what exactly did he do to the scrawny stranger who wriggled out from the past like a bug on a rose?

You need a shower and a shave, love.

You don't look so fresh yourself.

Well, it was a rough night.

You could say that.

Moses smiles as he speaks – the first proper smile of the morning.

You first, and watch that arm.

He goes for his shower and I pour the remains of the coffee. There is no milk left so I take bitter sips of the dark, cooling liquid and contemplate my small yard. One day I shall have to move to somewhere with a proper garden. My family history ties me to this house, which my parents loved so much. That link has kept me here, and it is a lovely house, but the garden is too small. Its lack of size depresses me. There is only so much you can do with a yard. Everything else in the house is perfect, especially the studio, but one day I shall move so that I can have that garden. My big garden sits in my mind, with long borders and trees – yes, trees would be good. Maybe a pond too, to attract the wildlife. And a shed for Moses. Boys do like their sheds. They always find a use for a shed.

Moses returns looking fresher, although there are bags under his dear blue eyes. I kiss him.

I'll have my shower and then I need to do some more work on collating my exhibition. It's only two weeks off.

SAM put down the diaries, rubbed his sore eyes and considered what he had read. The more he thought about it, the more he was convinced the skeleton in the allotment shed belonged to the stranger who had threatened Mundy.

But were there any scraps of traceable humanity left on those old bones? Somehow he doubted it. Perhaps Mundy had killed whoever it was in the shed, but he felt as certain he had nothing to do with killing Jane Wragge. Her death was linked to his past or to her past. An idea that art might have something to do with it floated into his mind just before he fell asleep in his lonely bed above the garage at the end of the garden.

CHAPTER TWENTY NINE

THE fog returned in the night, unfurling down on the narrow streets and filling the back yards. York Minster appeared to float as its solid connection with the ground was taken away. High above the blanket of fog, the Rose Window looked out over the city and down the straight line of Stonegate. One night in 1984, the Minster roof caught fire and York's most magnificent monument was threatened. The famous round window and the roof needed extensive restoration. Inside, high up, almost too far for the naked eye to see, there are 20th century carved bosses on the ceiling depicting lines from the Benedicite ("All ye works of the Lord, bless ye the Lord"). Children who won a competition on the BBC Blue Peter television programme designed six of them.

But it was not the Lord's handiwork that awaited discovery that morning. The fog remained as dawn broke and solid air filled the famous streets. In Stonegate, under the gaze of the Rose Window, the old flagstones remained invisible as the first delivery lorry of the morning nuzzled through the fog. The driver got out and rolled barrels of beer from the side of the lorry and clanked down an alleyway leading to a pub that claimed to be the oldest in the city, along with all the others that made a similar bid to be historically unique. A milk float edged by the lorry, its bottles tinkling as it tilted.

Across the way from where the lorry was parked, an alleyway ran off between the buildings, leading to other streets, most of which sprouted their own paths. This network of hidden alleys allowed those in the know to cut from the crowds and find a quicker way through.

It was going to be a clear day once the sun got going. Already there was a hint of brighter things to come as the first dull rays tried to find their way through. The fog clung on down in the alleyways between the streets. Two such alleyways formed a pointed junction where walls of bricks rose up steep as cliffs. Nearby was the back of a popular chain store that sold kitchen goods and expensive cleaning products. Two middle-aged women employed by the store as cleaners shivered as they stood for a moment before preparing to go in and start work. One was smoking and one was not. The one who wasn't told the other she ought to give up. It wasn't doing her any favours, not at her age. The other woman scowled above the smoke escaping her lips. She wasn't any sort of an age and what had smoking got to do with anything? She knew her friend was right, but she wasn't going to give her the satisfaction of admitting as much. She took one last drag and then let out a morning cough. Usually, she savoured the first cigarette of the day, but the fog was spoiling her enjoyment, making her cough more. In truth, it wasn't the first as she had had one half an hour earlier when she got up, with a cup of black instant coffee; normally she enjoyed the second almost as much as the first, but not this morning. As she went to stub out the cigarette, she told herself that she would give up. But soon she would quickly need another. She thought she was scrunching the cigarette into a wall but encountered something soft and wet. She dropped the fag end and lifted her hand to her face, then screamed. There was blood on her hand. With her cigarette-endangered heart pounding, she knelt down, feeling the cold damp stone through the knees of her jeans. Even in the fog she could see the girl, curled up by the rear door. Hair that only the day before had been blonde and shiny was now damp and bloodied. Shaking, the woman got to her feet and told her friend to ring the police. Then she threw up the coffee and withdrew to light another cigarette with trembling fingers.

AS MORNING broke the Rounder brothers were again engaged in contrasting routines. Rick had woken in the middle of the night, wondering how he had managed to cover himself with a blanket. He had risen from the leather sofa, which creaked at losing its burden, and walked stiffly upstairs, where he had undressed and fallen into a warm bed next to Naomi. When he had woken again, it was early morning and Naomi was standing naked by the window, peering through the fog. She shivered and returned to bed, where they cuddled for a moment, which closeness of flesh had a sudden effect on Rick. Soon they were making swift, sour-mouthed love of the early morning, urgent and quickly over. Then Naomi covered herself in an old blue V-necked jumper of Rick's she wore when it was cold in bed, and went to make tea.

"When I come back you can tell me what you've been up to. And how you got those marks on your legs."

"What marks?"

"You know what I mean."

Naomi returned with mugs of hot Darjeeling tea, which looked weak but always tasted so good.

"It's been a little while since we've done that, you know."

"I know, love, it's just that I've been busy."

"I didn't come half-way round the world for you to neglect me."

"I don't mean to but life gets in the way. I've got a job to do, you've got a job to do. But we need to make time for each other again. Perhaps we should have a holiday."

"That would be nice."

"Maybe a weekend away."

"Well, even that would be a start."

"Are you pissed off with me – pissed, as the American half of you would say."

"Am I pissed? Yeah, in a way. We seem to be drifting a bit, getting out of the habit of being with each other. Our lives have been too separate lately, not connected enough."

"I'm not drifting, I'm just busy."

"If you say so. Anyway, what happened in London?"

Rick sipped his tea, which gave him a moment to think. Then he told her everything, all the details about the two cases he had been working on, including being locked up overnight in London, and then being shackled and taken perilously close to what had looked like a watery grave.

"So that explains the ankles."

Then she started to cry, sobbing that Rick was going to get himself killed doing that stupid job. Tears over, she punched him on the arm, a hard punch that left a mark.

"Ouch! What was that for?"

"For nearly getting yourself killed again and for making me care."

"So you still care then."

"Don't push your luck."

They were quiet for a moment. Rick looked hopefully into his empty mug. He'd be chancing another punch if he asked for more tea. She looked at him, eyes bright and brown, cheeks stained with tears, and she went over what she had just been told.

"So you've been employed by the murder suspect your brother is looking for?"

"That's about the size of it, yes."

"And Sam doesn't know?"

"No – and you mustn't tell him."

"Boy, is his big fat foot gonna kick your skinny ass when he finds out."

"Well, he'll have to catch me first, won't he?"

"And when you weren't working for a man suspected of murdering his girlfriend, you were installing secret cameras to film a man up to no good with his secretary."

"Again, that's about the size of it."

"What a sordid life you lead, Mr Rounder."

"Well, yes, I guess I do, but it pays the bills, or at least some of them, and keeps me occupied. Anyway, let's do something civilised together right now. I could take you to Bettys for breakfast. We haven't done that in ages."

"We haven't done that ever, as far as I can recall."

"Haven't we? Well, that's strange, I must have imagined it."

"It must have been some other girlfriend, you mean."

"That would have been a long time ago. Anyway, so what about it?"

"Nice thought, but I'm working and I'm late."

Naomi got out of bed and was soon in the shower. Rick fell asleep again to the sounds of splashing and singing. What was that tune?

SAM spent a moment wondering about the bed. He always wanted to be in their big bed when he came to, but often he was alone in the room at the end of the garden. This proved to be the case again. He fumbled for the bedside lamp and sat up in a small pool of light. The dead woman's diary lay on the table. Alone in the early morning he felt a weight of sadness. Beneath the bluff exterior, behind the bluster and the teasing, he was simply a man whose life wasn't working out very well. He would like to say that it was her fault, not his. The blustering part of him would still say that, and believe it too. She strayed, not him; it was her who found someone else, not him. But had he pushed her away? Perhaps she simply no longer found him attractive. She liked a big man, but then he got bigger. In angry moments he blamed Michelle solely, it was all her fault. He shouted his complaints and she shouted right back. How did people end up like this? It just happened. Many of his mates were divorced or heading that way. One was stumbling towards a second divorce. The job didn't help, but the job was what he did.

Sam climbed out of bed and stood for a moment on solid but unsteady legs. He had slept in the old rugby shirt, which still fitted him, more or less so long as you discounted the tightness at the front. He'd not been this big when he had played, that was for sure. He stretched and as he did so he remembered to regret the beer. His head was hurting and his eyes had been rolled in grit. His legs were stiff from the walking, but at least he had done some exercise. That was the start of the new Sam, the Sam who took care of himself and bought flowers for his wife. Yes, the flowers had been a good idea, but he had allowed himself to get deflected. Well, sod it, at least he had bought her flowers – at least he had tried.

He stretched and yawned, frowned. His body was slowly coming back to him, and soon he would be in control again, ready to barge through the day. He put on his public persona in stages, incrementally building up the layers until the Sam people expected to meet was complete and standing before them in all his argumentative glory. He was moving towards this state of completeness and readiness when his mobile rang.

"Yes?" The single word was his only contribution to what followed. After he had learned what he needed to know, he flipped the phone shut, gathered his clothes from around the penitential room, and went down into the garden. It was foggy and chilled droplets clung to his bare legs.

As he entered the kitchen, the three women looked at him. Michelle was holding a box of salad that she took for lunch and eating a banana with the slow reluctance of someone who knew breakfast was the most important meal of the day, if only her body would play along with the idea. Lotte was dressed too, and ready for school, Sam Too was in her pyjamas.

Sam paused to catch his breath.

"There's a body been found."

Then he moved towards the kitchen door.

"Where, dad?"

"Behind that shop where your mother likes to buy expensive cleaning stuff."

Michelle bridled at this, sensing that she was being got at, but really Sam had only reached for the easiest reference.

"That's sad. Who is it?"

"How would I know that yet? A girl, that's all I know – a girl or a young woman. I've got to get myself showered and out of here. Can one of you girls make toast?"

"She'll have to do it, I'm late for school."

Lotte left as she said this, and Michelle went too, wordless.

"Looks like you're on toast duty, Sam Too."

He went upstairs to the marital bedroom. The pounding water of the shower cleared his head, but as he dressed the thick ache returned to his skull. Downstairs two pieces of more or less burnt toast sat on the work surface, their blackened edges hidden beneath pooled butter and subsiding gobbets of jam.

"Thanks, Samantha."

"Yeah, whatever."

He ate one piece quickly, then folded the other in two and hurried out of the kitchen, heading back towards the garage. It shouldn't take long to drive from here. Dots of buttery jam followed him down the path, and an escaped globule of butter landed on his tie and subsided into another greasy stain. By the time he reached the garage breakfast was over. He wiped his fingers on his trousers as he sought his car keys. Then he remembered that he had left the car at work. Swearing, he reached for his mobile. They would have to send a car for him.

Sam let himself out of the garden and into the wide alleyway that ran behind their terrace. He liked this hidden place which told a sort of truth. The front of the houses were uniformly attractive, with everything neatly ordered and in scale. Yet seen from behind, they presented a pleasing jumble of different walls and garage doors. It seemed fitting somehow for a man who spent his life patrolling what people didn't want seen. He walked to the end of the alleyway and waited for the patrol car.

Back in the kitchen, Samantha turned off the lights and stood for a moment by the flowers she had placed in a vase. Her dad hadn't noticed. Her mum hadn't done anything with the flowers last night and she had felt sad about that.

She discarded the battered blooms and found a vase. No one had mentioned the flowers this morning. Her mum was distracted before work, and as for her dad, he had been in a dad-daze. He often was. Samantha sighed and went upstairs to bed. Her first lesson wasn't until midday and she could manage another hour.

CHAPTER THIRTY

THE fog dissipated to reveal a cold blue sky. The officers crowded into the alleyway stamped their feet and hugged themselves warm. Sam knelt beside the body with devotional care. There was something of the fat priest about him, as if he were uttering the last rites. Instead, he was helping to usher in the bureaucracy of murder that would occupy so many people and hours. The woman was 20 or so. Her wallet was missing so there was no immediate key to her identity. Her damp hair was straggled with blood. She lay curled next to the rubbish at the back door to a store, and from such a position it was hard to gauge her height, but she appeared to have been quite tall and fit. She was wearing jeans, trainers and an expensive-looking waterproof, which was unzipped. Beneath that she wore a blouse which looked like it might have come from a walking shop. This had been ripped open and her bra had been removed. Her jeans were still zipped on.

The cause of her death appeared to be a trauma to the skull. A post-mortem would establish the medical facts. Inspector Iain Anders and Sergeant Sallie Lane were among the officers attending to the death scene, all wearing one-piece disposable hooded white suits over their clothes. A search of the area had already begun and there was hardly room to move.

Justine Haxby, the young pathologist, crouched next to Sam and the body. The Haxby woman, as Sam called her, hiding his fondness, placed a plastic-gloved hand over the wrecked skull.

"She's been hit once very hard with some sort of blunt

object, a brick perhaps. I should be able to tell for sure later. The blow appears to have been hard enough to fracture the skull and cause fatal brain trauma."

"What about the partial undressing?"

"What about it?"

Haxby was close and pale. She didn't look well, Sam thought, but it was early and they were kneeling over a body.

"I just wondered if you had any ideas or theories."

"Ideas and theories are your department, Sam. I just establish the facts via the careful application of scientific and medical procedure."

"I only asked."

"Perhaps he was just some male sicko who, having killed her, couldn't resist having a peek at her tits. You men can be funny about breasts. They are just sculpted from fat, that's all they are, yet men seem hopelessly obsessed by them."

Sam stared at the body for a moment longer and then hauled himself into a standing position, leaning on Haxby for support, panting until perpendicular. The hurried toast lay unsettled in his stomach and he had a headache from last night's beer. It was starting again, another body, another life cut short for whatever reason, whether calculated or random; caused, perhaps, by resentment of the victim, or maybe just by what she represented to the killer's lethally warped logic. Had she been killed because of who she was or merely because she had attracted the attentions of a man – surely it was a man – with inexplicable hatred in his heart? Sam had met a few murderers and sometimes they seemed perfectly reasonable, apart from the fact of having ended the life of another person; and sometimes they were obviously quite mad. The 'reasonable' murderers were the scariest because they were so ordinary, at least on the surface.

There was a diesel shudder as an anonymous black van reversed into the mouth of the alleyway, approaching as close as possible. The driver and his companion climbed out and opened the rear doors. The officers parted while the two men carried a stretcher. Soon the body was lifted and conveyed to the van. Haxby walked over and got in. As the van departed, Sam thought of a life, stretched out until it stopped. The woman had been young and her life had not stretched far before ending where two alleyways met behind the back of a store in York that sold kitchen and cleaning products. Crime so often mixed the awful with the mundane.

Her parents don't even know yet, Sam thought. We have seen their daughter dead on the ground and they have no idea anything is wrong. They would have worried and fretted, imagining the worst, to stop it happen. This time it hadn't worked.

Sam turned to Anders and Laine.

"We should be getting back to the station, but I need a coffee first. My body requires caffeine."

They removed their white suits and handed them to one of the scene-of-crime crew. As they left the alley, officers still wearing white suits scoured the area, crawling in search of clues. They looked like the wriggling larvae of insects waiting to emerge. Sam shook away the weird image and set off in search of a coffee shop. This didn't take long because the centre of York was full of the places. Close your eyes, spin round and you hit coffee. They chose an Italian chain on a corner and took their drinks upstairs.

Sam was drinking a cappuccino with an extra shot of espresso, while jogger Anders was on fruit juice of some description, and Laine was drinking tea.

"Good God, look at you two. I bring you to a coffee house and you drink fruit juice and tea."

"Bit early in the day for coffee for me, boss." Anders shook the bottle before opening it.

"Coffee doesn't really agree with me, not the real stuff."

Laine arranged her pale features into a tight smile. "It's a bit, you know, strong."

"That's the point of it. Good strong coffee shot through with God's own caffeine. Wonderful stuff. It tastes good and it gives your brain a kick up the arse. Well, I don't think a brain has an arse, does it, but you get my meaning. What more could you want?"

Sam savoured the bitter dark liquid beneath the foamy surface. They had chosen to sit on a sofa and armchairs, with a table between, Sam occupying the sofa, with the other two on the chairs. Framed posters adorned the walls. It was almost like being in someone's house. Windows along two walls gave a view of the street below.

"So how are your drinks then?" Sam put down his over-sized cup. He had chosen the largest one available. Foamed milk formed a moustache above his mouth.

"The tea's fine. Just tea, you know, but fine."

"The juice is good, too. Nice and re-hydrating after my run."

"Good God, what time were you out then?"

"Around six, but I didn't stay out long. Too foggy. The damp air plays havoc with the lungs."

"I did a bit of exercise myself yesterday."

"What, you walked twice round your car before getting in?"

"Or you took the long way to the chocolate vending machine at the station?"

"Very amusing, but you're both wrong. I walked all the way from the station to home."

"That's quite a walk, boss. I'm impressed. We'll have you out running yet."

"It's the new me."

The trouble was, the old Sam was desperate to go downstairs and buy one of the over-priced pastries or cakes on display in the large glass counter. But he told the old Sam to go away. He sipped again and remembered the walk, the wife-winning flowers, the accidental diversion to the pub, the three strong pints, the souring of the planned happy homecoming and his lonely night at the end of the garden. Small steps, Sam, small steps.

"So how's your domestic life, Sallie?" Sam asked.

"Oh you know, the usual. I keep thinking that one day I won't be tired, but it never happens. What with work, two kids and a husband who's just as tired as me, the days jam together into one endless mess of too much to do and not enough sleep."

"Well, you look fine today."

Sallie knew this wasn't true. She was just another woman with too much to do. Assorted images crowded her brain. She saw the body of the young woman with her skull bashed in, and she saw her children yawning over their breakfast before school. John started later than she did but he wouldn't have washed up, it would all still be there when she got home. It was his turn to pick up the kids, and his turn to cook, so she hoped he would remember. They were meant to be having pasta.

"Very gallant of you, boss, but a lie. I look fine in the same way that you look as fit as a fiddle."

Sam scowled over the remnants of his coffee. "Perhaps I am, fit as a very fat fiddle."

They were skirting what they should really be talking about. It was easier to engage in banter.

"So," said Sam, taking a final gulp, and then running his finger round the cup to scoop out the chocolate-tinged foam. "We've got another body. The Jane Wragge murder is still unsolved, and now we've got another one. Any observations?"

"Well, there's the obvious," said Laine. "They were both women, for a start. And they were both bashed about the head. There could be a link there, you know, a similar modus operandi."

"Don't come all fancy French with me, Laine," said Sam.

"It's not French, it's Latin, at least I think so."

Sam smiled slyly. "Yes, I know. I was just being my normal obstreperous self."

"Anyway, two victims, both female, and both bashed about the head."

"So what about the differences?"

Anders spoke this time. "Well, the settings for a start. Jane Wragge was killed in her own home whereas the new victim died in a public place. Wragge was almost certainly killed by someone she knew, possibly the boyfriend. The new girl was killed outdoors, presumably in the evening. This suggests she didn't know her killer. That the event was more random."

"And what about the similarities in method?"

"What, both victims having smashed skulls? That must say something – someone who kills out of anger maybe. That certainly fits with Wragge. The killing doesn't seem to have been thought out and planned, it seems to have just happened. The killer used something that came to hand. What was it?"

"A heavy glass juicer. We've got one at home. It's got a bulbous handle and the head is sculpted into fins that are shaped to push out the juice."

"Right, boss, well, Wragge was killed with whatever the killer could find. For some reason he chose a glass juicer. Unless there is some particular significance in that choice of instrument, it was what just came to hand."

"Forensics say there were traces of lemon pulp on the glass, which suggests it had been used recently."

Laine drained the last of her tea. "But she fell downstairs, all the way from the landing on to the hall floor. The juicer would have been downstairs in the kitchen, I guess. It doesn't quite add up."

Sam scratched his unshaven chin. There hadn't been time for razor-play this morning.

"Maybe she let him in, they talked in the kitchen, then went upstairs, perhaps to her studio. The killer picked up the juicer in the kitchen and kept it hidden until they got to the top of the stairs. Then he lost his temper for whatever reason and hit her with it."

Anders picked up the thread again.

"Well, that would make sense. The first killer was angry, but didn't go prepared, and improvised on the spot. The second killer also carried no weapon, at least nothing obvious such as a knife. The girl was hit with a blunt object, wasn't she?"

"Well, that's what the Haxby woman thinks, but she wouldn't say for sure. You know what pathologists are like, always hedging their bets until they've got back to the lab and done all the technical stuff."

Sam scratched again, sighed too. The day had only just begun but he was feeling incredibly weary. Exhaustion haunted his limbs. He fancied another coffee, but knew that they should be getting back to the station.

"So, two women, one middle aged, the other much younger. Both died after being struck about the head. And there's one main difference between the killings that we haven't mentioned yet."

"The partial undressing," said Anders.

"Yes, that bit. Why do you think our killer did that? The first body wasn't sexually disturbed in any way, was it?"

"No, boss."

"I wonder what that says? Some killers would have perpetrated some sort of sexual violence or act on the body, to vent anger or as a final humiliation or warped retribution. But Jane Wragge was left unmolested in death. The other victim, however, had her breasts exposed."

Laine frowned. "It could be something quite simple. Perhaps our killer just wanted a peek. You know, he wanted to have a look at her breasts, he was curious to see what they looked like."

"Yet she hadn't been assaulted in any other way, because her lower clothing was all in place."

"Maybe he just has a thing about breasts. You men often do."

Sam and Anders exchanged glances.

"And don't even think of saying it. I know I've not got much up top. Too much time running myself ragged, and what with having breast-fed two kids, I've been left with tits no man would be curious about."

"I'm sure that's not true," said Sam.

"Let's get off the subject, shall we."

"There is one thing," said Anders.

"What's that?"

"Assume for a moment that both women were killed by the same man. He knew the first victim and so felt no, you know, sexual curiosity about her. He was just angry. But perhaps he didn't know the second victim, and so wanted to satisfy his curiosity."

"And yet that's all he did, so far as we can tell. We should be able to discover later if he abused himself over her or anything."

"That's true. But there is one big blank in all this."

"What's that boss?"

"Well, if our killer didn't know the second woman, why did he want to kill her?"

"Maybe he got a taste for it after the first killing. Perhaps it gave him some sort of high and the only thing that would replicate it was killing again."

Laine looked between the two men, frowning.

"We're making a lot of assumptions here, aren't we? We don't even know if the two murders are related in any way."

Sam sighed, a gargantuan expulsion of air and frustration.

"True enough. But it seems to make sense to me. Anyway, we need to get back to the station and get things rolling. She was found in the city centre, so she probably visited somewhere in the evening, a pub or bar. Maybe she was a tourist, and if so she would have been staying somewhere in the city. It's time to start the ball rolling. Two women murdered in a short space of time – I can't remember anything like it. Surely it must be time for a bit of space now. There can't be any more deaths, can there?"

CHAPTER THIRTY ONE

WHEN people imagined York they tended to summon up the Minster and the walls, the cobbled streets and the ancient buildings crowded together. Such images only told part of the story. Many residents lived out of the city in old villages swollen over time into small towns. These satellite settlements usually had an old main street of attractive buildings that conformed to the archetype of a Yorkshire village, with a pub or two, a church, shops and farmhouse-style houses and cottages. Beyond this were newer streets of modern suburban homes. Some had reasonable amounts of land, with gardens and long drives, while other, more recent developments were less generously separated, the houses having been squeezed in to maximise profits. Such budget homes contributed to a sense that modern life asked more and gave less in return.

Miranda and Bill lived in one of the older new homes, with a drive, a smallish front garden, space round each side and a large back garden. Miranda was in the kitchen when she made the call, looking out over the late-autumn garden. It had been foggy, but now it was clear. The sky was a dazzle of blue and sun glistened everywhere. Miranda saw all this but did not take it in. Her mind was furiously elsewhere. Not that Bill ever knew. She feigned normality and kept up the pretence that everything was as it should be. She was making herself take her time, containing her fury.

Earlier she sat with Bill at breakfast, even though she wasn't at work. She made the tea and prepared the toast, slipping slices of bread into the weighty stainless steel toaster Bill brought home one afternoon. The toaster had been another extravagance and she did not understand why a machine that toasted bread had to be so big and ugly. The toaster annoyed her because it was too large and, well, because Bill had bought it, along with all the other useless things he insisted on owning. But she dutifully made the toast, and boiled the water in the too-large designer kettle before making tea in the small and tasteful teapot (her choice, that one).

They talked a little although it was early for conversation.

"We need to shop tomorrow."

"Fair enough."

"It would be nice if you could think up some meals for us to eat, and not just frozen pizza."

"What's wrong with pizza?"

"Nothing, it's just not very nutritious."

"All right."

Bill crunched his toast and Miranda was irritated by the way he ate. When had this happened? Had she been annoyed by the way he ate before he started having affairs or was it merely a consequence of extended proximity? When you lived with someone for long enough cherished eccentricities lost their sheen. Once she had liked the way he ate in a hurry of hungry distraction. The way he gobbled too quickly had seemed manly and impulsive. Now it just annoyed her. She took a small neat bite out of her toast while Bill crunched and crammed. She asked him about his day.

"More meetings. God, I seem to live my life in meetings, an endless chain of the things. Roomfuls of people either bored out of their skulls or justifying their existence by forcing other people to sit in the same room and discuss boring things."

"What's today's one about?"

"Third party employment opportunities, at least I think that's the phrase."

"What does it mean?"

"It means some poor sod is about to lose their job."

"How's that?"

"It's a what-do-you-call it? When you say something that sounds harmless to cover up a harsher truth. Like 'collateral damage' meaning some poor bastard just got killed."

"A euphemism."

"That's the word. Well, it's one of those. Third party employment opportunities means shipping jobs out to India. So instead of someone doing the job here in York, they are sitting in Delhi or wherever."

"Is that right or fair?"

"Right and fair doesn't come into it anymore. It's just the way the world is."

"And is your job secure?"

"Yeah, it's only the minions so far."

Bill shoved the last corner of toast into his mouth as he finished speaking. His crumbed lips touched her forehead in a dutiful, glancing kiss and he was gone. She wondered if he had cleaned his teeth, then felt irritated for caring. He probably had a toothbrush at work for when he didn't come home or to use before kissing other women, like that fucking secretary. She shook the image away and concentrated on the call.

★★★

RICK was asleep when his mobile rang. As he fumbled for his phone, he saw again the false faces of Bush and Blair, and imagined himself sinking in the Thames. He saw Naomi offering up her nakedness to him and heard her singing in the shower. He flipped the phone to silence the ring.

"Rounder here."

"Hello, Mr Rounder, this is Miranda Inchcliffe."

"How are you?"

"Fine, thank you."

"Did you get what I sent you?"

"Yes."

"And you watched the DVD?"

"Yes, I did."

"And are you all right?"

"That's my business, really, isn't it? As well as can be expected after an experience like that. But I'd like to meet to settle my account with you. There is also some further advice I would like from you."

"What about?"

"I'll tell you when we meet. Is this morning convenient?"

"Yeah, nothing else on yet. When and where?"

"That coffee shop where we met before. Would an hour be convenient?"

"What time is it?"

"Ten thirty."

"Right. See you in an hour."

"I'll be upstairs. Goodbye."

Rick sat up in bed. He wondered what she wanted, then put the thought away. She had money for him, which was more important. Being a freelance snoop was not easy. Sometimes he envied his brother's salary. Sam would able to retire in a few years on a good police pension, get himself a pub or something. Rick had a tiny police pension sitting somewhere, but it wouldn't amount to much. He could have been like Sam, solid and successful, set up for life. He didn't envy much about his brother's life, certainly not his weight and his marriage. There were the girls, of course – Sam was a father when he wasn't, and not likely to be if they didn't act soon.

Thinking of Sam, he glanced down at his own stomach. There was a modest roll of flesh around his middle, but that was because he was sitting. Rick got out of bed and stood naked and sideways before a long mirror. He was still slim, especially if he stopped breathing and held his stomach in.

He showered off the dried sex smell, shaved away three days' worth of stubble, dressed in dark blue jeans and a white linen shirt, and went downstairs for breakfast. He had not eaten well or indeed much during the past couple of days, and he felt in need of something healthy. He prepared chopped banana in natural yoghurt and poured a glass of orange juice. Naomi kept a healthily stocked fridge, crammed with fruit and veg, and a few creamy treats too, and bars of the bitterest dark chocolate. She liked her food and ate well, sweating off the weight. It was time he went for a run again or went out on his bicycle. He didn't want to end up like his brother. Not that there was much chance of that, he told himself, as he locked the door to the house in Ogleforth. He was too vain to be that fat. He sometimes wondered what Sam felt about himself, if he accepted the large alien person he encountered in the mirror. He'd have to ask him one day, so long as he could think of a way to frame the question. Beneath the bluster, behind the bluntness, Sam could be touchy. At the shop on the corner, Rick glanced at his reflection in the window, and admired the way the white linen shirt went with the long black leather jacket. He wasn't looking bad for a man who came close to drowning yesterday.

At the café, which was the same one his brother had visited earlier, Rick ordered a cappuccino. The girl behind the counter, who was pretty and had an accent of some sort, probably eastern European, turned to fiddle with the large machine behind the counter and then spun round with his coffee. She asked if he would like a cake or pastry with it, an automatic recitation that accompanied every purchase. It was a small example of the constant requirement to indulge, to feed the inner glutton. He declined and took his cake-less coffee up the narrow flight of stairs.

Miranda Inchcliffe was perched on the edge of one of the sofas, sipping chilled mineral water.

"Morning. You should try one of these next time. Much tastier."

Her smile was distracted, like she didn't mean it. She didn't have a lot to smile about. She was an attractive woman, but she looked tired and there were glinting threads of grey in her dark hair. Still, she had a lot on her plate, and he had put some of it there.

"So how are you coping with…?"

Rick wondered how to put it for a moment. "With the knowledge that I…"

"You mean with knowing that my husband is fucking his secretary? As he has done with other women too. I suppose he would say that they don't mean anything, that it's me he really loves, but it's all nonsense. And now it's gone too far and…"

The tears surprised her. She had been keeping herself together, she wouldn't let Bill make her cry, and now she was blubbing in front of a stranger. She took a neatly ironed hankie from her handbag and dabbed at her eyes.

"Sorry about that."

Rick reached across the low table between them and touched her hands.

"It's understandable what with…"

She snatched her hand away. "Don't touch me. What are you doing touching me? You don't even know me. And I don't want touching, not by anyone, especially not by a man who has filmed my husband having adulterous sex in a dingy guesthouse."

Rick withdrew his hand. "It was just instinct."

"What, you saw a little woman upset and you wanted to comfort her?"

"I'll remember not to be so concerned next time."

"No need to get touchy, Mr Rounder."

"Me, touchy? That's a good one."

"We seem to have got off on the wrong foot, Mr Rounder."

The smile seemed genuine this time. She thought this private eye man was really quite attractive. Rick occupied himself with his coffee. What a strange one she was, he thought, remembering the naked pictures she had enclosed to show what her husband was missing; what a funny mixture of ballsy and fragile. She blew hot and cold more often than a treacherous shower.

He put the coffee down.

"So how can I help you this morning?"

"Well, first of all, I've got this."

She gave him an envelope.

"There's a cheque in there, and you will see that I have added an extra hundred to your original bill. You did the work quickly and efficiently, so I've given you a bonus."

"Very kind of you."

"Oh, I don't know about that, but you did a good job And anyway, I took the money out of a shared account into which Bill puts all the money. So he is paying you a bonus for proving his infidelity. Something about that appeals to me."

"Yes, I can see that it would. You said on the phone earlier there was some further advice you wanted."

Miranda looked at him directly, ablaze with intent, then she glanced downwards, blushing slightly.

"I was just wondering…"

She looked up again. "I was just wondering if you knew someone who could teach Bill Inchcliffe a lesson. That man has put me through a lot of pain, and it seems only fitting that he should suffer too."

"I'm not quite sure I catch your drift here. How do you want him punished?"

"Well, castration would be a suitable punishment, but I am not quite that vindictive, not yet anyway."

She smiled distantly and sipped cold water.

"What it is…"

She lowered her voice, aware of the other customers. The shoppers taking a break from buying, the gaggle of girls from one of the city's private schools, at least to judge by their accents, and the solitary middle-aged man with a grey shadowy beard, who had just been served a pannini.

What she said next was delivered in a whisper. "I would like to arrange for Bill Inchcliffe to receive a fitting punishment."

Rick let his voice drop too. "What, you want him bumped off or something?"

"No, I want to hire someone to rough him up a bit. I just thought with your underworld connections, you might know someone who would do this for me. I hire men to do jobs around the house, and I even hired you to do a particular job for me. Now I would like to hire a man to teach my husband a lesson. You know, give him a slap, perhaps kick him in the balls. That would be fitting."

She seemed animated and the prospect of vengeance brought a flush of pleasure. "After all, it would only serve him right. So do you know anyone, or would you even consider doing it yourself? There would be another bonus in it."

"Look, lady, I did a job for you and you've paid me for it. But I'm not about to turn into a hired thug, however much you pay me."

"What about someone else?"

"All I can suggest is that you drop this idea and find some other way. Can't you have marriage counselling or something, or just leave him – rather than renting a thug to give him a beating?"

"So you won't even suggest someone?"

"Too right I won't. All I will do is warn you that you are getting into murky waters even thinking of doing something like this. Just leave him, walk out, or divorce him. But don't go looking to give him an arranged beating."

"So that's the end of it?"

"I'm afraid it is, as far as I'm concerned."

"How disappointing. Well, you'd better go then, hadn't you?"

"Look, whatever you had planned is illegal. My brother's a cop. Hell, I used to be one. I should report you for what you're planning to do. But I won't, because…" Rick stopped short of saying 'because I feel sorry for you.' Instead, he stood and made one parting shot "Don't do anything silly or dangerous that will get you into trouble. It's not worth it – he's not worth it."

"Well, thank you for the clichés, but our business is at an end now. Goodbye."

Rick went into the crowded street, stupid with moral outrage.

Christmas was a month or so away and York was crowded. Rick had nothing to do and could trudge around looking for presents, but he wasn't in the mood and besides it was too early. The week before Christmas would be fine. It usually was. He only bought presents for Naomi and his brother and family anyway, and that didn't take long.

He paid the cheque into his work account at the building society. The balance looked a lot healthier after that. This lifted his mood, until he remembered he didn't have any other work. There was still money to come from Moses Mundy, and maybe further work, although he couldn't imagine what more he could do for the man. Mundy may have saved his life, but he had put it at risk in the first place, so they were quits.

Rick decided to spend his bonus on an iPod. It would be good to have a distraction.

★★★

AS THE room emptied, Sam stood before the incident
board. He was used to talking to a roomful of officers,
but it still took it out of him. A set of photographs was
pinned to the board. The left-hand side contained images
concerned with Jane Wragge, including a photograph
found at her house. This showed a smiling woman who
seemed to combine youthfulness and middle age, and
gazed at the camera with a playful intensity. Next to it
was a scene-of-crime photograph of her body lying in
the hall. The juxtaposition brought home to Sam what
had been lost, what the murderer had taken. He sighed
and wondered about the cemetery, which haunted this
case with a shadowy persistence. Could the solution lie
somewhere in its acres of old bones? It hardly seemed
likely, but he should take a walk there again to see if the
place could inspire.

The right-hand side of the board showed images
connected to the latest murder. There was no name as yet,
because the young woman's identity remained unknown.
A series of photographs showed her body as it lay at the
scene of the crime, and another on which the face had
been cleaned up on a computer by some technological
smart arse. Sam had no idea what had been involved in
this process, but he could admire the handiwork. The dead
face looked almost alive again, although the reanimation
was a little spooky.

A series of words, marks and squiggles adorned the
display, asking questions about the victims and who might
have killed them. A small photograph of Moses Mundy
was placed next to the smiling picture of Jane Wragge. This
had been ringed and the words "prime suspect" written

next to it. On the other side of the board, the same words were accompanied by a large question mark.

A shaky vertical line divided the two halves, and at the top of the board a two-headed arrow embraced both cases. Beneath this Sam had scrawled: "Any connection?" He had also written "Links between victims: none known" and "Similarities: smashed skulls."

Sam was dog-tired, yet fully alive to the task before him Trying to discover who had killed these women gave his life a purpose. He sometimes wondered about what he did for a living and why he did it, but he never let on to anyone. Besides, he had been a policeman for so long he couldn't do any other job. He was stuck here until he had a heart attack and they took him out in a box. It would have to be a big box, he pondered gloomily to himself, before dismissing the thought.

AN hour later someone rang from the hostel in Micklegate. A young woman had booked in last night, gone out into the city for the evening, and never returned. Sam got Sergeant Sal to drive him there. As they parked on the steep cobbled street, the sun shone from a bright blue sky.

"Loveliest street in York, this is," said Sam as they got out. He spoke as if he were somehow responsible for the general fineness of the street. "Apart from all the other ones."

Micklegate led a double life. By day it was fine and handsome, with its bookshops, pubs and restaurants, and two churches. Sam recalled, dipping into his repository of dusty York facts, that the street took its name from the old English word "mickle" which meant great or main. Historically, this was the main street into York, starting at the most important city gate of Micklegate Bar and running down to the river crossing. Once this had been the main road from London and by tradition, visiting monarchs entered the city by this route. By night, and by way of another sort of tradition, young visitors and locals alike trooped between the pubs and bars, drinking too much and then relieving themselves of the excesses on the old cobbles.

Inside the hostel, the young man who had phoned was standing behind the reception desk, looking uneasy. Sam took note of this, but it probably meant nothing. People tended to be uneasy around the police, and those who had nothing to hide were often the most uncomfortable.

The man, who was called Stuart, said he had noticed the American girl the night before.

"She was attractive, you know. Like good looking, tall and blonde, if you know what I mean. So, like, I noticed her. You can't help it, can you, with girls like that?"

He apparently saw nothing strange or incongruous in discussing the inevitability of such sexual attraction with an overweight middle-aged chief inspector and a thin, harassed-looking sergeant and mother-of-two.

"So, like, I saw her and thought 'She's nice', if you know what I mean. Attractive, like. If I hadn't been working, I might have asked her out, shown her the sights, if you get my drift, like."

Sam sighed. The lean young man was wearing a skinny T-shirt and jeans so tight it was a wonder he could insert himself into them.

"I would get your drift a lot more quickly, lad, if you could complete a sentence without saying 'like' and 'know what I mean' all the time. It does tend to get in the way of easy communication. And incidentally, as for having sexual thoughts in those jeans, I'd be careful if I were you. Get yourself too aroused and you could do yourself a nasty injury."

"Well, like, that's bit a unnecessary. I was only trying to help, like."

Sallie Laine butted in, sensing it would be better if Sam said nothing more.

"And we appreciate that, sir. What you have to tell us could be very important. This is the first possible development since a body was found this morning, so we are very interested in what you have to say…"

"All right, but he could show a bit more gratitude."

Sam bristled, ready to answer back, but Sally settled him with a touch on the arm.

"Point taken, lad – and just take it as read that I am overflowing with gratitude – gratitude is flowing forth from every orifice."

"Apology accepted."

"Look, I wouldn't go so far as to say that I had apo…"

Sam was silenced by another touch.

"Fair enough. It's just that it's been a bad day, which started with me and Sergeant Laine here having to view the body of a young woman who had had her head bashed in. Not nice – not nice at all."

"Yeah, I can well see that – and what a waste. She looked like quite a girl."

"Any idea who she was?"

"Sorry, yes. Some of the guests like us to look after their passports, and she left hers with us before she went out last night. I'll just get it for you."

The lad disappeared, taking his skinny arse with him, pursued by a resentful glance from Sam.

"You were a bit hard on him."

"These cocky young blokes get on my nerves."

"What, just because they are young, and slim and still attracting the girls?"

"Yeah, probably. But don't forget, I've got two girls, two daughters, so it's understandable that I should be wary of young men like that."

"I bet your oldest girl would be thrilled to meet a handsome young chap like that."

"If he comes sniffing round my girls, I'll…"

"You'll do what? Get a bit cross perhaps, then give in anyway? I can just see you reacting like that – wanting your fill of indignation, then letting your daughters get their own way. Am I right?"

"I couldn't possibly comment on such a scandalous allegation. Now where is that lanky pretty boy?"

The lad returned almost on cue, but not soon enough to hear how he had just been described. He held the US passport out for Sam, who took and opened it. The photograph inside was heat-sealed into plastic and showed a girl who was certainly recognisable from the body. Now they could put out a better picture, which should hopefully get things going. The girl's name was Sherry Smithson and she was from Denver, Colorado.

"It's called the mile-high city or something like that," said Sam.

"You've been there?" said Laine.

"No, just read about it once. I've not been anywhere much, unlike my globe-trotting brother."

"Yeah, but he trotted right back to York."

"True enough."

He looked again at the picture. A mother had lost her daughter but didn't know it yet. When he got back to the station, he would begin a process that would let them know soon enough. It was unsettling to have such melancholy knowledge. Being a policeman got you to the front of all the unhappy queues.

"Thanks for your help, lad. I'll take this passport with me. I'll get a good copy from that photograph."

"What about her stuff? She had a big rucksack, packed with clothes and so on."

"What were you doing snooping around her belongings?"

"I wasn't, I mean, not like in a bad way. After I rang you, I began to wonder who she was, so I had a little root around."

"Anything take your fancy?"

"God, no – I'm not like that. You've got me wrong there. I was just curious, like."

"Cash, travellers' cheques – nothing like that?"

"No, well there was money, but I swear I didn't take anything. That's God's honest truth."

"Oh, I wouldn't go around invoking the Almighty to furnish yourself with an alibi. I'm sure he's got more important things on his celestial plate. As, too, do I."

"So what shall I do, you know, with her stuff?"

"Gather it all together and I'll send someone round later."

Sam and Laine left the hostel and the skinny Adonis, and returned to the station. Sam made a call to the American Consulate in London, passing on what information he knew. The person he spoke to was cultured and reassuring, rather than the more brash sort of American. He hoped whoever conveyed the bad news would be similarly sympathetic and comforting. He was hazy on the details and couldn't recall whether a consular official would relay the news by telephone, or if a local American policeman would be given the unhappy task. Whoever did it, it was a hellish job, and one that had to be handled carefully. The shocked relatives would remember what you said for as long as they lived, so you had to choose your words with care.

Sam ended the call, glad at least that the consular official had not been crass enough to depart with a "have a nice day". As he put the phone down, he thought of Sam and Lotte, then turned to his next task. Worrying about his girls wasn't going to get anything done, or make any difference. Fate would do whatever it wished, and fate could be a bastard.

He typed up the details from the passport and arranged for the picture to be copied and circulated. The picture made the last edition of the Evening Press and was shown on the BBC regional news.

It might be enough to get matters moving, he thought, as he went to waste more money on a coffee from the vending machine. The liquid he received in a thin plastic cup was, as ever, of horribly uncertain origin: it smelt vaguely of over-heated coffee, looked like Bovril with milk in it, and tasted like the product of a cruel experiment designed to torture the tastebuds.

"God, but this is awful," he muttered to himself, while continuing to think of the photograph. It wasn't possible to predict what sort of a reaction there would be from releasing a photograph, but something might come of it.

CHAPTER THIRTY TWO

MIRANDA Inchcliffe wondered at her lack of sadness. The dead American girl in the newspaper was pretty, so perhaps that was it. Just another pretty girl out to attract men like her stupid husband. She was surprised, saddened even, at her lack of empathy, but she had too much to worry about. Bad things happened to people all the time.

The meeting hadn't gone well. She had hoped to seduce him into doing what she wanted. Instead she had made herself look stupid. Worse than that, he had stomped out. Even more annoyingly, she had found herself attracted to him. Not that she had shown it. And the attraction had fizzled out when he went pious on her. All she had wanted was to pay him to rough up her husband. Where was the harm in that? The moral indignation annoyed her, but left her with a problem. Who could she hire to do this job now?

Miranda needed to stiffen her resolve. She made coffee, and then, composing herself, sat to watch again. As she sipped the coffee, her tears began to fall. By the end of the vile DVD, she felt drained, dirty and, oddly, the stirrings of sexual excitement. She didn't understand or welcome the latter emotion, and told herself to get over it. Then she switched everything off and went to the bathroom, her bathroom, the clean and tidy one, to wash her face, and then into the bedroom. She sat in front of the large dressing mirror and repaired the damage. She regarded the end result with a certain satisfaction. She wasn't holding up badly for her age, so long as you didn't look too closely, and the pretty deceits of make-up could hide most faults.

She almost managed a smile. Yes, she felt like shit but she looked all right at a glance. And a glance should be enough to suit her purposes.

SAM was tired and thinking of home, but the murder would keep him here for a long time yet. Sam read the newspaper and watched the news. The newspaper had a couple of details wrong, including the dead woman's name. Sherry Smithson had ended up as Cherie Smithsonian, but at least they had used the photograph prominently. He sent an email to the newspaper to correct the mistake and signed himself Chief Inspector Simon Squarer (a.k.a. Sam Rounder). The TV news had the name right but said the body had been discovered in one of the historical cobbled streets of York. It was true that the young woman had been found in a narrow space not far from an historical street, but cobbles had nothing to do with it. Sam wondered why they hadn't moved the body altogether and put it on the steps of York Minster.

Still, the newspaper and the TV news did the job, and soon the calls were coming in. After the calls had been sifted, Sallie Laine brought Sam a list of phone numbers.

"I'll leave that to you then, Laine. Do the ringing round, then get back to me. Someone round here should be able to help. I'm off to get something to eat."

"Yes, boss."

Sam had to eat soon or he would faint. His last food had been hours ago. He hesitated for a moment.

"Everything all right, Sergeant Sal?"

"Yes, boss, fine. Just, you know, a bit knackered."

"Me too. But that's the job for you."

Laine watched him go. "That's all right for you to say,"

she thought. "I'm the one left here making the calls." She sighed and wondered when or indeed if she would get home. How had she allowed her life to become so busy? She wasn't unhappy, not exactly. She didn't have time for happiness or unhappiness. Her life was a blur of distraction that allowed neither feeling nor emotion. Just getting through was enough. She rang home to check how things were going, and was drawn into a disgruntled conversation with her husband, who was just as tired as she was, and more prone to complaining about it. One of the boys had asked when she was coming home, and she couldn't give him any sort of answer. "Mummy will be home when she can." As she put down the phone she wondered who this Mummy person was.

Sam stood by the busy road. It was dark and headlights dazzled him as he waited for a gap in the traffic. Eventually, he got halfway across and then almost sprinted the last few feet. A car horn blared and Sam raised a finger skywards in retaliation. He was panting as he entered the small supermarket and sweat gathered on his forehead. He wiped his shirtsleeve across his face as considered the sandwiches. He supposed he should choose something with greenery in it and picked a cheese salad sandwich. Satisfied with the healthfulness of his meal, he bought a small packet of biscuits too.

He paid, left and, after safe delivery across the night traffic, made his way back to his desk. The sandwich was damp. He ate it anyway and even swallowed the soggy leaves. The biscuits were crisp and overloaded with sugar. He ate two and shoved the packet in a drawer, dissatisfied with the food and with himself for eating it.

★★★

THE house was on the scruffy end of Heslington Road, where the students lived. Once grand, it was weary from the careless passage of too many young people. The front garden contained more rubbish than bins. A punctured plastic football lay beneath a window patched with cardboard.

Sam and Sallie knocked and waited for someone to open the scuffed door. Eventually a young man let them in. He stood for a clueless moment, then remembered.

"You must be the police," he said. "Let's go to the kitchen."

Sam trod along the industrial-strength brown carpet, chosen with damage limitation in mind rather than aesthetics. His heart was sinking. He had been in student kitchens before. This one didn't disappoint. It smelt of neglect and misuse and, yes, of boys turning into men. A patina of grease covered everything and the work surfaces were cluttered with dirty dishes, used utensils and discarded packaging. Empty beer bottles lined the windowsill behind the overflowing sink. The backdoor was home to a dartboard and a halo of puncture marks. The one free wall featured a large flat-screen television. Sam glared at the TV thinking it was bigger and better than the one he had at home. The TV was on with the sound down, and music pumped from a hi-fi on the floor beneath. Sam didn't recognise the music but could tell it was loud.

"I'll turn that down a bit," the boy/man said.

"Off would be nice," said Sam. "Right, then, lad, so you have something to tell us."

"Yeah, it's about that girl, the American – the one who was murdered."

His lips trembled and his eyes began to fill. He pinched the top of his nose with his forefinger and thumb, and sniffled.

"Sorry about this. I never met anyone who was murdered before."

"Well, naturally, that would be upsetting. But when you say you've never met anyone who was murdered before, does that mean that you actually met the victim?"

"Sorry, no, not really. My mates were teasing me, you see. They saw me looking and told me I should go and talk to her. I wanted to but I was nervous, because she was, you know, gorgeous and all that. Also, well, it doesn't quite seem fair, does it?"

"What doesn't seem fair?"

"That us men always have to do the chatting up, make the first move."

"I thought that would have changed, what with women's liberation and all that." Sam had only a hazy notion of what women's liberation constituted, so he hurried on. "So you didn't speak to the victim then, lad?"

All colour drained from the young man's face. "No, like I say, I wanted to, but someone else got in first."

"Another man?"

"Yeah, that's right. He was too old for her, proper old, you know, middle aged at least. About your age, I guess."

The lad's outrageous youth was provocation enough, without the disparaging comments about age.

"You'll get here soon enough, lad. I used to be slim and handsome like you once – and about the same weight."

The young man's expression suggested such a thing could simply not be true. Sam sighed and glanced at Laine, who took over.

"What the detective chief inspector would like to know is what this man looked like, and how he appeared to be with the victim? Were they being friendly with each other, or did she perhaps appear to be uncomfortable at having to talk to the man?"

"Yeah, a little uncomfortable, at least I guess so. Like I said, he wasn't as young as her, by a long way. She'd have been happier talking to me and my mates, I'm sure."

"So why didn't you approach her?"

"Like I said, I was a bit anxious, shy, tongue-tied maybe, all of those things. I was going to, and I even had another pint to summon up the courage. But then I looked over and she was talking to this guy – the older man I mentioned."

"And what did he look like, this older guy?"

"Like an older guy, I guess. He was slim not, you know, like…"

The young man reddened and looked away.

"Yeah, he was slim, medium height, I guess."

"And did you see them leave the pub together at any point?"

"No, me and my mates left before they did. I glanced on the way out and she smiled at me. At least, I like to think she was smiling at me. It's nice to think that she noticed me and was smiling at me. But then, the thing is…"

"The thing is what?"

The young man was silent, and then he collapsed into sobs.

"What's upsetting you, son?" said Sam, reasserting himself. "What reason do you have to be upset? Usually the people I see crying have something to hide."

"No, it's nothing like that – nothing like that at all. It's just that…"

He looked away from Sam, turning back to Laine.

"It's just that I could have been the last person she ever smiled at."

"Yeah, lad, you could well have been."

The young man sobbed again and Sam stood to leave. Outside the house he kicked the deflated football while he waited for Laine. She came out and gave him what he regarded as a domestic glance – the sort of look he got at home when he had done something wrong.

"What?"

"You were a bit hard on him in there. He was really upset."

"Needs to toughen himself up a bit then, doesn't he."

"Just imagine what it's like for him. He sees a girl he fancies in a pub, he tries to summon up the courage to speak to her, someone else gets in first – and the next day he hears the girl has been murdered. Doesn't he have the right to feel upset? And that's the second time today you've got arsey with a young person. What's the matter with you – how come you are so pissed off with the young?"

Sam bristled at the criticism and walked back to the car. Laine wondered when the night would end.

IT WAS a while since she had been in such a bar and she was feeling old. The place was a heaving mass of booze, sweat, testosterone, cheap perfume and cigarette smoke. She took a deep breath to steady herself and regretted it. Smoking in pubs and bars was going to be banned soon. Shame it hadn't happened already, she thought, coughing again.

Miranda inserted herself into the scrum. While she waited she had time to enjoy the unwanted proximity of strangers. Everyone seemed to be underdressed. She was lost in a forest of armpits and cleavages. Eventually she secured a large glass of white wine. She took this to a place of relative calm by a window. Now she had room to breathe, but the noise was shocking. It wasn't music so much as an aural throwback to heavy industry. Once the young people in this bar would have spent their days surrounded by terrible noise and hellish heat; now they worked quietly in air-conditioned offices and spent their evenings being deafened in sweaty bars. She wondered if there was an irony in there somewhere. She gulped the wine and it was rotten.

Miranda tried smiling at a couple of tall young men, likely looking characters, lithe and strong, but they took no notice. She wondered what she was doing here, finished the wine and left.

Outside it was clear and cold. She walked along the quayside and saw the river, wide and inexorable, always on the move, never arriving. She hesitated outside the pub that flooded, but instead went up the steps by the bridge. There was a trendy bar on the other side. As she crossed the road, weaving between the taxis, a large man wearing leathers followed her. She slipped between the bouncers on the door and entered another place of noise and turmoil. She left immediately by a different exit. Outside in the cold again, she walked along Coney Street and its high street shops and stores. She felt very alone in the crowded night, although she was not as alone as she thought. She had a second white wine in a bar that overlooked St Helen's Square, just across the way from Bettys tea rooms, and a third in another place of cacophony round the corner. Yet she could find no way of approaching a suitable man.

When she left the third bar, it was all feeling like a foolish enterprise. What had she been thinking of? Bettys was in darkness as she went by its glass curves. She caught her reflection in the window but did not see the shadow some way behind her. That was where she belonged, somewhere genteel, not out here on the streets, getting drunker by the minute. She wondered where she could get a taxi. She could picture a street where the taxis lined up, but could not remember its name. Somewhere down there, she thought, as she cut across St Sampson's Square in front of the department store. There were two pubs in the square. The sound of a rock band blared from one, so she chose the other. She couldn't remember seeing this pub before, but hazily assumed it must always have been there. One more white wine, then a taxi home.

Entering the pub, she slipped through time. The place felt like a museum. It did not appear to have changed in years. It was not interesting or historic, just old the way pubs used to be; it was unfashionable and neglected, musty and unannounced. The jukebox was playing Matt Monroe or someone equally mothballed. The music was soothing after the noise. She ordered her wine and looked for somewhere to sit. She almost had the pick of the place. She chose a dusty corner and sipped the wine. She felt woozy with contentment in the shabby room. This wasn't her sort of place at all. She liked somewhere smart, yet she felt happy. She stretched her legs and looked down at the threadbare carpet. When she looked up again, a large man had loomed into view. He was wearing a leather waistcoat over a sleeveless T-shirt, leather trousers and biker boots, and had tattoos down each arm. On his face black stubble dashed with grey was forming into a beard.

"Good evening. Mind if I join you?"

The voice was deep and pleasant and did not match his demeanour. She invited him to sit.

"I don't think I've seen you in here before."

Miranda giggled, loosened by the wine.

"That's because I've not been in here before. Normally I wouldn't be seen dead somewhere like this. But tonight, I like it. It's nice. And you look nice too, even with all those drawings on your arms."

The man smiled and she saw what she took to be a flash of gold. This man was a regular motorbike-riding pirate.

"It's the only non-poncy pub in York. Either they are bars filled with noisy young people…"

"Tell me about it… I've just been through a few of them… horrid places…"

"…or they're haunted by the real ale crowd with their dreary reverence for beer. But this…"

He extended tattooed arms and raised his palms upwards to embrace his surroundings. "This is just a pub in the best sense. Somewhere to come for a drink, discuss this and that, and sometimes to meet someone you've not met before."

He smiled once more and she saw again the gold flash. Somewhere in the chilled core of her sensible being, she knew she was being foolish; but she silenced the hard little voice that guided her days. She was being led by a new voice, carefree and devilish.

"A nice attractive lady like you shouldn't be out on her own."

"I know, but I came into York looking for someone."

"Oh, didn't you find them."

"That depends."

"On what?"

She giggled again.

"I've got this husband, you see."

"I can see."

Miranda tried to pull off the ring, but it stuck fast behind her knuckle, so she gave up.

"He's been a bastard, you see. Messing around with his secretary, fucking her when he thinks I don't know. But I do know, you see, because I hired a man to spy on him. I'm always getting men in to do something or other at our house, and that gave me the idea. So I got a man in, a private eye, and he filmed my husband fucking his secretary."

The polite hell's angel, if that was what he was, looked a little put out.

"You swear a lot for a nice looking middle-class girlie."

Miranda sighed and gulped more wine.

"Not normally I don't."

She felt she was going to cry. She dabbed at her eyes with her sleeve, then finished her wine.

"You said you came into York looking for someone. Who was that?"

"Oh, that's the thing, you see…"

She dropped her voice to a whisper. Matt Monroe had given way to Frank Sinatra. She had found her stranger in the night and he was stranger than most men she knew. A rose climbed one arm and wasn't that…? She squeezed her eyes fighting tiredness and alcohol. When she opened them again she forgot what she thought she had seen.

"I wanted to get a man in to teach my husband a lesson. You know, rough him up a bit."

"I see. And do you still want to do this?"

"Yes, I think I do."

Miranda started to explain. She told the adorned stranger about the hated DVD of Bill fucking his secretary – "Sorry, swore again," she said, a finger held to unguarded lips – and how she wanted revenge. She supplied the friendly hell's angel with details concerning Bill, his secretary, and the guesthouse by the cemetery. Before she knew it, she was concocting a plan; money – quite an alarming amount – was being mentioned.

It seemed like a dream as they left the time-warped pub and stood by the motorbike. She hadn't been on a motorbike for years, not since that unsuitable boyfriend she had when she was 18. The thought hovered as she accepted a spare crash helmet – they have all been unsuitable in some way or other, all the men I've liked or loved, not one of them has been right.

Her tattooed saviour mounted the big bike and told her to hop on and hold tight. Her heart was beating too fast and her head was beginning to spin. Soon they were riding slowly through the centre of York, the engine ticking over as if impatient for proper use of its power. They passed the dark shadows of Knavesmire, then turned towards her village. Away from the busy road, the bike roared and whooshed forward, then swung low to the left to thunder beneath a bridge. Miranda clung on, hands clasping the stranger. She hadn't been so thrillingly terrified since she was last on a bike. That boyfriend had taken her on his old Honda to hidden places where they had al fresco summer sex. Was it a summer or a few weeks? She couldn't remember, but he had gone bad on her, mounting another girl on his bike.

The bike raced towards the village at twice the legal speed limit, then slowed to a stroll with the engine bubbling and burbling. As she dismounted, molten unease began to rise through her being. Was it her desire for the leather-clad stranger who had brought her home? No, the ride home had awakened memories of youthful, pre-Bill sex in fields and on cliff walks, but she had her self-respect, even in her drunkenness. Sex with someone you have just met wasn't a good idea. Besides, the forces surging through her were down to too much wine, the night's nervy progress, and the swift ride home. She made her farewells, and handed back the helmet. She rested a manicured hand on the leather shoulder, and then her new friend was gone, roaring into the night.

Miranda turned away from the departing motorcycle and vomited into her neighbour's hedge. That would give the nosy old cow something to complain about.

CHAPTER THIRTY THREE

SAM Rounder yawned widely as he tried to squeeze into one of the so-called chairs at a burger joint in the middle of York. Laine fitted snugly into her seat. Why didn't they design these things for proper-sized people? He fidgeted in the instrument of torture and scowled across the table. The teenage girl was picking at a cardboard envelope of chips. The smell was doing strange things to Sam's insides. He could die for some chips, or French fries as they insisted on calling them in this place, but he was trying to be good.

"So, you think that the murdered American girl came in here last night?"

"Yeah, that's what I said when I rang. Not much I can add. She came in here, she had a double cheeseburger, fries and a shake. She sat over there, near the window."

The girl gestured as she ate more chips.

"Would you like one?"

"I'm on a diet."

"Yeah, I can see that."

She giggled and popped another thin chip into her mouth.

Laine intervened before Sam could start up again. What was eating him tonight?

"So..." She read the girl's name-badge. "So, Sandra, she was by herself?"

"Yeah, like what I said on the phone. She sat by herself, ate double cheeseburger, fries and a shake, then left."

"Why did you notice her?"

"Might've been the accent, although we do get Americans in here, lots of them. Looking for a bit of home, I guess.

Yeah, the accent and the fact that she ordered all that food but was so slim. It didn't seem fair."

Sam's short silence ended.

"The poor girl getting murdered – that's what's not fair."

"Yeah, well, now you put it like that, I see your point. But she was tall and slim, like, and I noticed."

Sandra ate more chips. Working in a burger bar wasn't doing her any favours. Her uniform tugged and bulged, and her face shone with too much grease.

"Sure you don't want one?"

"Certain, thank you."

Laine said she would have one.

"Yeah, you can afford to. Another skinny one like that poor dead cow, but not so tall."

Sam sighed, expelling frustration, exhaustion and disgust – at the girl, the place where she worked, at himself, and above everything else at wasted lives, his own included. He recognised the symptoms, the anger and despondency that came with investigating a murder – two murders. It wasn't this girl's fault the American woman had been murdered; but it was her fault that she was wasting her life in a multinational grease pit.

"What do you want to do when you grow up, Sandra?"

"Dunno. Get a boy, a baby, maybe get me own council flat."

Sam thought of his own clever, infuriating, lovely girls, with their tantalising futures.

"Yeah, well, good luck. But maybe it might be an idea to set your sights a bit higher."

"What, two babies?"

"Something like that."

He handed the girl a card. Her nails were painted but bitten, so she had nibbled away at her own attempted glamour.

"Give me a call if you think of anything else about the American girl. Anything at all, the smallest thing, it could be important."

The girl put the card in the breast pocket of her overalls. Sam levered himself out of the chair and went outside. It was 11pm and he had been on the go since first thing.

"Give us a lift home, Laine, and then get off home yourself."

"Thanks, boss, I will – that's if I can still remember where I live."

THE house was quiet. Sam saw the flowers in the kitchen and wondered at his foolishness.

They had been married for more than twenty years, and what started out well went bad incrementally and neither of them noticed much was awry. The last pretence went when Michelle admitted to her affair. Sam had his own brief, unsatisfactory fling, more in retaliation than desire. Now he was alone and Michelle was – was what, exactly? He did not know if she was still seeing the other man.

The big man stood alone in the kitchen and ate an apple cold from the fridge. He crunched and mashed the glorious tart flesh. For years he had stopped eating apples in a sort of dietary suicide. He had cut most healthy food from his diet, opting instead for calorific self-harm. The results of this regime were apparent in the weight he carried, almost like half another person. He was still a strong man with an aura of physical power, but this had diminished as his weight had increased. The apples were a return to lost healthfulness. It would take more than an apple a day to put him right, more than a few flowers to soften his wife's heart, but it was a start.

He tossed the core into the bin and thought of the two dead women with their smashed skulls. The dead, injured or distressed took so much of his time, drained the sump of his humanity, that he didn't have much left for those he was meant to love. He would go upstairs another night, but now he craved solitary sleep, after another session with the diary.

Sam left the kitchen, locking the door behind him, and walked across the garden, retracing his steps from the morning, leaving heavy indents in the frost fur. Once inside the freezing room above the garage he undressed, put on the old rugby shirt and put himself to bed. Propped up on a pillow, he began to read, but the words would not settle. Exhaustion was doing strange things to his vision. He put down the diary. Almost finished, almost done.

Sleep swallowed Sam whole and then spat him out. It was dark and early. He shifted and sighed, trying to guess the time. At least he couldn't hear any carousing students, which was a good sign. Shouting students would put the time at around 2am, unless there had been a union ball. Then they could still be making a noise at breakfast time. He fumbled for his watch: 5am. Not too bad, the best part of five hours. He switched on the bedside lamp, climbed out of bed and went into the tiny bathroom to attend to his early morning bladder needs. After that he made a cup of tea with the small bed-and-breakfast-style kettle, returned to bed and started to read the last instalment of Jane's diary account of the year she met Moses Mundy. But he dozed off after a page.

★★★

MIRANDA woke with a hangover and a flimsy awareness of the previous night. Had those things really happened? It felt like a strange dream or a movie she had watched, yet arrangements had been made, details and phone numbers passed on, and locations given. She began to feel a nagging mournful regret.

Bill returned late and did not know she had been out, and he left for work early – if that was where he really went; she hardly knew what to believe any more.

Miranda dropped her face into her hands. What had she done? Her tattooed saviour had given her his mobile number, hadn't he? She would have to ring him and call everything off. She could just divorce the bastard. She rushed to the dirty washing basket and found the jeans she had worn the night before. They smelt of wine, exhaust fumes and vomit, but contained no scrap of paper with a phone number. She threw the jeans back and rummaged for the blouse. Tight black jeans and a grey and white check blouse, with just a suggestion of the cowgirl. How she liked that outfit.

She found the paper in the chest pocket. She sat on the floor in front of the dirty washing and dialled. All she got was a recorded message. She sobbed as she recalled something her tattooed saviour had said. "I never hang around, not when I've got a job to do. You'll get a result very soon."

The fluttering unease she had felt since waking rose to a fully winged panic. What could she do?

Chapter Thirty Four

SAM now had two bodies and he felt certain there was a link between the murders. Both women had suffered a smashed skull. He had no idea what the connection might be, so he decided to return to the three suspects he had for the murder of Jane Wragge.

He arranged for the three men to be brought into the station. He had interviewed the head teacher at his school and the artist at his house, and hadn't warmed to either of them. Laine and Anders had interviewed the one who called himself Himbo. Were these men even suspects? Two had come forward without prompting, while the third had been uncovered via a tip-off. Instinct told him the teacher and the artist were each hiding something, lying in some way or other, but about what? He had no idea, but he knew a lie when he saw one, even an old lie the teller thought long forgotten. As for Himbo, he was annoyed on that score. Why hadn't he thought to interview Himbo himself? Surely those two will have missed something.

Michael Stilton, the teacher, and Richard Whitty, the artist, were already in the station, and Sam could have started with either of them, but he wanted to speak first to Himbo, or Jim Whitehorn, to give him his proper name. Sam was about to relent and start with Stilton or Whitty, when Whitehorn was brought in.

So he went ahead with that plan.

The sight of the scrawny, shifty individual across the interview table made him feel even more annoyed. Guilt stuck to Whitehorn like dog shit to a shoe.

"So, Mr Whitehorn, I've read up what my officers said

about you in their report, and a few things don't make sense."

"Like what?"

"Oh, for starters, why a cultivated woman would choose you for a lover."

"You'd have to ask her that."

"Well, I can't, can I?"

"No."

"So what did she see in you?"

"Dunno. Liked a bit of rough maybe. Thought I had, you know, what's the word, potential as an artist."

Sam laughed at this. "I must make a note to go and check out your works hanging at York Art Gallery."

"Very funny."

"From where I sit, you seem to be hiding something. Did you go back and see Jane years later, to get your own back for the way she dumped you?"

"No. Hadn't seen her in ages, had I, so I couldn't have killed her."

"So what's your secret then?"

"What secret? I don't know why you keep going on about secrets."

"Secrets and lies, lad, there are always secrets and lies."

"Suit yourself, but I ain't got none."

Sam pushed the chair back and stood.

"Well, I leave you in here for a while to think about that."

"How long? I got things to do and that."

"As long as it takes."

As Sam left, he looked back through the small window in the door. Whitehorn was staring at his hands as if he thought they might contain an answer to his troubles.

As for Michael Stilton, he looked as if he were heading for apoplexy. His blood pressure was mounting and his face was turning purple. Sweat was running from beneath the swirl of hair with which he tried to disguise incipient baldness. He started up as soon as Sam walked in.

"Really, inspector, this is an outrage. Why on earth have you brought me here? My wife doesn't have the most robust of nerves at the best of times, and she will be worrying herself half to death. I am a respected figure, you know, a head teacher, who has taught generations of children in this city. So why the hell have you dragged me in here like some common criminal to suffer indignities ill befitting someone of my standing?"

Sam let silence do the talking for a moment. He found it helped sometimes. He pulled out a chair, sat heavily, and stared at Stilton, without speaking. He could hear himself breathing, slowly and calmly. Stilton's breath was coming out in intemperate bursts.

"You're enjoying this, aren't you, inspector? I think you have a taste for humiliation."

Sam stared at the man for a moment longer. He was right, of course. Sam did enjoy the power this situation granted to him. Why wouldn't he?

He decided to break silence.

"Chief inspector, not inspector. Bit like me calling you a teacher."

"All right, chief inspector, why have you brought me here?"

"We are still following up leads into the murder of Jane Wragge, and you are one of our potential suspects."

Stilton turned redder still.

"That is mad. Why would I kill her all these years later?"

"No idea, you tell me."

"I can't because I didn't."

"All right, but why do I feel that you are not telling me the truth? I have a nose for a lie, you know, it comes with the job. Bit like your line of work, I imagine. You must surely know when a child is telling a fib. So what aren't you telling me, Mr Stilton."

"Nothing, because I have nothing to hide, and I don't know what you are on about."

"So why do you look so shifty then, and why when you speak are your eyes raising up in that tell-tale manner?"

"I... I'm not saying anything."

"Fair enough. I leave you to think about it."

"You can't do that. I have things to do. I promised my wife I'd take her to Bettys."

"I'm sure Betty won't mind waiting."

Sam left and got himself one of the foul station coffees. Really, he should give up drinking this stuff. Now it was the turn of Richard Whitty.

The artist was much calmer and met Sam's gaze with equanimity. Yet Sam could still detect something, a hint of an old untruth, or maybe he just didn't like the man.

"So we meet again, chief inspector."

Good God, he spoke like a character in an old film.

"So we do, Mr Whitty."

"Any chance that you could give me an inkling of why you have summoned me here, away from my easel and the attentions of my doting woman?"

For being a smug arse of an artist with too high an opinion

of yourself. That was the first thought that came to Sam's mind.

"We are still chasing up leads over the murder of Jane Wragge, and I believe her death could be linked to the relationships she had. And you were one of those men."

"God, wasn't I just. Best sex of my life that woman gave me, though the present incumbent isn't half bad."

"So why do I sense that you are lying to me in some way, that something about your version of events isn't quite right. You seem to be offering me a self-serving account of your time with Jane Wragge."

"Not much of a hunch to go on that, is it? I think you'll have to do better than that before I cough to anything."

Whitty smiled at Sam, confrontational and cocky.

"When we met before, Mr Whitty, you said that you and Jane parted because of 'artistic differences'. Would you care to elaborate?"

"Not really."

"Looks like it's going to be a long day then."

Sam tried the silence trick again. The effect was different than with Stilton, but something in Whitty's demeanour did change.

"So let me get this straight. You've got me here because you think I could have killed Jane years after our affair ended?"

"Stranger things have happened."

"But why would I have done that?"

"You tell me. And while you're about it, you could tell me why I get the impression you are lying about something to do with Jane."

"Fuck knows."

"Manners, please, Mr Whitty."

"I honestly did not kill her. Christ, I hadn't seen her in ages. Besides, I've got my new younger girlfriend, who is about the age Jane was when I did that nude painting."

"So why don't you just tell me what really happened between the two of you?"

Sam was surprised by what happened next. He felt he was pushing up a blind alley on this one, but couldn't stop pushing. He wasn't expecting Whitty to tell him the truth, if that's what it was.

Whitty ran the palms of both hands over the grey stubble of his skull, stared at the table, then started to speak, without raising his eyes.

"It ended badly between us. It had been so lovely. Great sex, long conversations afterwards about art, and a bit of competitiveness on that score too. But it went sour very quickly. Jane just went off me. One day she was all over me, the next she said she didn't want me in her life, said I had a stifling aura or something ridiculous. And you see I couldn't take that, wasn't prepared to take it.

"So when I went back to get my stuff, I..."

There was a catch in his voice, which sounded weaker without the spring of self-regard.

"I said I wanted to have sex one last time. She laughed in my face and said she'd rather become a nun. So I pushed her over. She was only wearing a big old T-shirt at the time. It was warm you see and she'd been painting. I pulled her underwear off and forced her to have sex one last time, like I said I'd wanted. She hit me and bit me and screamed, but I didn't stop."

"So you raped her."

"Well, yes, I guess I did."

When he looked up there were tears in his eyes.

Sam returned to Stilton next. The head teacher had gone from flushing red to pasty white in the interim.

"You don't look very well, Mr Stilton, if you don't mind me saying."

"What do you expect, keeping me cooped up in here, for no good reason."

"So have you given any thought about what secret you might be keeping from me. If it's any help, my experience on this case suggests that it will have something to do with sex."

Stilton seemed deflated as he spoke.

"I liked Jane and we were good together. She was more experienced than me and I suppose you could say better at all that business too. I am not as physically demanding as some men. And Jane grew a little frustrated at my inefficiency."

"You mean you couldn't get it up?"

"That is not how I would put it. I prefer to call it occasional erectile dysfunction."

"And Jane wasn't happy about this?"

"No, chief inspector, she was not."

Sam left Stilton to his discomforting memories.

Whitehorn was looking sweaty and pale.

"I need a fag. It's been ages."

"Bad habit that, you know."

"What are you then, the government health minister or something?"

"No, just a policeman who is trying to find out why a woman was murdered."

"I already told you, I had nowt to do with that. It weren't me, I keep telling you."

"So why do I still think you are lying to me? I can always spot a lying bastard and you are ticking all the right boxes. So what really happened between you and Jane Wragge?"

Whitehorn was silent for a moment. Sam felt he could hear the cogs turning, the slow deliberation of thought. Then he signed and started to speak.

"It was like this, you see. I was pissed off with her for finishing with me. My whole life, everything had been crappy, then she came along and saw something in me. She lifted me up and that gave me hope, made me see some good in myself. Then she suddenly said she didn't want me any more."

"So you decided to hurt her?"

"No, I didn't. I couldn't, not her. I'm not saying I haven't hit a woman before, but not Jane, not her. I couldn't, you know, I liked her too much."

"People hurt people they love."

"Yeah, tell me about it. But I didn't do that. What I did was nick one of her paintings. I just took it when she threw me out, slipped it under my jacket."

"And did you sell it?"

"Tried, didn't I, but I bottled out. So I kept it. It's on my bedroom wall."

Sam told the three men they were still under suspicion, but let them go. He wasn't sure where the exercise had got him, other than to fill in more of the gaps. They still hadn't traced the suspect called Pablo. Sam considered the name and wondered if he should be looking for someone Spanish. Can't be too many of them in York, he thought.

CHAPTER THIRTY FIVE

BILL Inchcliffe went with the unstoppable flow. What a good day it was shaping up to be. Everything was going his way. It was his belief that you made your own luck. He had this familiar thought as he bounded up the stars to his first appointment. To fit with his mood, he emerged victorious from the meeting. One of the big bosses from corporate HQ, who passed through the place like undertakers with tape measures curled in their cold hands, eyeing up possible 'corpses', praised a suggestion he made, while a disliked colleague had his nose put out of joint. On the way downstairs he managed to dodge a colleague from whom he had recently cadged fifty quid. And, chiming with this perfect alignment of events, when he returned to his office Catherine was smiling at him playfully. Yes, it was going to be a humdinger.

"Looking forward to tonight," Catherine said, smiling. "It's been a while."

Bill was temporarily stumped, but wasn't going to admit it.

"Me too."

"Clever idea to use an intermediary to let me know."

"Yes, it was, wasn't it? Well, I am full of them. And you know what, it is good being me today. Everything feels just so right. The world loves me today, Catherine. And you can't put a foot wrong when that happens."

"Cocky bugger."

"Well, the world doesn't wait for those it favours."

He felt the lupine grin lick across his face. He knew it was wolfish because admirers and detractors had told him so, and because he had caught himself smiling in enough mirrors and windows. He thought the smile suited him, and it didn't hurt to be a wolf. They tended to get what they wanted. His knowledge of wolves was sketchy and did not include the fact that they tended to operate in packs; or that lone wolves were often old specimens driven from their pack.

Catherine reminded him about the unknown arrangements and the good day continued to shine. He had fixed up an evening's naughty entertainment without even realising it, which was such a fortuitous thing it made him smile all the way to his next meeting. This one went his way too and the disliked colleague again made a fool of himself. How gloriously were the planets aligned in his favour; fortune wasn't only smiling at him, it was grinning and showing all its teeth.

At lunchtime in the pub the girl he liked was behind the bar. She smiled and offered a gratuitous glimpse of cleavage while she pulled his pint. What a girl, a student of some sort, he shouldn't wonder. She told him once, but he couldn't remember. The details weren't important. But he could recall that face and those nicely sculpted breasts. What a terrible man I am, he thought, indulgently, warmed by his own charming awfulness.

He took his pint and his sandwich to a table some distance from the bar. There he supped and munched, while the barmaid told a colleague about the grinning creep, the one who always stared at her tits.

His mobile pinged once more, announcing another message. It would only be Miranda. She had sent him two or three already this morning, asking him to make sure he turned up at home in time for tea. What was the woman babbling about? The messages continued throughout the afternoon. Bill concluded his wife had gone demented in some way or other and so decided to ignore them. Then she tried to phone him but he cut the call and put his mobile on silent. That woman has too much time on her hands, he thought. Maybe we should have had children; perhaps I could still give her a baby. She might like that. It would give her something to do.

He wondered if her life hadn't become dull, with only that boring part-time job at the university to keep her ticking over. Yes, a baby might be an idea, women seemed to like babies. It might leave him with a bit of extra freedom too. She'd be too wrapped up in the baby to notice what he was up to. The more he looked at it, the better he liked the idea.

The working day ended and the evening lay ahead. He sought out Catherine to check the arrangements. He couldn't help noticing that she looked a little sheepish, even though he tried to ignore such nuances of female behaviour.

"Your wife has rung a couple of times. Said it was very important, imperative that she spoke to you – a matter of extreme urgency. What's that all about, Bill?"

"Oh, don't worry about that. I spoke to her just now on my mobile. It's all sorted out. No worries. So shall we be off then?"

"All right, you first, and I'll follow in five."

Bill remembered that he had no clean clothes or toothbrush, or any wine or nibbles.

"We'll stop for vino and food. We could pop into M&S and I could even get myself a clean pair of underpants – seeing as this is all rather unexpected."

Catherine looked a little concerned. "What do you mean by unexpected?"

"Did I say that? Oh, nothing at all, I didn't mean a thing."

A worried expression formed on her unlined features, then floated away to wherever it is that apprehensions hide.

Bill had a premonition about Miranda so he left by a different exit and slipped a safe distance away. Yes, there she was, fretting and fidgeting. She'll worry herself to death will that woman. Up and down she paced, glancing at her watch, at the door, and around. He dodged out of view just in time as she turned in his direction. When he looked again she was talking to another woman, to Catherine. The two of them were having a conversation, his wife and his mistress.

What would they find to talk about? After all, he was the only thing they had in common. Maybe they wanted to swap notes, score his technique out of ten, or something like that. They talked for a minute or so, and then Catherine left, looking flustered. Bill wondered about this as he set off for the arranged meeting place by Ouse Bridge, where Catherine caught up with him.

"She was there."

"Who was?"

"Your wife – who do you think I meant?"

"Oh, what did she want?"

Catherine frowned as she recalled the strange conversation she had just had.

"Well, she said that if I saw you, I was to tell you to go straight home. I thought she was going to have a go at me, slap my face or something. Scream at me there in the street, call me a harlot and a tart. But she looked worried, you know, genuinely scared."

"Oh, she's a worrier. Always has been, always will be. I'll give her a call later. You just put your frown away and let's go and enjoy ourselves. We need wine and food. Do you want to eat first or buy some deli-style nibbles to enjoy in the bedroom?"

Catherine smiled and relaxed. He was looking handsome today, she thought, animated and confident. Wine, salty food and sex enticed her, but perhaps she should slip some salad in as well. All this clandestine passion and eating wasn't doing much for her figure. She craved something healthy too. She promised herself she would run around even harder than usual at the squash club tomorrow. They held hands for a moment, then slipped apart. York was a small place and you couldn't go round holding hands without being noticed. Perhaps they should have gone to Leeds or somewhere to conduct their affair.

They kept their distance as they crossed the River Ouse. They went for a drink in the pub Miranda had avoided the previous night, the one that floods; and then they walked to M&S to stock up on food – pastrami rolls, crisps, nuts, cheesecake, a bag of salad ("Salad? What on earth do we want that green stuff for?") – and two bottles of wine. It was quite a spread.

AFTER the three interviews, Sam wanted time to himself. He had carried the diary into work that morning and felt furtive doing so. Technically, the dead woman's diary was evidence and he should have told someone about it. His defence was that he was following up a side-shoot and he wanted to learn as much as possible about the victim. It did no harm to fill in some of the blanks and these private thoughts might lead somewhere.

The growing closeness he felt was something he would only admit to himself. Was he falling for a dead woman while continuing to drift apart from the living breathing one he had been married to for more than twenty years? He dismissed this notion as being too fanciful for words. What would his fearful underlings think if they knew that blunt-speaking Chief Inspector Sam Rounder even had thoughts about having such thoughts?

The bureaucracy of murder continued to roll out. Laine and Anders and assorted PCs spoke to other young men from the group of students in the pub, and to another worker at the burger bar. The interviews filled in more details about Sherry Smithson's final hours. Nothing that emerged added anything new, or not that Sam could see. People's last moments could be so mundane and ordinary, and in other circumstances would merely constitute the dull minutiae in which lives are measured.

Around lunchtime, Sam withdrew to his office with a sandwich and a coffee of the usual foully dubious provenance, and shut the door behind him. With luck he might get an hour to himself; he might even finish the diary.

He had to flick back to refresh his memory. Jane and Moses were recuperating after the dark night with the disappeared stranger, and Jane was looking forward to her art show. The details pulled Sam in again and soon he was living once more in someone else's past…

March 16, 1987

MOSES has been his big happy gentle self once more.
The darkness has withdrawn from him and he is able to
smile again. I do not know how I could live without this
man, although I have existed without a fixed male presence
in the past and been perfectly happy. There is something
so reassuringly solid about my Moses. He is so male, so
much more of a man than those who came before. He
doesn't understand my art, and says he is puzzled by my
creativity, a little scared by it even, but he doesn't fuss me
about my work. He knows when to withdraw and leave
me to it, and that is to be cherished.

Anyway, painting is on my mind more than ever. There
is so little time left before the show. I still have to decide
which paintings to exhibit, and whether or not to include
my latest work. It will be an open show at the house, a
new thing, the first of its kind; other artists will turn their
homes into studios too. I have submitted the details and
will be given a sign to put outside the house. How odd and
exciting it will be to have strangers trooping through my
private spaces, looking at my paintings.

Most of them will be my garden works, things of tangled
dark beauty, or at least I hope so. The effect I am after,
I think – and it is always difficult to be too precise, too
certain – is to create something that looks beautiful in
itself, but with dark shadows. A tainted Eden, that sort of
thing. Some of the new paintings are of the cemetery, and
these show something ordered emerging from the tangled
neglect. It is my hope to catalogue the restoration, to paint
as we go along. In years to come, there will be a painted

record of the cemetery being brought back into order. It is such a special place for York, a sombre place, naturally, with so many stories to tell; all those people, all those lives. Yet it is our special place too, as it brought us together.

Moses is such a darling at the cemetery, working so hard. He really puts his back into it. Such a strong man, and yet that strength cost him dear.

My man suggested one of the paintings. It is of my favourite place, the corner of the cemetery that chimes with my other name, the one no one uses, not since my mother died; right up until the end she would say my full name occasionally, bringing back childhood memories of being told off. I finished the painting today, or I think it is complete. It can be difficult to know for sure, to pinpoint the moment when the worrying away at the thing has to stop.

Moses likes to come into the studio to look at what I have completed…

So you did paint your special place.

Yes, and now it's done. I didn't want you to see it until it was finished, but I can't think of anything else to add. If you overwork something, what makes it special can be spoilt. So there you are – it's done, finished.

Moses stands behind me and rests his strong hands on my shoulders. He makes me feel so slight and small, yet I am reassured by his presence. He is my rock and will stop anything bad happening to me. His hands are warm on my neck, which is exposed because my hair is up, like it usually is when I paint. He strokes my neck and kisses it gently. Then, still standing behind me, he runs his hands down the front of the man's shirt I wear to paint.

Such was my urgency to paint this morning that I did not dress properly, so his hands cup my breasts without any unleashing. Soon the shirt is off and Moses undresses and we make love on the rough floor surrounded by my paintings. We seem almost to be in a green place, a many-faced garden. Moses breathes near me and I fancy we can hear insects too, buzzing in the greenery. The painting I do is a sort of gardening, creating a green place heady with peace and an unsettling sense of something about to go wrong. We lie still together for a moment afterwards, looking up at the new painting, showing my favourite corner of the cemetery.

I'll put this one in the show but it's not for sale.

Why's that? It's lovely, someone would buy it.

Because I want you to have it, silly.

Are you sure?

Perfectly.

Thank you.

Anyway, let me go because I'm freezing. I need to get warm in the shower and then have something to eat. I forgot to have any breakfast and it must be lunchtime by now. What time is it?

Two o'clock.

No wonder I'm so famished.

In the shower the title for my little exhibition arrives amid the steam: Gardens of Death and Life. Warm and dry, I descend to the kitchen, where Moses has made lunch.

I didn't know you could make omelettes.

Oh, man of mystery, that's me.

We eat and I climb back to begin a new painting. This one won't be ready for the show, but I always have one on the go. Painting is what I do and I never want to stop, even when my head throbs, my back aches, my fingers are sore and my eyes are shot. I can see the paintings all the time, even those I have yet to paint. So I have to release those from my mind.

God, I'm getting carried away again. It's a good job Moses can't hear my muttered thoughts.

When I go down in the late afternoon, Moses has made sandwiches and coffee. Then we go for a walk until we reach the pub by Lendal Bridge, one of the ones Moses likes.

A perfect day, yet I am forgetting the one cloud. I haven't told Moses about Pablo and his plans. Moses now accepts my painted men – indeed he has become one of them. But men can be funny about past lovers. Now Pablo will be so near. It seems a funny thing for him to do, wanting to have guests. Not his sort of thing at all, or so I would have thought. Let's hope he cures that nasty personal habit before he makes them breakfast. God, how disgusting!

SAM was so wrapped in Jane Wragge's past that it took a moment for the significance to sink in. The former lovers had all been traced, except for Pablo. He put the diary back in his bag. He suddenly had an idea about Pablo, but before he could follow it up a call came through that jolted his heart. He wished things wouldn't keep doing that: he wasn't sure how many more jolts it could take.

There had been another attack on a young woman, a student out jogging this time. The adrenaline started up once more. It was happening again.

★★★

MAGGIE Motion was used to being teased about how she lived up to her name. She was lithe, fit and moved a lot, especially since she came to York. The running helped compensate for the excess alcohol and the dietary lapses. She knew how to eat well, knew how much she should and shouldn't drink, but it wasn't always easy to stick to healthy ways when you were a student. So she went running, most days if she could help it, apart from the other morning when she woke up in a boy's bed (a bit of a mistake, but another story). That way, part of the day was devoted to doing something healthy.

Her friends told her not to run by the river when it was early or late, but she ignored their fussing. She was young and fit, and besides she should be able to go anywhere: why should her life be contained or curtailed by fear? If you let that happen, the creeps and the perverts had won. This was what she said every time and eventually her friends stopped the sermon.

She had run along the river up from Lendal Bridge many times without incident, aside from the occasional over-friendly dog. It had been misty late this afternoon, instead of properly foggy.

"I wouldn't have gone if it was properly foggy," she said. "Well, I might, because I'm stupid like that. Stubborn, my mum says."

A hospital administrator had rung to say that a young woman had been admitted with a head wound. She said someone had attacked her while she was jogging by the River Ouse. The wound looked nasty, but was superficial, and the young woman was demanding to leave.

Sam put through a call asking that she be kept there, then rushed for his car. When he arrived, she was sitting on the edge of a bed in accident and emergency, looking drained and bored, but definitely alive. Sam knew that the first time they met could have been under much worse circumstances, with her pale dead body laid out at the mortuary, but he kept hold of that thought.

Sam introduced himself and asked if he could get her anything.

"No, I'm all right, they've given me a bottle of water. I could do with a coffee, but that wouldn't do my headache much good. I just want to leave this place and go back home."

"Looks like you suffered quite a blow."

"Yeah, there was blood everywhere, but head wounds are like that, aren't they? I've been stitched up and X-rayed, and they say there's no real damage. Aside from this headache, but the thing is, I had that before I started. I was trying to run off a hangover. It works some days, or at least those days when I don't get hit on the head."

"So tell me what happened."

"I was running along the river on the side near the railway museum. I'd just run over the footbridge next to the railway line, trotted down the stairs, and turned right. My head was hurting because I'd been mixing my drinks last night, but my legs felt all right, good really.

"At the bottom of the steps I saw a lace was coming undone. I went underneath the short tunnel and stopped the other side to do it up. While I was crouching, I saw something out of the corner of my eye, a shape or a person or something. It was getting dark so it was hard to tell for a moment. I looked up and there was a man, a middle-aged man, I guess, about the same age as my dad, forty or forty-five, something like that. About your age, probably. He had something in his hand, half a brick or something. Next thing I knew he was hitting me with it, only I dodged to one side and the brick didn't smack me as hard as it might. I hit out as well, scratched the creep. They took samples from under my nails earlier, in case they might help catch the man. I would have run after him, but the blood started pouring in front of my eyes, and I couldn't see. And I was scared."

She had been composed telling the tale, but now she started to cry.

"Why did he do that, Mr Rounder? I didn't know him or anything. Why did he want to hurt me?"

"No idea, love, but when I catch the bugger, I'll ask him."

The girl suddenly looked so young, not that much older than his daughters – "Eighteen, nineteen in two weeks," she said, when he asked.

"If the docs have finished with you, I'll give you a lift home."

Sam asked where she lived. She gave an address of Heslington Road.

"I'm going that way, as it happens."

He put in a call, then drove the girl home.

CHAPTER THIRTY SIX

RICK was cooking and trying to rid his head of clients. Generally they were trouble, but in his line of work, trouble was what you got. The untroubled had no need of private eyes to pick through the fibres of their lives. They got on with living instead.

He stirred the curry sauce, which he made from scratch, using individual spices rather than powder, heating the spices in a dry pan before grinding them in a pestle and mortar, then adding the mix to onions he had gently fried in ghee. The chicken had been introduced later, along with coconut milk and tinned tomatoes. The kitchen smelt invitingly spicy. The rice was almost ready and two bottles of Indian beer stood mottled with cold on the work surface. They were staying in tonight, just the two of them. Rick popped open the beers as Naomi came into the kitchen, fresh from the shower.

"This all smells fantastic," she said, accepting a beer.

"Oh, it's just a little something I rustled up after three weeks researching recipe books and a whole afternoon slaving in the kitchen."

Rick turned to chop fresh coriander for the curry. Naomi pulled him back round and gave him a kiss infused with beer.

"It's good to be together. We've not done that enough lately."

"I know, that's why I'm cooking."

"All that travelling, all those places we visited – we were always so close. Yet living back in York, it's been hard sometimes, especially when you keep disappearing on mysterious private eye errands."

"Well, they're not errands – it's my job."

"Sorry, yes, I know. I wasn't belittling what you do, it's just that sometimes it pisses me off."

"I know that, but what are you saying?"

"We should do more together. How about travelling again? That would bring us closer. Being on the road, never knowing what's coming next."

"We could book a holiday."

"I wasn't talking about a holiday, Rick."

"I know."

They were sharing a vision of sunny beaches and cold mountains, of open spaces and endless possibilities. But there was a divergence in their fantasies: Naomi was imagining dusty adventures still to be had, while Rick was recalling those already enjoyed.

Rick stirred the curry and checked the rice, a little fussily, Naomi thought. It was lovely that he was cooking for her and about time too. She did most of the cooking and it annoyed her; but tonight he was making an effort, she couldn't deny that, and everything smelt wonderful. She looked at her man and smiled. She felt good about what they had, yet her happiness was undermined by a nagging incompleteness. Would they stay here in York forever, her in a dull job and Rick running his fingers through other people's messes? She tried to put the thought away by drinking more beer, but her doubts were not so easily dissolved. Was this what she was for, was this why life had been granted her, to live cooped up in walled city where the sun didn't shine often enough and where she was trapped doing a job so dull?

Really she should stop being such a selfish cow and enjoy what she had. York was everything she had imagined and she lived in the heart of the city. She wasn't fully happy, it was true, but happiness was fleeting, hard to pin down, definable only by its absence, she knew that; and much was good in her life. Yet she wasn't part of where she lived, whereas Rick was at home, back where he belonged, even though he said he no longer felt as if he did belong. In truth, she liked not fitting in and as a tall black Australian-American woman living in mostly white York that was probably just as well. She enjoyed difference, felt empowered by standing out, and anyway there wasn't a whole lot she could do about it.

Naomi resolved to enjoy the evening and forget her dissatisfaction. Everything was almost ready and Rick was bustling about the messy kitchen. What was it about men and kitchens? He seemed to have cluttered every possible surface, used every pan and available implement. She bit her tongue and told herself that she would tidy up later.

"Nearly ready."

Rick bashed a pan and peered at the curry. She rested a hand on his shoulder but he moved away from her, breaking the contact, too busy to notice.

Then the doorbell rang.

"I hope that's not one of your new friends wanting to take you on another girlie night out."

Naomi might have felt she didn't belong, but she had more friends than Rick. Women were just better at friendships; they made the effort, and didn't sit around waiting for something to happen.

"I'm not expecting anyone."

She went downstairs and Rick concentrated on his final preparations. When Naomi returned, a cold autumn wind blew up the stairs, fluttering the gas flames on the hob.

"There's a mad woman at the door who insists on speaking to you."

"What?"

"She says she won't go until you talk to her."

Rick left the kitchen, with its warmth, smells and promised pleasures, and went downstairs. It was Miranda Inchcliffe, the last woman on earth he wanted to see at his door, aside perhaps from Margaret Thatcher. Her car was parked out in the narrow street with its engine running. She must have reversed in readiness for a quick getaway.

"You've got to help me. There's no one else I can turn to."

"I thought we were through. You hired me, paid me and then asked me to do something I felt wasn't right."

"I know, but everything has changed. I couldn't think of anyone else. Please, help me."

She explained quickly, gabbling with the urgency of what she had to say. Rick listened, sighed and said he would be back in a minute. He went upstairs to the kitchen. Naomi had turned off the pans and was drinking beer and watching television.

He said he would be back as soon as possible. Then they could eat, there would still be time. Naomi swigged her beer – his beer, in fact, as she had finished hers – and kept her head towards the television. EastEnders was on and two numbskulls were having a slanging match.

"You don't even like…"

"Just go, Rick."

He grabbed his leather jacket, went downstairs and got into the car. Miranda shot off over the cobbles before he had shut the door. The drive to York Cemetery was fast, illegal and left Rick feeling queasy. How could anyone drive this fast through the crowded streets of York?

"You should join the police with this driving technique. They'd bite your hand off."

Miranda stayed silent and concentrated on hurling her car through the darkness.

CLARENCE Smith enjoyed a secret. What was it they said about knowledge and power? He couldn't quite remember, but secrets were powerful. Thoughts of secrets and lies occupied him as he booked in the couple standing in his reception area. He knew they had been secretly filmed on their last visit, that the sex they shouldn't have been having had been recorded and was now captured in the unthinking innards of a computer somewhere or caught on a shiny disc. He knew this and they didn't, and this made him feel good.

"Turning cold, isn't it?" Clarence said, by way of a delay. "Soon be Christmas with all that entails. Now what names was it. Oh, yes, Harry Belafonte and Sally Bowles, that was it, wasn't it? Yes, as I was saying, Christmas will soon be upon us."

Bill grunted by way of a reply. Why was this man blathering on about Christmas? He didn't much care for Christmas: it required him to consider the wants of others. Still, he liked the parties and the opportunities they contained; yes, the parties were good, so there was something to look forward to.

Why wouldn't the ingratiating man stop talking? Bill wanted to go upstairs for sex and drink and unhealthy affair picnic food. Life was too short for annoying people who obstructed his desires.

Catherine could sense the man was annoying Bill and she wanted to be upstairs too. She had been feeling uneasy all day: not in the sense that she shouldn't be shagging a married man – she had accommodated her morals on that one. Besides, Miranda was clearly bonkers, so it was no wonder Bill would rather spend time with her. No, she had a vague and unsettling sense that something was wrong, that the situation was slipping out of control. There was no reason for this, so far as she could tell. She fought her way up the stairs, past the annoying man. She liked Bill, she really did, for all his egotistical quirks; he was fun, good company and he appreciated her. She knew it couldn't last and had toyed with getting herself a younger man, perhaps one of the boys at the squash club, with their leaner bodies and boyish enthusiasms. Some of them looked lovely, but she preferred older men, always had, finding boys her own age too callow.

Eventually, Clarence Smith let them through, making great play of his generosity, handing over the key and waving them up the stairs with an unnecessary flourish. He put his hand to his face as he watched the girl go up the stairs, pretty and slim, just the thing. Perhaps if his favourite girl had stayed faithful to him, everything would have turned out differently. He turned his mind away from what he didn't wish to dwell upon. He had always been able to do that and it was a useful skill. He diverted himself by remembering the other secret about the couple: the one about their friend who had arranged all this. It must be nice to have friends like that, he thought; or nice to have friends.

BILL and Catherine entered the familiar room. Bill dimmed the lights, removed his tie, unbuttoned his shirt, unscrewed white wine still cold from the supermarket fridge and filled the wineglasses he had bought. He remembered that the guesthouse only had tumblers suitable for stacking toothbrushes. He began undressing Catherine and soon she was almost naked. He felt excitement and need rise through his being. What a day this had been.

As for Catherine, desire removed her doubts. Yes, it's no wonder he prefers spending time with me, what with having a wife like that. She decided to enjoy what was coming. She was excited and ready. Bill unhooked her bra and she lent towards him, her smallish pert breasts – her favourite feature, one bit of herself she really liked; thank god she didn't have top-heavy tits like some girls she knew – pointing towards Bill's hairy chest. He reached out with his free hand, the one not holding the wine, and cradled her breast. They kissed passionately, so passionately Bill almost spilled his wine, but he had a steady hand where wine was concerned, and didn't waste a drop. She took the glass from his hand, but only after he had ambushed it for a final sip, and put in on the bedside table.

It was then, as they fell together on the bed, as Catherine fumbled with Bill's belt and his zip and felt him rising; it was then, as another joyous betrayal was about to take place, so quickly over and yet so lasting in the scars it left; it was then that they heard the bathroom door open.

Bill saw the man first.

"What the fuck?"

It couldn't be the alcohol, he'd hardly had anything. Who was that man and what was he doing here? He could hear a strange, piercing sound. What was that? Catherine was screaming. A moment ago she had been leaning towards him, her breasts had been nudging his chest; she had looked so lovely and sexual and ready for anything. Now she seemed so young and lost. She was grabbing around for her clothes and shouting.

"Bill – do something! What's going on?"

The man seemed to be dressed as a hell's angel and was wearing a leather jacket, with trousers to match. Perhaps he was a hell's angel. Bill had no idea. Everything was slipping away from him. He didn't understand anything. The stranger was speaking. His words were calm and deep, but at first they didn't get through. Bill felt as if he was underwater and the man was speaking above the surface. Then the words reached him. The man was telling him to get dressed and he was apologising to Catherine.

"I'm sorry, young lady, for causing you distress. But my complaint is with your partner, not you. Strictly speaking, you shouldn't be here, should you? Get dressed quietly and you are free to go."

Catherine, half-dressed now, although her skirt was still sloughed on the floor, screamed at the big man. Then she rained tiny punches on his chest. The man looked down at her and blocked her fist as she tried to punch his face. Then he picked her up, gently but firmly.

"As I said, my argument isn't with you, so just get dressed and behave yourself."

Catherine couldn't resist his grip. She felt puny and useless.

Bill stood, his trousers still unzipped, detumescence unmanning him. He stepped in to help Catherine, but the big stranger was ready for that. He placed her softly on the bed and grabbed hold of Bill.

"Get dressed now, please, and then we are going for a walk."

"I don't want to go for a walk, I want to…"

"I know what your want to do but I'm here to make you aware of what you have done in the past, the hurt you have caused."

"Christ, what are you? An avenging angel?"

"Just a man with a job to do, a man who found a distressed damsel in a pub, and came to her aid."

"What damsel?"

"The one you're meant to be married to."

"Miranda – you don't want to go around believing everything she says."

"Oh, but I do. That's just the way I am. Now get dressed."

Bill did as he was told and then left the room with the stranger. Catherine sat on the edge of the bed, face white, hands trembling. The debris of interrupted passion lay about her. Crumpled sheets, an open bottle of wine, an inviolate packet of condoms. Everything felt hurtful and she had no idea what to do next.

Her unsteady fingers tried to do up the buttons of her blouse as she took shallow, panicky breaths. She wondered what the stranger was going to do to Bill. She finished dressing, found the shoes she had kicked off moments earlier in a flurry of sexual anticipation, and left the room, rushing down the narrow corridor until she reached the stairs to the reception area.

BILL was incompletely dressed. His belt was undone, he'd lost his tie somewhere and his coat was still in the room. He noticed these sartorial defects as the stranger hustled him down the stairs. The annoying guesthouse owner was no longer by the desk and the lobby was empty. Bill had the feeling the man was hiding somewhere, keeping out of his way. He could almost sense his just vanished presence, as if he had scuttled at the first sign of trouble. He glanced around as he was manhandled into the street. It was cold and quiet outside. Bill noticed a motorbike parked in front of the guesthouse. Was that there on the way in, he wondered? A helmet was locked to the side of the bike. He couldn't recall seeing the motorbike, but supposed it belonged to his persuasive companion, who still held him tight.

"Why are you taking that mad bitch's side in this? There are two sides to everything, you know. You could hear what I have to say."

"If you want advice, go see a marriage counsellor."

"All right, I will, I will. Let go of me and I'll make the call right now."

"We have a little unfinished business first."

"How can we have unfinished business? We haven't started anything – hell, we've never even met. Are you sure this isn't a big mistake? That's it! You've got the wrong man. That explains it. You've got the wrong guy and this is all a massive misunderstanding."

"No, your wife is the one with the wrong man. Now get moving."

Bill was pushed towards the dead end of the street.

"Where are we going?"

"Over that fence and into the cemetery."

"Why?"

"So that I can teach you to value your wife."

"I will, I mean I do. Truly, honestly I do. The others,

they don't really count – Miranda's the one for me. She's always been the one, the one and only."

"Yeah, that's what it looked like just now when I interrupted you in that room."

"Catherine, oh she's my secretary. It was work really, that's all. You know, we were just getting a bit carried away. Work, that's all."

"Not what it looked like from where I was standing."

Bill fell silent. He could think of nothing else to say. He supposed he must be a bad man, but not so bad surely that he deserved whatever this hired-in hell's angel had in mind.

"I'll stop the shagging, go back to my wife, be a good and faithful man."

Even as he was speaking, babbling really, the words pushed out on a tide of panic, he felt depressed at the prospect. Was that all he had left, a dull life in the suburbs with his wife? Eyeing up other women at parties when he thought she wasn't looking, which she almost certainly was, or chatting up the young girls at the office, but nothing else. Sometimes the conquests were all that kept him going. Without those sexual challenges, what purpose would there be to his life?

Bill Inchcliffe was not much of a man, but he was too much of a man in other senses. He wanted to achieve and mostly he wanted to have; to have whatever and whomever he could, to live greedily and selfishly; and to do so with such wolfish charm that no one hated him for it. This had seemed a reasonable personal manifesto, one that had seen him through handsomely, aside from a few narrow squeaks. He had lived this way for years. How many women had there been? He lost count, although for a while he kept score, scribbling notes in a private book, until he panicked and burnt his private diary, fearing Miranda might find it.

He tried to remember how long he had been married. Was it 15 years? Something like that. Miranda had been so beautiful that day and so eager that night. He wondered how everything had gone wrong and why she had let it go wrong. He was not given much to self-examination and even in this moment of crisis, as a leather-clad hell's angel ordered him over the tall wrought-iron fence into the cemetery, he felt the prickle of justification. It's not my fault, she should have taken better care of me, she shouldn't have let me; why didn't she stop me?

They had honeymooned in the South of France, near Nice, in late spring, just out of season. Home for the week had been an apartment in the foothills, with a distant view of the sea. They had eaten in cafés and bars, and driven to the beach, or explored the hillside country, and then retreated to their honeymoon home, where they had quickly undressed each other, once only just getting through the door and making love on the hall floor. The unbridled urgency of their passion had stayed with Bill down the years, and if an explanation was sought for all the affairs, it was that he was always seeking to find those moments again, to experience that level of excitement and physical connection. That's what he would tell himself, for sure, even while knowing that he was making an excuse for himself. Bill was a man who mostly didn't see his own faults, and when they did become apparent to him, he indulged them, as he might a favourite but naughty child.

"I'll never get up there."

His voice sounded petulant and puny. He heard a car in the distance and thought someone might help him, but the car drove by the open end of the street and carried on up the hill towards the university. Then the silence settled again. He wanted to shout out loud; he did shout out loud. "Help! Someone please help!"

The man pushed Bill, winding him. Bill could taste the rust in the iron and a flake of paint stuck to his tongue.

"Just shut it and get over that fence."

"I can't, I…"

He felt himself being lifted, and then the man held Bill's foot in both hands and catapulted him upwards, until he was balanced precariously. Seeing no way out, Bill jumped into the dark cemetery, swearing as he fell in a pained heap. The big man climbed easily and leapt in one swift movement, bending his knees and rolling away.

"You've done that before." Bill was impressed, even in his terror.

"I've done lots of things before. Now get up and walk."

The limited light emitted by the street was soon diffused. A watery moon cast a pale glow over the cemetery, which became at night a place of deep shadows and unexpected fleeting vistas. Tall trees rose black into the sky, where bats darted and fluttered. An unseen owl hooted and a gust of wind stirred the dead leaves. Gravestones loomed and withdrew, holding on to their inscriptions. To the right of the gate a long walkway led to the road by the main gates, but the stranger led Bill away from this route, walking deeper into the cemetery. A cloud obscured the pale moon and Bill could see nothing. The big man kept on, placing his hand on Bill's elbow to guide and secure him. They walked in silence, two shadowy ghosts trapped on a gloomy purposeful journey and after a while the cloud moved on, letting the watery moon illuminate them again.

"A beautiful place, but a tragic one."

"Well, I suppose graveyards are," Bill sounded petulant, even to his own ears. "Full of dead people and all that."

"Sad stories are woven through this place, happy ones too, no doubt, but the sad ones stay in the mind. Even the land the cemetery is built on has sad stories to tell. Part of the land was originally a nursery run by a man called Thomas Rigg. He had two sons and both died young, predeceasing him by some time. One of the sons and his wife had twelve children, six of whom were lost to childhood diseases. As if that weren't tragedy enough for one family, the other six were drowned in an infamous boating accident on the River Ouse."

"Yes, very sad." Bill wasn't sure what to say, but had the momentary good sense to suppress the sort of quip that usually came to mind. He didn't think his kidnapper had much of a sense of humour.

They trudged in silence, until the stranger spoke again.

"It took years to get this place built. Originally most burials were in the parish churchyards dotted around the city, but they were overcrowded and often unsuitable. Even after the cemetery opened, bodies were still interred locally.

"A group of local worthies formed what we would now call a pressure group to campaign on public health. It was in 1847, I think, something like that, sometime after the first burials here. One of the issues they tackled was the unsuitability of parish graveyards, which were still being used at the time. The earth in those graveyards was often wet and swampy – loathsome mire, was one expression, I think. Disinterred bones and remains were found all over the place.

"Anyway, one of these worthies was Alfred Ely Hargrove, proprietor of the York Herald newspaper. His submitted thoughts included a gruesome little scenario about a dog and a human leg. I have committed it to memory. Would you like to hear it?"

"Go on then."

"Hargrove reported that 'A hungry dog entered the sacred ground and seized a leg bone in his mouth and bore it away in triumph to his lair, where he doubtless would feast on the putrefying remnants of mortality'. Quite something that, isn't it?"

"Lovely. I'm just glad you interrupted me before I had started eating."

The stranger made a deep sound that suggested mirth or menace, or both. Up ahead a building took shape in the darkness; it looked like a temple.

"What's this place?"

The stranger led Bill to the steps where they sat down.

"It's the cemetery chapel," he said. "Designed by the architect James Piggot Pritchett. He based his design on the temple of Erectheus in Athens. He completed the chapel in 1838 and it is considered by those in the know to be an excellent example of the late neo-classical style."

Bill thought he would die if he heard another fact, but kept that opinion to himself.

"You seem to know a lot about this place."

"If you live somewhere, you should know about its history, what's gone on before; you should appreciate all the threads of the past that lead to the present."

"Fair enough."

"There are catacombs below the building and when it was completed, interment was offered as a burial option.

But it was expensive and not very popular – only 17 people were interred here, the last in August 1881.

"The catacombs turned out to be a white elephant, but must have seemed like a good idea at the time. They offered a final resting place to people who didn't want to be buried in the earth – afraid of all those worms and so on. So their bodies were sealed in a coffin filled with formalin, which was supposed to preserve them, then placed on giant lead shelves under the cemetery chapel.

"It was very expensive to be deposited in the catacombs. It cost twice as much as an outside plot and they still had to pay for the coffin, a triple coffin: one of glass, one of metal and one of wood."

"Why are you telling me all this?"

"Why? Good question – because it is knowledge I possess after a certain amount of study and because it is interesting. I can tell you more or we can get straight to the bit when I deliver a message from your wife."

Bill suddenly felt drenched in despondency.

"Go on then, I'll have the history lecture before the telling off."

The big stranger paused for a moment. Bats zigzagged madly and shadowy birds twitched as they settled in for the night. Again, an owl hooted and somewhere in the distance a siren sounded.

"Among the bodies deposited in the catacombs are those of husband and wife John and Jane Johnson. They were Quakers, and when Mrs Johnson died she was originally laid to rest just outside the chapel.

"Three weeks later her husband came back and asked if she could be moved because she was getting damp. So she was moved into the catacombs. Mr Johnson joined her

26 years later, but only after causing a scandal among the Quaker elders after he remarried against their wishes.

"He fell in love with a farmer's daughter who wasn't a Quaker, so the Quaker elders objected to the marriage. But Johnson went ahead anyway, and then three years later took an advert out in the press stating he would not be responsible for his wife's debts.

"When he died in 1881, his will ran to five pages. He left £1,100 to be shared among many beneficiaries, but just one shilling to his wife."

Bill felt for a moment that he was going quite mad. A short time ago he had been undressing his girlfriend in readiness for a night of sex, wine and unhealthy food, his reward for a day that had been going so well. The luck had been running with him today, he had felt so confident, so certain. Now he had been kidnapped by a mysterious hell's angel and was sitting in the cold and dark, listening to a seemingly endless lecture about local history.

Bill sighed and decided to humour his captor.

"Just one shilling for the wife, eh?"

"Yes, some people don't know how to treat their wives, do they?"

THERE had been too many fast car journeys in Rick Rounder's life, starting from his days in the sixth form, when friends who passed their test early would display their virility by driving at speed along quiet rounds on the outskirts of York. Once two new drivers had raced each other, screeching in competition, with assorted friends as human ballast. Looking back it seemed they were competing to see who could be the first to die young. Luckily, no one won. Miranda Inchcliffe swerved the small car into

Heslington Road and accelerated up the lower reaches of the hill, before cutting violently to the right and shooting into the dark dead-end street. The tyres squealed as the car skidded to a halt outside the Cemetery View Guesthouse. Miranda leapt out, leaving the engine running.

At this point, events began to bounce off each other as everything started to happen at once.

Miranda ran towards the guesthouse. Rick lost sight of what was going on for a moment when he leaned over, cut the ignition and removed the key. By the time he had extracted himself from the car and locked it, Miranda was screaming at another woman, then trying to comfort her, before reverting to shouting. The other woman was the girlfriend. The last time he had seen her she had been making love and he had been filming her. Darkness hid the blush that coloured his face.

"So where the fuck is he?"

"I don't know. A big man took him, he was a hell's angel or something, huge and dressed in black leathers. Who is that man?"

"Someone who was going to give Bill a message from me about how he shouldn't be fucking little tarts like you."

"But I don't understand and…" Catherine slumped onto steps outside the guesthouse.

"He was my avenging angel only now I want him to stop. Enough harm has been done."

Miranda knew she was shrieking and she quietened herself. She felt almost sorry for the tearful girl hunched on the steps. What did this pretty little thing see in her treacherous wreck of a man?

"He's a man I met in a pub when I was very angry with Bill, and he came to my defence like a leather-clad knight on a motorbike charger. Only I think I got a little carried away in what I asked him to do."

Rick stepped between the women.

"His bike's still here so he's not gone on that. We didn't see anyone on the way in, so my guess is they've gone into the cemetery."

Rick ran towards the tall gates and climbed until he was balanced on the top. He wanted to turn and let himself down gently, but there was no room for the manoeuvre, so he had to jump. As he hit the ground, he felt something jar in his ankle. Headlights swung into the road. First one car, then others with lights flashing and sirens blaring. Rick stood and looked back into the street. People were starting to come out of the houses. Miranda and the girl were walking towards him. Rick was about to turn away into the dark cemetery when he saw his brother lumbering out of his car. He had never told Sam about Moses Mundy and he still felt bad about that omission, but now wasn't the time to worry about the ethics of his job versus the requirements of brotherly honour. Sam was back-lit by headlights and blue flashing lights. He stood on the other side of the gate lit up like an overweight angel, panting in the cold. His breath smoked the night air.

"What are you doing here?" The question was not friendly, put by the policeman in Sam rather than the brother.

"Helping a client. What are you doing here?"

"It's to do with the murdered artist. Anyway, where is your client?"

"She's standing next to you. That's Miranda, my client, and the girl she's with is her husband's lover."

"Was," said Catherine, emboldened to speak up. "Not any more, this night has cured me of that if nothing else."

"Proper little soap opera you've got going here, Rick."

Sam turned away as a woman from one of the houses close to the cemetery came up and said she had a key to the gate.

"I wish I'd known that earlier," said Rick.

Sam asked the woman to go and get her key, then turned back to the fence.

"I'll send a couple of my officers in after you, once the gate is open. That's so long as you don't mind their big feet tramping all over your private eye sensibilities. But I can't have them jumping over. The buggers might sue me or report me to health and safety."

"Yeah, thanks."

Rick wasn't sure about his route, but decided to follow the path alongside the houses and the high wall. The path dipped and ran ahead of him, mysterious and half-seen. Behind him the headlights shone through the gates, throwing shadow patterns into the cemetery. He was some distance away when the gates swung open.

Dead people were all around yet he felt surprisingly calm. The dead had their stories, carved into stone, and he had read them on walks round the cemetery, but now their legends were dark and unreadable. The lost generations kept him company as he jogged on as quickly as he could, trying to forget his ankle. Branches from a shadowy tree brushed across his head and above him bats scattered into the sky, as if the very darkness had fragmented and its pieces had come to life. He reached Cemetery Road and ran along the wall. A car drove by and its headlights raked the wall, dazzling him for a moment. Rick paused by the gatehouse, trying to decide which way to go.

★★★

BILL Inchcliffe felt gloomy and cold. He had started to shiver. Once his teeth began to chatter he wouldn't be able to stop himself. Cold always got him that way, seating deep inside, reluctant to let go. He stood and hugged himself, trying to tease warmth out of his body, and fidgeted his frozen feet across the hard ground.

"Well, thanks for the history lesson. All very interesting and that. And you've done what my wife asked, because I won't be straying again after a night like this. I'll be a one-woman man, faithful and true."

This was the truth, so far as Bill could foresee, marital fealty never having been his thing. Perhaps loyalty, honesty and all those other mysterious virtues would be a good idea; you never knew until you tried something. Once again, the faithful life rolled out in his mind, contained and dull. But there would be Miranda and she wasn't too awful, if only he could concentrate on her.

"I'll stick with Miranda. She's not that bad really, is she? How did you two meet, by the way?"

Bill might have wondered at the stranger's silence, especially since moments earlier he had become almost animated while going on about those catacombs and all the history. The details escaped him. Bill's concentration wasn't good, unless he was concentrating on how to turn a situation to his advantage.

The big stranger spoke slowly.

"We met in a pub. Miranda, your lovely wife, had gone out looking to find a man to teach you a lesson. She looked in all the wrong places, until she found me. We forged an arrangement, she gave me all the details I needed – where you worked, your lover's name, and your favoured place of betrayal, that sort of thing – and then I set up tonight's entertainment for you and your girlfriend."

"That's a lot of trouble to go to, just for a woman you met in a pub."

"Her story touched and affronted me. I can't abide a woman being hurt. And she arranged to pay me a lot."

A certain flip insincerity had always characterised Bill's approach to life, a tendency to find a smart phrase to see him through. Mostly this approach seemed to work and sometimes it was almost charming, although such charm was a risk, as likely to annoy as to soothe. A lifetime of chancing it, trying it on, giving it a go; that had always been Bill's way, so why would he change at the end?

The stranger had his orders and he had delivered what was required, hadn't he? Bill felt duly chastised: lessons learned and all that. He wouldn't be a naughty boy again, or not for a while, he could promise that much. Incorrigible was a word people had used to describe Bill in the past, Catherine among them. She had called him that in the days before they were lovers, when she had started to work as his secretary. He was flirting, trying on the charm, standing a little too close, and flashing that wolfish grin. "You're incorrigible, that's what you are." He hadn't been sure if this was a compliment or not and had looked it up in the dictionary he kept at work. "Incorrigible: adj. Not able to be corrected or reformed: she's an incorrigible flirt." It was next to incorruptible, which was a laugh.

Bill had shown a degree of good sense and restraint since the stranger kidnapped him. This was partly because his captor was big and clearly much the stronger man. Also, his confidence was shot. His good day had turned into a hellish day, the worst possible, and he was starting to feel annoyed. He weighed up the possibility of attacking the stranger, but knew he wouldn't have a chance. He had seen Catherine lifted clean off her feet, her pretty puny fists bouncing off the man to no effect.

This was when Bill made his mistake, a fatal mistake, although not in the sense people often intended – "This is when I made my fatal mistake" – when relaying a story, usually a heavy-handed one weighed with leaden wit. This mistake truly was fatal.

"You've gone to all this trouble for the mad bitch. What's wrong with you? Why didn't you just shag her? That's what I would have done. Shag and move on – shag and move on."

Bill did not see the fist. For a big man the stranger had fast reactions. One second he was sitting on the steps while Bill hopped around, complaining, and trying to get warm; the next he was on his feet, aiming his fist.

It was a lucky blow or an unlucky one, depending on perspective. It caught Bill beneath the chin and felled him. A soft landing would have seen him with little more than a broken jaw, a fate which might almost have been in keeping; and one which would have shut him up for a while.

RICK thought he could hear voices. There was a chapel here somewhere; he remembered going inside once. It had fallen apart and then been saved. He recalled something about the cemetery being sold for a pound to the people who now looked after it. Black trees brushed against him as he ran towards the voices. He was panting now, out of breath and hot, even though it was a cold night.

Not enough exercise lately; too much beer and wine.

Up ahead two shadow men were squaring off against each other. One silhouette was much larger. This dense shadow hit out and the slighter shape fell backwards.

Rick limped up as the larger man disappeared into the dark. The man who had been hit was spread-eagled on the ground. Rick crouched and felt the faintest of pulses. Even in the dark he could see blood spreading from the man's head. He sat on the ground next to the almost lifeless form of Bill Inchcliffe and rang for an ambulance. Before that could arrive he heard other voices and saw torches dancing in the dark. The constables sent by his brother had arrived.

Rick Rounder, ex-policeman, one-time globe-trotter and private eye, had seen people die before. He didn't want to hold the door open for Bill Inchcliffe. Someone who loved the man should be there to see him off, but the departing soul of the unfaithful man would have to make do with him. If Rick hadn't been hired by Miranda, then Bill Inchcliffe might still be vertical and going around annoying people. Then again, the man had caused his own downfall. If he hadn't been an inveterate shagger, he wouldn't be lying on the cold ground, all too close to all the other dead people. Rick knew this to be true, but he knew also that he had precipitated events more than he liked to admit.

THERE was no sign of Clarence Smith at the Cemetery View Guesthouse. Sam Rounder cursed the noisy arrival they had made. If he'd come by himself, Smith would still be around. He probably was still around, Sam thought; we just haven't found the little sod yet.

Uniformed officers wearing bright yellow reflective jackets trooped through the guesthouse. There had been no other guests that night, aside from Bill and Catherine. The officers went upstairs and crashed about the place, opening doors, peering under beds and in wardrobes.

Sam went into the kitchen for a drink of water. He was dehydrated from the long day, too many vile machine coffees, and the low-level hangover that seemed to accompany him most of the time. Water was good, like the apples he had started eating again; water and apples – he'd be the picture of purity before you knew it. He ran the cold tap for a minute, then filled a glass. A glass in his hand always felt good, even if it was only water. He felt the cold spread of the liquid. When he put down the glass, he saw that the kitchen door was slightly ajar.

Outside there was a small walled garden, space for guests to sit in the summer. Sam could see no back gate, so Smith would have had to climb over the wall at the back, which was fairly high, or the lower walls at either side, into the adjacent gardens. Light flooded from the windows upstairs as his officers continued their search. Sam looked up at the house, then did a slow revolution, his breath visible in the cold night air. There was a shed against the back wall. He walked over. The door was shut but it wasn't locked. He stepped inside, filling the door, head stooped. He thought he could hear something. Another man's breathing accompanied his own. Smith was curled behind an old bike. He stood shakily and started to speak. Sam remembered the petulant tones and sighed.

"Ah, chief inspector, I was just looking for something. Some, er, oil for the back door. Can I help you? I'll need to start preparing breakfasts for the morning soon. I always like to get everything sorted the night before; it makes my mornings easier. I'm a busy man, you know, this place doesn't run itself. There's always something to do."

"I'm sure there is, but I shouldn't worry. Your guests have gone and won't be coming back, and you will be breakfasting elsewhere. And I'm sure someone has started cooking your breakfast already: they always taste like they've been on the go for a few days."

THE ambulance couldn't get in by the main gates, which were locked, and had to set off again, lights flashing, siren blaring, and approach by the side gates. A stretcher was carried through the dark graves to the chapel. A mournful tableau presented itself. Rick had relinquished his place and stood some feet away, watching. Miranda squatted next to her husband, sobbing and then breaking off to swear and remonstrate with him. She didn't mean for anything so bad to happen; but it was his fault for being unfaithful and unkind; oh Bill, my Bill, you stupid, treacherous bastard, how have we ended up like this?

Miranda had made some accommodation with Catherine, who crouched at the other side, pale as icing, quiet and drawn. The man who lay between them seemed to be dying. His breathing was shallow and an awful lot of blood had escaped his head and was pooling at her feet. There would be blood on her clothes, blood of the man she had been having an affair with, blood of the man who belonged to the woman opposite. Miranda was older than her, ten years or so, but with more curves than she had and very attractive, she noticed, wondering.

Catherine wondered what Bill had seen in her as she sat working outside his office, organising his days, or why he had wanted her so much. He wanted her, she realised with a sob, because she was available, she was there, and he could have her. She had been another slight challenge in the amorous life of Bill Inchcliffe. Other girls had warned her, but she hadn't cared; they were just jealous, spiteful and wanting to spoil her fun. The affair had been fun: exciting, the good sort of wrong, forbidden. Now she felt stupid and dirty and frivolous. It wasn't all her fault and she wouldn't take the blame for everything. Bill was the one who shouldn't have been playing around; she hadn't been unfaithful to anyone – ever. Catherine, a clever and intuitive woman, smarter than she was sometimes given credit for, especially at work, knew she was fooling herself. She may have been free to have sex with Bill, but in doing so she had betrayed another woman and supposed she should feel bad about that.

The ambulance officers lifted Bill Inchcliffe on to the stretcher and carried him through the cemetery. The others followed in line, the two women, Rick Rounder, and the constables, leaving the cemetery to resume its mournful quietude.

SAM was preparing to leave with Clarence Smith as the procession reached the ambulance. The motionless form of Bill Inchcliffe was conveyed away speedily in case medical intervention would do any good. Miranda went with the ambulance and Catherine was driven to the police station, to be interviewed. She would face no charges, having broken no law, but her statement as a witness was needed.

Before Sam left for the station, he squared up to Rick.

"You need to tell me what all this is about."

"Well, I suppose I do."

"So you were working for the wife?"

"Yes, confirming her worst suspicions."

"Which you did?"

"Yes, completely and in full colour, all delivered to her on a DVD."

"So how do we get from there to what happened tonight?"

"Miranda Inchcliffe wanted to hire me again to rough up her husband, but I declined."

"So what were you two doing here together?"

Rick sighed and returned his brother's angry glint of a stare.

"She hired in someone else to do the job, then had second thoughts. She couldn't get hold of the man she had hired or Bill, her cheating husband, so she came round and made a scene at my house, insisting I came with her. I was bang in the middle of cooking a meal for Naomi too; proper pissed off, she was."

"And that's it?"

"Pretty much – except for one thing. I've…"

He wondered how to tell his brother about Moses Mundy. They were standing in the street outside the guesthouse, framed by the night sky. Clarence Smith hunched sullenly in the car.

"I've been working for Moses Mundy, too – more or less since the case started."

One of the yellow-jacketed officers was listening in to their conversation. Sam turned to him and gave him a blast of authority.

"Why don't you stop eavesdropping and get yourself back in that cemetery and starting looking for the bugger who hit the other poor bugger. Now."

"Okay, boss, but it's dark in there and goes on for miles. What chance have I got?"

"About as much chance as you have of getting a boot up your skinny arse if you stay around here complaining."

"Understood."

The officer walked towards the open gates and contemplated the dark acres before him. It didn't seem fair. How would that fat inspector like it if he had to trudge around a spooky old graveyard in the middle of the night?

Rick expected Sam to be blazing with anger, and he did looked pissed off; but the full fury was missing. But he still wanted to say his piece, to savour being affronted.

"So you thought it was all right to go behind my back and work for the chief suspect in a murder case – someone we hadn't even found?"

"Yeah, that's about the size of it. That's the way it works – I'm available to hire for whoever wants me."

"Sort of like a prostitute."

"Well, I don't normally sleep with them and bodily fluids are kept to a minimum."

"But all this time we've been looking for Moses Mundy, you've known where he was?"

"Only some of the time. He's a man of mystery who likes to move around."

"Look, I don't have time for all this now. I've got to get back to the station and interview this creep."

"Looks familiar. Who's he?"

"Clarence Smith, owner of the Cemetery View Guesthouse."

"So what's he done?"

"He murdered Jane Wragge – well, that's my theory."

"So how did you get on to him?"

"I've had a little help – and I've been keeping secrets too. I'll tell you about it after tonight. But I wish you would stop getting your scabby freelance nose in my official police business – I always knew this would happen when you set up as a snoop."

Sam leaned closer. "We'll talk later, brother to brother. I'll tell you summat for nothing, though."

"What's that?"

"I never did think Moses Mundy killed her."

"Why's that?"

"Well, you could say the dead woman herself told me."

Sam drove off with Clarence Smith, leaving behind a team to search the guesthouse. Rick wondered how he was going to get home and what sort of mood Naomi would be in when he got there. As for the reluctant search party, sent on a fool's errand by his angry boss, he edged into the darkness, gloomily speculating on how long he would have to stay in the cemetery. Everyone, in other words, was occupied; and so no one saw the large dark figure leap over a wall next to the guesthouse and mount his motorbike.

Rick turned as he heard the roar of the bike's engine. He ran towards the bike, a useless gesture, made in the name of doing something. He was still ten or fifteen feet away as the bike thundered off, sparks flying from its footrest as it rounded the bend a little too fast. The bike wobbled, then righted itself, and flew nosily into the night.

CHAPTER THIRTY SEVEN

RICK got a taxi home to a cold curry and a colder shoulder. Naomi would be in a rotten mood or deep in resentful sleep. It was usually his fault or so she would say in the morning. So the warm curry smells surprised him as he walked up the stairs. He had assumed the evening dead and gone.

Naomi was relaxed and a little drunk.

"No beer left for you," she giggled.

She had heated the meal and cooked more rice. It was late and Rick's head was full of a dying man, cautionary tales of illicit sex and a mysterious stranger on a motorbike. But he was ravenous and Naomi had passed through various shades of sulk to emerge happy. They ate the unexpected midnight feast and she pulled him upstairs to bed ("Leave all that, we'll tidy up in the morning") and they fell into bed and into each other, a little uncomfortably thanks to the weight of the late food. After the sex, they fell asleep, together and complete, until something else got in the way.

Sam was in for a longer night, with rotten food and no chance of sexual distraction. The police station felt drained and over bright, as if someone had forgotten to turn off the lights and tell everyone to go home. He'd been on the go since first thing this morning – yesterday morning now – and was zombified with exhaustion. He got himself another cup of the suspicious, murky liquid that the machine said was coffee – never mind thinking the unthinkable, this was drinking the undrinkable – and went into the interview room. Iain Anders sat behind him, trim and surprisingly fresh looking; how did someone look human at this time of night? He appeared to have had a shave. Sam's own face was cast in shadowy stubble.

Sam pulled up a chair and fiddled with the tape machine. Clarence Smith was tired and scared, but defiant too. Sam had seen all this before, seen most things before, guilt, innocence and all the shades in between, and he was happy to pace himself.

"I'm sure this is all some terrible misunderstanding, chief inspector. I'm just a man who runs a guesthouse. Putting tourists up for the night, giving house room to couples who are up to no good, that sort of thing. I don't know why you want me in here. What do you think I have done wrong?"

Sam was silent for a moment.

"All right, Mr Smith, why do you think I've brought you here in the middle of the night?"

"That's just playing games and I'm not in the mood."

"Well, I'd rather be at home in bed with the wife instead of stuck here with you, but life's a bitch sometimes, isn't it? It's not fair that you have to be here, it's not fair that Inspector Anders has to be here either. We're keeping him from his beauty sleep too. And if this goes on for too long, he'll be excusing himself to go for his morning run.

"It's not fair on me either, because I've had a very long day. But mostly, it's not fair on that poor, talented artist whose head you bashed in. And I haven't even mentioned the other girls yet."

"What other girls?"

"The young American we found in the middle of York with her pretty head caved in. And the jogger."

Smith gazed at Sam, eyes flicking, then said nonchalantly: "I read something about the American girl in the paper. But I don't know anything about any jogger."

"Well, we'll get to her later – and the American, too. But let's begin with Jane Wragge, artist and a neighbour of yours."

"She lived opposite me, but so what? Plenty of people live in that road. Anyway, I thought you were looking for the boyfriend."

"Maybe we are, maybe we aren't. But I now believe there is also a connection between you and the dead artist: you used to be lovers and she once painted you in the nude, along with four other of her lovers."

"This is mad – I don't know what you are talking about. You're raving. I want it put on record that I think you are mad."

"It is on record, it's on the tape."

Sam paused for dramatic effect, then turned over a piece of paper on the desk.

"That's you, isn't it, Mr Smith – or should I call you Pablo?"

"Pablo? I don't know what you are talking about."

"Oh, Mr Smith, I think you do."

A spark of defiance ignited somewhere deep inside Clarence Smith. He didn't have to do any of this.

"I'm not in the mood to talk. It's too late and all you've got are bullshit theories and crackpot suggestions. Other than that, you've got nothing. And besides, I'm tired."

Smith yawned ostentatiously and lay his head on the table. Sam left him like that for a moment, fitting in a quick yawn himself, and then leaned over and slapped the desk next to Smith's ear. That got him sitting up all right.

"Ow, that was loud!"

"Well, sue me for busting your eardrums. But if you really want to hear something loud, you should carry on pissing me off."

Smith sat up, slim arms crossed over his chest.

"I'm not saying anything else tonight. I want a solicitor. I'm allowed one, aren't I?"

"Fair enough, I could do with some sleep myself. I'll have you put in the cells until morning, when we can resume our nice little chat."

IT WAS nearly 2am. Sam poured a malt whisky and went into the front room and sat in his favourite chair. He hadn't been in this room for ages and felt like a lodger in his own house. No one else was up and even though it was horribly late, he enjoyed the silence and the space. Being the only man in a house full of women was hard work at times. The whisky warmth spread through his body like a friendly virus. He picked up the diary and started to read the final instalment...

March 17, 1987

THE paintings are complete – or as complete as they ever are, letting go, knowing when to stop can be difficult – and the show is today. I am up early, making the final arrangements. Most of the furniture has been removed from the front room, which is being turned into a gallery for the day. Moses did most of the shifting. He is good at moving things, so strong. I try to forget the ends to which that strength has sometimes been put. He is kind and good to me, and I can't deny that his bad-boy past doesn't have a certain attraction: the others mostly inhabited the straight

343

and narrow, although not Himbo; he was a bit of a rough boy, was Himbo.

I have invited all my boys. Does this display wisdom? Almost certainly not, but I couldn't help myself. Moses says he understands, although he looked hurt when I told him. Well, the boys are on display, so they might as well come along in the flesh too. The boys will be in the hall, away from my garden paintings. The front room is all garden, the hall a miscellany of other paintings, including my boys. Moses looks the best, naturally, and I told him this when he began to complain. He was not mollified, but resigned will do for now.

Anyway, he was right: inviting the boys was a mistake, as I shall explain soon in these notes to myself. I don't know why I am keeping a record of my life in this way, turning my life into a sort of fiction. It just helps, that's all I can say. Call it an artist's indulgence.

A few small jobs remain to be done – chill the white wine, open the red, put nibbles on display, scatter sweets in bowls.

Moses is staying to help, although he says the other 'boys' will annoy him. I laugh and tell him not to be such a silly. Now I realise I was the one guilty of silliness. How was this ever a good idea – not my lovely deathly gardens, but the boys, my naked boys?

The gardens go down well and I am pleased – and richer too, as all the big works sell quickly. Soon I am sticking small red dots on to all the main pieces, three of them sold to the same buyer. My naked men were not for sale.

★★★

SAM splashed more amber liquid into his glass, then embraced the lovely solitude and the final pages of the diary…

…EVERYTHING goes so well and I am thrilled: all these people here to see my work. Painting is a slow lonely business, and yet now everything is lively and exciting – so many people traipsing through my painterly garden.

I cannot say when I first realise something is wrong. I am in the 'gallery', standing where the television is normally, talking to the man who has bought three. He is a managing director of a company here in York and thinks the paintings will match the new colour scheme his wife fancies for their hallway. "More of a room than a hall, really," he says, musing on his good fortune. "As big as most people's living rooms."

I want to tell him my paintings are too important to match his wife's fucking colour scheme, but smile sweetly; too sweetly, for his eyes begin to scan me. It is as if he thinks I might match the colour scheme in his study, where he keeps his private collection of erotic art. I do not know this, but sense it to be true; and a truth sensed is as good as a truth discovered. It is then that I hear a scuffle out in the hall and voices becoming too loud. I excuse myself from my lecherous patron. My boys are in the hall, Mick, Rich, Pablo and 'Himbo', along with Moses, my dear Moses. They are in front of the paintings and had, so Moses will tell me later, been quiet, a little embarrassed perhaps, but contained. Then Himbo and Pablo start arguing – about me, apparently; Pablo saying it was Himbo's fault that I left him. Mick and Rich stand around, gazing at their shoes, but Moses steps in and separates the other two. The shouting stops and the situation seems to have been recovered, until Himbo darts round Moses and punches Pablo on the nose so that blood drips on to the hall floor. Himbo runs off, Pablo slumps against the wall, swearing. Somehow the afternoon has disintegrated and it is my fault.

A period of reflection is now called for.

SAM had finished the malt. It was horribly late and he was fully exhausted and pleasantly fuzzy. One page left but the words refused to settle, until Sam forced them to be still...

HERE ends the first lesson. Well, I've certainly learned something. Which is this: don't bring painted former lovers together; it won't be a happy reunion.

I am going to stop writing this diary. I was kind of blue when I started, but have written my way towards contentment, happiness, whatever. I shall keep these private pages to read again one day when I am old and saggy. They constitute as true and honest an account as I can manage of how I met and fell in love with Moses Mundy. One day, consumed by wrinkles and regret, I shall pick up this diary and re-enter the past, but now I want to live my life forwards. So that's it with words and I; henceforward, it is painting only... probably just as well if I will insist on using words such as henceforward...

SAM felt the sadness of leaving a good book. He had spent many hours with Jane F Wragge, squinting over her gold lettering, and he would miss her. He went upstairs, undressed and climbed into bed next to the sleeping stranger he called his wife. He was too tired for the long walk down the garden.

CHAPTER THIRTY EIGHT

THE stranger thundered along roads wide and then narrow, finally twisting to a halt. He switched off the ignition and propped up the motorbike. The engine ticked away its heat until silence enveloped him. Stars studded the night and breath smoked from beneath his helmet. He had lived only in cities and had not thought he would seek solace somewhere so quiet. The locals didn't bother him beyond the demands of bluff politeness. The lack of a pub in the village helped to stifle inquisitiveness, and he was glad of that. There was a pub deeper in the valley, which he had visited, drinking only one pint, because the bike was a new rediscovery and he didn't want to chance his luck.

The cottage was tiny and he had to stoop through the front door. Two rooms up, two rooms down, with the addition of a small conservatory. He took off his helmet in the kitchen and poured a glass of water. Nothing stronger would be needed to induce sleep tonight. He removed the biking jacket, which left his tattooed arms bare, and then shrugged off the leather waistcoat with the studded design on the back. She would have laughed to see that. The illustrated arms would have amused her as well. The ink was barely dry on those and the pain had surprised him, but it was worth it, and he liked the results, even if he did have to menace the tattoo artist into doing so many so soon. And the gold tooth, that would have tickled her too.

He went upstairs and washed his face, admiring the beard as he did so, and dabbed water over his grazed knuckles. The punch had been harder than he had intended and it would get him into trouble, or would do if they found him. He regretted the violence, but some things just happened, whether you wanted them to or not. The stranger relieved himself noisily with the door open – no one to complain now – and then went in the bedroom, undressed and collapsed into bed.

While the stranger slept, doctors fought to save the life of the man he had hit. It was to prove a vain struggle. Bill Inchcliffe died in the early hours. He never regained consciousness and so was unaware of the efforts made on his behalf. Being hit by a leather-clad stranger was the last thing on earth he knew. He saw the fist, then nothing. His body had continued to function for two hours while doctors tried to save him. When their efforts came to nothing, they moved on to try and save another's life or mend other bones.

Miranda was numb with disbelief as the police drove her home. She needed to sleep but was too tired and shocked to lose herself that way. She would have to sell the house, it was much too big. There were phone calls to make. What should she say? An accident would cover it for now, until the fuller truth emerged. There would have to be an inquest, wouldn't there, and the newspapers would get hold of the story. Everything would come out, all the sordid details, and everyone would know about Bill and his serial infidelities.

A woman constable stayed. She made coffee and withdrew when Miranda said she had to let people know. She would have to tell Bill's parents first. They would be devastated, seeing only charm in their eldest son, or so she supposed. She wasn't close to them. They had taken against Miranda early on for reasons now obscured even to her, and would blame her. Everything would be her fault. She sighed and made the call.

"There's been an accident," she said. "And I'm afraid Bill is dead."

AFTER sleep comes the waking.

Sam still had whisky in his veins as he emerged from too short an interlude. Yet he felt better than he should have, all things considered. Michelle brought him tea and got back into bed.

"Haven't you got work?"

"It's Saturday."

"Ah, so it is. No rest for me. Got a murder suspect to interview."

"The artist woman?"

"That's the one."

Too many unsaid conversations stood between them and Sam wasn't sure where to begin. Michelle made it easy for him.

"You came to bed with me."

"So I did. It was late and…"

The words were struggling to form.

"How's the health kick?"

She laughed as she spoke. He couldn't remember when she had last smiled at him. Sam looked down at the billowing mound of his stomach.

"I've been eating apples," he said. "And walking. Well, you know, one long walk the other day."

"What – the day of the flowers?"

"Yes, the day of the flowers. You don't seem as pissed off with me today."

Michelle was quiet and, when not smiling, looked

tired and drained, and older too. Sam noticed lines were beginning to form round her eyes.

"Well, something has happened."

"Good or bad?"

"Depends. The man I was seeing…"

"Yes."

"He got bored and moved on to someone else."

She was drained and tearful, but smiled at him again, a weak, distracted smile, but a smile nonetheless.

"Oh. So where does that leave us?"

Sam's voice was gruff from the whisky and emotion had nothing to do with it.

"It leaves me bringing you a cup of tea in bed."

"Well, that's a start."

"It is, isn't it?"

Sam let the steam from the tea obscure his tears. He didn't cry, he was a bluff fat Yorkshireman. Tears were for other, lesser, men.

Michelle looked at him and saw the hidden tears. She rested her hand on his.

"It doesn't mean everything's right between us, Sam. We've got our problems. The things that were wrong when I went off, they haven't gone away."

"But you're going to give the old Rounder boy another go?"

"Looks like I am. But I'll tell you one thing."

"What's that?"

"There are going to be a lot more apples in this relationship. And walks."

NAOMI was lying next to him, her black nakedness touching his white. He didn't often think about the racial thing, which was other people's problem. They were lovers and fellow travellers, friends. That mattered, nothing else did. Skin, that's all it was. Yet the difference could still surprise him: she so dark and he so white. He wasn't white anyway; he was pinkish. Underneath they had the same organs and bones, nerves and cells, the same blood. Before Naomi, Rick hadn't given much thought to race. He had not held racist views as such, or no more than the average Yorkshireman living in a mostly white city. Loving Naomi had made him see the world differently, but it didn't make him a better or worse person.

And this morning, he wasn't feeling good about himself at all.

Rick put on a dressing gown and went down to the kitchen. He made tea and while it was brewing he rang the hospital. The confirmation hit hard. He had come home and enjoyed a late meal and later loving, while Bill Inchcliffe lay dying a mile away. That was how life worked out, he told himself, you won or you lost. Well, we all lost in the end, but that was another philosophical story. His life was still going on and he was going to try to enjoy it. He didn't know if that made him good or bad, caring or heartless, but that didn't make any difference.

He took the tea upstairs to Naomi.

CLARENCE Smith hadn't slept well in the police cell, and the fat copper had been right about the breakfasts. As a self-acclaimed aficionado of the fry-up, Clarence knew what he was talking about. This was a fat-soaked balls-up of a breakfast. It had distressed him. People should know how to do things properly, even if it was just cooking breakfasts for criminals. Suspected criminals, he reminded himself.

He ate around half of the bad breakfast, leaving the rest to congeal. The fat was settling into ridges on the plastic plate when they came to bring him back to the interview room and the overweight copper. The thin watchful man of the night before had been replaced by a slight, tired-looking woman.

Sam Rounder started the tapes and said for the record that the interview with Clarence Smith was continuing, and that also in the room was Sergeant Sallie Laine, and a solicitor, Georgina Greene.

Smith spoke up first.

"You were right about the breakfasts, inspector. Proper crap it was, terrible."

"Chief inspector. And I'm sorry our catering isn't up to your high standards. It's been a while since Egon Ronay popped by to assess our hard-working chefs. They'll be worried about losing their Michelin star next."

Sam felt nothing but contempt for the man across the table; no, he felt more than that, anger too, and a temptation to do the man violence. Reading the diary had brought him close to Jane, too close; and this man was going to pay for what he did.

"Well, here's a funny thing: you'd better get used to rotten food. I hear that prison breakfasts aren't any better, and you'll be eating those for a long time, for the rest of your life with any luck."

The solicitor made a crisp interjection: "Chief inspector, I feel your language and bearing are threatening my client."

Sam turned and smiled at the young woman. "Fair enough, Mizz Greene. I'll consider my wrists slapped, so long as you consider my rights to question the prime suspect in a murder inquiry – two murder inquiries, in fact. And I still have that injured jogger up my sleeve."

Smith blanched. "Two – what are you talking about? I'm not owning up to one, and I'm certainly not admitting two."

Sam let the unfriendly silence settle. It helped, it always did. That feminist lesbian girl in the corner couldn't complain about him saying nothing, although she was shifting in her chair and looking uncomfortable; well, good.

"Let's return to that nickname, shall we? So why did Jane Wragge call you Pablo?"

"That was her idea of a joke."

"So you did know her then?"

"Doesn't mean I killed her."

"So what was the joke?"

"She called me Pablo because of an incident I would rather not discuss."

"We're not here for a nice chat. This is a murder inquiry and everything is important. So tell me about the nick-name."

Smith glowered, then sighed.

"She said I used to scratch my bottom."

"And?"

"And it was her idea of a joke."

"How come?"

"Picasso… do I have to spell it out?"

"I wish you would."

"Picasso… sounds like 'pick arse'. She called me Pablo Pick-Arsehole, or Pablo for short."

"Doesn't sound very ladylike."

"Well she was, a real lady, but there was another side to her, too. She could be quite crude at times."

"So how long were you lovers?"

"Eleven months, best part of a year – and the best part of my life."

"Eleven months – it's not long for a 'best part' is it? So you must have spent the intervening years stewing in resentment, especially when you opened a guesthouse opposite where Jane lived happily with her new man."

"The house came up, I could afford it and I liked the location."

"A nice locale, true. But weren't you torturing yourself, all those years spent living opposite the woman you once loved?"

"You learn to put up with these things."

Smith flashed a look of contained, capped-off anger, and Sam felt certain he had him.

"How did you find out about me and her?"

Sam paused, aware that what he was about to say was being recorded. "Certain evidence came to light during our investigation of the dead woman's home and belongings."

Sam sat back, forcing a creak of complaint from the chair.

"Well, here's a funny thing, you see. While you and I were getting our beauty sleep – me at home in bed with the wife, you alone on a hard mattress in one of our cells – my officers worked through the night at your guesthouse.

"They found a number of items of interest. Oh, while I remember, I'd like to interrupt the interview in order to get someone to take a DNA sample from you. I hope you don't mind."

An officer was admitted into the room and secured the sample from the inside of Smith's mouth, then took it away for analysis.

"One thing they found was this…"

Sam held a bag containing what looked something dead and furry.

"We found this wig in your bedroom. Now why would you have such a thing?"

"It's not much fun losing your hair. It made me feel better on dates, built up my confidence with the women."

"Well, a wig can also be a disguise, can't it?"

"Plenty of people wear wigs."

"Well, perhaps they do."

Sam decided on a break. "Tea or coffee, Mr Smith – or perhaps you would like something from our à la carte menu?"

RICK and Naomi were going out for the day, to Whitby, which was always rewarding, at any time of the year, even a chilly Saturday close to Christmas. Rick asked Naomi to reverse the Golf out of the garage.

"I've got a call to make – only the one, I promise."

"No more mad women?"

Rick smiled. "No more mad women."

He waited until he heard the engine start on the ground floor. Then he rang the number stored on his mobile. His side of the conversation went like this:

"Rounder here. He's dead, you know, died in the night. Did you have to hit him so hard? The wife wanted him taught a lesson, she didn't want him dead.

"You might call it an accident, I don't know if the courts would agree – manslaughter at the very least.

"I know I asked you to do this job after I refused. I don't know why I did that. I felt sorry for the woman, I suppose. You met her, she has something about her, even if she can be more than a bit mad. I should have left things as they were, but for some reason you came into my head, so I asked you to watch out for her.

"Yes, and that's how you 'accidentally' met her in that pub. I know all that, it was my idea, that you should watch her from a distance, follow her round and then introduce yourself. You did all that brilliantly. What I don't understand is why you had to kill the stupid man."

Rick ended the call and succumbed to thoughts of innocence and guilt. Sometimes the two bled together to form a moral mess that was neither one thing nor the other. Perhaps this was one of those occasions; or maybe he was kidding himself.

Naomi beeped the horn. Rick went downstairs and locked up. They had a day by the seaside to look forward to.

THE interview was going to take a long time, but Sam was happy enough with that. He was in his element, squaring up to a suspect. Seeing Smith squirm was making him feel better and compensated for the exhaustion and the whisky-smudged head.

Smith was uncomfortable. The colour had drained from his face and his skin had a waxy sheen. Sam prepared himself for a long bout of argument and denial. He would win such an attritional exchange, but hours might have to be spent wearing away at the man.

"So how did you meet?"

"At York Gallery, at an opening. For some reason Jane

357

noticed me and chatted to me. I was thrilled, Mr Rounder, thrilled. This lovely woman was showing an interest in me. Couldn't believe my luck."

Smith was lit up by a look of faraway contentment that took him from his confinement. They went on a date, then another, after which they ended up in bed together.

"I was so excited at the sight of her naked I let myself down, Mr Rounder."

"I don't need all the details."

"I made up for it, mind you, later on. I think I gave her a good time."

Sam chewed on his lips, to prevent himself from having a premature verbal ejaculation.

"We went out for 11 months, like I told you. We lived together for much of that time. Friends, lovers – she meant everything."

"But she didn't feel the same?"

"No... yes! No, she didn't – not in the end. She said she had a low boredom threshold and that I had pushed her across it."

The interview ground on throughout the day. Outside it was sunny, but Sam would be lucky to see daylight today.

THE stranger put down his mobile and looked at his knuckles, still sore. He stepped out to enjoy the sunshine. The air was so pure here, the countryside so elemental. He would like to stay but that might not be possible. The sky was clear and the surrounding hills patterned with dry-stone walls that seemed to defy gravity, clinging like necklaces.

He went back inside to make a coffee, the proper stuff, a taste he had picked up from her, and sat in the small kitchen. On the wall behind there was a painting. It was called Felicity's Gate and showed a favourite spot in York Cemetery. Jane's middle name had been Felicity, something he used to tease her about.

There was a story about the gate, a true story he heard from a man he met once. The cemetery used to be owned by the York Cemetery Company, which went into liquidation. The council pulled down the eastern boundary wall, which was considered unsafe. That gave unrestricted access to the cemetery and a local couple used it on their walks. The woman called Felicity became a trustee and when the boundary wall was rebuilt by the York Cemetery Trust, it provided a gate that would give access to the outside of the wall. When the gate was being built, another trustee, who was also a stone mason, carved the stone that names the gate and commemorates Felicity's connection with it.

That was the official story, but he preferred the one about the night when he had made love to Jane Felicity Wragge in watery moonlight on a blanket under the gate ("Like in that country song").

Moses Mundy was really called Harrison Hill and maybe even that name wasn't real. He liked the name, which he had borrowed from the inscription on a gravestone in the cemetery. Besides, that was the name Jane had known him by – "my Moses," she called him, even after she discovered the truth.

Moses would never forget Jane, not least because his tattoos were lifted from her paintings. Her gardens of death and life were etched into his skin. He even had her dead name embroidered into the back of his leather biker's waistcoat. She would stay, whatever became of him, however he shaped up. Moses regretted hitting the shagger in the cemetery: it was as if his old self, long buried, had rushed back to the surface, and a man had died because of this renaissance. It was a moment of foolish brutality, he could see that now, as he sat in the quiet kitchen in the Dales and began to wonder about himself, what he had been, what he had become. Had the love of one woman turned him away from being a thug-for-hire into a decent man? He thought that she had, but now that she was dead, did that mean he had to revert back to what he had been? These questions hung heavily on him and he let out a guttural sob, alone in the kitchen. That is where we leave the man who wasn't really Moses Mundy, alone and wondering which identity was the real one, and how he could shape up in a world without Jane.

SAM continued the interview, Clarence Smith persisted with his dull defiance, and the search carried on at the guesthouse. Smith's computer was taken away to be examined, furniture was emptied and shifted, cupboards spilled, and floorboards prised. In the back yard, Iain Anders, who knew how to lay a patio, was puzzled by the unevenness. Someone had done a good job, and then it had gone wrong by the shed. Bad workmanship, he supposed, then began to wonder. The small shed was not held by concrete and so could be moved. He had the shed shifted and arranged for the slabs to be lifted.

Sam ordered a break in the interview and went into his office for a sleep, making sure he locked the door behind him and pulled down the blinds. While he was asleep, Smith's computer, which contained a weight of pornography, the legal sort, unpleasantly gynaecological perhaps, but not revealing in any other way, gave up its secret. This was printed out and given to Sam, when he emerged bleary-eyed from his office. He read what the paper had to say, and walked back towards the interview room, yawning. It was almost evening now in his subterranean day.

HE TURNED over the paper and made a play of looking at what it contained, then across at Smith.

"Some of my officers are quiet technically minded and can do all sorts of things inside a computer. A good job really, as I can barely turn the bloody things on. One of my men has been working on yours. And do you know what he found?"

"No, but I guess you are going to tell me."

"Lots of pornography for a start."

"All legal, none of that paedophile stuff or anything like that."

"So I am told. No, it's what was written on this paper that interests me."

"What's that?"

"Something between a boast and a confession, I'd say."

Smith looked puzzled, then annoyed.

"But I deleted that."

"Did you now? Well, as I said, some of my officers are quite the technical geniuses. They can prise all the secrets there are out of a computer, raise the dead, as it were."

Sam started to read:

WHAT does a murderer look like? Much the same as anyone else. But I would say that, wouldn't I? All I have to do is look in the mirror. Murderers look like you and me.

Well, certainly like me, that goes without saying. And how do I look? Unexceptional, ordinary, much the same. I have the appearance of an everyday person…

"Sounds like a confession to me – so how do you answer that?"

The solicitor piped up again, advising Smith to remain silent. But Smith had been given his moment, he was the centre of attention. He looked shifty, then smiled.

"It was an exercise for a writing class I took at college, an evening class, you know, to try and improve myself."

"Oh, and where was this class?"

"At the college."

"And who was the teacher?"

"I forget."

"I bet you do."

Smith suddenly became oddly animated.

"I think I might be bi-something or other."

"Bisexual?"

"No, I've only ever liked women."

"Killing them seems a funny form of appreciation."

"Bipolar, that's the one – a split personality. I don't know why he does these things."

"Who?"

"The other me – the bad me."

Sam paused for a moment. He had a gambit ready for such situations, but it didn't always work. He tried it anyway.

"Why don't you ask the bad you to tell me what happened."

"With Jane?"

"Yeah, we'll start with Jane Wragge."

★★★

HE NEVER forgot her. There were other women, flings and one-night stands, or dreary dates with women who wouldn't let him fuck them, and the Australian woman, the one who never wrote; but then she couldn't, could she? But Jane was always on his mind, and just across the road.

"All that time and I never forgot. She was there each morning when I woke up, there again at night. She never left my mind. But if she saw me in the street she… she didn't exactly ignore me, but she didn't take much notice of me. A watery smile if I was lucky."

"You put up with this for years. So what happened to make things different?"

"Why did I…?"

The solicitor interjected. "Mr Smith, you are being led into areas which it would be advisable to avoid."

Smith glanced at the young woman, but carried on anyway.

"It went like this, Mr Rounder…"

HE watches until the man goes out, then steps into the road. To his left the gates to the cemetery offer a view of verdant, barely controlled greenery. Clarence has been inside the cemetery only once, even though he named his guesthouse after the place. He wonders at his lack of curiosity, but isn't really curious about that, for his attention is directed at what everyone in the street calls "the artist's house." No one mentions the man; it is the artist's house. The presence of another pains him; never stops hurting, he thinks, his finger on the bell. No one comes so he pushes again, watching his finger as if it belongs to someone else. His courage falters and he thinks he should leave. He has no plan, no idea of what to say. He is about to go when she takes shape through the stained glass, then opens the door.

"Oh, it's you. Hello, Pablo – what on earth do you want?"

He finds this hurtful. He wishes she wouldn't use that name. His name is Clarence. The woman he loves should be pleased to see him.

"Just to talk."

Jane looks at him with blank disregard. Then for some reason she relents.

"Come in then. But you can't stay long, I'm painting."

Painting, she was always painting. It got in the way, all that painting.

She makes tea in the kitchen, tea-bag tea, nothing special. She keeps the special leaf tea for her good friends. He used to drink that tea and remembers where it is kept, in an old Christmas caddy from Taylor's of Harrogate. They sip the tannic mahogany liquid and exchange the stilted conversation of lovers turned back into acquaintances. She asks about the guesthouse, he about the paintings. Then they are done with the tea and the polite conversation.

"I think you should go now, Pablo."

That name again. She shouldn't call me that. It is unkind of her.

She has been cooking, or someone has; perhaps the man is the cook. Husks of lemons lie on a chopping board next to a glass juicer, and he wonders what the lemons have been used for. He thinks to ask but she walks out of the kitchen and to the bottom of the stair.

"You can let yourself out."

He picks up the juicer and follows. He is not sure why he has the glass implement in his hand, but its weight is a comfort. He starts to follow her up the stairs.

"You could show me your paintings."

"Look around, you, Pablo, they are all over the walls."

That name again, she is using that name again.

"Your new paintings, the ones you are doing now."

"They are private, now will you please go! I don't know why I let you through the door – shit, I don't know why I ever let you into my life."

"But I don't want to go, I still love you."

"Don't be ridiculous – it was years ago, years and years."

"Maybe, but it's true. The years don't mean anything and I do still love you."

"Well, I love someone else so that won't get you anywhere. Now please go – piss off out of my house. I'm losing my inspiration, I need to get upstairs again before it leaves."

He doesn't understand how she can be so cruel and disheartening.

"Didn't you ever feel anything for me?"

"Years ago, fleetingly. But I didn't really love anyone until my Moses came along. I'm sorry if that hurts, but as people seem to say nowadays, get over it."

That's the man's name, Moses, what a ridiculous name. How has she ended up giving herself to a man called Moses?

Jane pauses as if thinking better of saying something; then she says it anyway, cross because she wants to paint. Her life is complete: she has her painting, she has her Moses, so why is this man – one of her mistakes, one of the many – standing in her house spouting all this misguided romantic nonsense?

"Pablo, you were nothing, an entertainment, a stage I went through, a bit of transient fun. Shit, you weren't even any good in bed. That first time you shot all over me like an over-sexed virgin teenager who had only ever seen pictures of a naked woman, never the real thing."

She is now at the turn in the stairs. Below in the hall light floods through the stained glass window, throwing filigreed patterns of colour across her paintings. Why has this man entered my world? This is almost the last thought she has. The actual last thought is more prosaic: why is Clarence holding the glass juicer from the kitchen?

Her words taunt his love-soured brain and he jumps up the stairs, quickly for he can move if he has to, being fitter than you would think to look at him, and smashes hard on her skull. She buckles into a heap next to him, then rolls and thumps down the stairs until her head hits the tiles of the floor below, making a horrible hollow smacking sound. He will hear that sound for ever, can hear it now as he tells the fat policeman about what happened, how he hadn't meant to do it, not really. She shouldn't have said those things, shouldn't have used that name, then everything would have been all right. There would have been no need.

The improvised weapon splinters across the tiles, where blood is beginning to pool. Shards adorn the blood like jewellery. Her life, her creativity, everything she was, all she managed to be, the love she has given, the friendships, it all flows away across the tiles.

Clarence steps gingerly round Jane. As he leaves the house he notices that his hands smell of lemons.

★★★

SAM wondered how someone so pathetic could kill someone. Two people, and attack a third. He decided to chance his arm on the tourist.

"So what happened with the American girl?"

Smith looked at him blankly: the question unimportant, his mind still occupied with the woman he loved.

"Yes, the poor girl we found in an alleyway, with her head all bashed in. Killed more or less the same way as Jane Wragge. We have taken a DNA sample from you and will compare that with any evidence found on the body. The science will catch you out in the end. Why did you kill the American girl too?"

Smith looked thoughtful for a moment, as if trying to remember where he had put something. The girl did have an accent, he remembered. She was on holiday, touring Europe, first time in York. She was going to the Minster in the morning.

"I don't know, Mr Rounder."

"You don't know what?"

"I don't know why I did what I did – why he made me do it."

"Why who made you do it? Oh, let me guess – the bad you."

"That's the fellow."

Sam sighed and then slapped the table, making everyone else in the room jump. He leant over towards Smith.

The solicitor spoke up. "Can I just say no touching please. Make sure you keep your hands off my client."

Sam did not look at the woman as he spoke. "I wouldn't want to sully my hands on the creep. I just want to find out why he killed that American girl."

Sam sat back and continued facing Smith.

"I can see the logic with Jane: you loved her but she rejected you, and you never got over it. There is some sense in your murderous logic there. But why on earth would you kill a complete stranger?"

Smith remained silent, sighed and spoke.

"I suppose I – by which I mean the bad me – got a taste for it or something. We were both still angry with Jane and decided to take our anger out on someone else. They're all the same, these women, they all do you wrong in the end."

"But why an innocent girl who had never done you any harm? You didn't even know her."

"Why not? I suppose I liked the look of her."

Sam felt weighted with glum resignation. To an extent we were all at the mercy of hazardous strangers, at risk of being stabbed by someone possessed by paranoid delusions. Or pushed under a train by someone who had been avoiding their medication, possibly in the belief that the doctor was trying to poison them. There went plenty of strange, mad or twisted people in the world. It was Sherry Smithson's tragic ill luck to meet one of them in York.

"I was still angry at Jane and I – by which I mean us, you know, him again – took it out on that girl. I could see she didn't really want to talk to me in the pub, but I coaxed her along anyway. We walked and talked a bit, and when I hit her – or when he did. I wasn't looking at a girl I didn't know, I was hitting Jane again. Smashing her deceitful skull all over again."

"And why did you partly undress the girl afterwards?"

"I wondered what she would look like without her top on."

He spoke the words simply, as if it was the most natural thing in the world to do.

"Christ, we all do that, but we leave it to the wondering. We don't bash their heads in and then have a peek. You could have bought a magazine, watched a porno film, Googled your favourite actress to see if there were any saucy pictures of her on the internet. Christ, I don't know, all sorts of things. But you didn't have to go and kill that girl. She had family, loved ones, friends – think of all the people she knew, and all those people whose lives you have screwed up, just through a casual, pointless act of violence.

"And then you had to go and hit that jogger. That was you too, wasn't it?"

Smith looked blank. What was the fat man going on about? Why was he talking about a jogger? Then he remembered the fit young girl down by the river, her legs lean and muscled, her body slim and shapely, and he nodded.

"Yes, he did that one too."

"Well, at least she survived."

Smith hadn't been looking good all morning. Perhaps it was the rotten breakfast, the airless room or the angry fat policeman. Whatever the cause, something was making him feel very odd. Before Sam's eyes Smith went waxy white to greenish, and then vomited across the table, ejecting his breakfast with great splashing force. Sam jumped up, brushing the flecks of sick from his tie, and opened the door.

"Cleaner in here, now, please. And can someone put this creep back in the cells."

★★★

THE following day, it turned out that Iain Anders had been right about the paving slabs around the shed.

"So I suppose being good at DIY isn't a complete waste of time then," Sam said. "Mind you, I prefer GSOBTDII."

Anders smiled warily and said: "I know I shouldn't ask, but go on."

"Get Some Other Bugger To Do It Instead."

Sam laughed and Anders thought he seemed to be in a better mood.

The remains had been found two feet beneath the surface in the shallow grave Clarence Smith had dug. He told them later that there had been no guests because he had put up the "No vacancies" sign. It had been such a good week until she had started to argue with him.

"You see, Mr Rounder…" Smith had been called back to the interview room for one last time, "…she wouldn't let up about it."

Sam wished he didn't have to ask. "About what?"

"Well, you see, she thought that I was incapable of love."

"What, after a week's introductory shagging? That seems quick."

"She said I had to let go of my old hatreds, and re-energise my love aura, or something. She was a bit, you know, New Age-y."

"And did you re-energise it?"

"No, I hit her on the head. Or rather he did, my troublesome other half. Then between us, we rigged up a tarpaulin in the yard by the wall, removed the slabs and buried her there. After that, I ordered a shed and had it put over her."

"And no one ever traced her back to you?"

"One of your lot came asking questions once, but I said the last time I saw her she was heading for the station and Edinburgh."

"Fortunately," said Sam, brightening, "it's all boys where you are going to end up, so womankind will be preserved from your loathsome attentions."

Epilogue

PINTS of beer bonded the Rounder brothers and dissolved the sibling rivalry, at least until the next resentment popped up.

They were in the tiny Blue Bell pub near the top of Fossgate. The pub liked to boast that its interior was unchanged since 1904 or something; and sometimes Sam felt he had been coming in here since then. They were in the back room, where a fire burned in the grate. The pub had two small rooms, divided in the middle by the bar. The bar faced the front room, and beer was served to the back room via a small hatch in a wooden screen. The barmaid on duty this afternoon was particularly busty and when she leant down to pass the beers through, her cleavage was framed perfectly, as if in a jolly seaside picture postcard.

"Do you reckon the landlord picks his female staff by interviewing them through that hatch?" said Sam, as he put the first pints on the table. He sat and made a frame with his hands, and laughed. "Big bangers that girl's got."

Rick glanced over, feigning casual indifference, but his eyes widened at the perfectly framed view as more pints were served through the hatch.

"Jane Wragge was buried the other day," said Sam, supping his pint of Timothy Taylor's.

"Where?"

"York Cemetery, fittingly. Just over the wall from where she lived. The gravestone has flowers carved into it, taken from one of her paintings. It was a moving ceremony, no religion, but nice and respectful."

"You seem to have been quite touched by Jane Wragge."

"Nah, it was just a case, another crime wrapped up and solved."

"Oh yeah?"

Sam thought of telling Rick about the diary, and how close he had come to the dead woman, and how she had helped him solve the case. But he hadn't let on to anyone else and he wasn't going to tell his brother.

For his part, Rick, decided to file the topic away. He had his own secrets where Moses Mundy was concerned. He had no intention of telling his brother that Moses and the motor-biking stranger who killed Bill Inchcliffe were one and the same. To admit as much would call his behaviour into question in a way he wished to avoid. He had earned good money on that case, but a man had died. It was Sam who brought the motor-biking stranger into the conversation.

"That Miranda Inchcliffe woman, the one whose husband was knocking off the little secretary, she said that the hell's angel type she hired was called Vincent B Lightning."

Rick laughed when he heard that, surprised to discover Moses had an unexpected sense of humour.

"It's a motorbike and a song," he said.

"What are you bollocks-ing on about?"

"It's a reference to a motorbike and to a song. 1952 Vincent Black Lightning is a song by Richard Thompson, and I think that's where the name comes from. It was like a biker's joke and a musical reference. Here have a listen."

Rick fiddled with his new iPod until the track came up, then handed the earphones to his brother… "Said Red Molly to James, that's a fine motorbike / A girl could feel special on any such like…"

Sam looked nonplussed. "Are you sure you know what the fuck you are talking about?"

374

Rick laughed. "No, not always, Sam. But I think I'm right about this one."

AS THE Rounder brothers drank their beer, and offered graduated versions of the truth to each other, the funeral of Bill Inchcliffe was taking place in the main chapel at York Crematorium. The chapel held 90 people and was about half full for the occasion. The funeral tribute had been tricky to arrange, seeing as so many of Bill's 'friends' were inappropriate for the occasion.

In the end Bill's brother, who had driven up from Bristol, gave the tribute, which was touchingly done. Bill's remains were sent for incineration while The Beatles went along their long and winding road. Bill had liked the song and once mentioned that he would like it played at his funeral, imagining an event far into the misted future. Miranda wasn't sure it was right, but demurred to the wishes of her dead husband.

Other guests wondered about the small pretty blonde woman who sat next to Miranda, holding her hand during the service. It was explained that she was Bill's secretary, and left at that.

The two women were embarking on a surprising friendship, brought together by the same misbehaving man. Eventually, Catherine moved in, which meant Miranda could stay in her big house in the suburbs. The mortgage had been paid off in full, thanks to the financial benefits of Bill's employment, so they were well set up. Before they knew it, the women were living and loving together, and neither of them had expected that.

THE END

AUTHOR'S NOTES

Felicity's Gate is set in the very real city of York, where the writer lives. The story concerning the naming of the gate is true and was relayed by Hugh Murray, York Cemetery historian and expert in all things to do with York. Hugh's informative history, The Garden Of Death, The History of York Cemetery, 1837-2007, supplied some of the background history about the cemetery; any mistakes or misunderstandings are entirely of the author's own making.

The dead-end road leading to the cemetery is similar but different to an actual one, as the buildings have been rearranged for the writer's convenience. It would not be advisable to try and book into the Cemetery View Guesthouse, which is entirely a figment of imagination. But it is thoroughly advisable to visit the cemetery, one of York's loveliest places.

ACKNOWLEDGEMENTS

The author would like to thank literary agent Shelley Power for all her efforts, Adam Kirkman of Quick Brown Fox Publications for keeping faith, and Gina for being there.

AUTHOR'S NOTES

Felicity's Gate is set in the very real city of York, where the writer lives. The story concerning the naming of the gate is true and was relayed by Hugh Murray, York Cemetery historian and expert in all things to do with York. Hugh's informative history, *This Garden of Death: The History of York Cemetery, 1837–2007,* supplied some of the background history about the cemetery; any mistakes or misunderstandings are entirely of the author's own making.

The dead-end road leading to the cemetery is similar but different to an actual one, as the buildings have been rearranged for the writer's convenience. It would not be advisable to try and book into the Cemetery View Guesthouse, which is entirely a figment of imagination. But it is thoroughly advisable to visit the cemetery, one of York's loveliest places.